JAG IN SPACE

AGAINST ALL ENEMIES

JAG IN SPACE

AGAINST ALL ENEMIES

JACK CAMPBELL

WRITING AS JOHN G. HEMRY

TITAN BOOKS

JAG IN SPACE: AGAINST ALL ENEMIES
Print edition ISBN: 9780857689436
E-book edition ISBN: 9780857689627

Published by Titan Books
A division of Titan Publishing Group Ltd
144 Southwark St, London SE1 0UP

First edition: April 2012
10 9 8 7 6 5 4 3 2 1

Visit our website: **www.titanbooks.com**

What did you think of this book? We love to hear from our readers.
Please email us at: readerfeedback@titanemail.com, or write to us at the
above address.

To receive advance information, news, competitions, and exclusive offers
online, please sign up for the Titan newsletter on our website:
www.titanbooks.com

A CIP catalogue record for this title is available from the British Library.

Printed and bound in Great Britain by CPI Group UK Ltd.

For Carolyn, Jack and James,
for all you are and all you will be.

And for S, as always.

ARTICLE 106A – ESPIONAGE

(a) That the accused communicated, delivered, or transmitted any document, writing, code book, signal book, sketch, photograph, photographic negative, blueprint, plan, map, model, note, instrument, appliance, or information relating to the national defense;

(b) That this matter was communicated, delivered, or transmitted to any foreign government, or to any faction or party or military or naval force within a foreign country, whether recognized or unrecognized by the United States, or to any representative, officer, agent, employee, subject, or citizen thereof, either directly or indirectly; and

(c) That the accused did so with intent or reason to believe that such matter would be used to the injury of the United States or to the advantage of a foreign nation.

RULES FOR COURTS-MARTIAL
MANUAL FOR COURTS-MARTIAL, UNITED STATES

1

There were times when the bridge of the USS *Michaelson* became a nerve-wracking maelstrom of activity, with orders being hurled at the watch standers and emergencies from every quarter demanding their immediate attention. Most other times, the bridge simply held the tension of watchful waiting as the crew members there kept alert for internal surprises and external threats.

But then there were times like this. Late at night, the lights on the bridge lowered to accommodate the day/night cycle the *Michaelson*'s crew had carried with them from Earth, the infinite stars glowing with amazing brilliance on the viewscreens and dimming the soft green status lights on the control panels. No tension, no special activity, just quiet and boredom on top of too many long days with too little sleep.

Lieutenant Junior Grade Paul Sinclair felt his eyes drooping. He couldn't seem to stop the wave of fatigue settling over him, couldn't seem to force his eyes open. He felt a surge of fear which somehow didn't penetrate the fog falling across his vision. Falling asleep on watch had to be one of the worst things an officer could do. It would disgrace him, place the entire ship in danger if something happened when he was supposed to be alert and watching for the unexpected, and doubtless deal a deathblow to his career.

Paul's eyes fell further. He couldn't keep them open. With a titanic effort born of anger and fear, he wrenched himself fully awake.

And found himself staring at the nearby, dim patterns of the ducts, cables and wiring which ran across the overhead just above his bunk in his darkened stateroom. The moment's disorientation passed, then Paul clenched his eyes shut again. *A nightmare. I had a nightmare I was falling asleep on watch so I woke myself up for real. Great.* He opened his eyes again long enough to check on the time. *And in less than forty minutes I need to get out of this bunk and actually stand watch. I can't believe I just woke myself up when I'm only going to get about four hours' sleep tonight as it is.* He tried to calm down from the stress induced by the nightmare, breathing slowly, hoping to get back to sleep quickly. *What a dumb thing to do. I guess as nightmares go that one's pretty harmless, though.*

Much better than the ones he sometimes had about something happening to Jen.

About an hour later, Paul pulled himself onto the bridge, wishing that he was still asleep and dreaming this watch away. The time counters in the corner of each bridge display screen all provided the same annoying information – 0345 on the twenty-four hour military clock. "Dawn" on the *Michaelson* wouldn't take place for more than another two hours, but Paul's work day had begun.

"Howdy." Lieutenant Junior Grade Brad Pullman yawned even as he greeted Paul. He waved one hand toward the screen facing the junior officer of the deck watch station. "It's still there. They're still there. We're still here."

"I know. I checked the situation out in Combat on my way up here." Paul studied the screen, even though it held nothing new or unexpected. A fairly large asteroid filled most of the screen, slowly tumbling over and over just as it had for however many millions of years it had wandered through space. As the asteroid's surface turned, the *Michaelson*'s fire control systems painted a constantly changing set of aim points and firing solutions on temporary structures scattered across the bare rock.

The next screen showed a much larger view, in which the asteroid occupied only a small section. Scattered around it were the highlighted symbols which announced the presence of an even dozen warships and hired merchant ships. All the other ships carried temporary "friendly" identifiers, but they, too, had firing solutions pasted over their symbols.

Pullman followed Paul's gaze. "Is it true this is the biggest gathering of warships in space? Ever?"

"Yeah," Paul confirmed. "My chief checked."

"So this is what making history feels like."

"Do you mean boring but tense, or just tedious?"

Pullman grinned and stretched. "Both. Any other questions?"

"Is anything scheduled for this morning? I didn't have anything listed in Combat."

"If we had anything, the Combat Information Center would have it, too. And I guess they'd tell you, Mr. Combat Information Center Officer." Pullman smiled again.

Paul snorted. "Yes, they would, but sometimes different orders get passed to the bridge and somebody forgets to tell Combat. It never hurts to make sure that didn't happen."

Pullman yawned once more. "To answer your question formally, no, there's nothing new laid on this morning. Unscheduled events can occur at any time, of course."

Like somebody starting to shoot at somebody else, Paul thought bleakly. "Otherwise just hold position and monitor events."

"Otherwise just hold position and monitor events," Pullman agreed. "Same old."

Paul scanned the status panels one more time, noting what equipment was ready to go and what rested in standby. "Okay, I got it." Paul saluted. "I relieve you, sir."

"I stand relieved." Pullman returned the salute. "On the bridge, this is Lieutenant JG Pullman. Lieutenant JG Sinclair has the conn."

"This is Lieutenant JG Sinclair. I have the conn." Paul kept his hand locked on the nearest hold while Pullman unstrapped and swung himself out of the watch stander's seat, then pulled himself down and refastened the straps without having to look at them. The gesture had been repeated so many times by now, on so many watches, that Paul was sure he could fasten those straps in his sleep if he needed to. "I'll try to keep things quiet so you can catch up on your beauty sleep, Brad."

Pullman rolled his eyes. "Wow. A couple of hours until reveille. Isn't there some regulation about letting us get enough sleep?"

"Yeah. Every officer is supposed to get at least the necessary minimum hours of sleep in each twenty-four-hour period."

"So what's the necessary minimum?"

"The regulation doesn't say. It leaves that up to the individual ship. Which of course means the XO." Which meant the ship's executive officer, the second in command. Which on the *Michaelson* still meant Commander Kwan, who still didn't particularly like Paul. But in any case XOs had never been known for their kindly and casual ways.

"The XO sets the minimum," Pullman mused. "Which I guess means the minimum is whatever you manage to get."

"Bingo. But cheer up. If the minimum wasn't good enough..."

"It wouldn't be the minimum." Pullman waved a farewell with his free hand as the other grasped a nearby handhold to propel him toward the hatch leading off the bridge.

Paul grinned, turning to offer his own farewell to Lieutenant Kris Denaldo as she finished turning over officer of the deck duties to Lieutenant Val Isakov. Kris nodded back, then raised one hand with the thumb and forefinger held out parallel to each other and only a short distance apart. Paul grinned wider at the hand gesture signifying that Kris was "short," as in not long left before she transferred off the ship. "You're not gone, yet," he reminded her.

"No. But another day's gone. I'm very, very short." She smiled. "Soon I'll be short enough to walk under the lines painted on the deck. And soon after *that* I'll actually get to sleep every night instead of standing watches."

"I thought you intended doing other things during your free nights."

"Depends if I find the right guy. Has Jen told you to take a hike, yet?"

"Nope."

"Fine. I'm tired of waiting. You're off my list. I'd love to stay and chat the rest of the night away, but my bunk is calling."

Paul waved again in farewell, then noticed Lieutenant Val Isakov giving him a sour look as she strapped in at the officer of the deck watchstation. *Uh-oh. Now what's she up to?* "Something wrong?"

Isakov shrugged elaborately. "Of course not. You have your little cliques and old friends. I'm just the newcomer."

"Val, you've been on the ship for about a year."

"And you and her," Isakov noted with a jerk of her head toward the hatch where Denaldo had left, "have been onboard for about three years. But that's okay. I don't expect to be allowed to feel part of your group."

Paul kept his expression noncommittal, carefully avoiding nodding or otherwise seeming to agree with her. He thought of Isakov as sort of a reptile, not bad to look at but not something he wanted to get close to, either. He also suspected that Isakov knew that Kris Denaldo usually referred to her as "Crazy Ivana," a name Paul also thought fit Val Isakov perfectly.

"But then your old Academy pal shows up," Isakov continued, "and you go through all that ring-knocker bonding nonsense. It's a bit much."

"What ring-knocker nonsense?" Paul had never been bothered by the standard nickname for Naval Academy graduates, which mocked their alleged tendency to knock their class rings on objects as a way of drawing attention to themselves.

"'If the minimum wasn't good enough...'"

This time Paul shrugged. "It's sort of an unofficial motto. That's all. Brad Pullman wasn't a big friend of mine at the Academy. We're classmates, and we shared a few courses over the years, so I know him and he knows me. No big deal."

"Sure." Isakov subsided into sulky silence.

Paul pretended to be concentrating on his display. He never knew whether Isakov would try to aim a heavy-handed come-on his way or try to bite his head off or just ignore him. *Personally, I much prefer being ignored by her.*

"Mr. Sinclair, sir?"

Paul twisted his chair so he could look at the bosun mate of the watch. "What's up?"

The bosun tilted his head toward the messenger of the watch. "I've been tryin' to explain what we're doin' here to Valejo, and damned if I can."

"That's okay, Boats. It's not in your job description."

Val Isakov bent another sour look toward Paul. "Keep it professional."

Paul followed an old piece of advice and just smiled back at her. "Yes, ma'am." Then he addressed the messenger. "Seaman Apprentice Valejo, you just came aboard, right?"

She nodded quickly. "Yes, sir. I came on with Mr. Pullman and Ms., uh..."

"Commander Moraine?"

"Yes, sir."

"Okay, then." Paul hooked a thumb toward the display dominated by the craggy surface of the asteroid. "There's a rule, one of the few rules *everybody's* agreed to up here, that nobody gets to set themselves up on an asteroid without international approval, supervision and inspection." Valejo nodded again, but her face was puzzled. "Do you know what killed the dinosaurs?"

"Oh, yeah. I mean, yes, sir! Some big rock hit the planet."

"Right." Paul indicated the asteroid again. "A big rock like that. We don't really want any more big rocks hitting Earth anytime soon, but if somebody was allowed to just settle on one, they could maybe set up a propulsion method to kick that rock toward Earth. Hopefully, we could intercept and divert it. Hopefully. No one wants it to get to that point."

The bosun spoke again. "That's what I don't understand, Mr.

Sinclair. Why'd anybody do something like that?"

"I don't understand it either, Boats, but every once in a while some group of people does something that's really scary for the rest of us." Paul indicated the structures on the asteroid's surface. "This particular group calls itself the Church of One. 'One' as in the only one they think should exist, apparently. They received approval to set up a remote settlement on Mars. No big deal. That sort of thing's been done before. It makes a small group of people happy, helps pay for stuff on Mars for everybody else, and pretty much renders any anti-social types harmless since they're out in the Martian equivalent of east nowhere."

"But they didn't go to Mars," the bosun noted.

"No. They hijacked the ship carrying them. They did a good job of it, too. No alarms. No alerts. They diverted the ship here and did it so quietly that no one realized what was happening in time to stop them. That ship, there. It's just a regular merchant named the *Jedediah Smith*." Paul pointed with one finger at the symbol representing a ship hanging perilously close to the asteroid. The *Michaelson*'s combat systems had a half-dozen aim points fixed upon the ship's hull, ready to blow holes through critical areas if need be. "Then they offloaded their stuff, which seems to have included a lot of gear for living on an asteroid and not all that much for living on Mars, and pretty much dared everybody to do anything about it."

"And we're goin' to take 'em off, right, sir?"

"Right. Not you and me, but those modified cargo carriers loaded up with cops."

"Cops? Not Marines or SEALs?"

"No. This isn't a combat mission. Nobody's supposed to get shot.

Combat troops like Marines are trained to shoot. Cops are trained to try to avoid shooting."

Valejo nodded again but the bosun looked perplexed. "Then why are *we* here? And all them other guys?" He made a gesture encompassing all the other ships shown in the displays.

Paul pondered the question for a moment. *Do I really want to get into all the politics here? The fact that everyone is here to keep an eye on everyone else as well as the illegal settlers and the cops? That these Church of One types not only have made hostages of the crew of that ship they hijacked but are also threatening to kill all of their own kids if force is used against their "settlement?" I can't go into any of that. The rules of engagement that tell us under what conditions we're allowed to fire, and who we're allowed to fire at, are classified pretty high and the bosun doesn't have a need to know.* "Everybody's here to keep an eye on things." The bosun let his skepticism show. "Boats, that really does sum it up. And that's as detailed as I can get."

Paul became aware that Lieutenant Isakov was watching him narrowly. *Just waiting for me to spill something I shouldn't? I wonder what Crazy Ivana would do with knowledge I'd broken security regulations? Not keep it to herself, I'm sure.*

The bosun nodded. "Yes, sir. I understand you officers can't tell us everything. Thank you, sir."

"No problem." Paul noticed Isakov going back into a solitary sulk. He relaxed against his own seat, eyes on the surface of the asteroid, watching as it completed rotations and the same structures and aim points came into view time and again. At some point he realized the repetitive motion was becoming hypnotic and began cycling through other views to remain alert.

An external communications circuit chirped for attention, breaking the silence on the bridge and startling everyone; then it spoke in the clear, unaccented English which meant whoever was sending the message was speaking or typing it into a verbal translator that rendered the words into another language. "This is South Asian Alliance Ship *Gilgamesh*. I am altering my position two kilometers along a bearing of one three five degrees relative, down angle two zero degrees relative. Over."

Paul tapped his own communications controls to acknowledge the *Gilgamesh*'s message, letting the other ship know the message had been received and understood. "This is the USS *Michaelson*. Roger, out."

He glanced over at Isakov, who looked back at him and nodded toward the general area of the captain's cabin as she answered his unspoken question. "You go ahead and call him."

"Okay." Paul reached for the comm switch, then hesitated and went to his display controls instead. He manually moved the *Gilgamesh*'s position along the track it had announced, then told the combat systems to update their readings and studied the results for a moment before finally calling the captain. "Sir, this is the junior officer of the deck. The *Gilgamesh* has informed us they're changing position slightly."

"Slightly?" Captain Hayes sounded grumpy, but then he hadn't had much sleep lately.

Probably less than any of the other officers had, Paul realized when he thought about it. And Paul hadn't been getting very much. "Yes, sir. Two kilometers along a track one three five relative and two zero down from his current position. Our combat systems don't reveal any change in the tactical situation as a result."

"Hmmm. No reason given for the shift?"

"No, si—" Paul's answer was cut off by another call to the bridge.

"Bridge, this is Combat. We've analyzed the *Gilgamesh*'s position change. In his previous location the asteroid's tumble would produce an occasional momentary line-of-sight blockage between the *Gilgamesh* and the *Saladin*. This change will make sure they have continuous line of sight."

"Thanks, Combat. Captain, Combat reports the *Gilgamesh* probably moved to ensure a continuous line of the sight to the other SASAL warship present, the *Saladin*."

"Hmmm. Okay. Thanks. Keep me informed."

"Yes, sir." Paul listened to the circuit click off, feeling a tight knot in his guts. *I should've gotten that analysis from Combat before I called the captain. But what if Combat had taken a while to figure out that line-of-sight thing and something had happened before then so that I'd have had to tell the captain I hadn't informed him of the* Gilgamesh *shifting position when it took place? I would've lost a piece of my hind end if that'd happened. I got lucky. Or maybe I helped make my luck. After all, I've been leading those operations specialists in Combat for a long time, now.* He pressed the comm switch again. "Combat, this is Mr. Sinclair on the bridge. Who ran that analysis on the *Gilgamesh*?"

"That was me, sir. Kaji."

Operations Specialist First Class Kaji. "Damn good job. That was fine work, Kaji."

"Thank you, sir."

Paul didn't bother looking toward Val Isakov. He knew she wouldn't offer any praise and he didn't want to look like he expected any. *Besides, that message from the* Gilgamesh *rattled me. It felt too much like it woke me up from a daze. How can I be drifting off when there's so much potential for trouble? But let's face it, that was probably the only two minutes of excitement we're going to see in this four-hour watch and I'm working on a serious sleep deficit.*

But if anything else exciting happens, I don't want it waking me up.

If there'd been another officer standing watch with him, they could've played trivia games to pass the time and keep awake. *I'll take emergency maneuvering systems for four hundred,* if they were in a professional mood. Or *I'll take late twentieth-century movies for two hundred,* if they weren't. But not with Isakov.

He did the next best thing, calling up the detailed information on the other ships present, both warships and freighters. He'd already looked at them too many times to count, but if an emergency arose he might need to know something right off the top of his head.

It worked well enough to pass the time that Paul was surprised when the bosun cleared his throat. "Permission to sound reveille, ma'am."

Isakov, who didn't seem to have moved for hours, nodded without looking back at the bosun. "Permission granted."

The bosun raised his pipe, an archaic little device the Navy had clung to even as efficiency experts tried to sell the virtues of digital recordings played automatically with canned announcements. In the deliberate inefficiency of his human presence, the bosun represented one of the US Navy's constant rearguard battles against change. The bosun keyed the ship's internal broadcast system, took a deep breath, then sounded the drawn-out whistle which tradition insisted upon for declaring the ship's day had begun. "Reveille, reveille," the bosun chanted immediately after the last note faded. "All hands turn to and trice up."

Paul stretched and yawned as Isakov made a face and dialed up the captain's cabin. He knew she didn't like giving the captain his wake-up call, but Isakov knew that was one task she had to handle in person instead of handing it off to Paul. He half-listened as Isakov ran through the standard spiel. "Good morning, captain. It's 0600. The ship is on-station..."

The darkened bridge gradually brightened as the ship's lights came to their "day" settings. Occasional sounds came to the bridge team as the rest of the ship stirred to life. The bosun passed mess call for breakfast. Paul glanced at the hatch, hoping their reliefs would show up on the bridge before the captain did. He both liked and respected Hayes, but the captain could be a real bear first thing in the morning if he hadn't got at least a few good hours of sleep.

"Yo, Paul."

Paul turned and smiled. "Yo, Randy."

Ensign Randy Diego smiled, too, though the gesture was aimed mostly at Isakov. Paul tried not to let his reaction show, instead running through the details Randy had to know in order to assume the watch, repeating some of it when Randy's attention seemed to be wandering. "Okay. That's it. Any questions?"

"Uh, no."

Paul pointed to the display. "Don't forget the captain's going to ask questions about *Gilgamesh* after that position change."

Randy blinked with apparent surprise, then nodded. "Right, right. I'll be ready." He saluted. "I relieve you, sir."

"I stand relieved. On the bridge, this is Lieutenant Junior Grade Sinclair. Ensign Diego has the conn."

"This is Ensign Diego. I have the conn," Randy repeated.

Paul unstrapped wearily and pulled himself out of his chair. "Later, Randy." He glanced over at Isakov, who was busy turning over her duties to Lieutenant Bolen and ignoring both Paul and Randy, then pulled himself off the bridge using the handholds set at convenient intervals in any spot that wasn't occupied by some other equipment.

Living in zero gravity most of the time didn't do much for the leg muscles, but the arms got good workouts.

He went through Combat on the way aft, stopping to once again praise Petty Officer Kaji for his quick work a few hours previous.

Most of the passageways on the *Michaelson* were still relatively free of traffic this early on the ship's morning, but Paul still found himself squeezing past other members of the crew whenever they passed. He'd seen some specifications which declared that the passageways on the ship had originally been designed to be wide enough for two people to pass without any trouble, but it didn't take a genius to look at all the equipment, wiring, ducting and piping sticking out from the bulkheads and realize that a few things had been added on to the ship after those specs were drawn up.

The compartment grandly labeled the wardroom was still empty when Paul pulled himself inside to grab some coffee. He paused, looking toward the chair at one end of the table that dominated the wardroom. *Commander Steve Sykes' chair. Suppo always seemed to be sitting there, but he got more done than any supply officer I've ever heard of. It feels funny not having him onboard anymore.*

He was still hanging there when Kris Denaldo came in, looking like she'd spent half the night standing watch. Which she had. "How's the coffee?" she mumbled.

"Terrible."

"It's good to know there's some things we can always count on," Kris remarked, shuddering as she took a drink. "Too bad Suppo's not here for us to complain to." She looked toward the same chair. "I miss the old Suppo."

"Who doesn't? I have to admit the new guy has a hard act to follow. But I don't see much of the new guy," Paul confessed.

"Nobody does. Commander 'Silent-E' Smithe spends a lot of time in his stateroom. I don't know what he's doing in there, but it's not anything that's helping me get the spare parts I need."

"Yeah. I'm having more trouble getting parts than I used to. Mike Bristol tells me he's doing his best to get us what we need, but it's not like it was with Commander Sykes and his forty thieves 'acquiring' whatever we needed. Smithe insists on doing things by the book."

"Heaven help us." Denaldo made another face, either from the coffee or the situation. "We'll never get the stuff we need if it all has to run through official channels." She shook her head, then took another look at Paul. "Hey, you look worse than I feel. Anything wrong?" Paul hesitated. "I saw that."

"Kris, you've got enough troubles of your own—"

"Shipmate, when I walk off the *Merry Mike* for the last time you'll be the longest-serving officer onboard. The old guy who personally remembers the ancient past a couple of years ago. Until then, you and I are still friends of some years standing who can lean on each other. What's up?"

Paul shrugged. "Nothing. Not really. I haven't been getting much sleep."

"None of us have. Are you sure there's nothing else?"

"Um..." Paul grimaced. "I guess I haven't been able to sleep some of the times I could've."

Denaldo looked alarmed. "You haven't been *able* to sleep sometimes? You know that's bad in a sailor. What's the problem, Paul? Level with me."

Paul hesitated again. *I need to get this off my chest, and Kris is probably the last person left on the ship I can talk to about something like this.* "I have these nightmares every once in a while. You remember when the *Maury* blew."

A shadow fell across Kris' face. "That's not something I'll ever forget. But you're still having nightmares about that?"

"Sort of. I mean... I went over there."

"Yeah. Most of us did at one point or another. But I remember you were on one of the first teams sent over to help."

"It's sort of about that." Paul took a deep breath. "I dream I'm back on the *Maury* right then, climbing through the wreckage, assessing the damage, wondering what'd happened to Jen."

He paused for a long time, while Kris watched him closely before she spoke again. "We found out Jen had survived in the after part of the *Maury*. After you got back. You just didn't find her."

"In the nightmares, I find her."

Kris frowned, then her eyes widened. "Oh. Nightmares. You find her in the wreckage."

"Yeah." Paul looked away, feeling immense relief as he finally blurted out the story. "Caught by the explosion and the decompression."

"Mary, mother of God." Kris shuddered. "You see *that?* No wonder you can't sleep sometimes. But it didn't happen, Paul. Your mind's torturing you over something that didn't happen. You didn't find Jen's body. She was safe, and she's still alive now."

"Accidents still happen, Kris. Could happen anytime."

Kris Denaldo sighed. "That comes with the territory, Paul. Jen's not going to live in a gilded cage. Not for you or anybody else. She's a Navy officer, like you. Hell, she's not even on shipboard duty now. Jen's sitting safe in a temporary job on Franklin Station while you and I cruise around out here with various foreign warships and religious fanatics pointing weapons at us. She's the one who ought to be worried. About you. But she'll never tell you she's worried, you know."

Paul smiled wryly. "Yeah. I know."

"Jen's a lot safer than you are. Is this about something else?"

"What? What else?"

"I don't know." She made a vague gesture. "Some problems your subconscious might be twisting around. Are you and Jen doing okay?"

"Uh, yeah. Sure we are."

"The wedding's still on?"

Paul knew his irritation at the question was showing. "Of course it's still on. Right after I detach from the *Michaelson*."

"All right. Don't bite my head off. Something's got you worried, that's all."

"Not with me and Jen." Paul felt a slight twinge inside as he made the firm declaration. *There isn't anything wrong! Jen's not the easiest person in the world to live with, but I'm not exactly perfect, either.* "Maybe it's just all the stress here. I've only got a few months left onboard, I'll make lieutenant in a month, we're facing off with all these other warships and the civilians, and... well, everything."

Kris smiled sadly. "Oh, yeah. Everything."

They both looked over as two more officers came in. Commander Garcia, Paul's department head and immediate superior for the past two and a half years, gave Paul his habitual glower. Paul suspected there were times when Garcia wasn't in a bad mood, but he'd never caught Garcia at it. "No work to do, Sinclair?"

"I just came off watch, sir," Paul answered.

Garcia turned to look at the nearest clock, obviously implying how many minutes ago Paul must've actually come off watch, then shook his head and headed for the coffee. Paul and Kris slid to the side to avoid him and leave the wardroom, but had to wait as another officer followed Garcia inside.

Commander Angie Moraine nodded absent-minded greetings to them, her attention focused on Garcia. She was Garcia's relief, due to take over as Paul's new department head and busy trying to learn everything Garcia could show and tell her about the job in the next couple of weeks. Then she'd become Paul's immediate superior, and determine just how pleasant or unpleasant his own last few months on the ship would be.

"Sinclair." Paul stopped himself halfway out the hatch and looked back at Garcia. Garcia tilted his head to indicate the general direction of the asteroid. "Anything happen last night?"

"No, sir." Paul became aware that Moraine had also fixed her gaze on him, watching him with unnerving intensity. "Just a minor repositioning by *Gilgamesh*."

Garcia's scowl deepened. "Why wasn't I told?"

Oh, hell. Why didn't I tell Garcia? He didn't need to know it even though he's the Operations Department boss. But I should've guessed he'd want to know. "We informed the captain, sir, and—"

"Did I ask you if you'd told the captain?"

Paul fought down a flare of anger and tried to keep his voice level. "No, sir."

"I expect to be kept informed of *any* change in the situation, Sinclair."

"Yes, sir." *At least I've learned that when somebody like Garcia is screaming at me the best thing to do is to just keep no, siring and yes, siring. He wants me to say something else he can scream at me for, but I'm not going to give him that.*

Garcia turned away. Moraine's gaze on Paul had sharpened, but she looked away as well to follow Garcia's movement.

Paul took advantage of the moment to finish exiting the hatch. Kris glowered toward the wardroom. "I can't wait to get away from him," she snapped in a voice too low to carry far. "At least you'll have Moraine for the next few months."

"Yeah, but what's she going to be like?"

"She can't be worse than Garcia."

Paul shook his head, not trusting himself to make any other comment as some other officers came into view. But he thought to himself that so far experience had shown him things could always be worse.

Half an hour later Paul and Kris Denaldo were facing Garcia and Moraine again for officers' call. Along with them was Ensign Taylor, the ship's electronic materials officer. Despite her lowly officer rank, Taylor was a mustang, a former enlisted sailor who'd come up through the ranks and therefore had immensely more knowledge and prestige than the average ensign. As a result, she also had a lot more attitude than the average ensign.

Garcia's temper had obviously stayed bad. "There's a meeting in the wardroom at zero eight thirty. Make sure you're there. Nobody better be late." His glower focused on Taylor as she raised one hand with deliberate casualness. "What?"

"Commander, you told us to run electronic systems checks this morning."

"So?"

"Your last instructions to me were that I was to be 'directly supervising critical systems checks.' You said that was top priority for me." Taylor spread her hands. "Just asking for guidance, sir."

"You—" Garcia broke off whatever he'd been planning to say, took a deep breath, and spoke again. "The meeting takes priority."

"Should I postpone the checks, sir?"

Garcia visibly wavered as his face reddened, then he shook his head. "No. Any more questions?" He looked toward Paul and Kris. "How about you two? No? Good." Garcia leveled his index finger at them. "No screw-ups, people. Do you understand? Nothing goes wrong." Then he turned, grabbed the nearest handhold and yanked himself toward the hatch.

Taylor waited until Garcia and Moraine had both left, then chuckled. "I love messing with that son of a bitch."

Denaldo looked upward beseechingly. "'Nothing goes wrong'? How the hell do we make that happen?"

Taylor grinned. "Don't worry, sweetheart. Garcia's just trying to make sure his butt's covered until he gets off this ship."

"Is that why he's being even worse than usual?" Paul asked.

"Sure. He wants to be relaxing and handing off the job to Moraine. His tour of duty's almost over and he's got halfway decent orders for his next job. But if something screws up at the last moment he could still end up with his butt in a bight. And here we are facing off with a bunch of other warships and some religious fanatics. Yup. He's worried." Taylor grinned again, apparently finding great amusement in the prospect that something might go seriously wrong. "Aren't you worried about that, Kris darling?"

She shrugged. "I guess. But I've done everything I can to get my division ready. We're trained, we're prepared, we're working our tails off to stay that way. Going ballistic isn't going to help things."

Taylor nodded. "Pretty dammed smart for a college kid."

"You went to college, too."

"Did not. Not a real one. Not like you and our buddy Paul here." Taylor gave Paul a grin.

Paul smiled back. "I didn't go to college. I went to the Naval Academy. Remember?"

"How can I forget, with you waving that ring in our faces?" Taylor sighed. "Ah, well, I'd best get going to pass on Garcia's inspirational words to my division. See you kids in the wardroom."

Paul met Senior Chief Petty Officer Imari and the rest of his division in Combat, running quickly through the few items he had to pass down. "Stay sharp," he advised. "Dismissed." Then he gestured to Imari as the other sailors scattered to their jobs. "Senior chief, I'll be in a meeting in the wardroom."

Imari nodded. "I hope it's good news, sir," she said.

"Me, too."

Paul made it back to the wardroom by 0820, wedging himself into a corner in the back with one arm through the nearest handhold. In zero gravity, that was about the most relaxing position possible as the room filled with other officers.

Garcia and Moraine entered, claiming seats at the table. After Garcia had strapped in, he manipulated some controls and the main display screen on the bulkhead lit up.

A rustle ran through the wardroom as those present looked to see whatever was shown on the screen. It only took Paul an instant to recognize the information, a read-out of the capabilities of the foreign warships present around the asteroid. He'd studied the same material a thousand times in recent weeks.

All of the other ships were roughly comparable to the *Michaelson* in terms of size and armament. So far, at least, no one had shown any desire to build space battleships, and as far as Paul knew the state of technology and the laws of physics meant that huge warships wouldn't make any sense in space at this point in time. Not that everything governments sank large sums of money into necessarily made sense, but in this case no one had succumbed to the urge to build a bigger ship just because it would be bigger. Ships significantly smaller than the *Michaelson*, on the other hand, tended to be kept near bases where their small capacity for fuel and other supplies wasn't a handicap.

Paul went down the list of Earthside powers represented here. *That Brit ship, the* Lord Nelson, *I wonder if she still has that insane captain who played chicken with the SASALs that one time?* There was one other Euro ship, the Russians, the Southern Africans, the two ships from the South Asian Alliance, and one from the Han Chinese state. Eight warships total, counting the *Michaelson*. In one corner, the four hired merchant ships were listed, almost an afterthought except for the security forces they carried.

Commander Kwan, the executive officer, swung himself inside the wardroom and scanned the officers present before looking at the department heads. "Are all your officers present?" he demanded.

The department heads all assured the XO that their officers were present and Kwan left to get the captain. Paul frowned as it occurred to him that something wasn't right, then he realized there was a department missing. *Supply. Neither Smithe nor Mike Bristol is here. Kwan would've noticed that if he'd wanted them present. This must be more serious than usual if they're deliberately excluding the Supply Department.*

"Attention on deck!"

Everyone began to try to stand to attention in the crowded, zero-gravity environment, but Captain Hayes came through the hatch on the heels of Kwan's announcement and gestured for them to relax. "Carry on."

Captain Hayes looked slowly around the small compartment, his eyes meeting those of every other officer in turn. Then he tapped his data pad. "We have reason to believe the current stand-off will not last much longer." Everyone watched him, wondering what sort of ending would take place and whether or not they'd be told of it in advance.

Hayes paused and rubbed his forehead. Paul realized the captain looked haggard from tension and lack of sleep, just like all the other officers in the wardroom. "I want to personally ensure all of you are fully aware of the rules of engagement under which we are operating. There must be no uncertainty in anyone's mind. Everyone present has to be fully familiar with the exact limits on our ability to act. I will remind everyone as well that these rules of engagement are classified Top Secret and are only to be divulged on a strict need-to-know basis as determined by me. They are not to be divulged to anyone outside of this room. Is that clear?" The other officers all nodded or murmured understanding.

Hayes leaned back, his expression unhappy. "You'll all reread these rules and indicate you understand them before you leave this meeting. The most important thing to remember is that we're forbidden to initiate any military action against any other ship present." He paused while everyone absorbed the statement. "We're forbidden to make any provocative actions, anything that might in any way trigger hostile action. That includes our ability to respond if someone else starts shooting. Even if they seem to be shooting at *us*. We're to do nothing against anyone except and unless," Hayes leaned forward and raised a single finger, "we are first deliberately fired upon *and hit*."

Ensign Taylor cleared her throat. "It might be a little late to power-up weapons at that point."

The XO and both Commanders Garcia and Moraine glared at Taylor, but Hayes just showed his teeth. "That's right. But those are our orders."

"Sir." Commander Destin, the chief engineer, was frowning. "I didn't read these rules as prohibiting verbal warnings."

Hayes shook his head. "That's incorrect. We're not allowed to issue verbal warnings. We're not allowed to threaten military action of any kind. That'd be... provocative." The captain looked like he had something bitter in his mouth as he said the last word.

"Why are we here?" Kris Denaldo blurted out, ignoring a fresh set of glares from both Garcia and Moraine as well as the XO. "Captain?"

Hayes twisted his mouth. "That's a reasonable question. We're here to deter any adverse actions. That hasn't changed. But it's a bluff, Ms. Denaldo. We want our *presence* to prevent anything from getting out of hand. That can only work if the other ships present are sufficiently unsure of our own intentions and ability to act if and when we see fit. I hope that makes it crystal clear why the limitations on our ability to act must remain very tightly held.

"The rules regarding the people on the asteroid are different. If they fire upon us, we are authorized to take out any weapons firing at us. That's all. Nothing else. No power supplies. No inactive weapons. Nothing else. Pure self-defense on the most limited basis possible."

Commander Destin spoke again. "The people on the asteroid have threatened to use their children as human shields."

Captain Hayes grimaced. "We're all aware of that. We'll cross that bridge when we come to it, if we come to it. We have to hope the cops can prevent any firing from taking place. They're supposed to have some new non-lethal stuff that'll incapacitate the defenders before they can do any shooting."

"What about the other ships?" Brad Pullman asked. "Do we know what rules of engagement they're operating under?"

Garcia gave Pullman an annoyed look.

"No." Hayes paused as if thinking for a moment before he spoke again. "As I said, I have reason to believe this stand-off is coming to a head soon. I know this ship is as ready as human effort can make her, and I want you all to know I recognize the extraordinary effort the crew has put forth in the last few weeks. But I need to make sure you're all ready, too. Mentally ready. If somebody throws a punch, we need to ready to react in the most appropriate means possible."

Silence followed the captain's last statement. Paul wondered how many of the others were thinking what he was. *Just what will be the "most appropriate means possible"? Especially since we can't really do anything if someone "throws a punch"?* He felt frustration boiling up inside. *It's not the captain's fault. Hell, it's not the fault of anyone on this ship. We've been sent into this mess with orders that tie our hands. But if anything goes wrong, it'll be our fault.*

2

The watch rotation had rolled its way to that point where Paul came off the 1800–2000 second dog watch knowing he didn't have another watch until 0400. It wasn't anything like a full night's sleep by normal standards, but the promise of several hours of uninterrupted sleep seemed like heaven.

Until a messenger came to his stateroom and woke him up. "Mr. Sinclair? You're needed in the captain's cabin."

Paul pried his eyes open and checked the time. Half an hour until midnight. He ran through most of the obscenities he'd learned since joining the Navy, adding in the ones he'd picked up from Ensign Taylor, as he struggled into his uniform.

Commander Kwan was waiting outside the captain's cabin when Paul arrived, with Lieutenant Bolen right behind. Kwan jerked his thumb to indicate they should enter, then followed, pulling the hatch shut behind him.

Inside, the captain's cabin was dimly lit by nighttime illumination and crowded with figures. Paul ran his eyes over the group, seeing that in addition to Bolen and Kwan those present were Commander Garcia, Commander Moraine and Commander Destin. The Combat Information Center officer, the weapons officer, the Operations Department head and his relief, and the chief engineer. Captain Hayes was sitting on his bunk to allow room for the others since the cabin could hardly hold the small group.

Hayes looked at them, his expression hard to read in the weak light. "We've been notified that the security forces will begin their operation against the settlers at oh one hundred tonight. Nobody outside of this room is to be told. Is that clear?" Everyone nodded. "I want each of you to be prepared. Hopefully, everything will go well and those cops will take down the settlers without any trouble. But if things don't go well, we may have to improvise some very quick responses."

Garcia nodded heavily. "Will we get copies of the operation plan or will we have to read yours, sir?"

"Neither. I don't have the plan and you won't have it. All I know is the start time."

For once, Paul agreed with Garcia's outrage. "Captain, that's nuts! They're carrying out this op right under our noses. We need to know exactly what's going to happen and when! Otherwise—"

"I know." Hayes cut off Garcia in a way that made it seem the captain agreed but couldn't do anything about it. "But we don't see the plan. Security is regarded as too important."

Garcia seemed to be struggling with himself but managed to keep silent.

Hayes looked around again. "I don't know how many of you were ever scouts when you were kids, but at oh one hundred I want you to be prepared. Clear? That's all."

They pulled themselves out of the captain's cabin. Paul caught Garcia's gaze, looking for any further instructions, but Garcia shook his head like an angry bull and headed rapidly off down the passageway. Moraine eyed Paul, then turned without a word and followed Garcia. Kwan and Destin stared at Paul and Bolen in a way that conveyed a desire for privacy, so the junior officers left, Bolen quickly angling off in his own direction.

Paul stopped moving, hanging with one hand locked on the nearest hold, and checked the time. Just after midnight. Sleep was obviously impossible at this point. But he couldn't do anything, either. Anything he might do could cause people to wonder what was about to happen, and the last thing Paul wanted was to have the captain, the XO and both his current and future department heads accusing him of violating a clear order to avoid tipping anyone else off.

What did that leave? As he hung there, Randy Diego came by and gave him a surprised look. "What're you doing up, Paul?"

Good question. Randy had just come off watch, but what explanation could Paul give? "The XO wanted to see me," Paul explained, reasoning that it was a truthful statement as far as it went.

"Oh. Paperwork?"

"Yeah." Paul seized on the explanation. "Legal officer stuff. There's some reports the XO wants to see."

Randy winced. "That ship's legal officer job really sucks, doesn't it? Uh, have they told you who's going to get it when you leave the ship?"

"Not yet." Every officer had collateral duties, extra jobs they got to be responsible for in addition to their primary jobs. Paul had been given the legal officer job, responsible for advising the captain on legal issues, by virtue of a three-week-long course he'd taken before reporting to the ship. With Paul's own transfer off the ship coming up, he'd heard that the other junior officers were in mortal terror of being assigned the legal officer job. "Are you volunteering?" he couldn't help adding.

"No!" Randy suddenly seemed to realize he needed to be somewhere else and started down the passageway away from Paul. "I'm too busy all the time now! Check you later!"

"Sure." Paul watched him go, then headed for the wardroom first. He'd need coffee.

The only person in the wardroom when Paul entered was the new supply officer. Paul blinked in surprise as he realized Commander Smithe was watching a video on the big display screen. Smithe gave a non-verbal and non-committal greeting to Paul and then paid full attention to the screen while Paul got his coffee.

Paul checked the title of the video as he got his dose of caffeine. Slaughterhouse-Five? *Oh, it's a twentieth century video. Old junk.* With time to kill, he pulled out his data pad and called up a description of the movie. It sounded mostly incomprehensible, but Paul locked on one section of the description. *"The aftermath of Dresden." Dresden? Air raid. Good God. Now I remember.* He looked at the screen, where two men were climbing up some huge pile of rubble. *Dresden. They still don't know how many people were killed there. For no reason. No military reason, anyway.*

The comparison bothered him. *We're here watching these civilians. They're not harmless, though. Well, some of them aren't. But some of them are likely to die tonight. And we're helping that effort even if we're not directly involved in what's going to happen on the surface of that asteroid. What if the civilians fire at us? What if we have to kill kids to stop them? What a lousy choice.*

We're supposed to use these weapons of ours against other military forces.

That's the way it's supposed to work. Honorable combat against people who follow the same rules we do. That sounds stupid and archaic but it's true. But how many times do we end up pointing them at civilians, instead?

And we don't have a choice. What the hell else are we supposed to do?

He didn't know. So Paul headed for Combat, nursing his coffee and hoping his fears would prove meaningless.

He tried to move without any sign of unusual haste or tension, though Paul realized that if he did move with speed and apprehension then everyone seeing him would assume Commander Garcia or the XO had just called him in for another chewing-out. The darkened nighttime passageways of the *Michaelson* were once again almost deserted except for a few personnel conducting physical inspections as a backstop for the automated sensors which had too great a tendency to fail just when they were most needed. The quiet and sparsely populated passageways made a strange contrast to the turmoil inside of Paul as he thought of the upcoming operation and everything that might go wrong.

He arrived in Combat a good half hour before the operation was scheduled to begin, nodding casually to the watchstanders who looked up at his entrance. He talked to them for a few minutes, the sort of quiet interaction that just reassured Paul that they knew what was going on and reassured them that Paul cared about them and their work. He was sure they were wondering what he was doing up here, but also sure the enlisted sailors would simply chalk it up to the mysterious and strange world of officers.

The sailors turned back to monitoring their watch stations as Paul strapped into his own and called up a view of the entire situation. He spent the next ten minutes trying to again commit every important fact about the familiar situation to memory, then paged Senior Chief

Imari on her data pad. "Senior Chief Imari? This is Mr. Sinclair. Could you come on up to Combat?"

The reply took a minute. Senior Chief Imari was surely unhappy at being awakened at a time very close to the legendary "o-dark-thirty," but had to realize upon thinking about it that Paul must've had a very good reason. "Uh, yes, sir. Give me ten minutes."

"Fine." No need to rush her, and no wisdom in doing so. If he did, every other chief would be aware before Imari left their quarters of something very short-fuse about to go on in Combat.

Paul played with the displays at his watch station, looking at views of how the tactical situation would appear from the point of view of some of the other ships. It felt odd, seeing a symbol labeled USS *Michaelson* hanging out in space, just where one of the SASAL warships would see her. He noticed the weapons simulators automatically calculating firing solutions for the SASAL ship to target the *Michaelson* and cut off the view.

Senior Chief Imari entered, eyeing Paul with mild curiosity. "What's up, sir?"

Paul waved toward his watch station. When she got close, he nodded toward the time display, which now read 0055. Catching the senior chief's eye, Paul held up his hand with five fingers splayed out, then closed his hand into a fist.

Senior Chief Imari looked from the time to Paul's hand, then nodded, her face impassive. "Okay, sir. I guess I ought to check that on my watch station." Imari strapped in, checked the situation display, then gave Paul a quick thumbs-up.

She's ready. And I didn't tell *her anything. I'm sure Garcia or Kwan would rip me apart for getting Imari up here at all, but if something's going to happen I want my senior chief here.*

He checked the time, trying to fight down his nervousness. Three minutes to go. Did 0100 mean that's when the cops would move in, or was it just the time when the merchant ships would start launching the cops toward the asteroids? He'd seen pictures of the system they'd use. Just big tubes with spring-loaded platforms on the bottom. The cops would climb in and be launched toward the asteroid on just the right course with just the right amount of force and without using any active propulsion system that might give them away. With the latest stealth gear hiding their presence, the cops would hopefully remain invisible to the people on the asteroid until they were ready to move.

And if some of them somehow missed landing on the asteroid, the *Michaelson* would eventually help retrieve any cops heading on a one-way trip to deep space.

"Sir." Paul jerked his head over at the sound of Imari's voice. "Transients," she reported. "From both the *Gilgamesh* and the *Saladin*. They may be charging weapons."

Oh, hell. Paul focused on the other watchstanders. "Bayless. Chen. I want three pairs of eyes on those read-outs. Give me your estimates." He called up the information himself, feeling a heavy sensation in his guts. The transients were there, sure enough. Tiny leakages of power that almost certainly indicated the two SASAL ships were charging up their weaponry in preparation for firing. Nothing else could produce readings like that.

"Sir." Senior Chief Imari again. "The system gives a ninety-five percent level of confidence on those transients."

That meant a very high probability that they were accurate. "What about you, senior chief? What's your confidence?"

Imari gave Paul a hard look. "My gut feeling is ninety-nine percent confidence, sir. They're real solid."

Damn. What're the SASALs up to? He couldn't help remembering an incident years ago when Combat had reported picking up transients. The transients hadn't been real, that time. He'd been on the bridge then, a brand-new ensign watching as the *Michaelson*'s captain mistakenly fired upon and destroyed an unarmed ship. Paul hesitated for a fraction of a second. *But this time it's Senior Chief Imari telling me those are real transient readings, and I know those are warships, and I know a lot more about this job.*

He hadn't heard anything from the bridge, yet, but Paul figured they were fixated upon the asteroid just as Paul had been. He keyed the communications circuit. "Bridge, this is Combat." He heard his voice starting to rise with tension and lowered it. "We have high-confidence transients from both SASAL warships indicating they are charging their weapon systems."

He had only a moment to wonder how his information was being received. It was all too easy to imagine the report had landed like a bomb on the quiet bridge.

Instead of the officer of the deck responding, he heard Captain Hayes' voice, sharp and uncompromising. "Combat, how high a confidence?"

"The system says ninety-five percent, sir. My people say ninety-nine percent."

"What do *you* say, Mr. Sinclair?"

"Ninety-nine percent, captain." Paul didn't have to hesitate. He knew his job and he knew his people.

There was a pause. Paul checked the time. 0102. Whatever was happening on the asteroid had already started.

This time Captain Hayes' voice was more controlled. "Is anyone else doing anything, Paul? Any other ships?"

"No, sir, not—"

Chief Imari's voice interrupted him. "The *Peter Ville*'s started chargin' weapons, too, sir," she reported, using the sailors' nickname for the Russian ship. "High confidence."

Paul swallowed and continued his reply. "Captain, we've just picked up high-confidence indications that the *Pyotr Velikiy* is also charging weapons." Were the Russians coordinating their actions with the SASAL ships, or were they responding to the SASAL actions? There wasn't any love lost between the South Asian Alliance and the Russian Federation, but that didn't mean there weren't areas of mutual interest.

Captain Hayes sounded very unhappy, making Paul glad he wasn't face to face with the captain at the moment. "No one else, yet?"

"No, sir. Yes, sir." Chief Imari had highlighted information on Paul's display. "The *Middle Kingdom* is charging up now, too."

Commander Garcia was suddenly there at Paul's elbow, glowering ferociously at the display. Unable to find anything wrong, he slammed a fist onto the nearest surface. "Captain, the Han Chinese don't like the South Asians at all. They can't be working with them. They must be charging up in response to seeing the SASAL ships doing it."

"Self-defense?" Hayes questioned.

"Yes, sir. Captain, recommend—"

"No." Hayes cut Garcia off before he could recommend that the *Michaelson* charge up her own weapons.

Garcia flushed, then switched his anger to Paul. "Run a tactical simulation of what'll happen if the SASALs and Russians open fire on us and the Europeans."

"Sir," Senior Chief Imari interposed. "We're all at dead stop relative to each other, fairly close together and all our positions known exactly. We don't have to run a sim to know what'd happen if those ships open fire on us right now, sir."

Garcia glared at Imari, but nodded sharply. Any "battle" would last for only seconds as the ships with powered-up weapons riddled those who'd refrained from the provocative act.

"Sir?" Paul looked toward Senior Chief Imari as she spoke. "Captain's activated Big Brother."

Paul nodded, staring back at his display. Normally, warships stayed very quiet, communicating only in very short bursts when absolutely necessary, in order to keep their locations uncertain. But that made no sense now. Big Brother was a fairly new system, one designed to fire-hose as much information as possible from the *Michaelson* back to fleet headquarters. All internal and external communications, sensor readings, orders given and received, the status of equipment onboard. Whatever happened to the *Michaelson*, the records of the event would be known with certainty to those receiving the Big Brother transmission.

Garcia slammed his fist down again and pointed wordlessly. Paul followed the gesture, seeing indications springing to life on the display, indications that said some sort of combat using hand weapons was erupting on one end of the asteroid. *The cops got spotted going in. Can they—*

An alert sounded. "Alliance ship *Gilgamesh* is firing," the *Michaelson*'s combat systems computer announced with its unvarying calmness.

Heads all over Combat jerked to focus on the combat action symbology which had flashed onto display screens. Paul had the briefest moment of dread as he wondered if the SASAL ship had targeted the *Michaelson*. He'd barely had time to realize that the ships were so close that if the *Michaelson* had been shot at, the *Gilgamesh*'s blows would strike home at the same time as the combat systems warning sounded, before he saw the freighter which had been hijacked by the religious fanatics staggering under repeated blows from the SASAL weapons. *They're targeting the* Jedediah Smith. *Why?*

Senior Chief Imari's voice sounded. "Bridge, this is Combat. *Gilgamesh* is targeting the bridge and engineering sections of the freighter."

Paul tore his eyes away from the display to shoot a quick nod and look of thanks across the compartment to the senior chief. *I should've been focusing on that, too, instead of being shocked into just watching.*

"Combat, this is the captain. That freighter should've been knocked out by the first volley. Why are they still shooting at it?"

"Unknown, captain. *Gilgamesh's* fire is shifting to other portions of the hull, now."

The answer came to Paul in a flash, perhaps because of his remembrance of Dresden earlier in the evening. "They're trying to kill everyone aboard."

Garcia and Imari both stared at Paul. Then Garcia flushed an even deeper shade of red. "Tell the captain."

"Sir, I'm just guessing—"

"Tell the captain!"

"Yes, sir. Bridge, this is Combat. Assess the *Gilgamesh* is attempting to kill everyone onboard the *Smith.*" That should include at least some of the *Smith's* crew as well as the people who'd been holding them hostage. Apparently the SASAL ship was willing to sacrifice the innocent crew members in order to ensure the hostage takers were eliminated.

The reply took a moment. "Thank you, Combat. Unfortunately, I think you're right."

The alert sounded again as the *Michaelson*'s combat systems made another announcement. "Alliance ship *Saladin* is firing."

Once again eyes jumped to the displays, watching the combat systems highlight the almost invisible particle beams and lasers leaping from the other warship, and trying to determine the targets.

"It's the asteroid," someone said.

Any sense of relief Paul felt at his own ship not being the target vanished as he watched damage markers pop up on structures located on the asteroid within line of sight of the *Saladin*. As the asteroid rotated beneath the other ship, new targets became available and were shattered by the barrage.

Paul felt his hands clenching uselessly, unable to think of anything he could do. By his side, Garcia was rigid with anger as he watched the destruction. *We can't do anything. Captain Hayes must be feeling even worse than we are, if that's possible.* Paul saw the enlisted sailors staring at him with confusion. Unaware of the orders restricting the ship from acting, they were wondering why the *Michaelson* wasn't doing something. And even now he couldn't tell them.

A speaker came to life. Paul instantly recognized Captain Hayes' voice, even as he realized he was listening to a message sent to the other ships. "South Asian Alliance Ships *Gilgamesh* and *Saladin*, this is the USS *Michaelson*. Cease fire immediately. Over."

Garcia's lips stretched into an ugly grin. "Good one. He didn't threaten them or threaten to do anything. He just told them to stop. The orders don't say we can't do that."

But the SASAL ships ignored the transmission, not replying and seemingly unworried by the presence of the *Michaelson*. The *Gilgamesh* had finally abandoned its death strikes at the helpless freighter and had joined in the bombardment of the asteroid.

Paul watched more and more damage symbols appearing on settler structures, feeling sick inside. Involuntarily wrenching his eyes from the surface of the asteroid, Paul focused for a moment on the wreck of the *Jedediah Smith*. Then he blinked and looked again. *The wreck's moving. How can it be moving? The hits from the Gilgamesh couldn't have imparted enough momentum... Venting.* "Bridge, this is Combat. The *Jedediah Smith* is being pushed out of position by venting of gases and fuel."

There was a brief pause, then the captain's voice came again, the furious tone in contrast to his words. "Good catch. Where's it going?"

Paul frantically ran some extrapolations. "The wreck looks like it's falling off to starboard and down toward the asteroid surface. The trajectory is still shifting. Unable to tell if it'll clear the asteroid." He didn't bother saying what would happen if the wreck got in the way of the asteroid, let alone what that would do to anyone still miraculously surviving onboard the *Smith* and anyone on the asteroid's surface where the *Smith* impacted.

"That does it! There's one other thing we can do and we'll damn well do it. Combat, I want a course to put us between the *Gilgamesh* and the surface of that asteroid."

Paul hesitated, unsure what he'd heard, and listened as Garcia questioned the order. "Captain? Between the *Gilgamesh* and the asteroid?"

"Yes! We're going to block their line of fire. I may not be able to do anything else, but we can damn well do that! We'll see if those bastards are willing to shoot through us."

Senior Chief Imari signaled she was working the problem, so Paul just tried to keep track of what else was happening. *Even if we can block the* Gilgamesh, *that still leaves the* Saladin *with a clear shot—* The thought hadn't finished forming when he heard the captain broadcasting again, this time on the movement coordination frequency.

"All ships, this is the USS *Michaelson*. I intend placing my ship between the asteroid and those ships firing upon its surface. I say again, I am maneuvering to interpose myself between the asteroid and those ships firing upon its surface. Out."

General quarters sounded, the strident bongs of the alarm echoing through the compartments of the ship and bringing the *Michaelson* to the highest state of battle readiness. "General quarters, general quarters," the bosun on the bridge recited. "All hands to battle stations. Set airtight integrity condition Zebra." Those members of the crew still sleeping were shocked awake, grabbing uniforms and racing to their combat duty stations. The sounds of the ventilation fans changed as the ship automatically sealed off compartments and shifted to local air purifiers.

Paul pulled on the survival suit stowed near his seat, rapidly fastening the seals even as he scanned Combat to ensure all of his sailors were suiting up. The hatch to Combat cycled open and a last few operations specialists pulled themselves hastily inside, resealing the hatch in their wake, then launched themselves on direct routes across the compartment to their duty stations, depending on helping hands from their already strapped-in comrades to guide them. Senior Chief Imari swung her index finger from sailor to sailor, checking each one's presence and that they were in their survival suits, then gave Paul a quick thumbs-up. Paul turned to look at Commander Garcia, who'd strapped himself into an observer's seat nearby. "Combat is manned and ready, sir."

Garcia nodded gruffly, his attention focused on the situation displays.

Paul took an instant to breath in deeply and calm his thoughts, then checked the *Michaelson*'s weapons status on his display. No change. *We're not getting ready to fight. But we are getting ready to deal with anything else that might happen.*

Maneuvering alerts sounded as the *Michaelson*'s thrusters fired, pushing the ship around to a new heading. Paul's body slammed against the straps as the acceleration forces jerked around everything inside the ship. He watched the projected course track which had sprung to life, seeing it for the series of compromises it was. Momentum and mass were the problem. Going too fast to get into position would make it impossible to stop in time and stay in position. Just how much slower to go was a matter of judgment. The captain's judgment. Paul knew that as the *Michaelson* came around the other ships would be quickly figuring out exactly where she was going and how fast she'd get there.

But what good blocking only one ship's fire would do...

A woman's voice came on the communications circuit, its light British accent sounding unnaturally calm under the circumstances. "All ships, this is HMS *Lord Nelson*. We are maneuvering as well. All ships are requested to remain clear of us."

Captain Hayes' demand came on the heels of the *Nelson*'s captain's announcement. "Where's the *Nelson* going, Combat?"

I don't know yet! Paul thought desperately. He knew the captain knew they needed to see the *Nelson* start moving to even guess on her course, but he also knew the captain didn't want to hear that now. "Working on it, sir," he replied.

But at that instant another message arrived on a secure communications circuit. "USS *Michaelson*, this is HMS *Lord Nelson*. We estimate you are placing yourselves between *Gilgamesh* and its targets. We will position ourselves to block the fire of *Saladin*. Is this agreeable? Over."

Hayes' response held the first note of joy Paul had detected this night. "Absolutely, Captain Vitali. *Michaelson* welcomes the actions of *Lord Nelson*. Over."

"Lord Nelson was never one to hesitate in the face of a need for action, Captain Hayes. The Royal Navy can scarcely do otherwise than live up to his reputation. Out."

"Thank God for the Brits," Garcia muttered.

The *Michaelson*'s maneuvering systems fired again, pitching the ship around and jerking her crew against their restraints. Paul shook his head and blinked to clear his vision, then looked back at his display. "*Gilgamesh* is maneuvering."

Garcia studied the display, then grunted. "He's trying to sidestep us. Captain, the *Gilgamesh*—"

"I've got it," Hayes replied, his voice cool now. "They're complicating our move to block their line of fire to the asteroid, but that's all." Thrusters fired again, augmented by the *Michaelson*'s main drive. Paul rolled with the forces pulling at him, grateful that he was experienced enough at space operations that his stomach could handle the erratic shifts and sudden returns to zero gravity.

Combat systems emitted several short, sharp cracking sounds to warn of shots from the *Gilgamesh* coming close to the *Michaelson* as the SASAL ship tried to keep pounding targets on the asteroid. The *Gilgamesh*'s energy weapons didn't make any actual sound as they blazed past too close for comfort through the vacuum of space, but system designers had realized that the fastest and most effective way of alerting a crew to incoming fire was to simply simulate sounds that might be made by such weapons if they could be heard. Paul, trying not to duck at the sounds, realized the idea worked very well indeed.

He checked the read-outs on his display and felt himself sweating. The shots had been far too close, less than five kilometers away, a distance the *Michaelson* covered in seconds at her current velocity. *If those SASAL ships keep trying to shoot past us, they run a real risk of accidentally hitting us, even if it's only a graze on our hull.* The thought brought a surge of anticipation. *If they hit us, we can shoot back. That'll stop this.* Caught up in the battle, Paul momentarily forgot his chances of dying in a battle with the SASAL ships. Then he remembered and felt the heaviness inside him again.

Another alarm sounded, the high-pitched squeal of the collision alarm. "Warning," the *Michaelson*'s maneuvering systems stated. "Current track will bring the ship inside asteroid approach limits. Closest point of approach on current track will be—"

The warning cut off abruptly, telling Paul that the captain had ordered it to be shut off. Despite all the activity, his mind conjured up a brief image of a court-martial in progress and a trial counsel pointing to a diagram with a point labeled "Captain shuts off maneuvering system warning." *No. We're not going to hit it. We're just getting too damned close for comfort. That's all.*

Another set of symbols and a probability cone sprang onto Paul's display. The *Nelson* was moving. "Captain, this is Combat. Confirm the Brits are underway and heading to get between the *Saladin* and the asteroid."

The captain's response was once again drowned out, this time by another incoming transmission. "All ships, this is the *Alsace*. We are maneuvering. Request all ships remain clear." Then, on the heels of that announcement. "This is the *Heavenly Mountain*. We are maneuvering."

Paul felt his guts tightening. All those ships swinging close by each other and close to the giant menace of the asteroid. Which way were the Franco-Germans and the Han Chinese heading? Out away from the mess or—

The collision alarm stuttered into life and *Michaelson*'s warning systems spoke again. "Warning. Multiple ships maneuvering along projected course close to current position. Unable to calculate closest points of approach—"

The alarm and warning shut off, doubtless again in response to orders from the captain. Paul didn't blame him. He felt a sort of stunned fascination as he gazed at the maneuvering display, watching the overlapping course projections cluttering nearby space, the firing tracks from the SASAL ships, the looming presence of the asteroid, and the assessments of what was happening on the asteroid's surface. *What a goat rope. What a gawdawful goat rope. This can't get any—*

"Watch the *Smith*!" someone yelled. Paul half-turned to snarl at the offender for yelling, then halted, his eyes back on the wreck of the freighter. Against the much faster-moving actions of the warships, the freighter's slow, staggering path had been easy to overlook. But its venting gases had carried the wreck further down toward the asteroid and not far enough to the side. The *Jedediah Smith* was fairly large as human spacecraft went, but its mass was nothing more than roadkill in the path of the asteroid's majestic tumble. Paul watched, horrified, as the freighter fell slowly down to meet the equally gradual movement of the millions of tons of asteroid, until the freighter merged with the rock for a moment before breaking into scores of fragments hurled outward from the point of collision.

"Captain, this is Combat. The *Smith* has collided with the rock. We have multiple fragments from the *Smith* being projected outward. Some are closing on our intended track." On the already cluttered display, the paths of the wreckage cut straight across the areas several of the warships were approaching. Paul jerked his head up in momentary shock as the overhead lights dimmed, then he fixed his eyes on his display to check weapons status. The *Michaelson* was finally powering up her main batteries and close-in defenses. *To deal with the wreckage. Hitting any pieces heading for us will divert them... quite likely toward another ship's path.* And if somehow by some miracle someone on the *Smith* had survived the firing from the *Gilgamesh* and the collision with the asteroid, then the defensive fire from the other ships would surely kill them.

The maneuvering drives fired again, then several more times, and the main drive chimed in with a quick, massive slam that checked the *Michaelson*'s movement and left her drifting unsteadily across the area directly between the *Gilgamesh* and the asteroid. Paul waited, trying to control his breathing, waiting to see whether *Gilgamesh* would try to slam shots past the *Michaelson* and risk hitting the American ship. *They don't know we can't fire on them unless they hit us. If they do hit us, will the captain fire on them? Will they take the risk of hitting us?*

They didn't. The *Gilgamesh*'s weapons fell silent as *Michaelson*'s thrusters kept kicking in from various angles to cause sudden changes in the *Michaelson*'s course and position so that the SASAL ship couldn't predict where the American ship would be from moment to moment. The *Lord Nelson* skidded into position between *Saladin* and the asteroid, braking hard with remarkable precision, and the *Saladin* stopped firing as well. The maneuvering display began to lose its insane web of projected courses as some of the ships settled in to new positions. Nothing and no one seemed to be headed for collision with *Michaelson* at the moment, though a lot of things were too close for Paul's peace of mind.

Paul took a long, deep breath, then studied the display for remaining trouble. Though the space above the asteroid had calmed, scattered symbols revealed that some sort of ground combat was still going on between the cops and the settlers on the surface of the asteroid.

"Mr. Sinclair."

Paul shook his head to clear it, feeling slightly stunned by the press of events and the recent chaotic movements of ships in the small area around the asteroid. "Yeah, senior chief."

"Sir, there's two main pieces of the *Smith* heading outward. If there's still any survivors, they'd most likely be on one of them."

Paul eyed the symbols the chief had highlighted, taking long moments to comprehend why she'd emphasized the point. Then the reason finally came clear. He glanced at Commander Garcia, who was watching the situation on the asteroid's surface with a sort of horrified fascination and seemed unaware that Imari had spoken. "Thanks, senior chief. Bridge, this is Combat. We have two primary pieces of wreckage from the *Smith* headed away from us. They may hold any survivors."

Hard to say how the information would be received, given everything else the captain and the rest of the bridge crew had to worry about right now. The maneuvering thrusters punched a couple more times, jarring Paul and countering an attempt by the *Gilgamesh* to clear its line of fire to the asteroid.

The commonplace sound of a bosun pipe shrilled across the general announcing system. "Gig crew to the gig, on the double."

Paul grinned and gave Senior Chief Imari a thumbs-up. There wasn't any doubt that the gig would be sent out to try to catch those big pieces of wreckage and see if there was anyone left alive on them.

But his elation faded as he took another look at the combat display. The Russians and Southern Africans hadn't moved, holding their positions as the situation swirled around them. Both the *Alsace* and the *Middle Kingdom* were finally sliding in between the SASAL ships and the asteroid, further limiting the ability of both the *Gilgamesh* and the *Saladin* to fire or maneuver. Paul almost shuddered as he saw how close the other ships were now. If somebody zigged when they were supposed to zag, there'd be a collision for certain.

The combined obstacles of the *Michaelson*, the two Euro ships and the Han Chinese had finally brought a halt to the SASAL firing on the asteroid, but the temporary structures Paul had spent so many long hours watching had all been shattered and breached. The *Michaelson*'s own sensors and the data links to the police teams couldn't tell him how many had been destroyed by the SASAL ships and how many by ground fighting or the suicide attacks the fanatics had threatened. *Dammit. Most of those people must be dead. Dammit. We were here to stop something like this from happening and we couldn't.*

Paul blinked as the last traces of action calmed with amazing quickness. One moment the situation was a swirl of action, with weapons firing and ships moving too close too fast, the next the weapons had fallen silent, the ships had settled into new positions that might be too close but were nonetheless almost stationary relative to each other, and even the battle symbols on the asteroid had dwindled to nothing.

It almost felt peaceful. Except for the scattered wreckage of the *Smith* tumbling outward. Except for the venting of gases still taking place at a few sites on the asteroid where wrecked and probably lifeless structures now littered the bare rock. Except for the smoldering anger and sense of futility Paul felt as he watched the SASAL ships pivot under the push of their thrusters and begin accelerating away from the asteroid.

"Secure from General Quarters. Set Readiness Condition One Alpha."

There was still so much to do. Support the cops. Coordinate moving the *Michaelson* and the other warships further out from the asteroid again. See if they could help anybody, somehow. Paul looked around, his head aching and fuzzy with fatigue, as he heard reveille being sounded. *Have I been in Combat that long?*

Senior Chief Imari yawned, rubbing her face. "I need a drink," she announced.

Paul managed a smile. "Coffee? Yeah, me, too."

"I didn't mean coffee, sir. Not after tonight. But it'll have to do, won't it? It's times like this I wish I was on the Brit ship with a fully stocked bar."

One of the operations specialists was sent to get coffee from the mess decks. When he returned, the sailor also carried a carton of battle rations. Paul and his sailors studied the food dubiously. They were all hungry, but if ordinary Navy food could be atrocious, battle rations could be inedible. In the end, Paul cautiously nibbled on some sort of food bar, which seemed fairly tasteless, and drank his coffee gratefully.

Officers' call was held that morning in a corner of Combat. From the way he glared at his division officers, Commander Garcia's anger from the night before didn't seem to have diminished much. "For those of you who haven't heard, the cops have recovered seven members of the cult alive. Everybody else they've found so far is dead."

Paul tried not to openly flinch at the news.

Garcia paused, glowering down at his data pad. "The entire crew of the *Smith* is confirmed dead. Our gig found no survivors on the wreckage. Neither did the *Alsace*'s gig." He looked up again, his expression seeming to blame Paul and the others for the bad news. "The cops are securing what's left of the structures on the asteroid. We're to return to Franklin."

Only Ensign Taylor had the nerve to ask the inevitable question. "Have the cops found any heavy propulsion devices? Anything that those people could've used to kick that rock toward Earth?"

Garcia's face shaded a little redder. "No."

Taylor grimaced and nodded.

Garcia shook his own head, his mouth tight, then turned and left. Commander Moraine left with him, her expression an odd mix of relief and dread.

Taylor, Paul and Kris Denaldo exchanged glances. Finally, Taylor shook her head. "Some days this job really sucks."

Paul nodded in agreement. "Yeah."

"We did our best," Kris insisted. "We did everything we could."

"Yeah. Everything we could do just wasn't good enough, though," Taylor observed. "Well, boys and girls, it's been real fun talking with you but I need to see my division and pass on the happy news. See ya."

Kris watched her go, then looked at Paul. "Yeah, let our sailors know what happened despite our best efforts. Then what do we do?"

Paul shrugged, too weary to think anymore. "You heard Garcia. We go home." Part of him knew that should be good news, but the rest of him was too numb to care.

3

The chartered freighter *Prometheus Rising* arrived near the asteroid that afternoon. Paul was on watch again on the bridge when the *Prometheus*'s captain called the *Michaelson*. Paul, not being a fool despite operating on hardly any sleep for the past couple of days, immediately called Captain Hayes.

Hayes came onto the bridge, looking as tired as Paul felt and in a lot worse humor. The bosun mate of the watch was still crying "Captain's on the bridge" when Hayes pulled himself into the captain's chair and glared at Paul and Val Isakov. "What the hell does that merchant captain want?"

Val Isakov looked at Paul, who faced the captain. "Sir, he said he needed to talk to you. He's standing by on frequency channel eight."

"Great." Hayes glowered at the displays before him for a moment, then reached to punch the controls. "*Prometheus Rising*, this is Captain Hayes of the USS *Michaelson*."

The captain of the *Prometheus* had a Midwestern American twang to his voice and the casual manner of a civilian. "Hey, thanks for calling back. My passengers wanted me to talk to you about helping them out."

"Passengers?"

"Yeah. I'm carrying forty US citizens."

At that news, Captain Hayes got a "why me?" expression on his face. "What are they doing here and what do they want from me?"

"Well, they're, uh, here to, uh, sort of protest against you guys."

"What?"

"Maybe I didn't say that right. They're with a couple of church groups. Mainline stuff, none of the cult outfits. They were coming to try to intercede here. Try to, you know, get this resolved without any loss of life."

Paul couldn't read Captain Hayes' expression, but the captain's voice didn't betray the frustration he surely felt. "I'm afraid they're a little late."

"Uh-huh," the captain of the *Prometheus* agreed. "We saw bits of that from where we were, and we got some news updates flashed to us. So, uh, you see, they know pretty much what happened."

"Then I suggest you and they depart," Hayes advised shortly.

"Well, captain, they'd like to do something first, and the guys in charge on the asteroid won't talk to them. They figured you might help."

Hayes pressed both palms against his face for a moment, then lowered his hands and spoke carefully. "I'm sorry, but—"

"All they want to do is lay a couple of wreaths, captain. That's all. For the dead, you know."

Hayes sat silent for a moment, then looked over at Paul. "Did we receive any heads-up that this ship and those people were coming?"

Paul thought before answering, not entirely trusting his memory.

"We knew the *Prometheus Rising* was on her way to this area, sir. But I don't remember seeing anything about her carrying protestors."

"I don't remember anything about that, either. Funny no one knew." Hayes stared at nothing for a moment. "But it's even funnier that the cops went in the night before that ship got here. If those idiots kept important information from me..."

Paul didn't know what to say to that. Had someone rushed things to avoid having to deal with the people on the *Prometheus*? If so, they'd bungled things badly. And if the fact that protestors were on the way had been known to the cops but not shared with the *Michaelson*, somebody had been exceptionally stupid.

Captain Hayes addressed the captain of the *Prometheus* again. "I don't have control over what happens on the surface of the asteroid. You need to talk to the head of the law enforcement people on the surface."

"Captain, they won't talk to me."

"Hold on. I'll get back with you." Hayes drummed his fingers on his arm rest for a moment, then hit another communications control. "This is Captain Hayes of the USS *Michaelson*. I want to talk to Colonel Trey."

"I'm sorry, sir. Colonel Trey is not available. This is Major Veshak. May I help you?"

"Yes. I've got a merchant ship up here with US citizens on board who want to lay a couple of wreaths on the asteroid. I understand they can't get anybody down there to talk to them."

"Sir, we're exceptionally busy."

"Did you people know they were coming?"

The circuit stayed silent for a moment, then instead of replying to Hayes' blunt question, Veshak passed the buck. "Sir, I believe

Colonel Trey is available now."

Hayes glanced around the bridge. "I think I'd better handle the rest of this in my cabin." He unstrapped and pulled himself off the bridge.

"Captain's off the bridge!"

Paul gave Val Isakov a questioning glance. She shrugged.

Twenty minutes later, Hayes called the bridge from his cabin. "The people on the *Prometheus* are legitimate, but the cops on the surface won't let them take any transport from the merchant down to the asteroid. I agreed to use our gig. Notify the XO that we're going to send it to the *Prometheus* to pick up a couple of representatives and their wreaths. They'll be taken to the surface, brought back to the *Prometheus*, and the gig will return straight here. Any questions?"

Val Isakov frowned. "Captain, when is our gig to depart?"

"I want it at the *Prometheus* in one hour."

"Aye, aye, sir."

"Oh, one more thing. Paul, you're going along."

Paul stared at his display. "Captain?"

"You're the legal officer, and you've got experience dealing with protestors. You'll be in charge on the gig."

"Aye, aye, sir." Paul felt a headache starting to come to life. *Oh, Garcia's going to love this. He hates it any time my legal officer job gets in the way of my primary job as Combat Information Center officer, and he hates it when the captain tasks me directly because I'm the legal officer.* He wondered what the protestors would be like. They couldn't be anything like Greenspacers or the captain wouldn't have agreed to help them even if he was ticked off at the cops for keeping the Navy in the dark. *I hope I don't fall asleep in front of them.*

Garcia turned out to be just as angry as Paul had expected.

Commander Moraine just gave Paul a suspicious look. But neither could override the captain, so Paul found himself twenty minutes later strapping into a seat on the gig after hastily turning over the watch to a perturbed Randy Diego. "I'm the first lieutenant," Randy had complained. "I should be commanding the gig."

"Randy," Paul had stated wearily, "if you can convince the captain to let you go instead of me, be my guest."

Randy hadn't seemed interested in trying that, however. Even Randy had learned that there were times when you just did what the captain said.

Paul checked his straps, then glanced over at Ivan Sharpe, the *Michaelson*'s master-at-arms. "It's funny seeing you in khakis, Sheriff."

Sharpe shrugged. "I was bound to make chief petty officer someday, sir, with an officer of your caliber mentoring me."

The two bosun mates sharing the gig's cabin grinned.

Paul nodded, keeping his expression serious. "I'm glad you appreciate that, Sheriff. That's why I make sure you get to participate in outstanding training opportunities such as this."

"I thought I had you to thank for drafting me on this mission, sir. Thank you so much. There ain't nothing I'd rather do than chauffeur a bunch of hippies around the solar system."

Paul leaned back against his seat, closing his eyes. "They're not hippies, Sheriff. They're strictly mainstream people who happen to believe in peace, love and understanding."

"I believe in those things, too, sir. And I have some very effective methods for keeping everything *peace*ful because I *understand* what it takes."

"You left out love."

"Love? All my love is for the Navy, sir."

Paul opened his eyes and snorted in derision. Sharpe was smiling with exaggerated insincerity. "Sheriff, sometimes I wonder about you. Just help keep an eye on the peaceniks and help keep those cops on the asteroid happy until we leave."

"I'll try, sir, but those cops are probably not going to be happy with us."

"I have every confidence in you, Chief Master-at-Arms Ivan Sharpe. After all, you're a cop, too. You speak the same language they do."

"Sort of. These are paramilitary, SWAT guys. They're a bit different."

The chief bosun signaled to Paul from the conning station. She wasn't going to let anyone else drive the gig on this run. "All ready, Mr. Sinclair?"

"Yeah, Boats. Let's go."

"*Michaelson*, this is the gig. Request permission to get underway."

"Permission granted." Paul had no trouble recognizing the XO's voice. *Commander Kwan's going to keep a personal eye on this little mission. Great. I'd better pray nothing goes wrong in even the smallest way.*

The chief bosun tapped her controls. Paul felt force pushing him to one side as the gig's cradle pushed it gently out and away from the *Michaelson*. Then he was back in a zero-g state again as the gig drifted out of its dock. Only when it was well clear of the ship did the bosun once again reach for her controls, using thruster firings to bring the gig up and around, then triggering the gig's main drive to propel it forward.

Paul craned his head to see the maneuvering display. The gig's systems were well capable of auto-piloting their way to the *Prometheus*, but he could tell the bosun was controlling the gig manually. Officially, that was frowned upon except during training for loss of automated control. Unofficially, experienced spacecraft drivers loved to eyeball their way through maneuvers, depending on experience and skill to do everything any automated control system could do, but often with more style.

Paul leaned his head back again and closed his eyes once more. The flight should take about fifteen minutes, and no experienced sailor would let that time go to waste.

"Reveille, reveille, Mr. Sinclair."

Paul popped open his eyes at Sheriff Sharpe's droll wake-up call, yawned and then stretched as well as the straps holding him to the seat would permit. "I think I just doubled the amount of sleep I've had in the last twenty-four hours," he remarked.

Sharpe put an expression of exaggerated interest on his face. "Sleep, sir? What would that be, sir? Some privilege restricted to the exalted ranks of junior officers?"

"Sheriff, you sleep more than anyone on board except the supply officer."

"That, sir, is the worst insult I've ever received." Sharpe grinned. "And even if I did, at least I work for a living when I'm awake."

"Is that what you call what you do?" Paul peered at the maneuvering display again. The bulk of the *Prometheus* loomed close by now. Even as he watched, the bosun hit the main drive again, braking the gig to bring it to a halt relative to the freighter, then using gentle taps on the thrusters to bring the gig close to the freighter's dock. A magnetic grapnel launched from the freighter, slowly heading for the gig while its line trailed out behind. Then the grapnel locked onto the gig's mooring plate and the line began very gently retracting, pulling the gig behind it.

The *Michaelson*'s chief bosun watched intently, ready to react if the gig started moving too fast toward the dock or if anything else went wrong. Navy sailors never trusted their merchant counterparts to do things right. But the gig came to rest gently against the padded surface of the dock cradle. They could hear a humming transmitted through the hull of the gig as the freighter's air lock moved to mate with the gig.

The bosun finally turned and nodded to Paul. "All secure, sir. It's okay to crack the hatch."

"Thanks, Boats. Good driving." Paul unstrapped, pulled himself to the hatch, and cycled it open.

There were three people awaiting him. One, obviously the captain of the *Prometheus*, wore a bright coverall betraying the sheen long use. He grinned at Paul. "Did you drive that gig in here?"

"No, sir." Technically, the civilian captain of the *Prometheus* didn't have to be addressed as "sir," but Paul felt it was only appropriate when dealing with the commanding officer of another ship. "That was our chief bosun."

"Any chance I can hire her off of you?"

"No, sir. Sorry."

The captain extended one hand. "Grady Perseus."

The commanding officer of a ship named Prometheus Rising *is himself named Perseus? Figure the odds.* Paul shook hands. "Lieutenant Paul Sinclair."

"I really appreciate the help from you guys." The captain of the *Prometheus* turned to point to his companions. "These are your passengers."

Both of the others wore new coveralls, and neither had hair cut short in the usual manner of professional spacefarers. The woman, some of whose long blond hair had escaped from its bun and was drifting in front of her face, smiled politely as she used her free hand to bat at the annoying hairs. "Reverend Alice Fernandez."

Her companion, tall and dark, nodded with equal politeness to Paul even though his expression remained noncommittal. "Doctor William Chen-Meyer."

Paul glanced behind them, where two wreaths formed from cloth were fastened to the bulkhead. "If you're ready, we can leave immediately."

"Thank you," the blond replied. Reaching back to gather in one of the wreaths, she used her other hand to propel herself awkwardly toward the gig's hatch. Paul steadied her, gesturing to the two bosun mates waiting inside to help her to her seat. The dark man followed with the same lack of low-gravity skills.

Paul looked back at the freighter captain. "We should be back in about one and a half hours."

"No problem, sailor. I'll be here."

Paul sealed the hatch and returned to his seat, fastening the straps again quickly. Physically tired and emotionally exhausted from events of the last day and a half, all he wanted was to get this extra job over with. "Let's go, Boats."

"Aye, aye, sir." Several minutes later, the gig was on its way toward the asteroid's surface.

Paul averted his eyes from the screen, which displayed the looming mass of rock they were to all appearances falling onto, and found himself looking at the blond. The reverend, he corrected himself.

Her smile was gone as she stared at the asteroid. Then she looked at Paul. "The reports we received weren't sure how many of the settlers survived."

Paul bit his lip before replying. "Seven."

She winced as if in physical pain. "How many children?"

"Only two."

The dark man was shaking his head. "I just don't understand."

Paul felt anger growing. "We did all we could——"

"No. I'm sorry. I didn't mean to imply... that is." The man took a long, slow breath. "I don't understand the South Asians. Or the settlers. Why fire upon the settlement when other options remained? Why kill your own children? What possible reasons could justify either act?"

Paul met his eyes. "I honestly don't understand myself, sir."

"We hoped we could stop something like this from happening. If the police had just waited——"

"Bill," the blond interrupted. "We don't know enough, yet." She looked at Paul. "Do you know why the police moved in last night?"

"No, ma'am, I don't." At least he could be honest about that, and there was no way he was going to share Captain Hayes' suspicions that the cops had moved early to try to forestall the *Prometheus*'s arrival.

"We understand you tried to stop the attack by interposing yourselves between the South Asians and their targets." She leaned forward as far as her straps would allow. "That was a tremendously courageous act. All of my comrades want to express our thanks to you."

The dark man nodded. "I personally feared someone would start shooting and everyone would join in. We'd have had a major war triggered. I don't know what kept you from firing, but it was the right thing to do."

Paul stared at him. *We couldn't fire. We wanted to, but—— Is he right? What if we had started shooting at the SASAL ships? The Brits would've backed us, I bet. The others? Who knows. Warships would've been destroyed. Would it have triggered a big war, here in space or on Earth as well?*

Was there nothing else we could've done that wouldn't have been worse than what actually happened? I've hated those orders not to fire, but would I have wanted to live with a war started by those stupid fanatics on that asteroid? How many other people would've died because of that?

Wait a minute. These people are thanking us for what we did. I thought they'd be all over me about what'd happened. Courageous? No, we were just— He remembered the simulated sounds of SASAL shots ripping past the *Michaelson. We could've died, I guess.*

The blond was nodding to Ivan Sharpe and the bosun mates. "Yes. You all risked your lives to save others. Thank you. I know your training is to kill—"

Sharpe coughed loudly, but one of the bosun mates just grinned and nudged her comrade. "Hell, ma'am, I spend most of my time keeping people alive. War's just kind of a hobby."

Both of the visitors looked at Paul, who shrugged. "That's pretty much true in a way. We train for what we might have to do, but war's pretty much the last option after all else has failed." *At least it's supposed to be the last option.*

The dark man looked skeptical but nodded. "I wish we'd had a chance to fail."

Paul nodded back but said nothing.

The chief bosun handled the approach to the asteroid with the same skill and aplomb she'd shown earlier. As the gig came to rest several meters above the surface of the asteroid, Paul gestured to the guests. "How do you want to do this?"

The blond looked distressed. "We don't have suits. We should've thought—"

"We can drop 'em internally," the chief bosun advised. She pointed downward. "There's a drop chute there. Put in your, uh, objects and I'll open the chute. There's a little spring-loaded launch pad that'll push them down toward the surface."

"Thank you. That will do very nicely."

As the two visitors cautiously loaded the wreaths into the drop chute built into the deck of the gig, Paul panned the visual display around. On the surface below, he could see scattered remnants of the settlement. No bodies were visible, but at least twenty security personnel were in place and watching the gig.

The chief bosun tapped Paul's arm and pointed to another display. "They got weapons trained on us."

"What?"

"Yeah. Light anti-orbital stuff. Only good for taking out tourists and boats like this."

Paul glanced back at the visitors and kept his voice low. "What the hell do those cops think we are?"

"I guess they figure better safe than sorry, sir."

"Well, they'd better do a better job of recognizing real threats, then. And of trusting people on the same side."

The drop chute safely sealed, the chief bosun triggered the drop while both of the visitors prayed. The blond watched the wreaths fall toward the asteroid, tears from her eyes drifting away from her face. The female bosun scooped the errant spheres of water up with a cloth, her face impassive.

Paul watched the wreaths, too, then looked at the security forces arrayed below. He caught Sheriff Sharpe's eye and Sharpe shook his head. *As soon as we're gone they'll get rid of those wreaths. Hell. What's wrong with grieving for the innocent dead?*

A few minutes later they were on their way back to the *Prometheus*. Paul was trying to decide whether or not to report that weapons had been trained on the gig when he realized both of the visitors were watching him intently.

"Excuse me," the dark man stated. "But I wonder if you could tell me, in your own words, why you do what you do."

Paul tried to sort the question through his weary brain. "Why I'm in the Navy, you mean?"

"The Navy. The military. Why you wear a uniform and, as you said, train to kill if your superiors should find it necessary."

"That's a rather complicated question and I've had a very long day." Paul thought about it for a while. "I guess because it's important."

"But, why? Why do you think so?"

"Because... look, we take this oath. Yes. An oath. When I put on the uniform I swore I'd, um, 'support and defend the Constitution of the United States of America against all enemies foreign and domestic.' There's more, but that's basically it."

The blond looked intrigued. "Then you don't swear to defend the country, or to follow orders, but to defend the Constitution?"

"Well, yes, we swear to follow orders, but they have to be legal orders."

"Legal orders?"

"Yes. You know. They can't violate the law. Or the Constitution. You can't be ordered to do something illegal. Well, okay, you can be ordered to do something wrong but it's your responsibility not to obey an illegal order."

"Such as one violating the Constitution?"

Paul nodded. "Yeah."

"Any part of it?"

"We swear to defend the entire thing."

She laughed, then looked at her companion. "Did you hear that, Bill? They're here to defend the Constitution. Including the Bill of Rights! People with guns and uniforms to defend freedom! It's funny, isn't it?"

"Why?" Paul asked.

"I'm not sure. Maybe funny is the wrong word. Incongruous. Ironic." She sighed. "We don't really understand you. The military, I mean. And you don't understand us, do you? But, really, you've got the weapons. *You've* nothing to fear from *us*."

Paul found himself smiling lopsidedly. "You've got a point there."

They were almost back at the *Prometheus* when the blond reverend spoke again. "Your captain told our captain that your ship will be leaving here soon to return to your base."

"If he told you that, then, yes, that's so," Paul said.

"We're going to request permission for the *Prometheus Rising* to accompany your ship back."

Paul frowned. "Why?"

She hesitated, looking over at the dark man, who nodded reluctantly. "To put it bluntly, we'd appreciate your escorting us to ensure we reach home safely."

Paul was sure his eyebrows were rising in surprise. "Escort?"

"Yes. Isn't that the right term? Those ships, the South Asians, they're still out there. We'd like your protection."

Surprise was putting it too mildly. Maybe shock, Paul decided. "I can't promise anything like that."

"We understand that. The captain of the *Prometheus Rising* will make a formal request to your captain. If you could do us the favor of letting him know the request will be forthcoming, we'd be grateful."

Paul nodded. "Sure. I'll tell him." *I can't wait to see how Captain Hayes reacts to that.*

Ten minutes later the gig was docked and the two pacifists made polite farewells to Paul and the sailors with him. Five minutes after that the gig was headed back to the *Michaelson*. The chief bosun looked back at Paul and grinned. "They were kinda nice, weren't they?"

"Yeah." Paul saw Sharpe rolling his eyes. "Give me a break, Sheriff. They were nice."

"Probably just deception, Mr. Sinclair. Get us off guard."

"I can't tell if you're joking this time."

Sharpe grinned. "I'm not telling. Don't fall for their act, sir. Maybe they are really nice people. But they don't understand how the world works. How people work. They just cause trouble for you and me."

"Sheriff, honest to God sometimes I wonder how much I do understand how things work."

Sharpe pointed to Paul's uniform. "You're wearing that, sir. That means you understand something. Of course, that officer's rank means you don't understand too much. That's why you need enlisted around to explain things."

"Very funny. You know as well as I do that there's always more than one way to handle a situation."

"Yes, sir. The Right Way, the Wrong Way and the Navy Way," Sharpe recited.

"Uh-huh. Maybe sometimes their way might work. Or at least make things a little easier for us."

Sharpe scratched his cheek meditatively. "Mr. Sinclair, I don't mind admitting you've got good instincts sometimes. In this case, though, I figure letting misguided idealists get involved would just make our problem worse."

"Would it?" Paul stared at the deck for a moment. "You know what, Sheriff? When push came to shove on and around that asteroid all our weapons couldn't make any difference. *Before* that our weapons hadn't resolved things. There's limits to what we can do."

Sharpe didn't try to hide his skepticism. "You think those peaceniks could've really made a difference?"

"We'll never know, Sheriff. Maybe they could've talked some sense into those settlers. Maybe their presence would've made the SASALs a little less likely to take out as many settlers as possible. Maybe. But I do know one thing. Things couldn't have turned out any worse than they did. I wish those people had been given a chance to try."

"What the hell were they doing there?"

Paul looked over at Lieutenant Mike Bristol, surprised by the junior supply officer's uncharacteristic outburst. Meals in the wardroom had been subdued lately. They were on their way back to Franklin Naval Station, the civilian freighter *Prometheus Rising* following five thousand kilometers astern, far enough away to avoid giving away the *Michaelson*'s exact position or colliding with the warship by accident, but close enough to be within easy reach if protection was needed. One of Paul's few enjoyable moments lately had been watching the expressions on the faces of Commanders Kwan, Garcia and Moraine when he told Captain Hayes in their presence about the civilians' impending request for escort home. But Hayes had agreed. "Why was who where?" Paul asked.

"Those people on the asteroid."

Paul had seen the reports. "The survivors claim God told them to settle the asteroid."

"Why?"

"Hell, Mike, I don't know. God hasn't talked to me lately. Next time he does, I'll ask."

Something about his tone of voice got through to Mike, who nodded. "I know you don't know. It's just…"

"Yeah."

"And the SASALs," Bristol continued. "Using a ship named the *Saladin* for that kind of atrocity. Saladin himself never murdered civilians. He was a decent, honorable soldier."

"What I want to know," Randy Diego asked, "is why they did it? I mean, why kill those people? What was the point?"

Paul glanced around, but no one else seemed willing to answer the question. "We don't know for sure, Randy, but best guess is that the SASAL leadership didn't want these settlers getting off easy. They wanted to make an example of them so no other groups would try to settle asteroids without oversight and monitoring."

"So they tried to kill them all?"

"Apparently."

Kris Denaldo made an angry face. "Anybody else planning on setting up rogue settlements will know the SASALs are willing and ready to slaughter them. And they'll know we won't stop the SASALs from doing it," she finished bitterly.

"We couldn't," Paul insisted. "You know that."

"Sure. We had our orders. And those orders gave the SASALs a free hand. How'd they know?"

"They didn't—"

"Are you sure? Look at what they did. It's just like they knew we couldn't do anything, that we'd have to sit by and watch them fire on those guys."

Paul scowled down at his food, not feeling the least bit hungry and unable to think of any response to Kris' statement. *They couldn't have known our orders. But they sure acted like they did. They even stopped shooting when there was a risk of hitting us by accident, as if they knew that would allow us to shoot back.*

"We saved two kids," Ensign Gabriel noted.

"Is that supposed to cheer us up?" Kris demanded. "Between the SASALs and the settlers' own suicide pact a lot more died."

"I know," Gabriel agreed helplessly. "I just... I don't know. It's something."

Mike Bristol nodded at her. "That's right. Does anybody know if the captain's going to get in any trouble because of this?"

"Why would he get in trouble?" Kris asked.

"You know."

"No, I don't."

Bristol made a face. "A scapegoat. What if they want a scapegoat?"

Paul shook his head. "The captain deserves a medal for what he did, not any kind of reprimand."

Randy Diego spoke again. "But all those people on the asteroid did die. If the politicians need someone to blame—"

"They can't nail it on Hayes," Paul explained with an outward patience he didn't real feel. "I know for a fact that word's gotten around in the press that our ship was put between those SASAL ships and their targets."

"But I thought we weren't supposed to do *anything,*" Randy insisted. "If they need someone to blame and the captain did something they can claim was wrong—"

"Or didn't do something they can claim he should've," Val Isakov chimed in. "They could court-martial him. Make him the fall guy."

She smirked at Paul. "You might get a chance to nail another captain, Sinclair."

The fatigue and frustrations of the last several days boiled over inside of Paul. Only the straps holding Paul into his seat kept him from launching himself at Isakov, his hand clenched into a tight fist. Isakov's eyes widened, but before anything else could happen Kris Denaldo had reached across Randy and grabbed the front of Isakov's uniform. Randy stared straight ahead, his body rigid at being caught in the line of fire between Isakov and Denaldo.

"You stupid bitch," Denaldo stated in a voice which seemed all the more menacing for not betraying any emotion. "Paul Sinclair testified on behalf of Captain Wakeman. Nobody else had the guts to do that, but he did because he thought even somebody like Wakeman shouldn't be blamed for the things they couldn't control. Either know what you're talking about or keep your damned mouth shut." Denaldo released Isakov's uniform and leaned back again, then unstrapped with quick, angry gestures. "I'm not hungry, anymore."

Val Isakov, her face still red with anger, watched Kris leave the wardroom, then unstrapped herself as well. "By your leave," she spat, then she was gone, too.

Silence settled. Paul rubbed his face, then found himself looking at the chair at the head of the table. Commander Sykes, the old supply officer, had sat there during the junior officer meal shifts. The new supply officer had chosen to eat with the senior officers, and no one else had stepped in to provide a steadying hand to the junior officers. *Sykes would've kept that situation from blowing up. Sykes would have had some good advice for us.*

Bristol followed Paul's gaze and nodded in understanding. "I miss him, too."

"We're tired as hell and too strung out to think straight." Paul pushed his own food away. "We could use some calm center of gravity right now."

"Yeah. The guy was almost a father figure. Of course, if we'd told him that he'd have said 'could be' and asked us who our mothers were." Bristol sighed. "It's hard having Smithe for a boss now. Sykes gave us plenty of free rein, but Smithe wants to know every time I need to push a button on my keypad so he can sign off on it first."

"Ouch. My sympathies."

"I bet you're looking forward to Garcia leaving."

Paul grinned. "You could say that. I haven't got a good feel for what Moraine is like, though."

"She doesn't seem to have Garcia's distemper problem."

Paul smiled again. "No. But she seems sort of... twitchy."

"Twitchy? Nervous?"

"Yeah. And every time she looks at me she has this expression like I'm another ship on a collision course with her and five seconds from impact." Paul unstrapped. "I've got twenty minutes left to grab some sleep."

Instead of heading straight for his stateroom, though, Paul went by Kris Denaldo's quarters. She was sitting in her chair staring morosely at nothing, but she looked up as Paul knocked on the open hatch. "Hi, Paul. Sorry I blew up at Crazy Ivana. Unprofessional."

"It's not like you weren't provoked."

"I'm turning into Jen."

"Careful, that's my fiancée you're talking about. Are you calling Jen unprofessional?"

That brought a half-hearted smile to Kris' face. "Perish the thought."

"Besides," Paul added, "if Isakov had been within reach of me I would've beat you to her." He grinned. "Did you see the look on Randy's face when you reached across him to get at her?"

"No. Was it priceless?"

"'Deer in the headlights' doesn't begin to describe it."

Kris smiled again, then went somber. "Three years is a long time to do this sort of thing, Paul. I feel burnt out and sucked dry. That's how I felt *before* the asteroid incident. Now it's even worse."

"Will you be okay?" Airlocks were too easy to find for someone who thought they couldn't handle life anymore. It had happened on other ships to other sailors who couldn't handle their personal or professional pressures.

But Kris shook her head. "I'll be fine. Me big strong space warfare officer. Underway is the only way. Do I sound perky enough?"

"Try a 'hoo-rah.'"

"I will *not* try a 'hoo-rah.' I'm not a Marine."

"Hang in there, Kris. In two weeks you'll be walking off of this ship for the last time."

"I'll believe it when it happens. Who's going to look out for you for Jen when I'm gone?"

Paul smiled. "I'm a big strong space warfare officer, too. I'll be okay."

"Sure you are." She waved him away. "Go get some sleep."

"Do I look that bad?"

"Frankly, yes. And before you tell me, I don't want to know how I look."

"Watch out for that guy!"

Paul jerked in reaction to the warning from Isakov, then cursed to himself before answering her. "I see him. The system shows him tracking clear of us."

"He's too close." Isakov kept her eyes riveted on the maneuvering display where dozens of contacts within the five thousand kilometer danger zone around the *Michaelson* moved along their own trajectories. "I hate being this close to base. There's too much crap out there to worry about."

Paul privately agreed but didn't say so since he'd yet to forgive Isakov for her latest verbal jabs at him. Franklin Naval Station had spent weeks being just a bright dot in space, then with apparently shocking speed had become a great hollow disc rotating majestically before them, as the *Michaelson's* velocity had closed the final thousands of kilometers within a short time. "Braking maneuver in five minutes," he reminded Isakov.

"Handle it."

Yes, ma'am. Paul turned to look at the bosun mate of the watch. "Give the five-minute warning, Boats."

"Aye, aye, sir." The bosun raised his pipe, triggered the internal broadcast circuit and blew the notes that called attention to his announcement. "All hands prepare for maneuvering in five minutes. Secure all objects and materials. Undertake no task which cannot be completed prior to maneuvering."

Paul reached to call the captain, only to have his gesture halted in mid-reach as the bosun spoke again. "Captain's on the bridge!"

Hayes pulled himself into his chair and strapped in even as he scanned the maneuvering display and shook his head. "There's a lot of traffic out there today."

Isakov nodded. "Yes, sir. Request permission to begin final deceleration and approach to station."

"Permission granted." Hayes looked over as Commander Kwan entered the bridge and hastily went to his own chair on the opposite side of the bridge from the captain's. "XO, let's go ahead and get the crew to stations."

"Yes, sir." Kwan pointed at Paul and Isakov. "Do it."

Isakov in turn looked at Paul, who couldn't help smiling at the absurdity of the way the chain of command was playing out on the bridge as he faced the bosun again. "Pass the word for all hands to man stations for entering port."

"Aye, aye, sir." Another blast on the whistle. "All hands man stations for entering port. Department heads make reports of readiness for entering port to the officer of the deck on the bridge."

Paul checked the time. Two minutes to the final braking maneuver. "Boats, give the two-minute warning." Hayes and Kwan were talking across the bridge to each other, but he couldn't pay any attention to that now. One minute. "One-minute warning, Boats. Captain, request permission to initiate final braking maneuver."

Hayes nodded without taking his eyes off of his own maneuvering display. "Permission granted."

Paul watched the countdown scroll down to zero, then pushed the button confirming the maneuver. Thrusters fired, pitching the *Michaelson* to the side. On the maneuvering display, her trajectory toward Franklin showed as a broad curve. More thrusters fired, halting the ship's stern on the right bearing, then the *Michaelson*'s main drive slammed them into their seats as it roared to life and began braking the ship's velocity. Paul swallowed, wondering if his stomach would ever get fully used to the rapid changes in apparent gravity caused by such maneuvers.

The curve of the ship's trajectory flattened out until the *Michaelson* was aimed at a point just above the station and coming in at an angle that would allow it to match the station's rotation at the point where its berth awaited the ship. Paul glanced at Isakov out of the corner of his eyes. *Who's taking the ship in for final? If I ask, they'll give me the job for sure since it'll sound like I'm volunteering.*

An instant later his unspoken question was answered by the captain. "Paul, why don't you take her in today."

"Aye, aye, sir." *Lucky me. Again.* Driving the ship through open space could be great fun. Driving the ship into her berth, where the slightest mistake could cause a collision and lots of damage, was never fun.

He keyed the communications circuit. "Franklin Naval Station, this is USS *Michaelson*. Request permission to approach the station and dock at our assigned berth seven alpha. Over."

After a moment, Franklin replied. "This is Franklin Naval Station. Roger. Permission granted for USS *Michaelson* to approach the station and dock at assigned berth seven alpha. Follow standard docking procedure. Over."

Paul looked over at the captain, who waved one hand to acknowledge the message, then replied. "This is USS *Michaelson*, roger, out."

To his side, Isakov spoke. "All departments report readiness for entering port, captain."

Paul concentrated on the maneuvering display. The ship's systems could auto-pilot them into dock, but few ships used those systems routinely for close-in approaches. The tiniest problem in the electronic brains running the automated systems could translate into serious trouble too quickly for human intervention to correct it in time. Experienced people, for all their human flaws, were more reliable.

"Standby thrusters," Paul commanded as the *Michaelson* began gliding over the top of Franklin's great disc. Berth seven alpha loomed ahead and off to one side, the movement of the ship and the rotation of the station bringing ship and berth together with ponderous precision. He had to gauge the right moment to fire thrusters to halt the *Michaelson* relative to the station at just the right place. "Starboard thrusters all ahead two-thirds."

"Starboard thrusters all ahead two-thirds, aye," the bosun mate of the watch echoed. The *Michaelson* shuddered as the thrusters slowed the ship's sideways progress.

Paul tried to feel the ship's motion and match it to the need to reach the spot right above the berth. "All stop."

"All stop, aye."

It wasn't quite enough. "Starboard thrusters all ahead one-third."

"Starboard thrusters all ahead one-third, aye."

The ship quivered again, with less force, slowing even more. "All stop!"

"All stop, aye."

Watching the ship's movement and the rotation of Franklin below, Paul thought it felt very good. "Standby all lines."

"Standby all lines, aye."

They were drifting very slowly now, the berth coming into alignment with the ship. "Send over lines one, three and five."

The lines snaked out, leaping toward the berth and latching onto contact plates. The lines tightened as the *Michaelson* continued to drift. Paul studied the display, wondering if he'd need to tap the thrusters again. But the strain on the lines stayed within acceptable limits and the ship lurched only slightly as the lines brought her into a complete match with Franklin's movement. The bosun twirled his pipe again. "Moored! Shift colors!" The flag on the *Michaelson*, safely ensconced in a container aft, didn't actually move to another location as it would on a seagoing ship, but the *Michaelson*'s broadcast identity changed, telling anyone listening that the ship had ceased being a free-maneuvering object and was now tied to a station with a fixed orbit.

Paul took a deep breath. The hardest part was over. "Send over lines two and four." The last two lines latched on. "Take in all lines." With the greatest of care, the lines started being reeled in again, gently tugging the ship into the assigned berth. Paul leaned back, knowing all that was left was the tedium of waiting while the ship was winched ever so slowly into the berth. But even that had to be monitored. If the winches malfunctioned and started pulling too hard and too fast the final mating of the ship to its berth would just be another form of collision.

Eventually, they were nestled securely in their berth, feeling the apparent steady force of about one Earth gravity under the influence of Franklin's rotation. Paul ran through the final responsibilities of his watch, then faced the captain again. "Request permission to secure stations for entering port and to shift the watch to the quarterdeck, captain."

"Permission granted." Hayes unstrapped and got down his chair a trifle unsteadily. "Good job, Paul."

"Thank you, sir." While the bosun passed the word, Paul called up the camera on the quarterdeck so he could see the pier. There was a small crowd awaiting them. Paul searched for any sign of

Jen, noticing a commander standing waiting to go onboard the *Michaelson* first. He zoomed in on the commander's uniform and saw the Judge Advocate General's insignia. *A JAG waiting on the pier. That's never a good thing. What do you want to bet he's here to see me?*

He was. Paul had scarcely left the bridge, his legs a little wobbly under the unaccustomed steady feeling of gravity, when he was paged to the quarterdeck. Paul had met a lot of the JAGs on Franklin because of his legal officer responsibilities and involvement in too many court-martials, but he didn't know this commander, so he must be fairly new to the station.

The commander didn't waste time, hauling out some paperwork. "Lieutenant Sinclair? Good. I've been assigned to compile the official investigation into the recent action involving your ship. Nothing to worry about. We've already gone over all the material we received from your ship's transmissions during the engagement. We do need a few personal statements, though." He tapped the papers. "The list is here. Please get sworn statements from everyone listed and forward them to me as soon as possible."

Paul took the list, trying not to think of everything else he needed to do and how much he just wanted to relax for a few hours at least. "Yes, sir."

"That's all." The commander waved farewell and left while Paul was still scanning the list. Captain. XO. Operations officer. No surprises. Just a royal pain in the neck for Paul to get those officers to cough up the statements. Since they all outranked him, it wasn't like he could order them to do the statements right away, which meant he'd have to diplomatically ride herd on the process until he could get every statement completed.

"Request permission to come aboard."

Paul looked up quickly at the familiar voice. "Jen!"

She finished saluting the officer of the deck and came over to him. "Virtual hug." They couldn't really hug, not while they were in uniform.

"Virtual hug back. Virtual kiss."

"Fresh." Jen's smile faded. "You look like you've been rode hard and put away wet. Rough one, eh?"

"You know what happened out there."

"Yeah. What's your status?"

He knew she meant whether he could leave the ship or not. "Standard work day." Which meant at least twelve hours.

"You're kidding. You guys have been out for several weeks, you've been involved in tough ops, and they can't even give you a little stand-down?"

"Sorry, Jen, the XO told us the morning—"

Ensign Gabriel, the officer of the deck, waved a forestalling hand at Paul. "Wait a minute. The captain's about to make an announcement."

Captain Hayes' voice came over the announcing system. "This is the captain speaking. I want to thank all of you for the outstanding effort you've put forth the last several weeks. You've all worked hard and done the *Michaelson* proud. Now you deserve a break. I can't give you much of one, but I'm authorizing liberty for everyone except the duty section effective as soon as your department heads and division officers can release you. That's all."

Jen grinned. "Let's go."

"Jen, I've got to cut my own people loose and get permission from Garcia."

"I can wait. Kris and I can catch up on things."

"Okay." Paul held up the papers. "And I've got to get this started before I go."

"Paul Sinclair—"

"I just have to notify the officers who have to provide statements. It shouldn't take too long."

Jen shook her head, then smiled again as Chief Sharpe came onto the quarterdeck. "When did you make chief?"

"A month ago, ma'am." Sharpe saluted with a solemn face. "It's a pleasure to see you again, Lieutenant Shen. Though I have to confess I keep hearing about you constantly from a certain love-struck lieutenant on this ship who will remain nameless." He faced Paul. "Sir, a word of warning. There's going to be a hot time in the old town tonight. This crew is strung tight. They're really going to be blowing off steam. I'd appreciate it if you talk to your troops and—"

"Remind them to maintain control because if they don't they'll end up paying for it? Sure, Sheriff. I'll pass the suggestion on to the other division officers." He checked the time. "Jen, I'll look you up in Kris' stateroom. Request permission to proceed on duties assigned."

She shook her head in mock annoyance and flipped him a salute. "Permission granted."

Paul hastened off in search of the captain or the XO, his arms aching with the wish to hold Jen but knowing he couldn't leave the ship without passing on the JAG's need for statements. As he walked, he glanced down at the questions. Most of them were totally predictable, as well as totally superfluous since the answers to them were already known thanks to the material *Michaelson* had transmitted during the engagement.

But then he frowned and came to a halt, reading the last question over slowly again. *"Provide your assessment of South Asian Alliance planning for this event, including any indications that to your mind might imply SASAL foreknowledge of US intentions."*

Somebody does think our rules of engagement might've been compromised. But how?

4

Now that she was serving on "shore duty" on Franklin, Jen actually had assigned berthing on the station. Remarkably, she'd managed to score one of the few private single-officer compartments. Granted, there were a great many closets on Earth that probably had a larger square footage, but Paul didn't particularly mind the fact that just being in the compartment with Jen made them stay practically touching the entire time. "Nice place."

"Thanks. It's just a little hole in the wall, but it's home." She handed Paul a drink and sat down next to him on the bed/couch. "Relax."

"I'm trying." Paul made a conscious effort to let the tension out of his body. "Let's talk about something besides my underway time. You know what I was doing. What've you been up to?"

"I had dinner with my father while you were out."

Gee, too bad I missed seeing Captain Kay Shen. But Paul kept his sarcasm silent, knowing Jen couldn't be held responsible for her father's opinion of Paul. "How'd it go?" he asked instead, trying to keep his voice casual.

He apparently didn't quite succeed, as Jen gave him an exasperated look. "You two remind me of a couple of bears or something. The old leader trying to keep control and the young upstart circling and looking for an opening."

"I am *not* trying to take control of anything from your father!"

"It's an analogy, Paul. You're not bears, either. Usually."

"So, how'd it go?" he repeated.

Jen shrugged. "Dad insisted on instructing me in lots of schemes to make my career 'healthy' again."

"He's fairly senior and he's got a lot of experience."

"Yes, but he's not me! He says I should stay away from engineering from now on. But I love that stuff, both theory and practice. And I swear, some of the things he suggested come down to kissing every butt in the solar system and begging them to forgive me. For what? For my being unfairly accused of sabotaging my own ship and killing my own shipmates and then having my name dragged through the mud and almost being convicted of a crime I didn't commit? *I'm* supposed to ask *them* for forgiveness?"

"I can see where that'd be hard to swallow. You got a raw deal."

"It would've been worse if you hadn't been there. Incredibly worse." Jen gave him a weary look. "But as you've probably guessed, Father also suggested I dump overboard something that would immediately cause people to associate me with the court-martial."

Paul felt a flash of anger and stifled it in a short laugh. "Meaning me?"

"Of course. Good advice, huh? Give up my pride, everything I care about at work, the man I love, and hope that somehow I'll be able to salvage a 'career' out of what remains. Why the hell would

I want a career doing things I don't like, alone, after I've flushed my self-respect down the toilet?"

"What'd you tell your father?"

Jen sat a little straighter, put an obviously artificial expression of gratitude on her face, and spoke in a lilting little-girl voice. "Why, thank you, sir. I shall certainly give your suggestions all the consideration they deserve."

Paul coughed, choking on the drink he'd made the mistake of taking just as Jen started speaking. When he recovered enough to speak, he shook his head. "You didn't really do that to him, did you?"

She was laughing. "No. I was on my best behavior, Mr. Sinclair. Yes, sir. Thank you, sir. I'll think very carefully about what you've said, sir."

"You called him 'sir' that much?"

"Yeah. He knows when I do that he's stepping over the line. But he kept plowing ahead, anyway. Dad's one stubborn guy when he thinks he's right."

"Unlike his daughter, who's the soul of reason."

She grinned at him. "Or his future like-it-or-not son-in-law."

Paul grinned back. "What if the kids inherit it from both sides?"

"God help us." Jen smiled wistfully. "It's funny to be talking about kids. About having them."

"Funny? I think it's scary."

She laughed. "You're daunted by the prospect, Mr. Sinclair? You've been responsible for an entire Navy warship and all her crew."

He nodded. "Yep. But kids, I think, will be a lot bigger responsibility. I've never had to worry about screwing up someone else's entire life before."

"Really?" Jen came a little closer and slipped her arms around his waist. "What about my life?"

He looked into her eyes, marveling at the emotion he saw there. "What do you mean?"

"You know what I mean. You could screw up my life something terrible, Paul. If you left me, if you were unfaithful, if you lied and cheated."

"I'd never do that. Any of that."

"I know. At least, I believe that, which is why I've got my arms wrapped around you right now and why I'm going to do this." Jen kissed him, long and hard, then slowly pulled back enough to see into his eyes again. "And that's not all I'm going to do," she whispered.

Roughly half an hour later, Paul looked over at Jen where she lay next to him, awed once again at the emotion in her eyes as she gazed back. *I never thought someone would look at me that way. Never really believed it could happen. And there it is.* "I love you."

She smiled with unusual gentleness. "I bet you say that to all the girls."

"No. Only to the one I'm going to marry."

"Damn straight, sailor." Jen snuggled close. "Right now, in here, I can forget everything outside, and just be happy. Forget all about careers and ships and sailing out into space without each other. Oh, that's right. There's something I forgot to tell you."

"What's that?" Paul asked, unable to prevent a sudden sense of tension.

Her breath was warm against his ear. "Welcome home, sailor." Then she laughed.

Commander Garcia marched off the quarterdeck for the last time as if even that was a cause for aggravation. The petty officer of the watch bonged the ship's bell and announced, "Commander,

United States Navy, departing," then Garcia was gone and the other officers dropped their salutes. Commander Moraine shuffled her data pad and several other items, then lunged off the quarterdeck into the ship's interior as if headed off on a desperate mission.

Paul had come aboard the *Michaelson* that morning in the highest spirits he'd had for a while. A few more months and he'd be married to Jen and on shore duty here on Franklin along with her. He'd remembered to get a completed and sworn statement from Garcia before his old department head left the ship. They'd be inport for a while taking care of long-overdue maintenance, so while the work would still be brutal it wouldn't be quite as brutal. All in all, things could be a lot worse.

He went back to his stateroom and started scanning through all the messages which had downloaded upon the *Michaelson*'s arrival. While the ship was operating out in space, communications were always kept to a bare minimum to keep anyone from using the transmissions to help locate the ship's general position, speed and trajectory. Anything of high precedence or importance had been transmitted before the ship arrived at Franklin, of course, so he didn't expect to find anything except routine administrative and operational matters.

But Paul's scanning stopped when he saw a subject line with his name on it and the words "order modification." *What? They're modifying my orders? This close to my transfer? It's probably just adding some training courses before I report in to Franklin's Operations Department.*

It wasn't. Paul felt an odd numbness spreading across his body as he read. "*When detached USS* Michaelson *(CLE(S)-3) report to transportation office, Franklin Naval Station, for flight arrangements to Theodore Roosevelt Naval Base, Mars. Upon arrival, report to commander for duties assigned...*"

Mars? They can't— Mars? How the hell—? Paul realized he was standing up and heading for what he still thought of as Commander Garcia's stateroom. He was knocking on the hatch before he remembered Commander Moraine would answer. She gave him a nervous frown as she opened the hatch. "Yes?"

"Req—" Paul swallowed and spoke again. "Request permission to leave the ship, ma'am."

Moraine's eyebrows shot up. "Liberty call just expired."

"Yes, ma'am. But something urgent has come up—"

"It'll have to wait. I won't have one of my division officers absent for the first officer's call at which I'm head of this department." Moraine shut the hatch, leaving Paul steaming in the passageway and mentally counting to ten to keep from punching the hatch.

The morning passed in a haze. He didn't pay much attention to Moraine's little speech at officers' call. Senior Chief Imari and Paul's fellow junior officers could tell something was wrong, but Paul waved them off, determined to fix the problem before he vented about it.

Knock-off ship's work was announced for lunch and Paul was off the quarterdeck in a flash, heading for a phone terminal. It'd cost a mint to phone Earth real time, but that wasn't important right now.

A receptionist answered. "Naval Personnel Command."

"I need to speak to my detailer. Lieutenant Commander Braun." The time delay caused by the need for the signal to travel at the speed of light between Franklin and Earth wasn't too large, but large enough to be apparent and annoying.

"Thank you. Please hold."

The receptionist was reaching for the switch when Paul interrupted her, having anticipated her move and started talking before he heard her reply. "I'm calling from Franklin Orbital

Station. I can't afford to hold long."

"Yes, lieutenant. I'll make sure Lieutenant Commander Braun knows."

A screen saver appeared. Thrilling pictures of senior Naval officers giving no doubt inspiring speeches. Paul tried not to look at his watch, not to let anger get in the way.

The screen saver blinked, then gave way to his detailer. Lieutenant Commander Braun smiled at Paul, a gesture that came and went too quickly to have meaning. "Lieutenant Sinclair. Nice to hear from you."

Paul spoke with a carefully controlled voice. "Ma'am, I just received an order modification."

"Yes?" Braun's face and tone expressed friendly interest but nothing more.

"To Mars. But I'm supposed to transfer off of the *Michaelson* to duty on Franklin. I had those orders in my hands."

"Oh. Yes. Sinclair." Braun spread her hands with an expression of mild regret. "Yes. A sudden requirement came up and you were judged the best fill for the job."

"Four months out and I'm the only guy who fits the job?"

"Well, you were the best fit."

"Fit for what? This order mod doesn't even specify a particular assignment."

"Ah, well, you'd have to talk to the people at Roosevelt about that."

Paul tried to keep his temper from flaring. "That's not too practical. Real-time calls to Mars—"

"Oh, well, yes, it might be a little difficult."

"Look, ma'am, I'm getting married right after I leave the *Michaelson*—"

"Congratulations."

"—which I *know* is in your file on me, and I had orders to be stationed on Franklin, which is where my wife will also be stationed."

Braun spread her hands again. "Yes, well, needs of the Navy. Sorry."

"There must be some way to fix this."

"Fix it? No, no. Nothing to fix. Nothing that can be fixed. Mars assignments are locked in to allow transportation planning. If you had any objections, you should've let us know within forty-eight hours of message transmittal—"

"My ship was underway. I just got the message."

"We can't make allowances for that. Personnel policy is built around firm rules to ensure everyone is treated fairly."

"*Fairly?*"

Braun ignored Paul's biting rejoinder. "This is a great career move, Paul. Absolutely. People fight for the chance to serve on Mars."

"It's a hardship tour and if people are fighting for the chance why don't we let one of them fill this job you want to send me to?"

"Paul, I can't second-guess the judgment of the people on Mars. They judged you best qualified."

"For *what*? And why was my name even up for judgment when I already had orders to Franklin?"

Braun frowned. "Now, Lieutenant Sinclair, you should know by now that personal requests are given full consideration but the deciding factor always has to be the needs of the service. You're needed on Mars. End of discussion."

"I could put in my papers. Resign."

"Nooooo. You still have more than two years of obligated duty from your Academy time, and in any case you can't resign within six months of your transfer date."

"You won't even try to help me?"

Braun smiled again, looking for all the world like a sales representative on a used car lot. "I'm your detailer. I'm always here to help you. To balance your needs against those of the service. You know, coming off Mars duty you should be able to write your own ticket for your next assignment. Be sure to have a preference on file. We'll do everything we can to make it happen."

Paul just stared at her for a few moments, unable to think of anything else he could say. Finally, he nodded abruptly. "Thank you." Then he cut the connection. The tone of his words and his action were at least borderline insubordinate, but at the moment Paul didn't really care.

Who can I ask for help? Captain Hayes. Commander, no she's a captain now, Herdez. Maybe one of them can do something.

Once back on the ship, Captain Hayes listened, letting his anger show, then promised to do what he could. "But I can't make any promises, Paul."

"I know, sir. Thank you, sir."

Paul left a message for Captain Herdez, then slumped in his stateroom chair and snarled at people for the rest of the day. Once he could leave the ship he went straight to Jen's quarters to wait for her, but found her already home and poured out the story.

Jen slammed a fist into one of the small cabinets the compartment boasted. "I don't believe he did this!"

"He?" Paul was momentarily surprised out of his own anger. "He who?"

"My father! Who the hell else?" She jabbed a finger at the data pad where Paul's order modification was displayed for her to read. "Mars! That's a four-year assignment."

"I know. Believe me, I know."

"He pulled some strings. He got your orders changed, sent you off to Siberia. No. Siberia would've been a lot closer and warmer. He found a worse place. I guess he couldn't swing getting you sent to Persephone or he'd have probably done that." Jen made a choking motion with her hands. "I'm going to—"

"Why?"

"Why?" She glared at him. "Because he—"

"No, no. I understand why you're ticked off at your father, but what's the point of sending me to Mars? Does he think we won't get married now?"

"I doubt it. Of course, he might've had help from others who had other reasons to go after you. There's at least one admiral who owes you a payback for your helping to get his son kicked out of the Navy."

"Silver deserved it! He caused the death of one of his own sailors!"

"I know that. Don't yell at me. And then there's the people who weren't happy with you for getting me off and proving that someone in the office of the deputy assistant undersecretary of defense for acquisition and development," she recited the full title with angry emphasis, "had covered up problems with equipment being fielded to the fleet. You've got plenty of people who'd be happy to see you rewarded with a trip to Mars." Jen sat down and closed her eyes, obviously trying to calm herself. "But I'm sure my father's involved somehow. Maybe he figures if we're separated that long we'll divorce or something. Mars is notorious for breaking up marriages. Lots of people far from home for a long time." Jen opened her eyes and fixed them on Paul. "And I admit it. I'd worry about that."

Paul snorted a brief laugh. "I doubt there's any woman on Mars the equal of you. No, that's wrong. None of them could be your equal and I know there's no one better than you."

"Yeah. Sure. After, say, two years apart you wouldn't be eyeing some babe with a halfway decent body who likes to smile at you?"

"No."

"I hate it when you're so positive about something without thinking about it! You're human. You're going to be tempted being alone out there that long."

"So?" Paul gave a dismissive wave of his hand. "Being tempted isn't the same as doing anything. Hell, Jen, you'll be here without me. I'm not worried."

"Oh? You don't think any other guys would be interested in me?"

"No! Yes! Dammit, Jen. I trust you. I'll always trust you. And I won't betray *your* trust."

"Maybe we *should* rethink the marriage. To make sure you're not committed just in case—"

"No! Aren't you listening to me?"

"I'm thinking. That's all."

Paul lowered his head, looking down at the floor. *I'm in this mess because of everything I've done. Getting involved in things I should've let slide. If I'd just kept my mouth shut and gone along I'd being going to whatever job I wanted now. Wouldn't I? Nobody gunning for me, nobody wondering what the hell I'm going to do next.* He looked up again, his eyes coming to rest on Jen. *But I know pretty much for certain that Jen fell for me because I did do things I didn't have to do. Because I didn't go along and keep my mouth shut. Maybe I'd have the duty of my dreams... without her. Would I want that?*

Can't I even avoid second-guessing my own second-guessing?

"What are you thinking?" Jen asked.

"That I'm an idiot."

"Hey, I get to call you an idiot because I love you. Nobody else gets to call you that."

"Even me?"

"Even you."

"What are we going to do, Jen?"

"Have you talked to anybody about getting the order mod rescinded?"

"Yeah. The detailer—"

"Who lied?"

"Like a big dog. Yeah. 'Needs of the Navy,' my ass."

"Maybe your captain..."

Paul nodded. "Yes. I asked Captain Hayes. No promises, but he's going to see what he can do. And, uh..." He hesitated.

"And?"

"Herdez. I asked her."

Jen rolled her eyes. "I bet she told you it was a great career move."

"No. I haven't heard back from her, yet."

"Hmmm." Jen lounged backward and rubbed her eyes. "Talk about dealing with the devil."

"Jen, Captain Herdez is a very tough officer, but she respects you as an officer. You know that." Jen made a noncommittal sound, frowning toward one corner of the room. "I believe she'll do her best. Unfortunately, she's not very political."

"I'll give you that. Herdez worked us to death but she never played political games." Jen shook her head. "Four years. It's like I'm seeing you being sent to prison, with no visiting privileges."

"I'm not there, yet."

"No." She took a deep breath, her face hardening. "Excuse me. I need to make a phone call. In private. Can we meet somewhere?

Fogarty's. I'll come there when I'm done."

Paul nodded, knowing that she meant to call her father. Paul had been present during earlier blow-ups between Jen and her father and hadn't enjoyed the experiences, so he had no objection at all to taking a hike this time. "I'll be there. Jen, don't burn any bridges."

"I—" She glared at him. "Thank you. Go away."

"Yes, ma'am. Right away, ma'am."

Fogarty's hadn't changed, but then Fogarty's never changed. The bar that tried its best to mimic an old neighborhood pub somehow magically transported amid the metal and carbon fiber composites of Franklin Naval Station also tried its best to avoid redecorating so that crews returning from long cruises in space would find a familiar place to celebrate their return and drown accumulated sorrows.

Paul chose a small table and sat nursing a drink, imagining the conversation going on between Jen and her father, and more than a little relieved that he wasn't listening in personally.

"Hey, Sinclair! Aren't you the guy who used to have a career?"

Paul looked up, frowning at a short, heavy-set officer standing at the bar. The crowd around the short officer laughed, hoisting drinks in mock-salute toward Paul. He knew the man, knew him well enough not to want to talk to him, so he pretended to ignore him.

But the short officer sauntered over to Paul. "So, what's it like?"

Paul controlled his voice, trying to keep it even and calm. "What's what like, Kramer?"

Kramer grinned. "That sucking feeling as your career goes down the flush. Anything like a catastrophic reentry?"

"I wouldn't know. I've never had one. How many catastrophic reentries have you had?"

Kramer's audience chuckled a bit at Paul's reply. Kramer himself

kept his wide smile, though his eyes hardened. "None like yours, pal. Come on! Tell us how it feels!"

Paul just gazed back at Kramer, trying to keep his expression totally bland, as if nothing the other officer was saying mattered. "Go away. I'm not interested in talking to you."

"Aw, you're gonna hurt my feelings. What're you gonna do next? Everybody knows you're gonna screw up again."

Paul smiled humorlessly. "I won't bother telling you what everyone knows about you."

Kramer stopped smiling. "You'd better hope we're never on the same ship."

"I've been hoping that since the first minute I met you at the Academy."

The audience laughed a bit again and Kramer curled his lip. "I hear that girl of yours has finally left the *Maury*. They get tired of trying to keep her from getting anywhere near the engineering plant again?"

Paul's left hand, safely under the table, clenched into a fist and made an abortive jerk upward, but Paul managed to kill the urge to slug Kramer before the move was visible. Before he could say anything, one of the other officers with Kramer stepped forward and pulled on Kramer's arm. "Hey, that's enough. Not funny."

"It's true!" Kramer insisted. "Would any of you want her on your ship?"

An uncomfortable silence fell, while Paul sought for something he could say that wouldn't sound like he was defending Jen against something she never should've been accused of doing.

Finally, one of the officers with Kramer poked her finger at him. "Yeah. I would."

"Me, too," another muttered defiantly.

The officer who'd poked Kramer turned to Paul. "Sorry. He's a jerk." Kramer reddened.

Paul nodded, letting his gratitude show. "I know. Thanks."

Kramer raised his arm and started to speak but two of his comrades started guiding him out of the bar. The officer speaking to Paul shrugged helplessly. "Yeah. I had a friend on the *Maury*." Paul stiffened again. "I followed the court-martial real close, so I know what happened. Most people don't. They just remember the news of your girl being charged and stuff. Sorry," she repeated.

Paul rose and reached to shake her hand. "No. *You* don't have anything to be sorry about. Thanks. I mean that."

"S'okay." The officer followed her friends out of the bar, leaving Paul alone again. Very alone.

His data pad chirped, announcing an incoming call. "Captain Herdez? Ma'am, I need your help..."

Jen came in half an hour later, her face still flushed. "My father claims to be utterly shocked, shocked that I would think he had anything to do with this. Naturally, he says there's not a thing that can be done and he really thinks you should be happy at the opportunity to serve in such a cutting-edge assignment."

"Happy. That's one emotion that hasn't come up yet." Paul hesitated. "I just talked with Herdez. Turns out she got my message earlier and has been discreetly checking out options."

"Huh." Jen took a big drink from Paul's glass. "Do you mind?" she asked as she sat it down again.

"No, dear. Of course not."

"Very funny. So what'd Herdez say?"

"It's hopeless." Paul held up a hand to keep Jen from exploding again. "She didn't put it quite that bluntly, but that's what it comes down to. The orders are set in stone and nobody with the power to change them is going to change them." He paused, knowing Jen wouldn't like the rest. "But there is one possible option."

Jen gave him a suspicious look. "What?"

"You know Herdez is going to command a newly commissioned ship after her current tour is up. They always let captains of newly commissioned ships get their pick of any officers they want—"

"No!" Jen slammed her palm onto the table, drawing looks from others in Fogarty's. "Back to ship duty?"

"Jen. She can get me off Mars after only two years. She's sure of it. She can slip the orders in without anybody noticing. Yeah, it'll mean coming back here to another ship, but I'll be coming back *here*."

Jen hid her face in her hands. "Two years gone and then back here on ship duty where I may see you four months out of the year if I'm lucky."

"That's worst case, Jen. New ships need a lot of break-in. It should be spending a lot of time around Franklin."

"I hate this option, Paul Sinclair." She reached over and finished his drink. "But I hate the alternatives even worse. God! You're selling your soul to Herdez! And I'm agreeing to it! I'm letting that woman who hates me Shanghai my husband for her ship!"

"She doesn't hate you."

"I notice you're not disagreeing with the rest of what I said."

Paul ordered more drinks. *Did I ever think I'd get to a point where two years of hell on Mars followed by two more years of hell on a ship commanded by Herdez was the best option available to me?*

The next morning, Commander Moraine gave another little speech. She kept fumbling with her data pad and several other items as she spoke, and Paul found himself paying more attention to that than to her words. Then Moraine singled out Paul. "I need to see all of your training records."

"Yes, ma'am."

"I want them on file to me, with a dynamic link to any updates."

"Ma'am?" Paul tried not let his disbelief show. Was Moraine actually planning on constantly checking the progress of his division's training?

"You heard me. The same applies to you two," she ordered Taylor and Denaldo. "Maintenance records, too. For all equipment. I want continuous updates."

Taylor held out her data pad. "Maybe you just oughta take this, ma'am."

Moraine glared at Taylor. "You do your jobs right and there won't be any problems."

After she left, Paul slapped his forehead. "Where does she think she's going to get the time to continuously monitor every detail in our divisions? That's our job."

Taylor popped a wad of a synthetic substance the sailors called "chew" into her mouth. "Haven't you figured out Commander Migraine, yet, college boy?"

"No. You tell me."

"She's nervous. Real nervous. Nervous she'll miss something. Because if she misses something she'll get in trouble."

"If she tries to track everything," Kris noted, "she's not going to be able to do it. She'll be overwhelmed."

"Bingo to the college girl! Tell me whose fault it'll be if Migraine tries to do our jobs in addition to her own and gets overwhelmed."

Paul rubbed his forehead. "Ours."

"Bingo again! Kids these days sure know a lot."

"Fine," Paul agreed. "What can we do?"

Taylor shrugged. "Our jobs. That's all."

"Why does Moraine look at me different from the way she looks at you guys?"

"You noticed that, too, Paul?" Taylor grinned. "I could say it's because she likes your hot bod."

"But you won't."

"Hell, no. That'd be crude and unsophisticated and I'm an officer now." Taylor sobered. "She's scared of you, Paul."

"Scared of me?"

"Yup. Think about it. You're the guy who nailed that little jerk Silver. You're the guy who speaks up when he sees something's wrong. Now, imagine you're Ms. Migraine, scared to death of getting caught with your pants down. How'd you like to have you working for you?"

Paul made a fist and rapped his forehead this time. "I don't go looking for reasons to turn people in! How could she—"

"I ain't saying she's right." Taylor shrugged again. "Just do your best and try to avoid taking lots of notes when she's talking or doing something. Hey, on second thought, maybe if you did that when she gives her morning speeches she'd clam up real quick. Do that for me and I'll teach you some tricks next time we're on liberty together."

"Would you?" Paul asked with mock sincerity. "I bet Jen would be really grateful."

"That she would! Heck, it's no fun yanking your chain anymore. Any other wisdom you need from me?"

"Yeah. Why do you chew that awful stuff?"

Taylor spat the chew into her palm and frowned down at it for a moment. "Hell if I know." Then she popped it back into her mouth and waved. "Later, kids."

Kris clapped Paul on the shoulder. "Just a few more months, Paul. Keep telling yourself that."

"Speaking of time left onboard, where's your relief?"

"Pullman?" At the last instant, Pullman had been shifted from taking over as weapons officer to relieving Kris Denaldo. "He's got the quarterdeck watch."

Paul met with his division, giving them assignments for the day, then headed back for his stateroom. He hadn't made it there when he was paged to see the captain.

For once, there wasn't a line outside the captain's cabin. Paul knocked, announcing himself.

"Come on in, Paul."

Captain Hayes looked slightly uncomfortable, Paul realized. *Bad news? For me? Why else would he look like that?*

But Hayes just passed Paul a note slip with a compartment address on it. "I need you to go there and see the people who'll be waiting for you. Just tell the front desk who you are."

Paul frowned down at the compartment designation. The numbers and letters were only vaguely familiar, telling him the compartment was located somewhere well inside Franklin's administrative decks. "Can I ask what this is about, sir?"

"No." Hayes grinned briefly to take any sting from the reply. "Just go there and do what you can."

"Aye, aye, sir." *Do what I can about what? I guess I'll find out.* Paul turned to go but was halted by a sharp command from Captain Hayes.

"I'll let your department head know you left the ship. Don't check out with her, or anybody else."

"Aye, aye, sir." It all made Paul very uneasy inside. A personal direction from the captain to do something off-ship and not to tell anyone else. He found himself checking his conscience for any actions which might conceivably have merited the sort of treatment he thought Jen might have experienced when she was arrested for the incident on the *Maury*. But that was ridiculous. Hayes wouldn't do that.

Still, Paul's unease grew as he drew nearer to the compartment, and settled into a hard, cold lump in his stomach as he stared at the sign on the compartment. Navy Criminal Investigative Service. *Why did the captain send me to the NCIS offices on Franklin? Why am I seeing the fleet cops?*

A harassed-looking petty officer looked up as Paul entered. "Yes, sir?"

Paul swallowed to ensure his voice wouldn't betray any nervousness. "Lieutenant Paul Sinclair."

The petty officer waited a moment as if expecting something more. "Yes, sir?"

"From the USS *Michaelson*. My CO sent me here. He said there'd be someone waiting."

"*Michaelson*..." The petty officer's eyes fastened on something on her desk. "Oh. Okay, sir. Wait one, please." She stood and hustled back into the NCIS offices, leaving Paul alone with her desk and a few battered standard-issue office waiting chairs. Paul measured the discomfort of standing against the discomfort of sitting in the chairs and decided to keep standing.

A moment later the petty officer returned with two individuals in civilian jumpsuits in tow, one a middle-aged man and the other a younger woman. The petty officer indicated Paul, then sat back down as if he and the two civilians had ceased to exist.

The male civilian gestured Paul to follow, his face solemn. Paul considered asking for an explanation then and there, but decided against it. He followed the man, the woman taking up the rear, as they wound their way through a small maze of offices until they reached one with a fairly substantial door. The man fumbled out a key card, opened the door, and waved Paul in.

Fighting down images of himself being sealed away in a secret confinement facility, Paul went inside. As the two civilians entered behind him and swung the door shut, Paul's data pad chirped. He checked it, seeing it was informing him that he'd lost contact with Franklin's internal comm net. "A sealed room?" he said aloud.

The man nodded, his face now slightly apologetic. "Yes. This room's secured against electronic signals. And anything else that might allow someone to hear what's going on inside." He gestured to one of the chairs at the table which dominated the small room. "Have a seat, please."

Paul sat carefully, keeping his back erect and not relaxing in the least. "What's this about?"

Instead of answering directly, the man pulled out an ID wallet and proffered it to Paul. "Special Agent Bob Gonzales. This is Special Agent Pam Connally."

Paul looked the badges and cards over carefully, even though he knew he wouldn't have recognized fakes. "Okay."

Gonzales and Connally sat, watching Paul. Paul watched them. Finally, Gonzales sighed. "Sorry. Can I get you anything? Water?"

"I'm okay, thanks."

"You're not suspected or accused of anything. Nada. Period. That's not why you're here."

"That's a relief."

Connally grinned. As she shifted her seat, Paul noticed a slight bulge under one arm and realized she was carrying a weapon in a shoulder holster.

Gonzales quirked a brief smile, then went completely solemn again. "We need to ask you some things about your fellow officers. On the, uh, *Michaelson*."

Paul felt barriers going up in his mind. *Is this how they tried to railroad Jen? What do they want me to say about any of the other officers?* "I can't imagine what I could tell you."

Perhaps sensing Paul's reflexive suspicion, Connally leaned forward. "This is important. We'd appreciate your cooperation. Your captain said you were the best person to contact."

Captain Hayes. Great. No wonder he looked uncomfortable. But he wouldn't aid or abet anything wrong against me or anyone else. I'm sure of that. "Alright, ma'am."

Connally grinned again. "Don't make me feel old. Pam is fine."

"And I'm Bob," Gonzales added. "Like I said, you're not a person of interest. You're someone we're asking for help. Could you just tell us if you've noticed any of your fellow officers acting at all unusual?"

"Unusual?" Paul frowned and spread his hands. "How do you mean?"

"Uh, working extra-long hours, say. After the normal work day is over."

Paul stared at Gonzales and then Connally, trying to judge if the question was serious. "We all work extra hours."

"I mean, consistently. Not underway, but inport."

"So do I. We all work extra hours. Inport, too."

Connally gave Paul a searching look. "None of the officers works longer than the others? At times when no one else is around?"

"Somebody's always around. And as for longer... look. Our typical work day is maybe twelve hours. Inport. Every four days inport is a duty day for junior officers. We spend twenty-four hours straight at work on those days. Maybe you get one of the night quarterdeck watches on your duty day and it's pretty much just you and the petty officer of the watch awake. But that's *normal* for us."

Gonzales leaned back and laughed. "Your work patterns are consistently after normal working hours and on weekends? All of you?"

"Yes. Pretty much. That's right. Even if it's not a duty day. There's always some emergency popping up, something that has to get done and get done right now."

"How about money? Does anyone seem to have a lot on hand?"

Paul let his puzzlement show. "How would I know?"

"Uh, spending, uh..."

"Yeah. On what? There's nothing much you can buy and take on the ship, no cars up here, no private housing, a couple of fancy restaurants maybe." Paul shrugged. "Somebody could be a billionaire and I wouldn't be able to tell. There's nothing they could be spending it on in front of me."

Connally looked at Gonzales. "I told you we'd have to bring him in on this. He can't help us otherwise."

Gonzales nodded heavily. "You're right. Lieutenant Sinclair, I have to ask that you swear to secrecy what we're about to discuss."

Paul felt his internal barriers rising again. "I don't understand. But whatever it is, of course I won't reveal classified information."

Gonzales waved to Connally, who gave Paul a level look. "I'll be blunt," she stated. "We have very good reason to believe one of the officers currently assigned to your ship is engaged in espionage against the United States."

Paul simply stared at her for a long moment before he could speak. "Espionage? You think one of the officers in the wardroom of the *Michaelson* is a spy?"

Both special agents nodded. Connally spread her hands, palm down, on the table before her. "Yes, but it's a lot more solid than 'thinking' that's the case. We have confirmed information of ongoing espionage. We've been tracking it for some time, with assistance when appropriate from the FBI and other government agencies. Just to let you know NCIS isn't alone in this. I can sum up what we know by saying the espionage operation has been ongoing for several years. We know, from sources we will *not* divulge to you, that one of the primary players is a Navy officer. I know," she agreed, seeing the look of shock on Paul's face, "that's hard to accept. But we know it."

Gonzales leaned back, rubbing his jaw line with one thumb. "Recently, there was a disruption in the deliveries by this officer. Then one delivery. Then another disruption, lasting from June 16th to 2 August."

Paul looked blankly back at the special agent for a moment, until the information clicked. "That brackets the period the *Michaelson* was just underway."

"Exactly. The officer transferred from the assignment they'd held before. We know he or she transferred up here. We know they couldn't pass material to their foreign contacts while your ship was underway. Within a few days of your ship getting back, there was a drop to their foreign contacts. Pretty clear-cut, isn't it?"

"But most of our officers have been onboard for a long time," Paul protested.

"Right. But you had two new ones transferred to you recently."

"Yes—" Paul had to break his gaze on Gonzales to shake his head in disbelief. "Two of them." *Commander Moraine, a spy? Is that why she's so nervous all the time?*

Connally nodded, picking up the conversation. "A Lieutenant Pullman and a Commander Moraine."

"Yes, but Brad Pullman—"

"We can't rule out either of them. They both came from the area the spy was operating out of, and they both arrived on your ship at the same time."

"That's why you wanted to know if anybody was acting strange."

"But you say they're not."

"Not that way…" *Do I really want to bilge Commander Moraine this way? But if she's doing what they say… is she doing that? I personally watched Jen get court-martialed and almost convicted on evidence that didn't prove anything. Is this that same sort of thing? How can I know?* Paul became aware the special agents were watching him, waiting for the rest of the sentence. "Commander Moraine is usually pretty nervous. But," something made him add, "I've had some pretty experienced people say that's just because she's worried about her job, about not messing up."

"Do you work with Commander Moraine?"

"She's my department head. My immediate superior."

"Does she mess up a lot?"

Paul almost laughed at the question, but once again saw it had been asked seriously. "It's hard to tell. I've only been working for her a few days. I can say I've had worse superiors based on what I've seen so far."

"What about Pullman? Does he seem unusually nervous?"

"No, he—" *He's so confident about everything. Brad never seems fazed by anything.* "Not at all," Paul concluded.

The special agents exchanged a glance that Paul couldn't interpret, then Connally spoke with exaggerated care. "Paul, we'd like your help in investigating this."

"I'm answering your questions as best I can."

"Yes. You are. What I mean is that we need to take some steps to try to identify whether Pullman or Moraine is our guy. Steps on the ship itself."

"Herself," Paul corrected automatically.

Connally looked amused. "Herself. What I'm saying is we need you to actively help the investigation from the inside of the wardroom."

"Actively?" Paul eyed her warily, not liking what he was hearing.

"Yes." Connally leaned forward again. "What we'd like you to do is wear a wire. A tap, you know? And get into a conversation with Moraine and one with Pullman and bring up some subjects we'll provide you with. That may give us the answers we need to focus the investigation tightly on a single suspect."

Paul suddenly became aware he was holding his breath. *They want me to spy on my fellow officers. Good God, how can I do that?* He stared at the two special agents, knowing they could see his feelings clearly in his expression. "I can't do that."

"It's important."

"*I can't do that.* Those guys trust me. We work together. Twenty-four hours a day, seven days a week for months on end. How can

I go in there and spy on them? It'd be a... betrayal of trust. Their trust in me."

Special Agent Connally nodded in acknowledgement of Paul's words, her own expression understanding. "We know it's very difficult. But you have to consider what's happening."

"What you *think* is happening."

"No, Paul. We know, for certain, that espionage is taking place. I can show you the evidence for that if you swear not to reveal it, as well as the sort of material that's been compromised. Things like the capabilities of your weapons, your sensor arrays, your ship's internal layout, and contingency plans for open warfare in space if that erupts. You talked about betraying trust. Someone is selling you, and every other officer and sailor on your ship and every other ship, down the river. Literally selling you. We know money has changed hands."

Paul sat silently for a moment. "If you know money has been paid, then you must know who got it."

"No. We wish we could trace that. But international currency transfers have gotten very good at laundering money. If we can get enough specific information to get the right warrants, we can dig in the right places and find what we need to know. But if we try to dig now, we risk alerting the object of the investigation. Money launderers are very sophisticated. Lots of big-time criminals and assorted dictators need those kinds of services."

Paul nodded, then looked challengingly at the special agents. "I've heard our own intelligence services make use of that, too."

Connally shrugged and Gonzales made a noncommittal gesture as he answered. "I wouldn't know, lieutenant."

"You're just a cop."

"Right."

"We have a cop on the *Michaelson*. A real good one. Ivan Sharpe."

This time Gonzales nodded. "I met him when our team searched Lieutenant Silver's stateroom."

"I didn't know you were in on that."

"We lead busy professional lives, too," he responded dryly. "Your master-at-arms seemed very capable. But he's not in on this."

"Why not?"

"It's above his level. So far."

Quiet fell in the small room, Paul sitting silently and the two special agents watching him as if waiting for his next question. *Why me? Haven't I given enough blood to the Navy already? Am I the only officer on the* Michaelson *who could possibly do this?* He finally spoke again, openly stating his question. "Why me?"

Connally looked at Gonzales, who reached into one pocket as he replied. "The short answer is we called you because your commanding officer said you were the best one for the job. He told us you could be counted on." The agent held out an actual envelope to Paul. "This is for you."

Paul opened the envelope, fumbling at the unfamiliar task and ripping the envelope almost in half. Inside was a single sheet of paper, which Paul saw was on the same letterhead as the innumerable official e-letters he'd seen generated by the *Michaelson*'s systems. Instead of a computer font, though, the paper held a few lines of handwriting. *Paul. I know this is asking a lot. It's a lousy job. I can't order you to cooperate. But I am asking you to do so. This is very important. I know I can count on you to do what needs to be done and do it right.* The signature was Captain Hayes'. Paul read the brief note through twice, then blew out a long breath and gazed at the two special agents. "Do you know what this says?"

Gonzales shook his head. "Your commanding officer said to give it to you if you expressed serious reservations."

Paul turned the paper over in his hands several times. "I need to talk to someone else."

"We'd really prefer you didn't."

The tone made Paul smile. "Meaning I can't?"

"Basically, yes."

"I still need to think it over."

"Understood. Just please don't take too long. This guy, whether it's Pullman or Moraine, is doing damage every day they're free."

"Are you so certain it's one of them?"

Connally gave him a demanding look. "Lieutenant, if we wanted to railroad somebody, we wouldn't be going to you to help us generate evidence. Pro or con. Right? We wouldn't need you if we were certain who was guilty."

Paul looked away. "I'm getting married soon."

"Oh? Congratulations."

"To Lieutenant Jen Shen. Do you recognize the name?"

Connally had the grace to flinch, while Gonzales just nodded, his lips a thin line. "Yes. This isn't that kind of thing."

"How can I know?"

The special agents exchanged glances again. Gonzales finally answered. "All I can do is promise you it isn't. And point out that your commanding officer thinks it's real."

Paul nodded reluctantly. "That's true. But I need to think. I'll be in touch."

"Before long?"

"Before long."

The two special agents escorted Paul back to the entry area. "Ask for one of us when you come back," Connally advised.

Paul held up his data pad. "Why not just scan your cards into my pad so I have your contact info?"

"We don't want to do that. We don't know who might be looking at your pad besides you."

That took another moment to sink in. This spy, if he or she was in the *Michaelson*'s wardroom, might be going through Paul's own files. Paul's own data pad and personal files. Looking for things to sell. He felt a hot rush of anger at the idea, but just nodded abruptly to the two agents and left.

As he walked back toward the ship he remembered something. Earlier conversations in which he and other officers on the *Michaelson* had wondered how the SASALs could've been so confident at the asteroid that the American ship wouldn't actively move to stop them. *As if the SASALs knew exactly what our rules of engagement were.*

Maybe they had known.

5

He spent the rest of the day trying not to look distracted. Commander Moraine chewed him out for not having provided enough files to her and for wasting time on legal issues ashore instead of doing his primary job. Captain Hayes had apparently provided that as a cover story for Paul's absence from the ship. Paul refrained from telling Moraine that he'd gladly let someone else do the legal stuff if he could find anyone else naïve enough to take the job. But he figured he was stuck with it until he transferred off of the *Michaelson*.

He also, hopefully, refrained from looking at Moraine as if she were a spy. Which he felt she had to be, if there was truly an officer on the *Michaelson* committing espionage.

In the late afternoon, he passed the captain in a passageway. Hayes nodded casually as Paul flattened himself against the bulkhead to let the captain pass. "How'd that business go this morning, Paul?"

"Fine, sir."

"Keep me informed."

"Yes, sir." *Once I know what I'm going to do.*

Thankfully, he had one more night before duty would keep him on the ship for twenty-four hours. He went back to Jen's quarters at the end of the day, his mind whirling but focusing on nothing.

Jen knew him perhaps better than anyone else by now. She took one look at his face and gestured to the couch/bed. "*Now* what?"

Paul sat gingerly, trying to sort out his feelings and trying to figure out how to broach the subject. "There's something I need to talk to you about."

She nodded slowly, her face a mask. Watching her, Paul realized Jen could be misreading his hesitation. "It's not about us. Not that way."

"Your orders? Mars?"

"No. That hasn't changed."

"Then what is it?"

He looked down at the deck, knowing he should maintain eye contact but not able to do so. "Jen, I've been asked to do something, a professional something, that really bothers me. I wouldn't even be considering it, except my CO wants me to do it and I trust him and... and, hell, I don't want to let him down."

Jen gave him an arch look. "Gosh, you're so noble, Lieutenant Sinclair. I'm gonna haveta marry your sorry hide to keep you out of trouble, ain't I?"

Paul managed a smile. "I'm not sure that'd work, but I'm more than willing to try." Speaking quickly, he outlined what he'd been told and what was being asked of him while Jen listened without interruption, her expression unreadable. "They told me not to talk to anyone. But I couldn't *not* talk to you about it."

"Damn straight." Jen's face flushed and her voice came out a little ragged. "They have the nerve to ask you to help them? After what they tried to do to me? After trying to railroad me into prison for what happened on the *Maury*?"

"They know I'm marrying you. I told them."

"You're lucky they didn't accuse *you* of being a spy as soon as they heard that! Tell me you're not actually thinking of going along with this."

"Jen, I don't want to! But Captain Hayes is a good officer and I really think a good man. He's personally asking me to help. And if those agents are right, if somebody's selling our secrets, then we're all being put at greater risk."

"You can't trust them!"

"Do I know that?"

"They want to use you, Paul. They think they can, but they don't know you."

"No, they..." Paul's voice trailed off. *They know... just like the SASALs knew. Admit it. You think they had our rules of engagement. The SASALs knew they could shoot up that asteroid and we couldn't do anything against them.*

Whoever gave them those rules of engagement helped cause the deaths of those settlers.

"Paul? Hello. Lieutenant Paul Sinclair, please report back to your brain."

Paul blinked, focusing back on Jen. "I'm sorry. I was just thinking of something."

"Obviously something important," she prodded.

"You know what happened last time my ship was out. And you know how the SASALs acted. Like they didn't need to worry about what we'd do. Maybe they *knew* they didn't need to worry."

Jen paused, her mouth twisting as she thought it over. "Possible," she finally conceded.

"We've been trying to understand how they'd take the risk of opening fire. But if they knew it wasn't a risk..."

"Okay. I agreed it was possible." Jen let aggravation show. "That makes it personal, doesn't it?"

"Yeah."

"But... what does Sheriff Sharpe think?"

"He's not involved. He's leaving the ship real soon anyway."

"One more reason not to play, if you ask me. You *are* asking me, right? This isn't some roundabout way of trying to get me to think you've heard me out so you can go off and do whatever you've already decided to do, is it?"

He glared at her. "Jen, I don't deserve that. I've always been straight with you."

She sat still for a long moment, then nodded. "You're right. Do I have final say?"

Paul thought about that. "No."

"You're too damned honest for your own good, Sinclair."

"I can't let someone else decide this for me. But I can't make that decision without the input of a woman I not only care very deeply about but also admire as an officer."

Jen quirked an eyebrow at him. "Who is she?"

"Jen..."

"Herdez?"

"Yeah, right. Me and my old XO."

"*Our* old XO." Jen made a face, staring into a corner. "I wonder what she would think."

"She'd tell me to help NCIS, Jen. You know that."

"Yeah. All professional, all the time. Make sure you're looking out for..." Jen paused, her head down, then looked up and over at Paul.

"You know what? Thinking about Herdez and all cleared things up for me. I want you to cooperate with them."

Paul was sure his amazement showed. "Cooperate with the NCIS agents? You mean that? Why?"

"Because of that trust thing. You know how Herdez worked. If she trusted you, she'd keep giving you more to do. Because she knew you'd do it right. Well, I trust you. I trust you to be involved with this. Because I *know* if they try to do to someone else what someone tried to do to me, *you* won't play along. You'll make sure the truth comes out."

Paul looked away, shaking his head. "I'm not perfect, Jen." *And I'm tired of being the guy other people count on to do the right thing. Why can't somebody else do that? Especially when the right thing isn't so obvious.* "What about the guys I work with? I guess just about all of the ones you knew are gone, now. But, still, we're talking about me spying on my fellow officers."

"Two of them, from what you told me."

"Yeah, just two. But it's the act, not how many people are directly affected by it. Would you ever trust another officer if you knew they'd spied on other officers in their wardroom?"

She came close and knelt to look into Paul's eyes. "That'd depend on who and why. Really. Two things, Paul. First, make sure you're protected. Even if you do this, your role doesn't have to be known. Confidential informant, isn't that what they call them? And if all this stuff does is point them at the right target, they won't need you to nail that target. Second thing, I've lost a lot of shipmates. Don't flinch. I'm the one who saw the *Maury*'s crew gutted. They died because someone played games with them. Some bureaucrat who wanted to score points by moving a program forward and didn't care what might happen to the sailors on the *Maury* or any other ship. I hate that guy, whoever he or she is. And if there really is somebody selling important classified info to the other side, then they're playing the same kind of games and I want them stopped. Just like you do, because their little game might've caused the deaths of those settlers, and could cause the deaths of others. Including you or me."

"Yeah, exactly that had already occurred to me. But even if there's a chance the one who's accused might be innocent?"

"*You* get in there and *you* make sure their rights are protected, and then *if* the evidence you help find points that way, we'll know. We'll also know if it *doesn't*."

"*Why do I have to do it?*"

Jen eyed him for a long moment, her face close to his, then suddenly grinned. "You big dope. I told you this would happen when you stood up for that idiot Wakeman. I told you everybody would start counting on you to 'do what's right.' You didn't believe me. I was right, wasn't I? Admit it."

"Jen—"

"Admit it."

"Jen—"

"I was right and you were wrong," Jen declared in a mocking sing-song voice.

He wanted to stay mad, wanted to stay frustrated, but started laughing. "Am I ever going to get to be right?"

"I'll think about it." She leaned forward and kissed him, letting the gesture linger. "Too bad you have to get back to your ship in the morning. I could do with a full day of you."

He held her shoulders lightly, smiling back at her. "Having tonight isn't anything to complain about."

"Yeah." She leaned back, letting his hands drop. "First we need to eat."

"Fogarty's?"

"No. Let's just grab some sandwiches from a take-out."

"Okay." Paul paused as they walked toward the nearest take-out, looking at Jen. "Why does this stuff always seem to be my responsibility?"

"Because you keep volunteering."

"I could say no."

Jen shook her head, looking rueful now. "No, you couldn't. Not you."

"You could tell me not to."

This time she cocked her head and regarded him for a moment. "Could I?"

"If anyone could, you could."

"But I won't. Because every time you've taken a stand, Paul Sinclair, you've been right."

He gave her a rueful look back and walked on silently for a while, thinking that the paths of duty shouldn't lead to an assignment on Mars without Jen.

Special Agent Connally smiled encouragingly. "You made the right decision."

"Yeah. What do I have to do?" Paul felt uncomfortable in the sealed room, as if he were plotting against his friends outside their knowledge. He'd managed to get another officer to cover his duty on the ship for a few hours because he wanted to get this over with as soon as possible. Of course, he'd had to lie about why he needed to be off of the ship, but his fellow officer hadn't noticed. Apparently Paul was a better liar than he'd thought.

"You have to do two things." Connally leaned back and pressed her fingertips together. "First, stay alert for unusual activities by either person of interest. Unusual for you people on the ship, that is."

"So what's unusual?"

Connally looked thoughtful. "Secretive activities. You know, if it becomes apparent they're trying to hide something from the rest of the people on the ship."

"Isn't that going to describe me?" Paul couldn't help asking.

"In a way. Also watch for signs of interest in things they shouldn't be pursuing. Things unrelated to their jobs. Messages they shouldn't have access to. That sort of thing."

Paul rubbed his neck, grimacing. "Brad Pullman's the communications officer now. He could see any message on the ship. And since Commander Moraine is the operations officer, there's not a lot she couldn't see."

"I understand. That aspect of things is going to be hard. That's why we're asking you to do this other thing." Special Agent Connally held up a small, paper-thin disc. "This, believe it or not, is a wire."

Paul stared at it. "That's it? The entire thing?"

"Yeah. Beautiful, isn't it? Power source, microphone, storage media all in one." She leaned forward and reached inside his uniform to press it against the fabric. "See? It affixes here, under the collar. That's all you have to do. It'll monitor everything you hear for the next twenty-four hours."

"Everything?"

Connally laughed. "You don't have to wear it while you're with your girlfriend."

"I've got duty tonight, so I'm stuck on the ship. But that was just one of my areas of concern."

"I can imagine the others. Trust me, there's not a lot we haven't heard. We actually have a very good reason for having you wear it all day on the ship. We want you to forget, as much as you can, that you're wearing it."

Paul brushed his collar near where the wire rested. "I don't see how I could do that."

"Trust me. You'll forget it's there." The NCIS agent brought out a large data pad. "This can't leave our office, so I'll have to ask you to memorize it as much as possible. We'd like you to somehow bring up the following topics while talking to Pullman and Moraine."

Paul took the pad, reading slowly. The topics were fairly predictable, once he thought about it. Money troubles. Recent purchases. Investments and investment advice. Opinions on foreign policy. Opinions on the current political leadership. "I have a little trouble with some of this. It's not illegal to dislike whoever's in the White House and I don't want to entrap someone into violating Article 88 of the Uniform Code."

Connally looked at him in surprise. "Contempt Toward Officials? Not a lot of people even know about that one, let alone the right article number."

"I'm my ship's legal officer."

"Oh. In any event, nobody's going to get convicted of that charge nowadays unless they're standing on a mountaintop screaming obscenities and threats. You know that. All we're looking for is motivation."

Paul read the data pad again. "You think somebody would dislike the president enough to spy on their own country?"

"Stranger things have happened," Connally noted dryly. "How well do you know Pullman and Moraine?"

"Do you mean personally?" Paul made a dismissive gesture.

"Neither all that well. Both of them just came aboard a little while ago. I knew Brad in school a little, but just sort of in passing."

"Then it might be a little hard to start discussing personal opinions and finances with them. Just do your best."

Paul shook his head. "I'm not a brilliant conversationalist. If I could get someone else to help—"

"No. I'm sorry."

"I'm sure Captain Hayes—"

"That reminds me." Connally leaned forward again, her eyes fixed on Paul. "Don't talk to your captain about this."

Rebellion rose immediately. "I can't do this and not inform my commanding officer!"

"We'll tell him." She must have read Paul's skepticism. "I swear. He'll know this evening. But you can't talk to him about it. Where could you get enough privacy?"

"The captain's cabin. We shut the hatch—"

"There might be a tap in there."

That startled Paul into momentary silence. "Are you serious?"

"Absolutely. There's any number of devices that could be concealed in there and be effectively invisible. We don't know whether or not our target has planted one, and there's no way to sweep the cabin for it without tipping off our target." Connally pointed to Paul's data pad. "Not to belabor the point, but just a reminder to make sure nothing's put in your data pad about this either."

Paul couldn't decide if he was unhappier about being asked to spy on his fellow officers or unhappier about the real possibility that one of them was spying on him. "Understood. I guess I just come back here tomorrow and you take the tap off me?"

Connally shook her head. "No. We don't want you coming here

too often. That might tip off someone, too. Is there someplace we could meet tomorrow?"

"Sure. A private place?"

"No. Someplace public." Connally smiled. "I'm new up here so I won't be recognized easily as an NCIS agent. And we're old friends! Did I tell you?"

Paul couldn't help smiling back. "Really?"

"Oh, yeah. We go way back. When I see you I'll be sure to stop by and say hi. Might even give you a hug."

"Um... I'm engaged."

Connally's eyebrows rose. "Just a hug, Paul. I'm not *that* kind of friend. Or agent. You haven't been watching too many spy movies, have you?"

Paul laughed. "I didn't mean... That is, it might attract attention. People might talk about seeing us if you hug me because everyone knows I'm engaged and you're, well, pretty good looking."

"You silver-tongued devil you. And you said you weren't a good conversationalist. Don't worry. Bring your fiancée. It'll be good cover. As far as she's concerned, I'm an old friend, too. She's not obsessively jealous, is she?"

Paul thought about that. "Do comments about ripping my lungs out if I ever cheat on her count?"

"Uh, yeah, but we'll keep this friendly. That's all. Your lungs should be safe."

"One other thing." Paul pointed to where he'd seen her shoulder holster on his earlier visit. "Are you going to have, uh..."

Connally frowned, following the line of Paul's finger toward her underarm. Then her expression cleared. "Oh. Am I going to be carrying, do you mean?"

"Carrying?"

"That's what we call it when we've got a sidearm. Yes. I'll be on duty. Don't worry. With my jacket on no one will be able to see I've got a weapon in a shoulder holster."

"I just wanted to be sure I didn't react if I felt it."

"Don't worry," Connally repeated. "I'm the best shot on the station. Ask anybody. Carrying the weapon's just a requirement. I don't intend using it."

The idea of Connally using her weapon hadn't occurred to Paul at all. He spent a moment wishing he could discuss this with Sheriff Sharpe, then bade farewell to the special agent.

Paul returned to the ship, trying to forget about the little disc concealed under his collar, and therefore unable to stop thinking about it.

It was early afternoon before he saw Captain Hayes again. Hayes was standing in a passageway talking to the chief engineer. Paul flattened himself to the maximum extent possible to squeeze by without inconveniencing the senior officers, but Hayes stopped him at mid-point with a quick gesture. "Did you take care of that thing for me?"

"The legal thing, sir?"

Hayes cupped his hand to his ear as if he hadn't been able to hear, then nodded. "Yes."

"I'm on it, captain."

"Good." Hayes waved him on.

About ten minutes later Paul realized that Hayes' gesture to his ear had very likely been a tip-off that Hayes knew Paul had a listening device planted on him. If so, at least the NCIS agents had proven true to their word on that matter.

It was getting on in the day before Paul realized something else. He'd been avoiding talking to Pullman or Moraine. He'd been evading the job he'd agreed to do. Not that the extra time had helped him plan any conversational gambits. His mind stayed so stubbornly blank on ways to steer any conversation around to the right topics that Paul realized he'd have no choice but to wing it and hope he could improvise.

He went to his stateroom, the fabled "ensign locker" which he shared with Brad Pullman and two ensigns but which was nonetheless the closest thing to an oasis of quiet and privacy for him on the ship, and concentrated on remembering all of the possible topics that Special Agent Connally had shown him.

He'd only been at it a couple of minutes when Brad Pullman entered, sat down heavily in front of his small desk and yawned. "I had the mid-watch inport last night. I think if you look up 'terminal boredom' in the dictionary it'll refer you to a mid-watch inport on Franklin."

Paul smiled ruefully, thinking that was how he would've reacted to Pullman's comment normally. That is, if he wasn't hyper over the need to steer the conversation and record whatever his roommate said. "You got that right. Uh, how's your turnover with Kris Denaldo going?"

Pullman waved one hand. "Piece of cake."

"Really?" Paul thought about the long hours of work Kris had put in as communications officer, even when she'd had the help of Senior Chief Kowalksi before he'd transferred off the ship. "No worries?"

"No worries." Pullman leaned back. "No problems. I can handle the job in my sleep."

"Brad, there's a lot of things about being in charge of communications that can trip you up."

"Sure. I know that." But Pullman's dismissive tone didn't match the words. "Really, Paul, I can handle it. Don't sweat it."

"Okay." *Brad is sharp. I know that about him. Everybody says he's really smart. And Kris hasn't complained to me that he's slacking off at all. As a matter of fact, I haven't seen Brad slacking off at anything. He's a hard worker from all I've seen. So relax about that and do the unpleasant job you said you'd do, Paul Sinclair.* "Hey, Brad, mind if I ask you something?"

"Shoot."

"Have you ever looked into investments or anything? I'm building up a pretty good nest egg." Paul hoped he still sounded casual.

Pullman scratched his ear and appeared to contemplate the question. "A little bit. It's kind of cool watching the pay pile up while we can't spend it on much, isn't it?"

"Yeah. So, any advice?"

"Not really." Pullman looked mildly apologetic. "I've just sort of skimmed a few things. My money's picking up interest in my savings account and that's all. Investment stuff just isn't my thing. I've got enough money to get what I need, and if I can stick out the Navy long enough, I'll have the retirement package, so I'm cool."

"Oh. Okay. Just thought I'd ask." Paul let disappointment show, though he actually felt relief. Pullman obviously wasn't concerned with having too little money and certainly wasn't acting like he had more than he should.

"Why'd you bring it up?" Pullman asked. "Because you're getting married?"

"Yeah." Did that sound sincere? "Jen and I'll be both pulling in income, and with my orders to Mars I won't be spending much for the next couple of years, either."

Pullman shook his head. "They really screwed you, man."

"Tell me about it." Paul hesitated, then deliberately brought up another one of the NCIS agents' topics. "How could they do that? I'm plenty unhappy."

"With the Navy?"

"Yeah." Paul waited, certain that Pullman wouldn't take the bait but still trying not to show tension over simply dangling the bait before him.

As Paul had expected, Pullman just spread his hands in a helpless gesture. "You're not the first guy. Remember that joke about how being in the Navy guarantees regular sex, because you get screwed every day? Sorry I can't help. You can always punch out after Mars. By the time that's over your obligated service will have been completed and then some."

Paul pretended to agree, since he was keeping Herdez' offer secret to everyone except Jen. "Maybe I will. It's not like I'm getting major rewards for what I do." He hadn't meant to say the last, but it slipped out in what he knew must have been a slightly bitter tone.

Pullman just nodded again. "You've got to be smart, Paul. Smarter than the people calling out the orders."

"Like you?" Paul asked sarcastically.

"Yup." Pullman grinned. "Like me."

Paul couldn't help grinning back.

Commander Moraine scowled at Paul as he stood in the entry to her stateroom. It was getting late, and Paul simply couldn't afford to put off talking to her any longer. "You should have all the files from my division that you've asked for, ma'am," Paul reported.

Instead of replying directly, she picked up her data pad and began punching keys to check. Paul waited with outward patience as the minutes dragged. Finally, Moraine put down the data pad and nodded several times quickly. "It looks like it. Why is that new tracking software labeled as being in degraded status?"

Paul knew Moraine had already been told the answer because he'd been present when Senior Chief Imari explained it to her. But Moraine had looked distracted and had kept fiddling with her data pad and other objects, so Paul had been pretty sure his new department head had been so busy concentrating on other details that she'd missed the one being explained to her. "It's not handling all tracking functions up to specifications, ma'am. It occasionally drops an object, which we have to manually reacquire to restart tracking, and sometimes creates false echo tracks of real objects that we have to delete to keep the system from confusing itself."

Moraine stared at Paul, one eyelid twitching slightly. "Why is it doing those things? How can we fix it?"

"Uh, ma'am, Ensign Taylor believes the dropped objects are being caused by the anti-countermeasures subroutines being too sensitive and misreading real detections as fakes. She thinks the false echoes are being caused because the tracking subroutines are hyped up to be so sensitive that it's generating false targets from scattered indications off of real ones."

"I don't want our tracking system software degraded! *How can we fix it?*"

He decided to try to defuse things, because he would have to work with Moraine for some months, unless she was led off the ship under arrest for espionage, which event Paul was looking forward to seeing more and more with every minute. "Ma'am, Taylor suggested we target the anti-countermeasures subroutines against the detection subroutines and let the software fight it out." Instead of smiling, Moraine just stared at Paul. *Well, that didn't work.* "Commander, we're not allowed to modify the software in any way. The contractor has to make changes. We've been told the changes are being worked on."

"How long?" Moraine raised her data pad as if that held the offending tracking software. "How long until it's fixed?"

"We don't have an estimated time to repair, ma'am. The company says it can't provide one."

"That's not acceptable! I don't want a major capability in my department to be in degraded status!"

"Ma'am, Ensign Taylor has helped us with some work-arounds and my people can identify problem detections—"

"I want it fixed right now, Mr. Sinclair!"

Paul tried to keep his face expressionless. *I want another new department head right now. But neither one of us is going to get what we want, are we? Unfortunately, I appear to be the only one here who understands that.* Since every attempt to explain reality had failed, he fell back on the only possible reply. "Yes, ma'am."

"Maybe I should take a look at it. Personally. Yes. Tell Taylor I want to see that software."

"The... software?"

"Yes! The source-code! I've handled software acquisition and I'm sure I can evaluate the source-code for anything that looks odd."

Oh, boy. I wonder how many millions of lines long that source-code is? I can just imagine Taylor's reaction when I tell her that Moraine wants to see it. "Yes, ma'am."

"Are the tracking consoles active? Can we go up to Combat right now? I want to personally look at this and find a fix."

"I'm sorry, ma'am, but the consoles are down for system maintenance and upgrades. We can't even run any simulations," Paul stated carefully, trying not to let his relief show at the fact that Moraine couldn't personally go up and try to do his sailors' jobs right now. "It's in my division's status report," he added with apparent helpfulness. *Which means you'd know that if you weren't so focused on details that the big picture is lost to you.*

"Combat doesn't seem very capable, Mr. Sinclair. Perhaps you haven't been focusing enough on your *primary* duty."

Uh oh. Here it comes.

"You've been off the ship several times in the last couple of days supposedly dealing with legal issues. That's unacceptable."

Paul knew he'd never win this battle. He'd never won it with Garcia, and Moraine obviously wasn't any more inclined to be reasonable. But, still... "Ma'am, I've only left the ship twice in the last two days to deal with ship's legal officer responsibilities."

Moraine didn't seem mollified. "That's not what I recall. You haven't been around when I needed to contact you regarding your *primary* duty as Combat Information Center officer! One time I couldn't even contact your data pad! Was it *off* in violation of regulations?"

Paul hoped his reaction didn't show on his face. *She must've tried to contact me while I was in that NCIS isolation room. How do I explain that?* "It was not off, ma'am. I haven't turned off my data pad." *No lie, there. But how do I explain why she couldn't contact me?* "Some of the rooms down in the staff sections of the station are sealed against transmissions. It could be one of them blocked my signal temporarily." *Could be, hell. I was inside one of them. How many lies am I going to have to tell to get through this assignment?*

Moraine glared at him, then looked down at her data pad again, apparently seeking some new item on which to grill Paul. Given the break, Paul decided to go on the offensive. "Ma'am, we do need your sworn statement regarding the engagement at the asteroid."

Her head jerked up. "We? Who's been asking?"

"The XO asked me the status of that this afternoon, ma'am."

"I wasn't even the department head then! Why do they need my input, anyway?" Moraine grumbled. "All right. The sooner I can put that incident behind me, the better."

Perhaps that finally offered an opening for Paul. "A lot of things went wrong, ma'am." Maybe Moraine would express some opinions that he could guide toward seeing if any motivation existed to commit espionage.

But his department head just glared at him again. "Nothing I had anything to do with! I wasn't yet in the chain of command! Nobody had better try to claim I was, because I have documentation proving when I took over responsibility for this department and it was after we got back here. Nothing like that will happen now that I'm in charge. Whatever situation we confront, we will handle it perfectly because our equipment will be working perfectly and our enlisted personnel will perform perfectly. That's our only goal and I will accept nothing less."

Paul, at a loss for words, could only nod. *I wonder how screwed up a department can get while its boss insists on perfection in everything?*

Grumbling to herself about the statement, Moraine dismissed Paul. He left with a real sense of relief that outweighed disappointment at his failure to get Moraine to talk about any of the things the NCIS had been interested in.

Paul walked down the passageway, fighting a growing feeling of frustration and deflation as his relief faded. *Talking to Moraine didn't get me anything. All I ended up with is that stupid demand of hers for the source-code on the tracking software. What's wrong with her? There's no way she should be looking at that.*

Paul stopped moving so abruptly that a sailor coming along behind bumped into him. The sailor gave Paul an aggravated look as Paul moved to the side of the passageway to let the other past. Paul wasn't paying attention, though. He was considering the realization that had just come to him. *Moraine's job doesn't require her to look at sensitive source-code, has nothing to do with looking at source-code for software, but she insists on seeing it. Which is exactly one of the things that the NCIS agents told me to watch for.*

Not that he could do anything about it right now. He couldn't leave the ship again today, and in any event Connally wouldn't see him until tomorrow.

The day finally wound down, the senior officers leaving to spend some time ashore as evening officially came to Franklin and the lights dimmed in public areas all over the station. Now the entire ship, in one sense, belonged to Paul. As command duty officer he had responsibility for whatever happened onboard until his duty day ended tomorrow morning.

Despite his weariness, Paul walked, checking every compartment on the ship from bullnose to stern, looking for any sign of trouble or anything amiss. He paused, as he almost always did, outside of Forward Engineering. Chief Asher had died there, and the engineers on the ship insisted that his ghost still occupied the compartment, keeping an eye on things. One petty officer had told Paul of an incident where an accident had been forestalled when a broken switch miraculously functioned long enough to divert power. The rational part of Paul laid that incident at the feet of the transient malfunctions that plagued sophisticated electronics. But another part of him felt a sense of someone watching whenever he visited the compartment. Not that Asher should be mad at him, but Paul just wasn't too comfortable around ghosts.

Farther aft he passed the weapons bay where Petty Officer Davidas had died even longer ago. According to the crew, Davidas (like Asher) occasionally made his continued presence known. Paul stopped for a moment. *How's it feel?* he asked Davidas. *So many of the crew you knew back then are gone. I understand that feeling. Part of a ship is the hardware. The ship herself. But the biggest part is the crew. What happens when the crew changes? Does the ship become a different ship?*

I know I won't be able to visit again in years to come and feel that this ship is a familiar place. It's already full of people I hardly know, and in a few more years there'll be nobody left onboard who remembers me as anything other than a name on an old crew roster.

The next morning he handed off duty responsibilities to his relief and dove into work in an attempt to catch up and also forget his recent unconventional activities. As usual, he was interrupted by a page, this one on the ship's general announcing system. "Lieutenant Sinclair, Lieutenant Pullman, your presence is requested in the wardroom."

Grumbling, Paul hastened that way, keeping his eyes on the messages on his data pad as he entered the wardroom. Finally looking up, the first thing he noticed was Jen smiling at him. "Jen? What're you doing here?" She gestured to one side. "Captain?"

Hayes frowned with every appearance of displeasure, the frown also taking in Brad Pullman as he entered. "Didn't I ask for Lieutenant Sinclair and Lieutenant Pullman to report here?"

Paul nodded, trying not to look confused.

"But you're both wearing lieutenant junior grade insignia." Hayes consulted his own data pad. "According to this promotion message, you two are wearing the wrong insignia. I won't have my officers walking around out of uniform."

It finally sunk in. Paul's promotion had been authorized to take effect. Jen grinned a little wider.

Hayes kept his expression stern. "If you're going to be promoted, perhaps you ought to retake the commissioning oath. No objections? Good. Raise your right hands," he ordered Paul and Brad Pullman. "Repeat after me. I, state your name."

"I, Paul Sinclair," Paul recited.

"Do solemnly swear or affirm..."

"Do solemnly swear or affirm..."

The captain read through the rest of the oath, pausing to let Paul and Brad Pullman recite each section in turn. "... that I will support and defend the Constitution of the United States against all enemies foreign and domestic;"

"... that I will bear true faith and allegiance to the same;"

"... that I take this obligation freely without any mental reservation or purpose of evasion;"

"... and that I will well and faithfully discharge the duties of the office upon which I am about to enter; so help me God."

Paul lowered his hand and grinned at Jen.

Captain Hayes finally smiled as well and handed a set of lieutenant's insignia to Jen. "Lieutenant Shen, I understand we're jumping the gun a little bit on this, but as spouse-to-be I think the honor of pinning these on Paul should be yours."

"Thank you, sir." Jen took the twinned silver bars, removed Paul's single silver bar from his collar, then pinned the lieutenant insignia on. "Now that we're the same rank you've got an excuse for not saluting me when we meet in public," she teased Paul.

Captain Hayes pinned the insignia on Pullman, then Paul and Brad shook hands.

Lieutenant Sinclair. It felt good. It'd been a long time coming.

Jen waved in farewell. "I've got to get back to work. See you at lunch."

"Yes. Fogarty's," Paul reminded her.

Ensign Taylor contrived to look shocked when she saw Paul an hour later. "Damn. I'd better make sure I get those ice skates."

"Why?"

"Because I figure I've got a better than middlin' chance of going to hell when I die, and since you just made lieutenant that must mean hell has finally frozen over."

"It might thaw out again by the time you get there."

"Could be," Taylor agreed. "I ain't in no hurry. Where's Willy Wise Ass?"

"Who?"

"Our fellow division officer."

"Brad Pullman? I left him in the wardroom."

"Huh. If you see him before I do, tell him that if he tries messing about with comm linkages again without coordinating with my people first, I'll pin those new lieutenant's bars of his onto his forehead."

"You're kidding." Ensign Taylor usually acted easy going, but Paul had quickly figured you could get on her bad side real fast by messing with "her" equipment. "Why'd he do that?"

"Figured he knew a better way to do it. Maybe it is. But since he didn't talk to anyone about it, his little changes locked up half the linkages." Taylor shook her head. "There's such a thing as being too smart for your own good."

Paul found himself smiling. "I guess that's one thing I don't have to worry about."

"Probably not," Taylor agreed. "And if it starts to become a problem, we'll just promote you to lieutenant commander and make you a little dumber. Ah, hell, maybe I won't kill Pullman this time. But he better start using his head as well as his brains."

"I'll make sure to mention that to him. Hey, has Moraine talked to you about the tracking software?"

They were still deep in a discussion of the twin problems of how to fix the software and how to keep Moraine happy, when Paul's data pad reminded him of his lunch appointment. He ended up practically running to meet Jen on time.

"Wow. Lunch at Fogarty's," Jen remarked as they sat down. "What a lucky girl I am. I haven't eaten here since... the day before yesterday."

Paul grinned. "I haven't seen you for a couple of hours. I didn't want to wait any longer."

"Please. My stomach. I haven't eaten yet, and you're making me nauseous."

They ate, they talked. Paul tried not to look at the time any more often than normal. Even though he had every right to take lunch off of the ship, Moraine was watching him like a hawk and he needed to get back to the ship on time.

"Paul? Paul Sinclair?" The voice was right behind him. Paul turned and saw Special Agent Connally smiling at him with a surprised expression. "I don't believe it! It's me, Paul. Pam."

"Pam? What're you doing on Franklin?"

"I got me a government job. Come here, you." She pulled him up and they hugged, one of her hands reaching in to remove the wire so smoothly that Paul almost missed it even though he knew it was going to happen. Then Connally was smiling brightly at Jen. "Who's this you're with?"

Before Paul could answer, Jen half-rose to offer her hand. "Jen Shen. You're a friend of Paul's, huh?"

"Sure thing. Years ago. Is that a ring? Are you two engaged? That's wonderful!" Pam burbled on for a few moments, playing her role so well that Paul found himself wondering if she really was an old friend. "Look, I've got some place I have to be, but I'm sure I'll see you around every now and then. I'll call. Okay? Great. See you soon."

Paul sat back down and saw Jen giving him an arch look. "Old friend?" she asked.

"Uh, yeah."

"How good a friend? That was a nice lingering hug you two exchanged."

"She's just an old friend," Paul protested. "We were never involved." That, at least, was absolutely true.

"Where from?"

"Annapolis," Paul improvised. "She went to that civilian college located near the Academy."

"Oh, I see." Jen seemed to be enjoying herself. "You guys dated, then."

"No. I've never been on a date with Pam." It was a relief to be able to tell the truth about something even though the context was more than a little misleading.

"Why not? She seems nice."

"Uh, we just never clicked. You know."

Jen finally laughed. "Paul, you're allowed to have old girlfriends. It's not like I don't have a few old boyfriends floating around."

"I've never met any," Paul reminded her.

She grinned wickedly. "That's because I meant the 'floating around' part literally. My father spaced them out of airlocks."

Paul started to laugh, then gave her a questioning look. "Knowing your father, I'm not sure whether or not you're joking." His data pad beeped. "Time for me to get back. My new department head thinks I'm spending too much time off of the ship."

"And you're complaining? This from a guy who's planning to go back to working for Herdez? When she gets command of a ship she'll probably seal the quarterdeck for three years and keep the crew working nonstop the entire time."

"At least she'll know what she's doing. Catch you tonight?"

"Sure. My social calendar's open. Let's get you back to your ship. I'll walk a little ways with you." They were halfway back to the ship when Jen gave him a loving look. "Who's she really?" she murmured.

"What?"

"Don't look upset. Anyone watching can tell I'm saying sweet things to you. Who's this Pam person really?"

"I..."

"Is she related to that thing we discussed? Working on it?"

"Yes."

"That's what I thought. Don't worry that your cover's blown, Secret Agent Man. I know you well enough to tell you weren't really old friends with her. I doubt anybody else could've told. Just be careful. This isn't your game they're playing."

"I know. Jen, I really don't like not telling you the truth."

"I could tell, which is why I'm not upset. Besides, I told you to do this. Just keep any lies to me about this stuff to the bare minimum necessary, okay?"

"I promise."

Connally met with him again the next day. "We've gone over everything recorded on the wire."

"And?"

"It's... not very useful."

Paul shook his head. "But Commander Moraine asked to see source-code for our tracking software. That's not something she should be looking at."

"True." Connally smiled encouragingly. "I didn't say there wasn't anything on it. But the psych we had listen to her said that Moraine's request is also consistent with her apparent obsessive-compulsive tendencies. That means it's not as strong an indicator as it would be if the action were uncharacteristic for her."

Paul sagged backwards. "That was a lot of trouble for nothing."

"I didn't say it was for nothing!"

"It didn't help you focus on Commander Moraine."

"Or Brad Pullman," Connally agreed. "I've talked this over with my superiors. We think the only way to resolve this is to set a trap."

"A trap?" Paul knew he looked alarmed.

"Yes. Relax. This isn't a blazing-gunfire-in-a-dark-alley thing. Do you know anything about taps on computers?"

"Just that they exist. It's one of the things they talk about in security classes."

"Yes." Connally gave Paul another smile. "Taps can either broadcast information from the computer, or alert someone on the outside to actions taken by the computer. The second form is much easier to keep hidden, because a lot less data needs to be sent out."

"What does this have to do with catching whoever's committing espionage?"

As she spoke, Connally tapped the table surface gently with her fingers to emphasize her points. "Our target needs to download data onto portable storage media in order to pass it to his or her contacts. There aren't any uncontrolled computers on your ship. Your own security systems prevent any of those from operating or tying into the ship's data."

Paul nodded. "Right."

"Which means our target has to use their own terminal to do the dirty work."

"Then we'd have a record of it," Paul objected. "All we'd have to do is access the system records—"

Connally was shaking her head slowly. "No. There's software that hides the operations. We have a couple forms of it. So do various bad actors."

"Then you can search for that software—"

"It loads to do the job, then wipes itself out without a trace. Now, if we could catch our target with a data coin holding that software, we'd be in fat city, but odds are that our target only has the stuff when it's needed. We have to catch our target doing a download of sensitive information with one of our special taps which even that sneaky software won't be able to spot, then nail him or her when they walk off the ship with it. That'll give us probable cause to get search warrants enough to check out personal possessions and dig into financial records. Then we'll have our target just where we want them."

Paul found himself nodding. "That makes sense. How do we do that?"

"One part's easy. We'll contact your captain about it. All you need to know is that your ship is going to get some special sensitive information downloaded to it. The second part is a little trickier. We need to physically install the taps in the targets' personal terminals in their staterooms. We'll need your assistance to make that work."

More spying on his fellow officers. But if it was only two terminals, and the taps only reported illegal downloads, that wasn't so bad, was it? "Who does this installation? How many people do I have to cover for?"

Connally pointed to herself. "Me."

"You? Just you?"

"I'm a woman of many talents. Look, we need to do this without arousing interest. We can't have people openly showing up to work on those terminals during the work day, or even at night. Your own computer people would want to know what was going on."

"Ensign Taylor can be trusted."

"I'm sure... she? Yes? I'm sure she can. That's not the point. We don't want anyone else knowing work was done. I can install the taps in a few minutes and not leave any trace for anyone to see. You say you stay aboard the ship some nights?"

"Yeah," Paul agreed, wondering why he was feeling a sense of unease.

"When's the next night?"

"Day after tomorrow."

"Great! I'll come aboard in the evening as if I'm visiting you to catch up on old times—"

"Whoa!" Paul held up both hands, palms out. "You don't think anyone will notice if a good-looking young woman visits me on the ship at night?"

"That doesn't happen?"

"Well, yes, but it's always Jen. My fiancée. If you come onboard some people are going to... well, they'll talk."

Connally shrugged. "Not about taps on computers, I'm sure."

"One of those terminals is in my stateroom! I share the room with Brad Pullman! We can't go in my stateroom alone!"

"I promise not to do anything unladylike, Paul."

"That's not—" He could tell she was barely keeping from laughing. "All right, I know it sounds funny, but it does matter to me. I don't want people thinking I'm cheating on Jen. Besides, messing around on a ship is against regulations. I don't want everyone thinking I'm breaking regulations."

"Fair enough." Connally frowned in thought, resting her chin on one fist. "Can you think of any plausible way I can be alone in your stateroom, with the door closed, and in Commander Moraine's stateroom with the door closed? Just for a few minutes."

Paul thought, too. Then he finally looked back at her. "Yes. But I'll need one other person's help. An absolutely trustworthy person. I won't have to tell him anything, but frankly we'd have to tell him something anyway because there's too great a chance he'd recognize you as an NCIS agent if he saw you onboard."

"Who is this?"

"My chief master-at-arms, Ivan Sharpe."

"Hmmm. Tell me about this idea of yours."

So Paul did.

6

Once again, Paul found himself trying not to act nervous as he answered a call from the petty officer of the watch. "Mr. Sinclair? You've got a visitor on the quarterdeck, sir."

"Thanks, I'll be right there." Paul checked his uniform, feeling absurdly as if this was a date. He paged Sharpe, then walked at a steady gait to the quarterdeck.

Pam Connally was there, looking nice indeed and not at all like a special agent. "Paul, this is so cool. This is your ship?"

"Uh, not mine, exactly." He could see Chief Cruz, the officer of the deck, giving him an approving thumbs-up and wink from behind Connally. *Great. This'll be all over the mess decks by morning.* "It's great to see you again after all these years, Pam. Come on inside."

She followed him through the hatch, bending more than she had to in order to clear the hatch edge, in the way people who weren't experienced with moving around ships always did. They walked down the passageway, exchanging idle, generic chatter about non-existent old times. "Can I see your room?" Connally asked.

"My stateroom? Uh, sure."

Connally went inside, making remarks about the small size of the compartment. "They actually have four of you living in here?"

"Yeah." Paul pointed to the four small desks. "That's mine. That one belongs to a guy named Brad Pullman, this one is Randy Diego's and that's where Jack Abacha works."

"And this one... Brad?" Pam pointed to that desk again. "He's a lieutenant like you?"

"Right. Lieutenant junior grade. The other two are ensigns."

"Wow." Having discreetly confirmed that she knew exactly which terminal belonged to Pullman, Connally looked around the cramped compartment with a wondering expression as if she were touring the Sistine Chapel.

"Mr. Sinclair?"

Paul turned to see Ivan Sharpe. "Yeah, Sheriff. What's up?"

"Something I needed to talk to you about, sir. Oh, you've got a guest. Sorry, ma'am, I need to talk to Mr. Sinclair privately for a moment."

Connally looked disappointed. "Do I need to leave already?"

Paul shook his head. "No. This will only take a few seconds. Right, Sheriff? Why don't you just stay inside while I shut the door and the master-at-arms and I talk out here? When we're done talking I'll open it up again."

"That'd be great! Then I could really see how it feels to be in this small room."

Paul closed the hatch, reflecting that he'd never thought of being in that small compartment as anything anyone would seek to experience.

Sharpe cleared his throat. "Yada, yada, yada," he murmured.

"She's not bad lookin', sir."

"I hadn't noticed," Paul replied in a similar low voice.

Ensign Hosta came by on the way to her stateroom, giving Paul and the shut door a curious look. "The sheriff and I are talking about something my guest shouldn't hear," Paul explained. Hosta nodded and went on, hopefully to spread the explanation for the shut door to anyone who might wonder.

"I do recognize her," Sharpe continued in a near-whisper after Hosta had gone out of earshot. "Seen her a few times around the offices where she works. Good thing you clued me in she'd be here or I might've mentioned it to someone tomorrow."

"But now you won't mention it to anyone."

"I wouldn't dream of it, sir. Sure you can't tell me what's up?"

"No. Nothing's up, Sheriff."

"Aye, aye, sir. I don't know nothin'."

Connally rapped lightly on the hatch and Paul pulled it open. "Thanks, Sheriff," he said in a normal voice. "Keep me informed."

"Yes, sir." Sharpe nodded companionably to Connally. "Nice meeting you, ma'am."

"Likewise," Connally replied cheerfully as Sharpe left. "Can I see more of the ship, Paul?"

"Sure." They walked around a while, then back toward officers' country. As they were approaching Commander Moraine's stateroom, Paul checked his watch. "How much longer can you stay?"

"Not long. I had something come up at work. I need to go there right after this. There isn't a private restroom I can use around here anywhere, is there?"

"There's one in this stateroom," Paul advised, halting in front of Moraine's hatch. He knocked as if not knowing whether Moraine was onboard and in her stateroom, then opened the hatch. "Senior officers get their own. Go ahead."

"Thanks." Connally went inside, shutting the hatch, while Paul waited. A few minutes later she emerged. "I'm glad I got that done."

They walked back toward the quarterdeck, while Connally invented an imaginary social event she'd attended with Paul and some equally imaginary mutual friends in their college days and chatted gaily about the details. "I'm sorry I couldn't stay longer."

"That's okay." Paul realized close to an hour had passed since she'd come aboard. The cover activities had taken considerably more time than the actual installation of the taps. "It was nice having you here."

She waved as she walked off the brow. Chief Cruz waved back along with Paul. "Your secret's safe with me, lieutenant."

"There's no secret to keep safe, chief."

"With a fine lady like that? There ought to be."

Paul laughed and left the quarterdeck, knowing word would somehow filter back to Jen and hoping she'd understand that Paul's secret activities tonight had been professional, not personal.

Another day, another evening at Fogarty's. Paul wondered whether he was starting to become too much of a regular at the bar.

But it wasn't like he could pass up on coming tonight. Neither Kris Denaldo nor Mike Bristol had wanted to make a big deal of their farewells from the ship, but tradition had to be served. Jen sat quietly beside him as Paul raised his drink toward the pair. "Fair winds, you guys."

"I still can't believe I'm going to be feeling real wind again before long," Bristol remarked. "Should I send some up to you guys after I get back to Earth?"

"Nah. If you tried that the new suppo would probably reject it as nonstandard."

Bristol looked pained at the reminder of the state into which the *Michaelson*'s Supply Department had fallen. "I tried to give my relief a good turnover, but she's got to work with Smithe so there's only so much I could teach her. Smithe won't let us do a lot of the things Sykes did."

Paul looked around, finally spotting Bristol's relief, a small-framed, quiet, brand-new ensign. Paul had been so busy he'd hardly met her since she'd come aboard. Now he noticed her sitting nervously as if expecting a team of inspectors from Naval Supply Command to burst through the door at any moment and demand to audit her books. "I'll try to look out for her." He felt that as a duty, in a way. The lieutenants onboard when brand-new Ensign Paul Sinclair had reported in had helped him when they could, while still giving him enough slack to learn some painful but important lessons.

"Thanks. I know you won't have much time onboard with her yourself, but I'd hate to see her made into a whipping boy for Smithe's policies."

Kris Denaldo had been staring into her drink. Now she looked up with a wistful expression. "Young and innocent. We were like that once."

"Life goes on," Jen replied. "Keep in touch, Kris."

"I'll do my best. It's strange. You know what's really freaking me out? The next time the *Merry Mike* gets underway, I won't be on her. For the last three years, every time that ship left port, I was onboard. Next time, I won't. It feels wrong somehow."

Jen grinned. "Paul, if Kris tries to sneak back aboard the *Michaelson* after she's transferred so she can keep working, promise me you'll kick her back off."

"Even if she's doing some of *my* work?" Paul asked.

"Even if."

"Okay." He pointed a stern finger at Kris. "Begone and darken our wardroom no more."

"Screw both of you," Kris replied, sticking out her tongue. "Here I try to share my innermost feelings—"

"Save it for that lieutenant on the *Mahan*," Jen suggested. "Oh, yeah. Don't look so shocked. I have my sources."

Kris smiled. "I've spent a long time looking for someone as desperate as *my* lieutenant. Oh, there was always Paul, who was as desperate as they come, but *someone* else got their claws into him first."

Jen smiled back. "You snooze, you lose. Besides, you've been serving on the ship with him the entire time. That means you two were off limits to each other. I was clever enough to get transferred so I could snag the poor lad before he knew what was happening."

Brad Pullman came by, hoisting a toast of his own. "To the soon to be departed. Is this a private booth or can new guys join in?"

Paul moved over so Brad could join them. A few other junior officers came by and sat down, too. The conversation went on for a while, but it didn't have the same easy familiarity as when it'd been just among the four who'd served together for so long.

And when the night had ended and the next day came, Kris Denaldo and Mike Bristol detached from the crew of the USS *Michaelson*, walked off the ship for the final time, and life went on.

Commander Moraine had finished her daily little speech at officers' call. Paul was beginning to wonder of she had an entire book of them loaded into her data pad. Taylor was doing a good imitation of someone just barely able to stay awake after listening to the speech. Pullman appeared to be trying not to laugh at Taylor. "I have one other thing to announce," Moraine declared with icy looks at Taylor, Pullman, and Paul. "The captain has informed us that we'll be receiving an updated copy of the Fleet Tactical Action Manual. This has a Top Secret annex containing the latest intelligence on foreign space capabilities. You will be expected to read that annex and be familiar with its contents. It's a new format and Fleet Intelligence Center Space wants feedback."

Paul, already wondering why he'd gotten a fish-eye from Moraine when he hadn't been engaging in the same high-jinks as Taylor and Pullman, started wondering if this was the sensitive material Connally had told him would be provided to the ship. *The bait's here, the taps are in place. It's just a matter of waiting until the trap springs.* He looked at Commander Moraine, unable to keep from speculating if her days of giving speeches to them were numbered. The thought did cheer him up somewhat.

"Is something wrong, Mr. Sinclair?"

Paul focused back on Commander Moraine's aggravated expression. "Uh, no, ma'am."

"Then get to work. All of you." Commander Moraine stalked off, furiously punching the keys on her data pad.

Taylor blinked and looked around like someone awakening from a sound sleep. "Hello? What? Yes, ma'am!" Both Paul and Brad Pullman laughed as Taylor stood and stretched. "I'm really getting to enjoy these morning rest breaks. See you young 'uns later." She strolled off, singing "heigh ho, heigh ho," in a low voice.

Ivan Sharpe ran Paul down half an hour later. "Captain's mast, Mr. Sinclair."

"I know. I know. At 1300."

"No, sir. The captain had something come up and he needs to be off the ship then. Mast has been moved up to zero nine thirty."

"Zero nine thirty?" Paul checked the time. "Great. There goes the rest of the morning."

"Yes, sir. If you'll excuse me, sir, I need to notify everyone else involved."

Paul dropped what he was doing, calling up the charge sheets for everyone going to captain's mast, and ensured they were accurate. Unfortunately, Sharpe had been right about the crew blowing off steam when they hit port, and there'd been an unusually large number of incidents that needed to be handled by the quick and dirty form of military justice known to the Navy as mast even though its formal name was non-judicial punishment.

At 0915, Paul headed for the mess decks. Regardless of how Commander Moraine felt about it, the ship's legal officer was required to attend every captain's mast. Sharpe was already there, furiously checking off the presence of accused personnel, witnesses and the chiefs and division officers of the accused. Paul waved a brief greeting and left Sharpe to his work, going to the side of the compartment where'd he stand during the mast. "Mornin', Mr. Sinclair," Master Chief Maines greeted him.

"Mornin', master chief." The new senior enlisted on the ship had taken over that job when she joined the crew soon after the departure of Senior Chief Kowalski. Paul hadn't had too much interaction with the master chief, who worked in engineering, but had the impression she was solid enough at her job, even if not quite the paragon that

Kowalski had been. *Then again, maybe I'm turning into one of those "old guys" looking back at the good old days when gods allegedly walked the earth in human form.* Paul stood next to Master Chief Maines, waiting in a relaxed, almost-at-ease posture.

Maines checked her watch. "Gonna be a long one today, sir."

"Yeah. The crew went a little nuts on us the first days back in port."

"It happens, sir. Not that we didn't try to keep a lid on things, but after all the crap we went through during that last underway period, a lot of people had a lot of pressure to vent off."

"Too bad they couldn't have vented a little more gradually and avoided explosive decompression."

Before Maines could answer, Sharpe stuck his head in the compartment. "All present and accounted for, Mr. Sinclair. I'm going to get the captain."

"Very well." Paul let his mind wander, trying to plan which fires he'd concentrate on putting out for the rest of the day once mast was over.

Before he knew it, Sharpe was back. "Attention on deck."

Paul and Master Chief Maines straightened to attention as Captain Hayes entered. Nodding to both of them, Hayes ordered them to "carry on" as he went to the small podium set up facing the center of the compartment. As Paul went from attention to parade rest, Hayes pointed at Sharpe. "Let's go."

Sharpe leaned back into the passageway. "Petty Officer Timbale," he called.

Timbale entered, his uniform well turned out, marching up to stand at attention facing the captain. Behind Timbale, his division officer Ensign Abacha and the chief of his division entered and came to attention on the other side of the compartment, facing Paul and the master chief so that the accused sailor was in the center of a three-sided box formed by his superiors.

Hayes eyed the sailor for a moment, then looked down at his data pad. "Petty Officer Second Class Timbale. You are charged with violation of Article 92 of the Uniform Code of Military Justice, Failure to Obey Order or Regulation. You're also charged with violating Article 108, Damage to Military Property of the United States and Article 134, Disorderly Conduct/Drunkenness." Hayes fixed Timbale with a demanding look. "What do you have to say?"

Timbale licked his lips nervously before starting to speak. "Captain, I *was* drunk."

Hayes waited a moment, then prodded the sailor. "That's all?"

"No, sir. I mean, yes, sir. I wasn't disorderly, sir."

"Why were you charged with being disorderly?"

Timbale let his unhappiness show. "I believe that's the result of a misunderstanding, sir."

"A misunderstanding."

"Yes, captain." Timbale's expression became earnest. "I don't deny me and my shipmates had been hitting the bars and maybe hitting them a little too hard. But we weren't making any fuss. Maybe we were a little loud, but when we got thrown out of— I mean, when we decided to leave that last bar we was going to head back to the ship and sleep it off. But then Johnson started feeling a little dizzy and he laid down and we couldn't get him up again and we had a problem."

Captain Hayes waited again, then once more posed a question. "And?"

"Captain, we wasn't going to leave Johnson just lying there. He could've got in trouble. But he's a big guy, sir, and for some reason we was having trouble trying to carry him back to the ship. Then Petty Officer Ghi remembered there was a first aid locker real close."

"Did you think Johnson was sick?"

"No, sir. We knew he was drunk as a pig. But those first aid lockers have stretchers in them. So we popped open the seal on the first aid locker and pulled out the stretcher and put Johnson on it and carried him back to the ship that way. Then the officer of the deck got kind of upset when she saw Johnson in the stretcher and told us we'd messed up. But we never tried to hurt Johnson, sir!"

Hayes looked perplexed. "Who said you did?"

Sharpe cleared his throat. "Excuse me, captain, but the XO screened out an assault charge against Timbale and the others. It was brought because of some injuries Johnson sustained."

The captain looked around, then focused on Timbale. "How did Johnson get injured?"

"Captain, that wasn't my fault. Ghi dropped her end of the stretcher a few times—"

"Okay. I understand. To summarize, then, you all got drunk, Johnson passed out and you broke into a first aid locker to steal a stretcher." Hayes looked around the compartment again. "Why wasn't he charged with theft?"

Paul took a moment to realize that after all the captain's masts at which he stood by just in case he was needed, he'd finally actually been asked a question during captain's mast. "Sir, we couldn't charge Timbale or Ghi with theft because they didn't plan on keeping the stretcher. They were going to take it back."

"It's only theft if they plan on keeping it?"

"Yes, sir. Legally, sir."

"The Uniform Code of Military Justice says that?"

"Yes, sir. It's that way in civil law, too."

Hayes shook his head, then looked at Timbale again. "But you're charged with damaging property, so I assume the stretcher was damaged?"

Timbale nodded, his nervousness showing again. "Yes, sir. When it got dropped and when we were getting it out of the locker. And I guess some folks were upset that we popped the locker seal, and they said that was damage, too."

Hayes looked at Paul again. "What order or regulation was violated?"

Paul nodded toward Timbale. "The first aid lockers are only supposed to be opened to provide emergency medical assistance. That's by order of the station commander. The order is posted on the lockers."

"But, captain," Timbale protested, "it *was* an emergency. We couldn't leave Johnson just lying there."

"Why didn't you simply call for assistance?" Hayes demanded.

Timbale hesitated. "Uh, captain, we didn't want anyone to get in trouble."

Hayes shook his head again, looking down at his data pad for a moment, then gazed over at Ensign Abacha. "What kind of sailor is Petty Officer Timbale?"

Abacha looked almost as nervous as Timbale but spoke in a firm voice. "He's a good performer, captain. He rarely gives us any trouble. Just an occasional incident on liberty. There's never any problems on the job. He's a good petty officer when he's on the ship." Timbale's chief nodded in agreement.

Captain Hayes gave Timbale a searching look. "Petty Officer Timbale, do you think you handled that situation properly?"

"Captain?"

"Do you think you did the right thing or do you think you screwed up?"

Timbale nodded heavily. "I screwed up, sir. We shouldn't have taken that stretcher."

"Or gotten so drunk you got thrown out of a bar and Johnson passed out?"

"No, sir. Not that, either. But, captain, honest, we didn't think we were violating any order. It said open that locker in an emergency and it sure seemed like an emergency to us."

"All right." Hayes glanced at Ensign Abacha again. "Your division officer and your chief stood up for you here. But they also said you get in trouble on liberty sometimes. You're a member of the United States Navy twenty-four hours a day, seven days a week, Petty Officer Timbale. That means your job doesn't end when you walk off of this ship. You still need to think about what you're doing and make sure you don't get so drunk that damaging government property sounds like a good idea. Do you understand?"

"Yes, sir, I do."

"I could really hammer you, Petty Officer Timbale. Instead, I'll go pretty light because your chief and division officer say you're a good performer and you've got a clean record. But not so light that you won't remember this next time you have to think about what to do on liberty. I'm fining you one-half month's pay for one month and giving you a reduction in rate to seaman, suspended for six months. Keep yourself out of trouble and you won't have to worry about being busted to seaman. Understand?"

"Yes, sir! Thank you, sir!"

"Dismissed."

Timbale pivoted on one heel and marched out of the compartment, followed by Ensign Abacha and his chief. Master Chief Maines shook her head and muttered something under her breath. Hayes gave her a wry look. "What was that, master chief?"

"I was just commenting to myself on the eternal nature of sailors, captain. If they ever design a machine that can replace them, *it'll* probably go out and get drunk and do something stupid."

Hayes grinned. "No doubt. Next case, Sheriff."

Petty Officer Chi came next, getting the same treatment as Timbale had. Then a still slightly battered-looking Petty Officer Johnson, then more sailors, each with some variation on drunk and disorderly, provoking speeches and gestures, insubordination, and the occasional assault charge from a bar brawl. The captain varied his punishments depending on their individual records and the severity of the offenses. Hayes was shaking his head by the time the last case came up. "At least we didn't have a riot," the captain remarked. "What's this last one?"

"It's a bad one, captain," Sharpe warned before leaning into the passageway. "Petty Officer Vox."

Vox entered, his uniform neat but his face still bearing a black eye and a visible series of healing but deep scratches on one cheek. Hayes frowned, then checked his data pad as Lieutenant Isakov entered and took up position along with a female sailor who avoided looking at Vox. The captain's face visibly hardened as he read. "Petty Officer Vox. I see you're charged with violating Article 112(a), Wrongful Use of Controlled Substances, Article 134, Assault with Intent to Commit Rape, and Article 134, Drunk and Disorderly. What do you have to say?"

Vox's eyes flicked from side to side before he spoke, then looked straight ahead to avoid meeting the captain's eyes. "I don't remember doing any of that, captain."

"That's all? You just claim you don't *remember* committing these offenses?"

"Yes, sir."

"*Did* you commit them?"

"I... I don't remember, sir."

Hayes glared at the sailor, then over at Isakov. "Lieutenant Isakov, what's the story?"

Isakov kept her face expressionless as she spoke. "As command duty officer on the night in question, I was notified by the shore patrol that Petty Officer Vox had been placed under arrest. I arranged for his release into the custody of Chief Sharpe the next morning. As Vox's division officer, I investigated the report the shore patrol provided. The report states that Petty Officer Vox became belligerent while on liberty and was asked to leave a bar where he and a number of other sailors from the *Michaelson* were drinking. About one hour later, as Seaman Kanto was returning to the ship alone, she was assaulted by Petty Officer Vox, who attempted to rape her. Seaman Kanto fought off her assailant and called the shore patrol, who took Petty Officer Vox into custody a short time later not far from the scene of the attack. While Petty Officer Vox's injuries were being treated at the brig, blood tests revealed he had ingested an illegal synthetic substance known as Joy Juice earlier that evening."

Hayes gave Vox another hard stare, then looked over at the sailor next to Isakov. "Seaman Kanto, is that an accurate account of events as you know them?"

Kanto nodded, studiously avoiding looking toward Vox. "Yes, sir."

"How certain are you that Petty Officer Vox is the individual who attacked you?"

Kanto gave a brief, nervous smile. "I marked the son of a bi— Excuse me, sir. That's him."

Isakov spoke again. "The shore patrol investigation matched the blood under some of Seaman Kanto's fingernails to Petty Officer Vox, captain. One hundred percent certain match."

Hayes stared silently at Vox for several seconds. Vox quivered once but said nothing. Finally, Hayes shook his head with slow finality. "And you *don't remember* trying to rape a shipmate, Petty Officer Vox?"

"No, sir."

"Do you *remember* taking Joy Juice?"

"No, sir."

"Lieutenant Isakov," Hayes asked, keeping his eyes fixed on Vox, "what kind of sailor is Petty Officer Vox?"

Isakov's voice stayed cool and controlled. "Middling at best, sir. He does what's required and nothing more."

"Does he have a history of trouble?"

Isakov nodded. "Petty Officer Vox has had frequent minor disciplinary problems. He just came off a suspended bust to seaman."

"And now you've graduated to trying to rape a shipmate, is that right, Petty Officer Vox?" Captain Hayes' face had reddened as he glared at the accused sailor.

"Captain, I don't remember—"

"You said that. Even if it's true, it doesn't excuse the act in the least. Nor the use of a controlled substance which has long-term effects on a person's judgment. You're a menace to this ship and to your own shipmates." Hayes shifted his glare to Paul. "This is too serious an offense to dispose of at mast. I want this... individual... court-martialed."

Paul nodded. "Summary or special court-martial, sir?"

"See if the station will approve taking it for a special. If not, we'll do a summary." Hayes looked back at Vox. "Regardless, you are going to get hammered, Petty Officer Vox. Chief Sharpe."

Sharpe came to attention. "Yes, sir."

"I don't want this man on my ship. Will the brig take him for pre-trial confinement?"

"I believe so, sir."

"Make it happen. Today. Notify me if I have to talk to the brig commander in person. Master chief."

Maines also came to attention. "Yes, sir."

"I want to ensure Vox doesn't come back to this ship. If the court-martial doesn't discharge him I want to make sure he's transferred somewhere else."

"Yes, sir."

"Dismissed," Hayes snapped.

Vox, his face rigid, marched out of the compartment, followed by Isakov and Seaman Kanto. Hayes shook his head. "Inexcusable," he said to himself, then walked out.

Sharpe pointed to one of his deputy master-at-arms who was standing by and then to Vox. "Lock him up in the confinement compartment."

Paul let out a long breath as he relaxed. "Let me know how the brig goes, Sheriff."

"Aye, aye, sir," Sharpe replied grimly. "It shouldn't be a problem. I know they've got a few vacancies." He sketched a salute and hastened away.

Master Chief Maines rubbed her chin. "I'll go talk to Kanto."

"She handled Vox real good," Paul noted.

"Oh, yes, sir. Real damn good. But that sort of thing still rattles a person something fierce. I'll talk to her and listen to her."

"Thanks, master chief."

Maines shrugged. "It's my job, sir. Too bad I can't have a personal talk with Vox. If he'd attacked me he wouldn't be walking around right now."

"That's okay, master chief. I have a feeling that even if Vox isn't already real sorry for what he did, he's going to be real sorry before all's said and done."

"Are you sorry for him, sir?"

"Hell, no."

"I didn't think so." Maines gave Paul a fierce grin. "By your leave, sir." She left, heading in the direction Kanto had gone.

Paul exhaled again, then walked out of the compartment. He had a lot of other things to do.

Late that afternoon, Paul was standing on the quarterdeck, talking to Senior Chief Imari and a contractor who claimed the tracking software problem had been fixed even though the same problems kept popping up, when Brad Pullman came out as well. "Don't tell me you're still working," Pullman chided Paul.

"Yeah. Some of us have real jobs."

"Better you than me. I had duty last night and I'm ready to get off this tub and hit the bars."

"Have one for me."

"I'm a better shipmate than that, Paul. I'll have two for you." Pullman laughed and faced the officer of the deck. "Request permission to go ashore."

Paul shook his head and went back to arguing with the contractor. Then he heard something unusual and looked up again.

Brad Pullman wasn't far from the ship. He had three people standing by him, one in front and one on each side. The one in front Paul recognized as Special Agent Gonzales. As Paul watched, Gonzales used a small device to scan over Pullman, locating what seemed from this distance to be a couple of data coins. Gonzales dropped the coins into his data pad ports, read briefly, then nodded. A pair of hand restraints appeared and were clapped around Pullman's wrists.

Paul realized his mouth was hanging open as Pullman was led away. He shut it, then spotted Special Agent Connally near the ship as well. Seeing that Paul was looking at her, Connally gave him a discreet but triumphant thumbs-up and then followed the agents taking Brad Pullman into custody.

"Sir, what happened to Mr. Pullman?" Senior Chief Imari asked, staring at the departing figures.

Paul shook his head, trying to clear it. "I... I need to see the captain, senior chief." Ignoring the contractor, Paul went in search of the captain. He didn't feel triumphant, just sick to his stomach.

The wardroom was crowded with officers again and filled with a buzz of conversation. Paul hung near the back, trying not to look like the man who'd helped get Brad Pullman arrested. *And I still can't believe he's actually guilty.*

"Attention on deck!" Commander Kwan barked and everyone leaped to attention as Captain Hayes entered.

Hayes looked around the compartment for a moment, his expression unreadable. "As some of you may already be aware, Lieutenant

Pullman has just been arrested. He was apparently carrying highly classified information which had been illegally downloaded from the ship." Hayes paused while his audience absorbed that information. Paul, watching faces, saw various degrees of shock and disbelief registering. Commander Moraine had gone very pale, her cheek twitching spasmodically.

The captain cleared his throat before speaking again. "There'll be a full investigation into the charges against Lieutenant Pullman. You will all be expected to cooperate in that investigation to the best of your ability. Lieutenant Sinclair." Paul jerked his head up, staring at the captain. "You and Chief Sharpe will be our primary points of contact with NCIS during their investigation. Make sure the XO and I are kept fully informed."

"Yes, sir."

Hayes paused again, long enough for Commander Destin to interject a question. "Captain, exactly what is Pullman going to be charged with? Mishandling classified materials? That doesn't seem serious enough to warrant—"

"If I didn't make it clear before, Lieutenant Pullman is suspected of committing espionage. The extent and duration of the suspected espionage is one of the focus points for the investigation." Hayes grimaced. "I know this is unpleasant news. I expect you all to continue focusing on your jobs. If the crew poses questions about Lieutenant Pullman, you are to tell them that there is an ongoing investigation and you can't comment on it. That's all." The captain turned abruptly and left the wardroom so fast he was already out the hatch before Kwan could yell "attention on deck" again.

The XO gave them all a hostile look. "You heard the captain. Keep your mouths shut on this." Then he left quickly, heading in the same direction the captain had gone.

The other officers held themselves at attention a moment longer, too stunned to do otherwise, until Commander Destin snapped, "Carry on." She shook her head, speaking in a low voice to the other department heads near her.

Gabriel was staring into the distance. "Brad was *spying* on us?" she asked no one in particular.

Paul swallowed and nodded. "That's the... the allegation. It hasn't been proven."

"But the captain said Brad had classified material he'd taken off the ship."

"Uh, yeah."

Jack Abacha suddenly looked livid with anger. "He was in our stateroom. He lived with us and worked with us and he was spying on us? Why?"

"I have no idea, Jack. Look, there's a lot that needs to be looked into. It's possible the charges won't hold up, or won't be all that serious. It's going to depend on what the investigation finds."

Ensign Taylor had sat back down silently, but now she shook her head. "Too smart. He figured he was too smart to play by the rules. And I'll lay you odds, boys and girls, that Mr. Wise Ass Pullman figured he was too smart to get caught."

"We don't know that he's guilty—"

"I do," Taylor stated firmly. "My gut tells me he is, and my gut don't lie." Then she grinned without much humor. "I guess that means I don't have to worry about being a member of the court-martial, huh?"

The officers were trickling out of the wardroom when Chief Sharpe stuck his head in. "Mr. Sinclair? Need you, sir."

Paul followed Sharpe, feeling the eyes of his fellow officers upon him as he left the wardroom. Sharpe waved down the passageway in the direction of Paul's stateroom. "We got company, sir. I hope you have a spare toothbrush on you."

"What?" Then the likely meaning of Sharpe's words struck home and Paul headed for the stateroom he shared with Brad Pullman.

A woman in civilian clothes stood outside the stateroom, which had crime-scene tape strung across the hatch. Paul came to a halt before her, staring into his stateroom. He could see two other civilians in there, methodically searching the compartment.

The woman gave Paul a hard look, then read his name tag and her face cleared. "Oh, Sinclair. You're our point of contact."

Paul could only nod.

"Special Agent Connally sends her respects. She didn't think she ought to come aboard in an official capacity."

That took a moment to soak in. Then Paul nodded again. *If Connally came on as an NCIS agent, then everyone would know I'd been walking an NCIS agent around officers' country after hours, and everyone would start to figure out what role I played in this.* "Thank you. What needs to be done?"

She waved toward the agents in Paul's stateroom. "We're doing it. There'll be sweeps later on of places like the captain's cabin to see if any taps were placed there by Pullman. But first we need to go through this compartment atom by atom and see what we find."

Paul rubbed his forehead hard with the heel of his hand, trying to push away the dazed feeling inside him. "Any guess how long this compartment will be off-limits?"

"No. Sorry. It'll take as long as it takes."

"Okay." *I'll have to talk to Commander Smithe about him finding temporary berths for me, Randy Diego and Jack Abacha. But all our uniforms, other clothes, personal articles and everything else are in that stateroom. This is not going to be pleasant.*

"All your stuff's in there?" the agent asked.

"Yeah."

"We'll check out some of that as soon as we can and pass it on to you. Clothes and things like that."

"Thanks. Here's the link to my data pad. Please have somebody let me know as soon as your work is done in here."

"Sure. After all, we owe you one."

"Yeah, well, that's something I'd prefer not be widely known."

The NCIS agent gave a knowing nod. "Understood. We'll keep you up to date on anything that happens."

Paul turned and began walking, lost in thought until Sharpe made a sound to get his attention and began talking softly. "Excuse me, sir, but I assume this is what that thing I didn't know nothing about was about."

"Yeah," Paul confirmed.

"Good on you, sir. It couldn't have been easy deciding to work with NCIS on that. Not with a fellow officer involved."

"It wasn't. But there were some people I didn't want to let down." He gave Sharpe a look. "Like the local cop."

"And he appreciates that, sir. I'll tell you frankly that I'm proud to have worked with you the last few years. My relief's supposed to show up tomorrow and I'll let him know he'd better do a good job for you."

"Tell you what, Sheriff. I'll tell him that I learned a lot from a real professional, and that I was proud to work with you."

Sharpe grinned. "Damn, sir, if you wasn't marryin' Ms. Shen, we'd have to get hitched ourselves."

"That's not funny, Sheriff." But he was grateful for the brief distraction the conversation had brought. Everything still refused to make sense inside his head. Lieutenant Brad Pullman, a fellow officer and someone he'd trusted, arrested on suspicion of espionage. And Paul couldn't just blow it off as a mistake because he himself knew about the computer tap and the trap set to catch someone stealing classified information. Nothing made sense and the facts kept clashing with each other. How could it be true? How could Pullman actually have done something like that? It seemed cut and dried, Pullman caught red-handed, but how many things were there that Paul didn't know? Things that might exonerate Pullman?

Only one thing seemed certain, that Pullman would be facing a court-martial soon. Which meant Paul Sinclair's role in the matter was far from done.

7

Paul knocked on a familiar door, then entered. Commander Alex Carr, Judge Advocate General's Corps, looked at him from where she was hanging from the chin-up bar mounted on one side of her office. "Paul! Good to see you." Dropping lightly to the floor, she sat down at her desk, waved Paul to the chair in front of the desk, and smiled in welcome as she stretched her arms after the exercise. "Here we are again. Not under the happiest of circumstances, of course."

"It's under better circumstances than last time, ma'am," Paul noted.

"Oh, yes. I much prefer being on the same side as you are." She twisted her mouth. "How is Ms. Shen doing?"

"Pretty good."

"'Pretty good' or 'pretty good considering'?"

Paul hesitated before answering. "Pretty good considering," he finally admitted.

Carr looked away, her expression hard for Paul to read. "There's not a lot of things in my life and career that I truly hate having been involved with, but that case is one of them. Does she hate me?"

"I... don't think so."

"I wouldn't blame her if she did. I didn't bring the charges against her for what happened on the *Maury*, and I sure as hell didn't have anything to do with all that publicity about her being charged with causing all those deaths, but I did prosecute the case against her." Carr sighed. "Things you do because you have to in order to convict someone you figure is guilty are sometimes hard to stomach. Doing those things to someone who turned out to be certainly innocent of the alleged crimes is a crime in itself. Or so I think."

Paul nodded, not speaking. There didn't seem to be any proper response. He knew Carr was referring particularly to the parts of Jen's court-martial in which Jen had been implicated in an improper relationship with a fellow officer on board the *Maury*, as well as forcing Jen to publicly admit she'd become involved with Paul a few days before her transfer off the *Michaelson*.

Commander Carr fell silent for a moment as well. "How about you, Paul? How're you doing?"

"Well, pretty good, too, I guess."

She gave him an arch look. "No fall-out from your actions?"

Paul felt a small knot form in his stomach. "Fall-out?"

"Come on. You know what I mean. You've gone to the mat three times on matters of principle, done what you've believed was right despite the possible consequences. That scares some people, Paul."

He nodded slowly. "I'm beginning to see that, ma'am. Why?"

"Why? Hell, Paul, everybody's got some skeletons in the closet. Professional and personal skeletons. They're worried you might rattle them, or not go along when something bad pops up in the future and everybody else decides to just sort of sweep it under the rug."

Paul thought of how Ensign Taylor had explained Commander Moraine's attitude toward him. "I had someone warn me about that."

Carr's eyes narrowed, somehow reminding Paul of a great cat scenting prey. "Threateningly or in a friendly way?"

"Friendly."

"Good." She relaxed, then gave Paul a worried look. "You've damaged your career. You know that."

"Yeah." Paul let the bitterness show. "My orders got changed to Mars."

"Mars? Damn. Nothing subtle about that. Paul, I hate to see your career run aground because you did the right thing twice and stood by a friend the other time. I asked you before if you'd like to be a lawyer some day. That offer stands. If you put in for a transfer to the JAG Corps I can pull some strings, make sure you get one of the law scholarships and start a new career as a Navy lawyer."

"I..." *It's a great offer. I know that. But I also know it's not for me.* "Thank you, ma'am. Thanks very much. But that's not my road. Not yet, anyway. I know I've got some career baggage following me around now, but—"

"But you're not going to give up this easily?" Carr asked with a wry smile.

"Yes, ma'am."

"Fair enough. I respect that. But remember. If you want to contact me, the JAGs here or wherever you go can provide a link to wherever I'm stationed in the future. The offer will stand."

"Thank you, ma'am."

"Don't thank me. You earned the offer. And I owe you for your assistance with the Silver case. And, God help me, I owe Ms. Shen for things I can never make right. If *she* needs legal help, Paul, you let her know she can have everything I've got. Assuming she can stand to talk to me."

"She shook your hand after the court-martial was dismissed," Paul protested.

"Oh, yeah." Carr laughed again. "She gripped so hard I thought she was going break some of my fingers."

Paul grinned. "Jen complained you almost broke her hand."

"Only almost? I must be getting soft." Carr tapped her data pad. "But hopefully not too soft to nail Mr. Bradley Pullman for betraying his country. Fortunately, it's a fairly straightforward espionage case."

"Really?"

Paul's unease must have shown, because Alex Carr rested her chin on one hand and eyed him. "Misgivings?"

"Ma'am..."

"No, really. I want to know. Your misgivings could point out weaknesses in the government's case. They might even point out fatal flaws. I really don't want to convict innocent people, Paul. Though from what I've seen of the case against Pullman I'm as certain as I've ever been that he's guilty as sin." She tapped the data pad again. "This isn't a circumstantial evidence case. In the two months since Pullman's arrest we've been able to unearth a lot of new material thanks to search warrants. There's a lot of solid evidence against Pullman, not the least of which was that he was caught red-handed leaving your ship with classified material."

"I know." Paul made a frustrated gesture. "I don't really have anything specific. It's just that I can't believe Brad Pullman would do that."

"Nice guy?"

"Uh, sort of."

Carr made a note. "Friendly?"

"Yes. Very."

"Any friction with other officers on your ship?"

"No. He seems to be a really decent guy. He didn't... no, wait. He really got Ensign Taylor... She's in charge of keeping the ship's electronic systems working right, and she got really mad at him for messing around with them."

"Stupid stuff?"

"No. Smart stuff. He's really sharp. He just didn't coordinate what he was doing with the right people."

"Uh-huh." Carr made some more notes. "Smartest guy on the ship?"

"Uh..." Paul had to think. "Maybe. He's really intelligent. Which is one reason I can't believe he'd commit espionage."

Commander Carr gave a short laugh. "There's two kinds of people who commit espionage, Paul. The dumb ones usually get charged with *attempted* espionage because they screw up trying to be spies just like they screw up everything else and get caught before they can do any damage. The dangerous ones are the smart ones. They get away with it for a while. Maybe a long while. That's because they're smart enough to successfully betray their country but not wise enough to worry about the moral implications or anything else. They're smart, you see. They don't think they need to play by the same rules that you and I do."

"But they can't think the people around them aren't smart, and we don't do that kind of thing."

"They think that's because people like you and me *aren't* smart enough to do it. They figure they're the only ones clever enough. You and me, we're stooges in their eyes." She must have read Paul's reaction on his face. "I know. You figure Pullman was friendly. But the evidence shows that while he was acting like your friend he was betraying you personally as well as his country. Is that the action of someone who actually is a friend? There's some stuff on that data coin we pulled off Pullman that came from your personal files. Statements about the incident at the asteroid."

Even though Paul had already accepted the fact that Pullman had been arrested for stealing information, the news still came as a shock. "He dug through my personal data files?"

"Apparently."

"How do we know that coin didn't get planted on him?"

Carr gave a sad smile. "That'll be one line of defense his lawyer will use for sure. Paul, your captain sent you over here to help us get Pullman. I'm not asking you to buy into his guilt right now. It's my job to convince the members of the court, officers like you, that he's guilty. You'll be in that courtroom, you'll judge how I'm doing and help me spot weak points in the case while you're monitoring things for your captain. Okay?"

He thought about it. Alex Carr had agreed at almost literally the last minute to help pursue what proved to be evidence of Jen's innocence. She was tough, but unquestionably fair. "Okay."

"Thanks." Carr looked back at her data pad. "There's one new wrinkle in the case, at least from your perspective. Pullman is going to have a civilian lawyer assisting in his defense. Some guy Pullman's father is footing the money for sending up here."

"That can't be cheap," Paul observed.

"No, it's not." Carr's face reflected surprise as she read. "Boy, that's a strange coincidence. The civilian lawyer has the same last name that you do."

"He does?" Paul felt an icy sensation inside.

"Yeah. David Sinclair."

"David T. Sinclair? From a law firm in Washington, DC?"

Carr raised her head and stared at Paul. "Yes."

"He's my brother," Paul admitted.

"Your brother. Paul, I have to admit you keep making my cases more interesting. Is there any chance you'd be willing to share any insights into how your brother will try to help defend Pullman?"

"I would if I could." *Would I? Don't I want Brad Pullman to have the best chance to defend himself? I don't know that he's guilty.* "But I've never seen my brother handle a case."

"You've never seen him in a courtroom?"

"No."

"Never discussed legal issues with him?"

"No."

"Not even the court-martials you've been involved with up here?"

"No."

"I see." Carr leaned back, her eyes seeming to look through Paul as if she were reading his innermost thoughts. "What's he like?"

"He's okay."

"Do you have any reason to think he'd be unethical in any way?"

"No!"

"Good. Is he aggressive? Confident?"

Paul snorted. He couldn't help it. "Oh, yeah. He's confident." Full of himself was more like it, in Paul's opinion.

"I see," Carr said again. "He may be in for a surprise if he's never dealt with a military court-martial. Even if he's good, he'll also have a problem with the members of the court."

"Because they'll be biased against a civilian attorney."

"Yup. It's not fair, but that's the way it is."

Paul raised one hand slightly as a thought occurred to him. "Maybe that's why David got hired. He's not military himself, but he's from a military family. Both my mother and father are veterans. David may try to neutralize bias against him by bringing that in somehow."

"He might. Thanks, again. Are any more of your family members going to show up for this court-martial?"

"My parents will probably—"

"You've got to be kidding." Commander Carr was watching Paul as if waiting for the punch line to his joke.

"No. I'm getting married soon, you know. They'll be up here for the wedding, and if the court-martial's open to the public they'll probably want to see David in action." A not-so-small part of Paul felt a malicious wish that David would make some blunders in the case because of unfamiliarity with military law and perhaps finally have to admit to being a little less than perfect.

"Oh, yes. Married! To Lieutenant Shen!" Carr shook her head. "My sins keep coming back to remind me. Will *she* be at the court-martial?"

Paul realized he hadn't even thought about that before. Jen had plenty of bad memories about courtrooms, but if she thought she'd be supporting Paul or helping ensure justice was done with Pullman... "Maybe."

Carr laughed. "This'll be the first time one of my cases included a family reunion in the courtroom. I'll try to give you a good show."

"It sounded like you thought this would be a simple case."

"Did I say that?" Carr shook her head. "Not simple. The only simple ones are where the defendant pleads guilty right off the bat. This case is straightforward in a lot of ways, since we've got solid evidence to work with. But the members of the court are probably going to be a lot like you, Paul. They won't want to believe that one of their own has committed espionage. The defense will play off of that, try to give the members grounds for doubt."

"You don't think Pullman will go with a judge-only trial?"

"No way. They can't win on questions of evidence or the law. I'm certain of that. Manipulating the emotions of the members is their only hope." Carr pressed a couple of keys on her data pad, then turned it and pushed it in Paul's direction. "Take a look at this for me. It's the court-martial convening order, hot off the presses."

Paul studied the document, running quickly past the boilerplate standardized sections. There were few surprises, and he knew Carr really wanted him to see the list of members of the court, the officers who would serve as the "jury" to decide the guilt or innocence of Brad Pullman. He scanned down the names, starting with surprise at one. "Colleen Kilgary."

Carr raised her eyebrows. "You know her?"

"Yes, ma'am. Lieutenant Kilgary transferred off of the *Michaelson* a little while back. I know her real well."

"What's she like?"

"Professional and capable. She'll evaluate things herself and make up her own mind. She did a great job on the *Michaelson* and just about everybody liked her. Everyone respected her."

Carr made some notes. "That's my kind of member. Did she ever meet Pullman?"

"Not on the *Michaelson*. Like I said, she left a few months back. It was, let's see, about two months after she left that Pullman came aboard."

"Good. So she's an independent thinker?"

"Yes, ma'am. You'll have to convince her."

Carr flashed a smile. "I can do that. Do you know any of the other members?"

Paul pointed to another name. "This other lieutenant. Peter Mahris. He was a classmate of mine at the Academy."

"You knew him well there?"

"Yes, ma'am. He was in my company."

She made a beckoning gesture. "Meaning?"

"Sorry. The midshipmen at the Academy are divided into companies. There's between twenty and thirty members of each class in each company."

"Ah, so you did know him well. What's he like?"

Paul hesitated, then shrugged. "To be perfectly frank, ma'am, Pete Mahris is going to do whatever he thinks is best for his career. If he thinks the Navy wants Pullman to be convicted, he'll do it. If he thinks the Navy wants Pullman exonerated, he'll want to do that."

Alex Carr made a face. "A real suck-up?"

"Yes, ma'am. He'll probably take his cue from whatever the senior member of the court-martial does and says. Unless he's changed a lot, Pete Mahris always tries to do and say whatever he thinks his boss wants."

"Aiming to make admiral, eh? That sort of strategy doesn't always work, though unfortunately it does work sometimes. You knew Pullman at the Academy, right? Did Mahris?"

"I don't know. I just knew Pullman in passing. It's entirely possible Mahris never really met him."

Carr made more notes. "I'll have to check. It could effect Mahris' ability to serve as a member. Okay, do you know any of the other three members?"

Paul read through names again, ransacking his memory. "Captain Hailey Nguyen. She was a member of Wakeman's court-martial."

"Really? There's not any surplus of senior officers lying around up here to draw on, so some people do get tapped more than once." Carr checked something. "She's on her way to a new command. I guess that's why she was available. I don't think her involvement with Wakeman's case is any reason for questioning her membership on this court-martial."

Only two more names remained. Lieutenant Commander Pedro de Vaca from the Fleet Intelligence Center. Paul couldn't recall ever meeting him during intelligence briefings they'd received on the *Michaelson* or on Franklin, but an intelligence officer wasn't too likely to be sympathetic to someone accused of espionage. *At least, not sympathetic to someone spying against us instead of for us.* Finally, Commander Alan Sriracha, who had been pulled from the Operations Department on Franklin. *I'd have been working with him, maybe for him,* Paul thought, *if my orders hadn't been changed. Well, that's not going to happen now.*

At last, Paul shook his head. "I don't know anything about the last two, ma'am."

"That's okay. I can't complain with what you told me about two of the members." She looked over at her office clock and frowned. "Where does the time go? I guess that's all. I'll be in touch, Paul. See you in court."

Paul gave her a look as he stood up. "I can't say I like having a lawyer tell me that."

Carr laughed. "Believe me, you'll enjoy this court-martial a lot more than Mr. Pullman will."

Paul hesitated as he left the JAG office area, checked the time himself, then headed for the brig. The master-at-arms on watch at the front desk there recognized him but didn't try to make small talk as Paul signed in. They knew he'd been coming by fairly frequently the last few months to keep an eye on them, and regarded every visit by Paul as an unannounced inspection.

Brad Pullman was available, as he usually was during visiting hours. He and Paul sat in the small compartment set aside for visits. There wasn't a master-at-arms in the space with them, but Paul knew they were under constant surveillance. Confidentiality only applied to Pullman's visits with his lawyers.

Pullman grinned at Paul, apparently unabashed by his weeks of confinement and by having to wear a uniform stripped of insignia and ribbons. "How's it going, Paul?"

"That's what I came to ask you. Any problems?"

Pullman smiled again and waved around him. "They won't let me out." It was already an old joke. "But otherwise they're being pleasant enough. I think they suspect they're being watched."

"Do you need anything?"

"Not right now. Thanks for bringing that stuff earlier. It really helps to know you guys all still believe in me."

Paul nodded, not willing to say anything. He didn't know whether or not Pullman actually believed that the rest of the wardroom of the *Michaelson* was supporting him, but it wasn't Paul's job to tell him otherwise. Even if Paul knew for sure how all of the other officers felt. *I'm here to make sure he's being treated right before the trial. Maybe he's guilty. Maybe not. But until that court-martial decides, I don't want him treated as if he's already been convicted.*

Pullman leaned forward a little as if sharing a confidence. "I'll beat this, you know. No problem."

"Brad, Commander Carr is a real good lawyer, and there's some evidence——"

"No problem," Pullman repeated, waving away Paul's warning. "I've told my lawyers how to handle this. We'll get these stupid charges dismissed. Stupid and unfounded charges, that is."

Paul couldn't help being impressed by Pullman's confidence. *What does he know that I don't? Or that Commander Carr doesn't?* Still, he wasn't about to jump off this fence, to commit to believing Pullman, until he saw whatever legal tricks Pullman's lawyers pulled out of their hats. "This may be my last visit for a while. The court-martial is convening soon and I understand they won't want me seeing you while that's going on."

"Ah, I'll talk to my lawyers——"

"Your lawyers are two of the people saying they don't want me seeing you."

"Oh. Okay. I'll talk to them about that."

Paul gestured toward one of the cameras he knew were mounted in the walls. A door opened and two masters-at-arms entered, eyeing Pullman with disdain and Paul with wariness.

"All good things come to an end," Pullman noted. "Catch you later."

"Sure." Paul watched Pullman leave the visitors room to be returned to his cell, then signed out and began walking back to the ship, trying to reconcile Pullman's confidence and calm demeanor with what he knew of the government's case against him.

As Paul came back aboard, he saw Master Chief Maines talking to Petty Officer First Class Qui, the new master-at-arms. Ivan Sharpe had told Paul that Qui knew his stuff, and so far Paul certainly hadn't had any complaints. Except for wishing that he still had Sharpe's familiar, trusted presence to bounce ideas off of.

Maines gave Paul a big grin. "Mr. Sinclair. Petty Officer Qui's just back from the special court-martial of Petty Officer Vox."

"It's over?" Almost two months to get the special court-martial convened and only two days to conduct the trial. One less thing to worry about, although Paul knew he'd have to summarize the trial record for the captain and the XO to go over.

Qui smiled as well. "Yes, sir. Mr. Vox bought himself a Big Chicken Dinner."

"That'll make the captain happy." Big Chicken Dinner was slang for Bad Conduct Discharge. Not as bad as a Duck Dinner/Dishonorable Discharge, but not something any person would want in their life record.

"And a year at Leavenworth," Qui added.

"That'll make the captain *very* happy. Does he know, yet?"

"No, sir. Petty Officer Qui was just telling me." Master Chief Maines inclined her head in the general direction of the captain's cabin. "The captain told me a bit earlier to let you know that he wanted to see you when you got back to the ship anyhow, Mr. Sinclair. He wants you to brief Captain Agee on the progress of the Pullman thing."

Captain Agee. The new commanding officer, who would relieve Captain Hayes in about two weeks' time. It seemed impossible that Captain Hayes' time as captain of the *Michaelson* was already coming to an end. Impossible and cause for more than a little uneasiness in Paul. He'd grown to depend on the steady hand of Captain Hayes as his commanding officer. Now an unknown element would be taking over again, though Paul himself would be leaving the ship before much longer, so the practical impact should be very small.

Both Captain Hayes and Captain Agee were sitting in the wardroom when Paul poked his head inside. He gave Hayes a quick report on the outcome of Vox's special court-martial, earning a grin from the captain. "Vox was a dirtball," Hayes explained to Agee. "But he's gone. You won't have to worry about him."

"Good to hear," Agree said approvingly. "Sit down, Paul. I want to hear about this Pullman case."

Paul sat, keeping his back stiff. He knew better than to slouch in any official meeting with any captain, especially a captain who within a short time would be captain of the *Michaelson* and therefore in control of Paul's fate on a day-to-day basis. "Captain Hayes, sir, about the initial NCIS investigation—"

"I've already told Captain Agee about that. You don't need to cover it."

Agee nodded, eyeing Paul. It was hard to tell whether or not he approved of Paul's assistance of NCIS.

Paul ran down what he knew of the charges and evidence, trying to be even-handed.

Agee pursed his lips and glanced at Hayes. "It does look like a strong case."

"Yeah," Hayes agreed. "I'm personally convinced of Pullman's guilt, but it's not over 'til it's over. When's the last time you saw Pullman, Paul?"

"Less than an hour ago, sir. I stopped by the brig on the way back from the JAG offices."

"How's Pullman?"

Paul let his exasperation show. "Confident, sir."

Agee looked surprised. "Confident?"

"Yes, sir. Almost cocky. He says he'll be exonerated for sure."

"Any idea why he's saying that?"

"No, sir. Nothing specific. He just says he'll beat the charges."

Hayes pointed to Paul. "I've told Paul to be at the court-martial every day as an observer once it begins. It looks like that's going to overlap with the change of command, though."

Agee nodded. "It sounds like a good idea. Can your chief cover your division, Paul?"

"Yes, sir. Senior Chief Imari is very capable. My relief should also be coming aboard any day now."

"Fine. Do the JAGs mind us having a command representative present?"

"No, sir. Commander Carr has asked for my presence." Agee looked intrigued. "We've worked together before."

Hayes was apparently examining his fingernails. "Admiral Silver's son."

"Oh." Captain Agee gave Paul another look. "You're that guy. Okay, if the JAGs want you there, I don't see any reason not to grant their request. Do you give Captain Hayes daily updates during the trial?" Paul nodded. "Do that for me, too." Agee paused and frowned. "Have you been seeing Pullman in the brig on the captain's behalf as well?"

"Uh, no, sir. That is, I've kept Captain Hayes informed, but I've been keeping on eye on him on my own initiative."

"Why?"

It was funny how the shortest questions could require the longest answers. "I just want to ensure he's being treated appropriately, sir. I thought someone from the ship ought to keep an eye on him, and let the brig know that we were keeping an eye on him. It seemed the right thing to do."

"Huh." Agee gave Paul a searching look. "You sound like you know somebody who wasn't treated too well in the brig."

"Yes, sir." Paul paused but Agee kept watching him as if expecting more. "My fiancée, sir." Another pause. "Lieutenant Jen Shen."

"Oh." Agee glanced at Hayes, seeing the other captain nod to confirm Paul's statement. "Oh. You're *that* guy, too. Damn, Sinclair, you're high-level radioactive. Do you know that?"

For some reason the statement almost amused Paul. "So I've been told, sir."

"Where are you going from the *Michaelson*?"

"Mars, sir. Last-minute order modification."

"Well, hell." Agee glared at Paul but his anger seemed directed elsewhere. "Anything I can do?"

"I'm afraid not, sir."

"You let me know if there is."

"Yes, sir. Thank you, sir." He meant it, because he was sure Agee meant it. Despite everything, meeting those who were willing to openly stand up for him counted for a great deal.

After leaving the wardroom, Paul stood on the quarterdeck for a moment, not really aware of the officer of the deck and the petty officer of the watch, who were busy with their own jobs at the moment anyway. His eyes came to rest on the brow leading onto the station. It was odd how such a small walkway could have so much significance. But that was how people came and went from the *Michaelson*. Some day soon Captain Hayes would walk off that brow for the last time, and not long afterwards Paul would do the same.

Right now he was wishing some of those who'd left were still around. Commander Sykes would have good advice, or at least an absurd story to tell to get a junior officer's mind off his problems.

Sheriff Sharpe would be blunt and practical, a solid sounding board for Paul's own thoughts. Sharpe knew it, too, but had never tried to take advantage of his professional closeness.

The Sheriff had walked off the brow his last time a couple of weeks ago, grinning when he saw Paul there to say farewell. "Gonna miss me, Mr. Sinclair?"

"Yeah." Paul extended his hand and they shook. "Thanks, Sheriff."

"For anything in particular, sir?"

"For being one helluva master-at-arms and helping a certain new ensign keep his head on straight when he needed it the most."

Sharpe had grinned wider. "That's just my job, sir."

"And for being someone I could always count on."

The grin changed to a close-lipped smile. "Thank you, sir. And may I say the same back. I could always count on you. I know Chief Asher and I appreciated it even if no one else in the damned Navy did."

"A man's gotta do what a man's gotta do, right, Sheriff?"

"Right. I don't think that's one of the things I had to teach you, though. You seemed to figure it out for yourself." Sharpe stepped back and saluted. "See you around, Mr. Sinclair."

"Fair winds, Sheriff." Paul returned the salute, then for a moment watched Sharpe saying rough farewells to the other enlisted who'd come to see him off. Chief Imari came over to talk to Paul about a problem with one of their sailors, and when Paul looked over again Sharpe had left.

David T. Sinclair was taller than Paul. He'd always been taller, Paul thought, as well as better looking and smarter. Which wouldn't have been so bad except that through life David had demonstrated a tendency to bring up those advantages with enough frequency to make Paul want to kick holes in the nearest solid surface. Still, simple courtesy required Paul to go greet his brother after he arrived on the station.

"Come in." David had, naturally enough, rented a room at one of the two private hotels which rented space to operate on Franklin. Also naturally enough, he'd chosen the more expensive of the two. He was standing in the room when Paul arrived, and staring around as if not able to believe how little space the money he was paying actually bought on a space station. "Hey, little bro. Long time no see." David smiled widely and they shook hands. "Can you believe this?"

"Believe what?"

"This closet they call a hotel room. Do you know what this is costing me?"

"It's pretty spacious for private quarters up here, David."

"Unbelievable. I guess I can put up with it for a little while though."

Paul nodded, thinking how much time he'd spent putting up with considerably less personal space on the *Michaelson*. "Mom and Dad will be staying in the other hotel when they come up here. That's where family members usually stay when they come up to visit people assigned to the station or ships that dock here."

"Sure, they're not on an expense account for their law firm," David chuckled. "How long should this military trial take?"

"Not too long. I'm told it's a fairly straightforward case."

"Really?" David seem amused. "Who told you that?"

"Commander Carr, the trial counsel." He paused just a moment to let David puzzle over the title. "That's the prosecutor."

"Oh." David waved one hand. "Whatever they call him—"

"Her."

"Her. Whatever they call her won't matter. I don't lose cases."

"Neither does Commander Carr," Paul advised dryly.

David laughed. "Maybe I'll have a few surprises for this prosecutor. It wouldn't be the first time." He gave Paul an appraising look. "Do you know her? What's she like? What sort of courtroom tactics does she use?"

Paul pretended ignorance. "I haven't seen that much of her."

"I guess I couldn't have expected anything else. Besides, you probably couldn't tell me much about courtroom tactics even if you had." David rummaged through his bag, apparently oblivious to the flash of anger on Paul's face. "What are these military lawyers like? The defense lawyer, I mean."

"They're lawyers."

"No. I mean, who do they work for? The military, right? The same people running the prosecution. Is there any reason to believe this guy who's been appointed to defend Pullman is actually going to do any real work on Pullman's behalf?"

Paul simply stared for a moment, shocked by the statement. "Of course he'll work to defend Pullman. He'll do everything he can. That's how they work. I've seen them work. They don't roll over for the prosecution. They fight for their clients."

"Really?" David didn't bother hiding his skepticism. "Of course, you don't really know enough to judge."

"Yes, as a matter of fact, I do."

David frowned and gave Paul a serious look. "You sound upset."

"I know the military legal system. I've worked with it far more than I ever expected to, and I'm speaking from personal experience."

"Okay, okay. Pardon me for assuming you were just sailing around in spaceships up here."

Paul realized he could stay mad or he could try to educate his brother, which wasn't a bad idea since it would place him in the role of his brother's teacher. "You'll need to visit my ship." David gave him another frown, this one questioning. "To interview witnesses, get character references, get firsthand knowledge of the places that'll be referred to in the trial, that sort of thing."

David's expression changed. "You do know something about this game. Yes. I'll want to do that. Who do I talk to about setting it up?"

"Me." Paul grinned. "I'll also take you down to meet Lieutenant Owings. He's been appointed to defend Pullman."

"Where's Pullman? I understand he's in pre-trial confinement?"

"Yeah. In the brig. That's a military jail."

"Does Owings have any idea how well or badly Pullman's being treated in that jail?" David asked sharply, as if he already knew the answer.

"Yes," Paul stated. "So do I. I've visited him frequently to check on conditions."

David nodded, letting approval show. "Good one, bro. Consider me appropriately chastised for assuming you wouldn't have any kind of handle on this. How soon can we get going?"

Paul checked the time and shook his head. "I'm real limited on time right now, but I can take you down to see Lieutenant Owings. I'm sure he'll take you to see Pullman."

"Good. Pullman's old man wanted me to send him an update on how his kid's doing."

Paul hesitated, then asked a question that had been bothering him. "Pullman's father is the one who hired you, right? I know you're not cheap, and I know it costs a fair amount for you to come up here. Pullman's father is a retired warrant officer. I wonder where he got the money to afford you?"

David shrugged. "He didn't have to tell me that, but he volunteered that he'd had some investments pay off real well. You're not begrudging him spending the money on defending his son, are you?"

"No. Not at all."

Lieutenant Owings greeted David Sinclair politely when Paul brought his brother down to the JAG offices. Then both lawyers looked at Paul in a way which clearly conveyed that they wanted to be alone, no doubt to discuss how they'd defend Pullman. On his way out, Paul wondered whether he should drop in on Commander Carr, then decided after another look at the time that he needed to get back to the ship as soon as possible.

"Hey, Paul!" Randy Diego had the quarterdeck watch. "Guess what?"

"Am I guessing something good or something bad?" Paul asked, though from Randy's expression he knew it had to be good.

"Depends on whether or not you consider your relief coming aboard is good or not."

"My relief's aboard?" Paul didn't know how, even in the midst of everything else, he could've forgotten his relief would be showing up anytime now. "Where is she?"

"I think she's in Combat. Senior Chief Imari came down to pick her up."

"Thanks, Randy." Paul hastened up to Combat, where he found Lieutenant Junior Grade Jane Shwartz chatting with Imari. "Good to see you. Paul."

"Jane." She shook his hand. "This looks like the same set-up as on the *Rickover*."

"Pretty close," Paul confirmed. "There's a few minor differences. Did you work in Combat on the *Rickover*?"

"No. Engineering." They talked a while longer. Paul walked Shwartz around the ship, introducing her to other officers and senior enlisted. Shwartz seemed friendly and intelligent, which made Paul feel better about his impending hand-over to her of the sailors and equipment for which he'd spent the last three years being responsible.

Paul apologized for the amount of time he'd be off the ship for the next couple of weeks. "It's the legal officer job."

Shwartz nodded. "That legal stuff is so weird."

"You know something about it?"

"I just went through the three-week ship's legal officer course."

"Uh-oh."

She looked puzzled, then clenched her eyes shut. "I'm going to get stuck with ship's legal officer collateral duty when you leave, aren't I?"

"I'd put money on it."

Half an hour later, after Shwartz had met Commander Kwan, Paul could've collected on his bet if they'd actually made one. He took his relief to meet Petty Officer Qui. Paul hoped that after she took over the job Shwartz would have a less interesting time as legal officer than Paul had had.

He finally left the ship late that evening, having partially caught up on some of his tasks and having spent time jawboning with Shwartz about the wardroom of the *Michaelson*. Paul emphasized telling her which officers were the best in his opinion and could be trusted, while dropping a few hopefully discreet warnings about those who were less capable or should be watched. The *Michaelson* no longer had onboard any blatant back-stabbers like Smilin' Sam Yarrow had been, but he wanted to be sure Shwartz at least knew about Isakov. It turned out she did already. "A lot of people know about her. But thanks for the heads-up."

Paul paused outside the door to Jen's quarters for a moment, reveling in the feeling that the place was a home of sorts. Jen had keyed him into the entry system, but he still pushed the buzzer out of a desire to avoid seeming to take her or the quarters for granted.

"You're late. Rough day?" Jen asked.

"Busy day. My relief showed up."

"Good day, then." Jen held up her data pad. "Speaking of good days and not-so-good days, guess what? Your movement order came in."

Paul just nodded, not really wanting to look ahead that far.

"Aren't you curious as to when your ship leaves for Mars?" Jen prodded.

"Why?" Something about the question sparked concern in Paul. "When's it leave? About a month after I detach from the *Michaelson*, right?"

"Try three days."

"*Three days?*"

"The morning of the third day, to be exact. You will have two days between the time you detach from your ship and the time you leave Franklin for Mars."

"I don't believe this." A realization finally hit Paul. "The wedding. That's supposed to be a week after I leave the *Michaelson*."

Jen smiled mockingly. "Yeah. Sweet, isn't it?"

"What are we going to do?"

"I've done it." Jen sat forward, her face serious in that way Paul had seen it get when there was a job to be done quickly and right. "Miraculously, the chapel is available the day before you detach from the *Michaelson*. Only for a one-hour window, but it's open. We'll have to do the wedding then, quick and dirty, after which you'll have to go back to the ship the next day, go through your check-out, and detach. That will leave us a glorious two days for a honeymoon before you sail off to Mars for at least two years."

Paul sat there, slowly absorbing the information. "I don't believe it."

"Think of all the days of leave we're going to save."

"Oh, yeah," Paul agreed. Jen seemed about to laugh. That puzzled Paul for a moment, then he got it. What else was there to do? They could get enraged, they could scream bloody murder, and it wouldn't make any difference. They might as well start enjoying the ride because it wasn't going to get any better. "Somebody up there must hate me."

"No, somebody down here hates you, but somebody up there loves you. That chapel is never available on this short a notice. Talk about a miracle."

"Like my meeting you?"

"Oh, please..."

"Forty-eight hours." Paul thought about it. "That's going to be one short honeymoon."

"Short and intense, sailor," Jen advised with another smile. "Make sure you've been taking your vitamins. You'll need your strength."

This time he laughed, too.

To Paul's surprise, NCIS came aboard again just a few days before the court-martial was to begin. To his even greater surprise, Special

Agent Connally was with them. "Hi, Paul." She seemed unaware of the others watching them, some of them no doubt recognizing Paul's guest from the days before Pullman was arrested, but her next words belied that. "I didn't tell you that time I visited the ship, but I'm working for NCIS now. I thought I'd surprise you today."

The first part was, literally, true. She hadn't told him then. She'd told him before that. But those listening would draw another interpretation from the statement, that Paul hadn't knowingly squired an NCIS agent around officers' country. Another lie by omission, in the service of truth. It still didn't feel right to Paul, even though he couldn't think of any other way it could've been handled. There wasn't any doubt he'd been surprised by Connally's coming to the ship, though. "Really?" he managed to reply. "What brings you here now?"

"We're doing another sweep of the ship for bugs and taps." She grinned at the look on Paul's face. "No, we don't think we missed any. We don't expect to find any at all."

"Then why are you doing another sweep?"

"It's a request from the trial counsel. She didn't explain why, but we know the reason."

Paul made a questioning gesture. "What is it?"

"One of the things Pullman's lawyer is certain to try to claim is that Pullman isn't the one who planted the taps and bugs we found last time, that it was someone else who wasn't arrested. But if our sweep shows that no new bugs or taps have been planted since Pullman was arrested, it sort of sandbags that claim."

Paul nodded as comprehension finally hit. "If Pullman didn't do it and someone else who's still free did, then why haven't more been planted?"

"Right. It's not proof that Pullman did the original plants, but it undercuts any claim that the real bad guy is still running loose." She looked around. "Can you take me to your commanding officer?"

"Sure." Paul led the way.

Captain Hayes greeted Connally in a way that clearly revealed that they'd met before. They spoke for a few minutes as Connally described the sweep her team had come to perform and formally requested Hayes' permission. Captain Hayes, of course, granted it, then went on the general announcing system to order the crew to cooperate with the NCIS team to the best of their ability.

The NCIS agents and the technicians they brought with them went over the *Michaelson* carefully, searching painstakingly for any taps or bugs that might have been installed since the last sweep of the ship.

They didn't find any.

Special Agent Connally bade Paul farewell before she left the ship. "I'm one of the witnesses for the trial counsel, so I'll see you in court."

Paul pretended to flinch. "Women keep saying that to me lately."

"It must be the company you're keeping." She left, walking away with the rest of the NCIS agents.

Paul watched them go, thinking about the times he'd spent with Special Agent Connally and wondering if they would've really been old friends had they somehow met years ago. He thought so, that Pam Connally would've been a good friend to have, then and now. He couldn't help also wondering if she had felt the same, whether her friendliness was purely a public act or if she enjoyed being around him. *I'm not playing with fire here, am I?* he wondered. *No. I'm not getting any spark around Connally, like we'd get emotionally involved. She just feels sort of like Kris Denaldo. Somebody who'd be a friend.*

But then, given the odds he wouldn't be seeing Connally outside the courtroom again, the whole issue didn't matter. Perhaps that was just as well, given that Jen might have already heard about the fact that Paul had been seen with Connally after working hours on the ship. He knew it had been part of the investigation, and Jen would give him the benefit of the doubt (he hoped), but why risk anything else?

It wasn't like he didn't have enough other things to worry about. Not with Pullman's court-martial starting the day after tomorrow.

8

Paul walked slowly into the courtroom, taking his time since he'd arrived early and he knew Commander Carr had reserved a seat for him near the trial counsel's table in any case. The courtroom was one of three on Franklin, a multipurpose room able to fulfill other functions if necessary but currently dedicated to administering the ultimate form of military justice. Rectangular in shape, it was dominated by the slightly elevated judge's bench centered in the back, with the witness stand beside it. Slightly in front of and to either side of the judge's bench sat two tables. The defendant and his lawyer would sit at one table, the trial counsel at the other, all facing the judge. Off to one side sat a longer table, facing the judge's bench as well as the tables for the prosecution and the defense. This table, with five chairs behind it and a navy-blue cloth draped over the top to add some dignity to the furnishing, would be where the members of the court would sit.

Two blocks of chairs filled the rest of the room, facing the bench and divided by a path leading up the middle from the main entry door. There were two other doors visible, one behind the judge's bench that led to the judge's chambers, and from which the judge would enter and leave the courtroom, and one behind the members' table, which would be used by those officers to arrive and depart.

In the apparently bare walls, unseen cameras and microphones were emplaced to allow a complete and total record of any legal proceeding to be automatically recorded.

All in all, despite the color lent by the flags of the United States and the United States Navy posted behind the judge's bench, the room felt bare and utilitarian. It served the function of cradling the administration of military justice, and that was all that was demanded of it.

Paul reached the row behind the trial counsel's desk and sat down, though not without a glance to the other side of the room. He still felt oddly uncomfortable to be aligning himself with the prosecution against an officer who'd shared his stateroom, who'd stood watches on his ship, who'd been a trusted comrade right up until the moment of his arrest.

"Good morning, Lieutenant Sinclair." Commander Carr strode in with wide, quick steps, dropping her data pad onto the table but remaining standing, scanning the room. "Ready?"

"I guess so, ma'am."

Paul didn't turn around, but he could hear people entering and going to their seats. The court-martial was open to the public, and a fairly big crowd was expected due to the nature of the charges against Pullman and the fact that he was an officer charged with espionage.

Lieutenant Owings went past, walking to the defense counsel table, followed closely by David Sinclair. They stood talking to each other in low voices, then looked up as a sudden surge in conversation erupted in the courtroom. Paul finally looked back as well, seeing Brad Pullman entering in the custody of two masters-at-arms. The masters-at-arms walked Pullman to the defense table, then walked back to the main entry and took up sentry positions on either side of the door, their eyes constantly on Pullman.

Pullman talked to his lawyers for a few moments; then the three of them nodded and sat down at the defense table. Pullman glanced around and saw Paul, then grinned and made a small wave in greeting. If Pullman was feeling any uncertainty, he was doing a great job of hiding it. Paul just nodded back, wondering what Pullman made of the fact that Paul was sitting near the trial counsel.

The low surf of conversation which had risen when Pullman entered dropped noticeably. Paul watched as the bailiff walked to the front center of the courtroom to stand near the judge's bench. She waited, outwardly patient, as some conversations continued in the background, then finally cleared her throat loudly. "Quiet in the courtroom, if you please."

The bailiff waited a moment longer to ensure everyone was paying attention, then turned slightly to point toward the door to the judge's chambers. "I will announce 'all rise' when the military judge enters. Everyone is to rise at that time. You are to remain standing until the military judge directs everyone to be seated. The judge will direct me to summon the members of the court. Everyone will rise again. Once the members of the court have entered and taken their seats, the military judge will direct you to be seated. Are there any questions?"

The bailiff, apparently neither anticipating questions nor being interested in answering them, immediately went to the back of the courtroom. Paul thought she was the same bailiff who'd been present for Jen's court-martial. Barely opening the door behind the judge's bench, the bailiff spoke, listened to a reply, then came back to stand in her original position. "All rise."

Paul and everyone else in the room came to their feet, the military personnel also automatically coming to attention. The military judge, Captain Elizabeth Campbell, walked quickly to the bench and sat down, then looked around the courtroom. "This Article 39(a) session is called to order. You may be seated." Paul could have recited the same words in his sleep. Every court-martial started with them, invoking the legal article under which a court-martial was held.

Everyone sat, but almost immediately Commander Carr stood up again and began reciting the next words mandated by the Manual for Courts-Martial for opening the legal proceedings. "The court-martial is convened by general court-martial convening order 0330, Commander, United States Space Forces, copies of which have been furnished to the military judge, counsel, and the accused. The charges have been properly referred to the court-martial for trial and were served on the accused on 6 October 2102. The accused and the following persons detailed to the court-martial are present: Captain Nguyen, Captain Campbell, Commander Sriracha, Commander Carr, Lieutenant Commander de Vaca, Lieutenant Kilgary, Lieutenant Mahris, Lieutenant Owings."

Captain Campbell nodded. "Thank you, trial counsel. Bailiff, please ask the members of the court-martial to enter."

The bailiff went to the door behind the members' table, opened it, spoke briefly inside, then stood to one side. "All rise," she called again.

Paul came to attention again as everyone else stood. Captain Nguyen led the way inside, pointing out their seats to the other members of the court. Nguyen, as most senior, would sit in the center, the other officers alternating taking seats to either side in decreasing seniority.

Lieutenant Kilgary appeared to sweep her eyes across Paul when she took her seat, but didn't react. He hadn't expected her to. This wasn't exactly the time or place for renewing acquaintances. Lieutenant Pete Mahris looked pretty much like he had the last time Paul had seen him, during commissioning ceremonies at the Academy. Paul noted that Mahris had twisted his chair very slightly so that he could more easily watch Captain Nguyen out of the corner of his eye, no doubt the better to ensure he followed Nguyen's lead on events.

Judge Campbell waited until she was sure the members of the court were all seated, then looked out across the courtroom. "You may be seated." Then, after a brief pause while everyone took their seats again, she pointed her gavel at Commander Carr. "Continue, trial counsel."

Commander Carr turned to face both the members' table and the judge. "I have been detailed to this court-martial by order of the fleet Judge Advocate General's office. I am qualified and certified under Article 27(b) and sworn under Article 42(a). I have not acted in any manner which might tend to disqualify me in the court-martial."

Lieutenant Owings then stood up at the defense table. "I have been detailed to this court-martial by order of the fleet Judge Advocate General's office. I am qualified and certified under Article 27(b) and sworn under Article 42(a). I have not acted in any manner which might tend to disqualify me in the court-martial."

Judge Campbell turned her head toward the defense table. "Lieutenant Bradley Pullman, you have the right to be represented in this court-martial by Lieutenant Owings, your detailed defense counsel, or you may be represented by military counsel of your selection, if the counsel you request is reasonably available. If you are represented by military counsel of your own selection, you would lose the right to have Lieutenant Owings, your detailed counsel, continue to help in your defense. Do you understand?"

Brad Pullman gave a brisk nod as he answered. "Yes, ma'am."

"In addition, you have the right to be represented by civilian counsel, at no expense to the United States. Civilian counsel may represent you alone or along with your military counsel. Do you understand?"

"Yes, ma'am."

"Do you have any questions about your right to counsel?"

"No, ma'am."

"Who do you want to represent you?"

"I wish to be represented by civilian counsel, Mr. David Sinclair, along with my detailed military counsel, Lieutenant Owings."

"Very well," Judge Campbell stated. "Mr. David Sinclair, your qualifications to practice law have been provided to this court?"

Paul's brother nodded, his civilian suit looking out of place amid the military uniforms on all sides. "Yes, Your Honor."

"Counsel for the parties have the necessary qualifications, and have been sworn, except for Mr. David Sinclair, who will now be sworn." The judge waited while the bailiff marched to the defense table and swore in David Sinclair, then she said, "I have been detailed to this court by order of the Judge Advocate General's office of the Commander, United States Space Forces."

Commander Carr walked away from her table, then once again turned to face the members of the court-martial and the judge. "The general nature of the charges in this case allege the commission of acts of espionage against the United States by Lieutenant Bradley Pullman. The charges were preferred by Commander, United States Naval Space Forces, and forwarded with recommendations as to disposition to Commander, United States Space Forces." She fully faced the judge's bench. "Your Honor, are you aware of any matter which may be a ground for challenge against you?"

"I am aware of none."

"The government has no challenge for cause against the military judge."

David Sinclair looked over at Lieutenant Owings, nodded and made a gesture. Lieutenant Owings stood. "The defense has no challenge for cause against the military judge."

Judge Campbell focused her attention on Pullman. "Lieutenant Pullman, do you understand that you have the right to be tried by a court-martial composed of members and that, if you are found guilty of any offense, those members would determine a sentence?"

Pullman kept his voice and actions crisp and confident. "Yes, Your Honor."

"Do you also understand that you may request in writing or orally here in the court-martial trial before me alone, and that if I approve such a request, there will be no members and I alone will decide whether you are guilty and, if I find you guilty, determine a sentence?"

"Yes, Your Honor."

"Have you discussed these choices with your counsel?"

"I have."

"By which type of court-martial do you choose to be tried?"

"By members, Your Honor."

"Very well. The accused will now be arraigned."

Commander Carr spoke with a crisp authority that more than overmatched that of Brad Pullman. "All parties and the military judge have been furnished a copy of the charges and specifications. Does the accused want them read?"

Pullman glanced down at David Sinclair, who looked at Lieutenant Owings. Both lawyers nodded to each other; then Owings answered. "The accused wishes the charges to be read."

Paul wondered why, then noticed how his brother was intently watching the members of the court-martial. *He wants to see how they individually react to the reading of each charge. Clever.*

"Very well." Commander Carr looked down at her data pad and began reading, looking up often to scan the members and gauge their reactions as well. "Lieutenant Bradley Fielder Pullman, United States Navy, is charged with violations of the following articles of the Uniform Code of Military Justice."

"Article 92 – Failure to Obey Order or Regulation. First specification. In that Lieutenant Bradley Fielder Pullman, United States Navy, did onboard USS *Michaelson*, CLE(S)-3, then docked at berth seven alpha of United States Naval Space Station Benjamin Franklin, on or about 20 August 2102, violate a lawful general regulation, to wit: Secretary of the Navy Instruction 5520.5 dated 1 July 2100, Security and Handling of Classified Materials Onboard US Navy Ships and Installations, by wrongfully and without authorization downloading Top Secret documents from the combat support data systems of the USS *Michaelson* onto portable and transportable storage media."

AGAINST ALL ENEMIES

Paul, knowing the boilerplate part of the charges by heart, concentrated on watching the members, trying to gauge their reactions to the charges, and on watching Brad Pullman to see how he took hearing the charges against him being read in all of their grim formality.

"Second specification. In that Lieutenant Bradley Fielder Pullman, United States Navy, did... violate a lawful general regulation, to wit: Secretary of the Navy Instruction 5520.5 dated 1 July 2100, Security and Handling of Classified Materials Onboard US Navy Ships and Installations, by wrongfully and without authorization removing Top Secret materials downloaded onto portable and transportable media from onboard the USS *Michaelson*.

"Article 106(a) – Espionage. First specification. In that Lieutenant Bradley Fielder Pullman, United States Navy, did... with intent or reason to believe it would be used to the injury of the United States or to the advantage of the South Asian Alliance, a foreign nation, deliver operational orders and annexes classified up to and including Top Secret and pertaining to US Naval operations then soon to be carried out, to an agent of the South Asian Alliance.

"Second specification. In that Lieutenant Bradley Fielder Pullman, United States Navy, did... on or about 20 August 2102, with intent or reason to believe it would be used to the injury of the United States or to the advantage of the South Asian Alliance, a foreign nation, attempt to deliver intelligence reports classified Top Secret which directly concerned current knowledge of foreign military capabilities, to an agent of the South Asian Alliance.

"Third specification. In that Lieutenant Bradley Fielder Pullman, United States Navy, did onboard USS *Michaelson*, CLE(S)-3, on or about 20 August, 2102, with intent or reason to believe it would be used to the injury of the United States or to the advantage of the South Asian Alliance, a foreign nation, attempt to commit espionage by emplacing covert taps within selected compartments onboard his ship with the aim of covertly collecting information.

"Article 133 – Conduct Unbecoming an Officer. In that Lieutenant Bradley Fielder Pullman, United States Navy, did onboard USS *Michaelson*, CLE(S)-3... wrongfully and dishonorably engage in conduct unbecoming an officer, to wit: misappropriating classified information for personal gain.

"Article 134 – False or Unauthorized Pass Offenses. In that Lieutenant Bradley Fielder Pullman, United States Navy, did... have in his possession a station access pass which had been improperly tampered with to allow Lieutenant Pullman to access areas of the station without leaving any record on the station personnel tracking and security system.

"The charges are signed by Commander, United States Naval Space Forces, a person subject to the code, as accuser; are properly sworn to before a commissioned officer of the armed forces authorized to administer oaths, and are properly referred to this court-martial for trial by Commander, United States Space Forces, the convening authority."

As far as Paul could tell, Brad Pullman hadn't flinched from the charges at all, but had kept his expression cool and confident throughout the reading. If they'd been in a card game, Paul would've assumed Pullman had a very good hand.

Judge Campbell kept looking at Commander Carr for a moment after she finished speaking, then looked at Pullman. "Lieutenant Pullman, how do you plead? Before receiving your pleas, I advise you that any motions to dismiss any charge or grant other relief should be made at this time."

David Sinclair stood up, his expression respectful. "Your Honor, the defense would like to move for the dismissal of the violation of Article 133 on the grounds that it is duplicative and nonspecific as to the nature of the requirements which Lieutenant Pullman is alleged to have violated."

Judge Campbell shook her head. "The motion is denied. The Uniform Code specifically states that violations of Article 133 can be brought in addition to charges for specific actions if those actions substantiate a charge of conduct unbecoming an officer. As to the 'nonspecific' nature alleging conduct unbecoming an officer, the law presumes that all officers are aware of the special requirements placed upon by virtue of their holding a commission as an officer. Does the defense have any other motions at this time?"

"No, Your Honor." David Sinclair sat down again.

Brad Pullman stood at attention, speaking in a firm, clear voice. "I plead not guilty to all charges and specifications, ma'am."

"Very well. Does the prosecution have an opening statement?"

"Yes, Your Honor." Commander Carr took another two steps, placing herself in front of the judge's bench, but still partially facing the judge and the members. The members were watching attentively, no expressions betraying their feelings. As far as Paul had been able to tell, none of them had reacted when the charges were read, either. "The prosecution intends to prove that Lieutenant Pullman has engaged in multiple cases of espionage against the United States, that in the furthering of this espionage he has willfully and repeatedly violated United States Navy regulations and instructions governing the handling of classified materials, and that he has received monetary compensation from a foreign country in exchange for these acts of espionage. Lieutenant Pullman should be found guilty as to all charges and specifications, because by his actions he not only disgraced himself, he intentionally caused grave injury to the United States."

Commander Carr walked back to her table. Judge Campbell motioned toward David Sinclair. "Will the defense make an opening statement?"

"Yes, Your Honor." David Sinclair remained standing at his table as he spoke, his voice carrying easily across the courtroom. "The defense intends to prove that Lieutenant Bradley Pullman is innocent of the most serious charges against him, and that any mishandling of classified material which may have taken place was both inadvertent and not done with any intent to cause injury to the United States. Since Lieutenant Pullman will be proven innocent of any intent to commit espionage or mishandle classified material, he should be found not guilty as to all charges and specifications."

David Sinclair sat down. Silence fell for a moment. Captain Campbell pointed her gavel at Commander Carr again. "Proceed."

"Thank you. The United States calls as its first witness Ensign Akesha Taylor, United States Navy."

Ensign Taylor came down the aisle moving purposefully. As she sat down and looked Paul's way, one eye twitched in what might have been a surreptitious wink. Taylor seemed no more intimidated by a military courtroom than she was by any other aspect of the Navy.

Commander Carr stood before Ensign Taylor. "Do you swear that the evidence you give in the case now in hearing shall be the truth, the whole truth, and nothing but the truth, so help you God?"

"I do, ma'am."

"Are you Ensign Akesha Taylor, currently assigned as electronic materials officer onboard the USS *Michaelson*?"

"Yes, ma'am."

"Briefly describe your duties, please."

"Yes, ma'am." Taylor hitched herself over slightly so she partially faced the members' table. "In laymen's terms, I'm responsible for making sure all the electronic systems and linkages talk to each other properly. I handle the interfaces."

"Do you have much experience with electronic system interfaces?"

"Only about twenty-two years, ma'am."

Paul caught a glimpse of smiles flickering on the faces of the members of the court-martial.

Commander Carr gave a small smile as well. "Do you also oversee the software safeguards and hardware cut-outs designed to prevent unauthorized actions?"

"Yes, ma'am."

"Were all of those safeguards and cut-outs operational on the evening of 20 August?"

Taylor nodded several times. "Yes, ma'am, they were."

David Sinclair rose to his feet, looking serious. "Objection, Your Honor. How can the witness be certain none of the referenced safeguards and cut-outs malfunctioned for even a very brief time on the evening in question?"

Commander Carr gestured toward Ensign Taylor. "Perhaps we should ask the witness."

Judge Campbell nodded. "Perhaps we should. Ensign Taylor?"

Taylor shook her head just as firmly as she'd earlier nodded. "That couldn't have happened, ma'am. The system maintains a continuous track of the interfaces, the safeguards and cut-outs and everything else. Any failure, and lapse, even for a microsecond, gets tagged. I check the system reports every morning and they were clean."

"Ensign Taylor," Captain Nguyen spoke up. "What if the systems doing the monitoring fail?"

Paul looked at his brother, who seemed torn between distress that the senior member of the court was questioning the witness directly and happiness that a potential flaw in the prosecution's argument had been brought out.

But Taylor shook her head again. "Ma'am, if I had that kind of failure it'd mean the primaries and two back-ups had all failed simultaneously. I don't know the odds of that happening, but they're awful long. And if somehow it did happen, everything would start locking up and I'd get sparks spitting out here, there and everywhere. It'd be impossible to miss, as well as one tremendous mess to fix."

"Then," Captain Nguyen pressed, "in your expert opinion, it is virtually impossible that there could have been failures of not only the safeguards and cut-outs, but also simultaneous failures of the systems monitoring the working status of those safeguards and cut-outs?"

"Captain, the only way I could see that happening is if we'd sustained major battle damage and been totally knocked out of commission." Taylor looked from Carr to the judge to David Sinclair. "Can't happen, otherwise."

Captain Nguyen sat back, clearly satisfied. Commander Carr looked up at Judge Campbell, who looked over at David Sinclair. "Objection overruled."

David Sinclair nodded and sat down. Paul thought he might be the only one in the courtroom who could spot the tiny but tell-tail signs that his brother was seriously ticked-off. *Didn't you think Commander Carr would be prepared to handle such an issue? Maybe after this David will stop assuming he's head and shoulders a better lawyer than the JAGs up here.* Paul took a look at Lieutenant Owings and saw he was making notes with a carefully expressionless face. *I bet David didn't listen to you, did he? Well, David's smart enough when he wants to be. I have a feeling he'll learn fast.*

Judge Campbell gave Commander Carr a nod. "Proceed, trial counsel."

"Thank you, Your Honor. Ensign Taylor, do the safeguards and cut-outs to which you refer include functions designed to prevent the unauthorized downloading of classified material?"

Taylor nodded. "Yes, ma'am. They check to see if a specific terminal is authorized for access to that information, that is, if they can handle classified material and at what level of classification, then they check to see if whoever's logged in has high-enough access as well, then they allow viewing of the material but no copying, no transfers and no downloads of any kind. People are always complaining to me that the system is a pain in the neck, but I tell them that's the rules and if they don't like it they need to talk to somebody quite a bit higher in the chain of command than I am."

Paul hid another smile. He hadn't thought about what a persuasive and personable witness Taylor would make, but he was sure Carr had realized it immediately.

Commander Carr looked toward the members as she asked the next question. "Then your system works exactly as required, Ensign Taylor? No unauthorized modifications of any kind that would short-circuit any of those safeguards?"

"No, ma'am. And I've got inspection results to prove it."

"In your expert opinion, Ensign Taylor, is there any possible way for someone to accidentally download classified information in violation of regulations?"

"No, ma'am. It'd take a lot of work and you'd have to be doing it on purpose."

"Thank you, Ensign Taylor." Commander Carr gave her a small, professional smile. "No more questions."

Judge Campbell leveled her gavel at David Sinclair. "Defense may cross-examine."

David Sinclair rose, frowning slightly, but his expression cleared as he approached the witness stand. "Ms. Taylor—"

Taylor's eyes widened. "My mother's not here."

A brief chuckle ran through the courtroom. Judge Campbell rested her chin on one hand. "Please use military courtesies in my courtroom, counselor."

David Sinclair had flushed slightly at his error, but recovered quickly. "Forgive me, Your Honor. Both my mother and father are retired Navy officers so, as one raised in a Navy family, I shouldn't have made that error."

Paul almost let his admiration show. His brother had brought out his military family credentials as early as possible without making the revelation seem phony.

David Sinclair faced the witness stand again. "*Ensign* Taylor, does your equipment ever malfunction?"

"Sure it does. If it didn't, I wouldn't have a job."

"Does it ever behave in ways it's not designed to behave?"

"Sometimes. Within limits. It's—"

"Has it ever done anything unexpected?"

Taylor gave David Sinclair a look of grudging respect. "Yes. It has."

"Can you honestly say that it is absolutely completely impossible that the safeguards and the system monitoring software didn't suffer brief simultaneous failures, or that some combination of failures somehow led the system to approve an action which it should not have approved?"

"Nothing's impossible. But—"

"Thank you, Ensign Taylor. No more questions."

David Sinclair walked back to the defense table and sat down as the judge addressed Commander Carr again. "Does the trial counsel wish to redirect?"

"Not at this time, Your Honor. The rial counsel defers to the members."

David Sinclair looked up quickly, then frowned again as Judge Campbell addressed the members. "Do the members have any questions for this witness, Captain Nguyen?"

Paul saw his brother whispering to Lieutenant Owings. It was obvious to Paul, at least, that this aspect of military justice didn't suit David Sinclair at all. It allowed the military officers on the "jury" to use their own experience and expertise to draw out information which the lawyers might or might not want brought into evidence.

Lieutenant Kilgary spoke softly to Captain Nguyen, and at Nguyen's nod she leaned forward. "Ensign Taylor, would you complete what you were about to say in your last answer?"

"Thank you, ma'am. I was about to say that something might not be impossible, but that doesn't mean it's got any real chance of happening. I can't rule out my system suddenly becoming self-aware, deciding it's God, and trying to take over the world, but just because that isn't flat-out impossible doesn't mean I stay awake nights worrying about it."

Another brief smile flickered over Lieutenant Kilgary's face. "Thank you, Ensign Taylor."

Lieutenant Commander de Vaca leaned forward next. "Ensign Taylor, when was the last time your system was certified safe for the storage of and access to classified materials?"

"Sir, that was last done on the afternoon of 17 August." A murmur ran through the courtroom.

De Vaca looked impressed. "The system was certified and approved in all respects?"

"Yes, sir. No faults noted, no waivers required. There never have been," Taylor added. "Not on *my* systems. You can look it up."

Commander Carr stood. "If the member desires, trial counsel is prepared to enter the inspection report and certification into the trial record."

"Yes, ma'am." De Vaca nodded. "Please."

Paul noted that de Vaca looked pleased with himself for bringing out the point about the inspection. He wondered at what point Carr would've introduced it if one of the members hadn't. *She likes letting her points get brought out by the members or even the defense. They make more impact that way. Maybe David will learn a few things from her.*

Captain Nguyen looked from side to side to see if any other members had any questions, then gestured to the judge. "No more questions from the members, Your Honor."

Judge Campbell pointed her gavel toward the witness stand. "Ensign Taylor, you are temporarily excused. Please ensure you are available for the remainder of this court-martial in the event you need to be called again. As long as this trial continues, do not discuss your testimony or knowledge of the case with anyone except counsel. If anyone else tries to talk to you about the case, stop them and report the matter to one of the counsels."

"Yes, ma'am." Ensign Taylor stood and walked out, looking for all the world like she was actually the one in charge of the proceedings.

"The United States calls as its next witness Special Agent Pamela Connally."

Paul watched Connally stride purposefully to the witness stand, looking quietly professional. Commander Carr swore her in, then standing near her, began asking questions.

"Are you Special Agent Pamela Connally, currently employed by the Navy Criminal Investigative Service and assigned to the NCIS office on Franklin Naval Station?"

"I am."

"Describe your actions on the evening of 17 August."

Connally gazed calmly back at Commander Carr as she spoke. "I went aboard the USS *Michaelson* and placed a special tap onto the personal terminals of some of the officers."

"What was the purpose of this tap?"

"It would alert us if any classified information was downloaded in violation of the usual safeguards."

Commander Carr looked mildly puzzled. "We've just been informed that the computer systems on the USS *Michaelson* contain safeguards which would prohibit such downloads."

"Yes. That's right. If they haven't been deliberately interfered with. There is, however, software which allows a determined user to bypass those safeguards by essentially misleading them as to the actions being taken. The tap was designed to detect such bypassing despite the use of the software."

Carr nodded. "Then it would only report downloads which had deliberately," she paused for a fraction of a second, "bypassed the normal safeguards on the *Michaelson*'s systems?"

"That's right."

"And one of the terminals upon which you installed this tap was that normally used by Lieutenant Pullman?"

"Objection." David Sinclair was on his feet again. "Your Honor, I know this point was brought up in pre-trial arguments, but I must again protest against the use of evidence acquired from a terminal belonging to Lieutenant Pullman without benefit of a search warrant."

Commander Carr shook her head. "I must remind the defense counsel that the terminal did not 'belong' to Lieutenant Pullman. It was, as I stated, normally used by Lieutenant Pullman."

"Using semantics to avoid requirements for legally obtaining evidence—"

"It is *not* a matter of semantics," Carr broke in.

Judge Campbell rapped her bench with her gavel. "I'll remind trial counsel and defense counsel that they are to maintain polite and civil exchanges in my courtroom. Now, Commander Carr, did the terminal in question belong to Lieutenant Pullman?"

"No, Your Honor. The terminal was assigned to the desk used by Lieutenant Pullman, but it was and is the property of the US government. Further, the terminal was and is located within a stateroom onboard the USS *Michaelson*, which location is also on government property. Since the terminal was not the private property of Lieutenant Pullman, and since it was located in a working space on a ship owned by the government, Lieutenant Pullman had no expectation of privacy on either that terminal or within that stateroom."

"Your Honor," David Sinclair protested, "an expectation of privacy is perfectly reasonable if a piece of government equipment is so assigned to individual use, within that individual's living area, that it becomes de facto private property."

Commander Carr let apparent exasperation show. "*De facto* private property? Can counsel for the defense provide case law supporting the supposition that government property can by assigned use become the private property of the user? Especially in the case of military equipment?"

Campbell held up her hand to halt the debate. "Defense counsel, I must overrule this objection. Legal precedent is clear that both the terminal and living area in question were public property and that therefore no expectation of privacy existed for Lieutenant Pullman. That being the case, no warrant was required for US government personnel to access that terminal or that area."

David Sinclair grimaced and sat down again.

Commander Carr inclined her head toward Judge Campbell. "Thank you, Your Honor. Special Agent Connally, I'll repeat the question. Was one of the terminals upon which you installed this tap that normally used by Lieutenant Pullman?"

Connally nodded. "That's correct."

"There was no doubt it was the proper terminal?"

"None. It was positively ID'd to me and the ID was confirmed."

Paul tried not to look like he'd played a role in that. *It had to be done. At least I'm not up there testifying and giving away my role in things.*

Carr began walking slowly back and forth in front of Connally. "You installed the tap on the evening on 17 August on a terminal positively identified as that being normally used by Lieutenant Pullman. What happened after that?"

"We waited for any signal from the tap that illegal software had been used to carry out an unauthorized download of classified information. Late on the afternoon of 20 August, we received a signal from the tap notifying us of a large unauthorized download on that terminal."

David Sinclair stood again. "Objection, Your Honor. It has not been established that the download on 20 August was unauthorized."

Without waiting for Campbell to rule, Carr nodded. "I will ask the witness to use the term improper rather than unauthorized. Will that address defense counsel's objection?"

David Sinclair smiled politely. "Yes, it will."

Judge Campbell pointed her gavel again. "Then the objection is sustained and the witness is directed to use the term 'improper' to describe the downloading of classified information to that terminal on 20 August until such time as it is proven to have been unauthorized."

Connally didn't seem entirely happy with the instruction, but nodded. "Yes, Your Honor."

Commander Carr gave a brief, encouraging smile. "What did you do after receiving the signal from the tap on the terminal normally used by Lieutenant Pullman?"

"We positioned ourselves—"

"We?" Carr gently prodded.

"I'm sorry. There were four of us standing by, all NCIS special agents. We positioned ourselves discreetly near the USS *Michaelson* and waited. After a period of approximately fifty minutes, Lieutenant Pullman was sighted on the quarterdeck, dressed as if he intended to go on liberty. We waited until he left the ship, then closed in on him. Lieutenant Pullman appeared surprised by our appearance, but offered no objection when Special Agent Gonzales asked for permission to do a scan for contraband."

Carr held up a hand to stop Connally's testimony. "Did Lieutenant Pullman offer no objection, or did he consent to the scan?"

"He consented. We obtained a record of the consent."

"If the court wishes," Commander Carr announced, holding up her data pad, "a copy of the recorded consent can be entered into the record."

Judge Campbell looked toward the defense table. "Well?"

David Sinclair stood, then shook his head. "I do not think that is necessary, Your Honor."

"Ah, but I do," Campbell responded. "Trial counsel is directed to enter a copy of Lieutenant Pullman's consent to scan for contraband into the record."

Commander Carr rubbed her lower face for a moment. Paul was fairly sure she was concealing a smile, but couldn't be certain. "Please continue, Special Agent Connally," Carr urged.

"After receiving the consent from Lieutenant Pullman, Special Agent Gonzales conducted a scan of Lieutenant Pullman. The scan detected two data coins, one located inside the seam of Lieutenant Pullman's upper garment and one located inside his sock. Based upon what Special Agent Gonzales determined of the content of both coins, he directed us to place Lieutenant Pullman under arrest. Lieutenant Pullman was read his rights, placed in restraints, and escorted to the brig, where he was turned over to the custody of brig personnel. We returned to the NCIS offices to file our reports on the matter."

Carr nodded, not saying anything for a moment, while the members watched her and Special Agent Connally. "Thank you, no further questions."

David Sinclair approached Connally with what Paul thought was a wary look in his eyes, but nothing in his face or bearing betrayed concern. "Special Agent Connally. You testified you're absolutely certain that you placed this tap on the terminal normally used by Lieutenant Pullman."

Connally calmly gazed back at David Sinclair. "That's correct."

"Did you ever *see* Lieutenant Pullman using that terminal?"

"No."

"Did you *see* him using that terminal on 20 August?"

"No."

"Do you in fact have any direct personal knowledge that Lieutenant Pullman routinely used that terminal, and that he used it on 20 August?"

Connally gave David Sinclair a long look. Before she could answer, Commander Carr was standing again. "Your Honor, trial counsel has access to numerous witnesses who will swear to having seen Lieutenant Pullman routinely use the exact terminal on which the tap was placed. The trial counsel also has available the system logs for the USS *Michaelson* on the afternoon of 20 August which show that Lieutenant Pullman was logged onto that terminal."

David Sinclair spread his hands. "Your Honor, I would still like the witness to answer my question."

Campbell shrugged. "If it will make defense counsel happy, then by all means. The witness is directed to answer the question posed by defense counsel."

Connally had kept her eyes on David Sinclair. "In answer to defense counsel's question, no, I did not personally observe Lieutenant Pullman seated at the terminal on 20 August."

"Or on any other occasion?"

"Nor on any other occasion."

"Then how can *you* know whether or not Lieutenant Pullman was the one who downloaded the information that day?"

Carr stood again. "Objection, Your Honor. Defense counsel is questioning the witness on a point not covered in her testimony. The witness did not testify as to whether or not Lieutenant Pullman downloaded the information. Her testimony was that a download occurred and that Lieutenant Pullman was subsequently found off the USS *Michaelson* while in possession of data coins containing information her compatriot identified as containing improperly downloaded material."

David Sinclair pursed his lips, but before he could speak, Judge Campbell intervened. "I agree, trial counsel. Objection sustained. Defense counsel is reminded to cross-examine the witness only on matters she has testified about."

"Your Honor," David Sinclair protested, "the witness's testimony clearly implied that Lieutenant Pullman had carried out the download."

"Be that as it may, she did not explicitly state that as fact. If and when trial counsel makes that assertion of fact, you may address it. Let's move on, defense counsel."

"Yes, Your Honor. I have no further questions."

"Redirect, trial counsel?"

"Just on one point, Your Honor." Commander Carr stood, but remained at her table as she addressed the witness. "Special Agent Connally, were you certain that you had positively identified the terminal routinely used by Lieutenant Pullman before you placed the tap?"

"Yes. Without a doubt."

"After Lieutenant Pullman's arrest, when the tap was removed, was the terminal positively confirmed to be that routinely used by Lieutenant Pullman?"

"Yes."

"Have you been given any reason whatsoever at any time to doubt that identification?"

"No."

"Thank you. No more questions."

Captain Nguyen twisted her mouth in thought. "Special Agent Connally, I know terminals on warships are sometimes shared. How certain could you be that Lieutenant Pullman would be the one using that particular terminal?"

Connally didn't even look toward Paul, instead facing the members' table. "Captain, I was told Lieutenant Pullman used that terminal."

"By whom."

She didn't appear to hesitate. "One of Lieutenant Pullman's roommates."

"How many does he have? I'm sorry, how many *did* he have?"

"Three."

"And there are four terminals in that stateroom?"

"Yes."

Captain Nguyen nodded and sat back, her brow creased in thought.

Commander Sriracha raised a forefinger for attention. "Special Agent Connally, reading between the lines here it seems you had assistance on the USS *Michaelson* in planting this tap. Was the commanding officer of the ship apprised that NCIS was taking this action?"

"Yes, he was."

"And he had no objection to this plan or to the placing of the tap?"

Before Connally could reply, Commander Carr stood up, speaking with a tinge of apology in her voice. "Commander Sriracha, Captain Hayes, the commanding officer of the *Michaelson*, will be testifying later in the proceeding."

"Good," Sriracha approved. "I'd much rather hear it directly from him."

Lieutenant Kilgary spoke next. "Special Agent Connally, I'm frankly surprised that you were apparently able to covertly board the *Michaelson* and place that tap without being noticed by anyone in the crew."

"There was some deception involved," Connally stated. "The crew wasn't aware that I was a special agent or in any way connected to NCIS when I was onboard to place the tap."

Paul once again tried not show any reaction, but he found himself hoping Connally wouldn't veer so far toward implying things that weren't quite so that she'd end up committing perjury. Sure, the *crew* hadn't known about her status. But Paul had.

Kilgary looked impressed. "I wish I could ask how you managed that, but I have a feeling you won't want to answer in an open forum like this."

"No. I wouldn't want to go into details on how we conduct operations."

Captain Nguyen checked to see if there were any more questions. "That's all. Thank you, Special Agent Connally."

Carr was speaking again before Connally left the room. "The United States calls as its next witness Special Agent Robert Gonzales."

Gonzales went over much the same information as Connally had provided, except that he testified as to the contents of the data coins. "I only scanned the contents of the first coin briefly, enough to ensure it contained material classified Top Secret. The second coin contained a sophisticated and illegal software program designed to allow the download of classified material despite safeguards."

Commander Carr gave Gonzales a demanding look. "So Lieutenant Pullman had in his possession not only a data coin containing classified material downloaded from the systems on the USS *Michaelson*, but also a data coin containing the software which would allow an individual to successfully carry out such a download?"

"That is correct."

"Did Lieutenant Pullman attempt to offer any explanation to you for the presence of those coins on his person when you discovered them?"

"No, he did not."

Commander Carr once again held up her data pad. "The trial counsel wishes to enter into evidence a listing of the classified material found on one of the coins in Lieutenant Pullman's possession and a description of the software found on the other data coin in Lieutenant Pullman's possession."

Judge Campbell nodded. "The court orders those items to be entered into evidence."

"No further questions."

David Sinclair approached the witness stand with an openly skeptical look on his face. "Special Agent Gonzales, you testified that you found two data coins on Lieutenant Pullman. Did either of those coins bear any markings indicating they were possessions of Lieutenant Pullman?"

Gonzales pursed his lips and shook his head. "No. Neither coin had any markings on it."

"Did either coin have Lieutenant Pullman's finger prints on it?"

Another head shake. "No. Both coins had been wiped clean."

"Then you have no evidence that those coins actually belonged to Lieutenant Pullman?"

"He had them concealed on himself."

"Is it possible that someone else could have concealed those coins in Lieutenant Pullman's clothing?"

"Objection." Commander Carr shook her head at David Sinclair. "Defense counsel is speculating and asking the witness to speculate regarding matters not introduced into evidence."

"Your Honor," David Sinclair protested, "it is perfectly reasonable to point out alternative explanations for the presence of the coins on Lieutenant Pullman."

"Your Honor," Carr replied quickly. "Defense counsel has introduced no evidence to substantiate the argument that those coins were placed upon Lieutenant Pullman by some third party."

Judge Campbell blew out an plainly exasperated breath, holding up her palm to forestall David Sinclair's next statement. "If defense counsel wants to argue that someone other than Lieutenant Pullman placed the coins upon his person, then defense counsel must introduce some evidence to that effect. Do you have such evidence?"

"Not at this time, Your Honor."

"Objection sustained. The members are asked to disregard defense counsel's speculation in this instance."

David Sinclair lowered his head for a moment, then looked up again with his face composed. "Special Agent Gonzales, did you ask Lieutenant Pullman if the coins were his?"

"No. I—"

"Thank you. That's all."

Commander Carr, still standing, extended one hand toward Special Agent Gonzales. "Trial counsel wishes to redirect. The witness should please feel free to finish his last reply. I believe you were elaborating on whether or not you asked Lieutenant Pullman if the coins belonged to him?"

"Yes." Special Agent Gonzales gave a hard look toward the defense table. "As I started to say, no, I didn't ask Lieutenant Pullman if the coins were his. That's because when we read him his rights, Lieutenant Pullman stated that he desired a lawyer. As soon as Lieutenant Pullman expressed that wish, I was no longer able to question him without his lawyer being present."

The members had no questions for Special Agent Gonzales, who left with another glare toward the defense table.

"The United States calls as its next witness Captain Richard Hayes."

9

Captain Hayes gave off an air of command as he sat in the witness chair, seeming as if he were actually seated in the captain's chair on the bridge of the ship which would still be his for another twelve hours. Commander Carr approached the witness stand and spoke respectfully. "Sir, are you Captain Richard Hayes, United States Navy, currently commanding officer of the USS *Michaelson*?"

"That's correct."

"Was Lieutenant Pullman assigned to your ship?"

"Yes, he was." Captain Hayes' voice stayed flat, betraying no emotion.

"Captain, would you please summarize the events which led to Lieutenant Pullman's arrest on 20 August?"

"Certainly." Hayes chewed his lip for a moment, apparently ordering his thoughts. "My ship returned to port here about noon on 1 August. As you may be aware, in the course of our last underway period we had the misfortune to observe SASAL warships firing upon the civilians who had illegally settled upon an asteroid. On 4 August, while off the ship on what was supposed to be a visit to fleet staff, I was instead met by agents of the Navy Criminal Investigative Service who informed me that they had evidence that one of the officers assigned to my ship was conducting espionage against the United States."

Captain Hayes paused, then spoke again in the same controlled voice. "I was very disturbed by the charge, but I was shown evidence which convinced me it was very likely true. Over the next several days, I coordinated actions with NCIS to attempt to identify the officer involved. These attempts failed. NCIS then suggested placing a tap on one of the terminals aboard my ship to detect any illegal activities, and arranged for special classified material to be delivered to the ship to serve as bait. I heard nothing more until the afternoon of 20 August, when I was informed by my ship's legal officer, Lieutenant Sinclair, that Lieutenant Pullman had just been arrested as he was leaving the ship."

Another pause. "I immediately contacted NCIS and was told of the coins which had been found in Lieutenant Pullman's possession. I notified my officers and told them to cooperate with any follow-up NCIS investigation."

Commander Carr nodded. "Thank you, captain. Can you explain which evidence shown to you by NCIS convinced you that espionage had taken place?"

"Yes. I can. NCIS had conclusive proof that the operational orders under which my ship had just sailed, the orders we were following off that asteroid, had been provided to the South Asian Alliance."

Commander Carr turned quickly, facing midway between the judge's bench and the defense table, and speaking while David

Sinclair was still rising. "Your Honor, trial counsel would like to enter into evidence at this time a list of classified material which US government agencies have certified as having been compromised to the South Asian Alliance."

David Sinclair finished standing up. "Is the defense correct in assuming the orders just cited by the witness are among that list?"

"Yes."

"Your Honor," David Sinclair continued, "while the defense recognizes the need to protect the means and methods by which the US government collects intelligence, it is nonetheless of some concern that we have been presented with the list but provided no means to verify it."

Judge Campbell eyed the defense counsel. "Are you making an objection?"

"I am asking the court to rule on the admissibility of evidence which has been provided in such a way that the defense is unable to verify that evidence. The defense doesn't know the means by which the list was compiled, doesn't know the criteria used for placing items on the list, doesn't know the standards applied to assessing those criteria and doesn't even know exactly who compiled the list. Your Honor, Lieutenant Pullman has the right to confront his accusers. That is a fundamental principle of American justice. This list was compiled by individuals who are among Lieutenant Pullman's accusers, but those accusers remain anonymous, unavailable to appear and unavailable to be questioned in Lieutenant Pullman's defense. The defense submits that allowing this list to be entered into evidence will significantly prejudice Lieutenant Pullman's ability to defend himself against the charges brought against him."

Judge Campbell pursed her lips and sat for a moment without speaking. "Trial counsel? What do you say in response to defense counsel's argument?"

Commander Carr spoke firmly. "Your Honor, the government believes that this list represents a matter of fact, not an accuser. It simply lists documents confirmed to have been provided to a foreign country, documents which the government intends proving were provided to that foreign country by Lieutenant Pullman."

The judge sat silently for several seconds longer. "I am still troubled by this. American justice is not founded upon the use of secret evidence."

"Your Honor," Carr protested, "this is not secret evidence. Lieutenant Pullman's lawyers have been allowed to see this list after signing the appropriate nondisclosure agreements. They know what it contains."

"But they do *not* know how the list was put together. They have no means to question or refute the contents of the list. Is the government prepared to offer such information to the defense?"

Commander Carr shook her head. "Your Honor, I am not authorized to make such an offer. Extremely sensitive intelligence sources and methods are involved."

"Then how is this court to ensure the evidence is indeed a matter of fact, as trial counsel claims, and not an accuser at one remove, as defense counsel claims?"

This time, Carr nodded with every appearance of reluctance. "Your Honor, I am authorized by the government to provide you with detailed information on the means used to compile the list if absolutely necessary to the prosecution of this case. The government is prepared to give the court the necessary information under appropriate classification safeguards to allow the court to determine that this list is verifiably a matter of fact."

David Sinclair frowned and look back at Lieutenant Owings. Owings rose to his feet and spoke for the first time. "Your Honor, with all due respect, the court is not the defense counsel. You do not represent the interests of Lieutenant Pullman."

Judge Campbell nodded. "That's true. However, the interests of Lieutenant Pullman are not the criteria used for purposes of determining the admissibility of evidence, as you know. It's the court's job to decide which evidence can be brought to bear in this trial. Therefore, I will accede to the government's request and receive a private briefing on the means used to compile the government's list of compromised classified material."

David Sinclair spoke again, spreading his hands. "Your Honor, while defense counsel does not wish to call into question the court's integrity—"

"Good for you," Campbell noted dryly.

"— I nonetheless must object to this procedure. If there are reasons why a civilian such as myself cannot be provided with this same private briefing, surely Lieutenant Owings can be given that access."

Commander Carr shook her head again. "I'm sorry, but the government is not prepared to agree to that. Lieutenant Owings lacks the necessary background investigations and clearances, as did Lieutenant Pullman even before his arrest."

"Your Honor—"

Judge Campbell held up a restraining hand. "Defense counsel's objections and concerns are noted. The court will fairly evaluate the nature of the government's evidence and then rule on its admissibility. Is the government prepared to continue its arguments at this time without reference to the material on the list, or must the court-martial be suspended until my ruling?"

"The government is prepared to continue, Your Honor."

"Then do so."

Commander Carr faced Captain Hayes, who had listened to the argument without apparent emotion. "Captain, Lieutenant Pullman was a member of your crew. What is your assessment of him as an officer?"

Hayes frowned. "To be perfectly frank, commander, Lieutenant Pullman was a member of my crew for a very limited period of time. I only had the opportunity to develop preliminary impressions."

"Please share those impressions."

"Lieutenant Pullman seemed to be a capable officer."

"Would you describe him as knowledgeable?"

"Objection, Your Honor." David Sinclair gestured with one hand toward Commander Carr. "Trial counsel is leading the witness."

"Objection sustained. Let the witness use his own words, trial counsel."

If Carr was abashed, she didn't show it. "Yes, Your Honor. Captain Hayes, please provide a more detailed description of your impression of Lieutenant Pullman as an officer prior to his arrest."

"All right." Captain Hayes frowned again, this time in thought. "Lieutenant Pullman gave me the impression of being capable, as I said. His performance of duties was at least competent. He learned his new responsibilities as communications officer quickly. He seemed to get along well with his shipmates and presented a good military bearing."

"Did Lieutenant Pullman make many mistakes?"

"Not to my knowledge. I didn't personally observe any significant errors on his part."

"Did he demonstrate awareness of standard procedures on your ship, including the proper handling of classified material?"

"Yes, I believe he did."

"In your professional assessment, Captain Hayes, did you believe Lieutenant Pullman was sufficiently well trained and capable that he could be trusted to carry out tasks without committing serious errors?"

"Objection." David Sinclair shook his head. "Your Honor, it appears that trial counsel is attempting to get the witness to comment on hypothetical situations."

Carr shook her head in turn. "Your Honor, as commanding officer of the USS *Michaelson* it was Captain Hayes' responsibility to make such assessments of all his officers. It is not a hypothetical situation since such judgments are required on a constant basis."

Judge Campbell thought again, then looked toward the members' table. "I'd like the opinions of the members on this matter since it deals with issues of command responsibilities and the court doesn't have that experience. Do you believe such assessments are made routinely as a part of daily command responsibilities?"

Captain Nguyen, Commander Sriracha and Lieutenant Kilgary immediately nodded. Lieutenant Commander de Vaca, after clearly thinking for a moment, nodded as well. Lieutenant Mahris nodded apparently just as soon as he realized that Captain Nguyen was doing so. Captain Nguyen looked to either side to tabulate the responses, then nodded again to the judge. "It's unanimous. Any commanding officer has to make such assessments every moment of every day. That is why commanding officers are held accountable for failures by their subordinates. They're responsible for deciding whether or not those subordinates can be trusted to carry out tasks."

"Thank you, captain," Judge Campbell stated. "Objection overruled. Continue, trial counsel."

"Thank you, Your Honor. Captain Hayes, would you like me to repeat the question?"

"No, that's not necessary." Hayes' mouth worked for a moment. "Yes, I did assess Lieutenant Pullman as being well trained and capable enough to carry out the duties of a junior officer on my ship. If I'd thought he wasn't to be trusted to do his work or stand watches properly, I would've relieved him of his duties and had him transferred off of the ship."

Carr leaned closer to the witness stand, her eyes locked on Hayes. "Captain, did you feel you had any reason to doubt Lieutenant Pullman's understanding of security regulations?"

"No. None at all."

"Are you confident he knew it was contrary to regulations to download classified material onto portable media using his stateroom terminal?"

"Yes, I am."

Carr stepped back, raising her data pad slightly again. "At this time trial counsel would like to enter into evidence the security briefing papers signed by Lieutenant Pullman when he was granted his clearances, and the nondisclosure agreement signed by Lieutenant Pullman at that same time, which spells out the penalties for unauthorized disclosure of classified material. Trial counsel would also like to enter into evidence the page from Lieutenant Pullman's service record which certifies that he attended and passed standard security indoctrination training."

Judge Campbell, leaning her chin on her hand again, twisted her head slightly to look toward the defense table.

David Sinclair shook his head. "Defense counsel has no objection."

"Then the court orders those documents be entered into evidence. Continue, trial counsel."

Commander Carr faced Captain Hayes again. "Captain, did you ever, by any means whatsoever, order or instruct Lieutenant Pullman to download classified material onto portable media?"

"No, I did *not*."

"Are you familiar with the list of classified material contained on one of the coins found in Lieutenant Pullman's possession?"

"I am."

"Did you ever, by any means whatsoever, order or instruct Lieutenant Pullman to download any or all of those specific items of classified material onto portable media?"

"No, I did *not*."

"Did you ever, by any means whatsoever, order or instruct or approve of Lieutenant Pullman's removing from your ship coins containing classified material?"

"No, commander. You can ask any officer in my wardroom. I don't permit or encourage my officers to violate security regulations."

"Thank you, captain. No more questions."

David Sinclair stood a ways back from Captain Hayes, his posture respectful but not submissive. "Captain Hayes, I understand the commanding officer of a warship deals with a tremendous quantity of decisions and actions every day. Is that a fair statement?"

Hayes gave David Sinclair a sidelong look, but nodded. "I believe that's a fair statement."

"Have any of your orders, statements or instructions ever been misinterpreted or misunderstood?"

"Perhaps I should explain to you that orders are routinely repeated back, so that I and other officers can be sure they're properly understood."

David Sinclair smiled, unabashed. "Thank you, captain. I do understand the system is designed to *minimize* the chances of misunderstandings. But no system is perfect. What I asked was whether, in practice, any orders, statements or instructions of yours ever have been misunderstood."

Captain Hayes didn't look happy. "I can't honestly say that has *never* happened."

"Has anyone in your crew ever done anything, believing it was what you desired, even though you were sure you had given them no such instruction?"

Hayes spent a moment watching David Sinclair, then nodded. "That sometimes happens."

David Sinclair looked appreciative. "Captain, you have testified that in your opinion Lieutenant Pullman could be trusted to do his work. That he was capable, competent, and intelligent. Do you believe a trustworthy, capable, competent and intelligent officer would download classified information in the manner described without believing that his actions had been at least sanctioned, if not ordered, by his superiors?"

Paul looked at Commander Carr, expecting her to object, but though she frowned, Carr stayed seated and said nothing, watching Captain Hayes intently.

Captain Hayes sat back slightly, looking at David Sinclair and clearly thinking through his response.

"Captain?" David Sinclair prodded.

But Hayes refused to be rushed. After a few more seconds he spoke carefully. "I believe an officer who was *believed* to have all of those traits would be capable of such an act if they were motivated by a desire to circumvent security requirements for their own purposes."

Commander Carr smiled briefly.

David Sinclair nodded several times. "Thank you, again, captain. But my question was whether or not an officer you yourself have described as being trustworthy, capable, competent and intelligent could conceivably take such an action in error and not through deliberate intent."

"No, I don't think so." Hayes shook his head, giving David Sinclair a hard look. "This isn't a minor matter, and as I believe has already been discussed earlier, downloading classified material isn't easily accomplished. I would expect a trustworthy, capable, competent and intelligent officer to know better, even if he did think I wanted it."

David Sinclair didn't let any disappointment over Captain Hayes' answer show. "Captain, when your officers fail to carry out your wishes, do you make your displeasure known?"

Paul saw that Captain Hayes couldn't quite suppress a small and brief but ironic smile. He wondered how many others in the courtroom, all of whom had served under their own commanding officers, had the same reaction.

Hayes nodded. "I've been known to express displeasure." This time a murmur of laughter sounded in the courtroom. Judge Campbell glared around, bringing instant silence.

David Sinclair smiled himself, as if he were telling an inside joke. "Do your officers seek to avoid your displeasure?"

"I believe they do, yes."

"Is that a strong motivation?"

"You'd have to ask each officer in the wardroom, but I doubt it's their strongest motivation. That's not how I try to motivate my crew. I don't lead with a whip."

David Sinclair leaned closer, his expression serious now. "But you do use a whip, metaphorically speaking, when you believe it necessary."

Captain Hayes hesitated, then nodded. "Sometimes it may be necessary."

"And do officers and crew members sometimes act hastily, without thinking their actions through, in an attempt to avoid your displeasure?"

"I can't say that's never happened."

David Sinclair smiled briefly again. "Conversely, your officers seek your approval, correct, captain? Your approval of their work."

"I would hope so," Hayes agreed.

"That approval not only affects their day-to-day life on your ship, but also their long-term careers, doesn't it? Those officers who gain your approval receive good marks on their evaluations. They get promoted, they get good orders to new assignments."

Paul barely kept from making a small but probably noticeable sound of derision. *Like my marks got me good orders.*

But Captain Hayes nodded again. "That's true."

"Have any of your officers ever exceeded your orders in an honest attempts to gain your approval?"

Hayes twisted his mouth, but eventually nodded once more. "I'm sure that has happened."

David Sinclair came close to Captain Hayes. "Captain, have any of your officers or other crew members ever done anything downright stupid in a misguided attempt to earn your approval or avoid your displeasure?"

"Again, I have to admit that sort of thing happens on rare occasions."

"Thank you, captain. No more questions."

Commander Carr waited until David Sinclair had sat down, then stood with every appearance of calm confidence. "Trial counsel wishes to redirect. Captain, have any of the misguided incidents just described which *may* have taken place involved major or serious issues?"

"No. Of course not."

"No hazarding of the vessel? No danger to human life?"

"There is *no* possibility that any of my crew, no matter how misguided, would believe I would approve of such actions."

"Violations of major rules and regulations?"

"Certainly not to my knowledge. There's a common-sense factor that needs to be applied here. No one capable of occupying any position of responsibility could believe that I'd approve of something like that. I've never given them cause to believe such a thing."

"Never? You're certain?"

"Absolutely certain." Hayes had reddened as he spoke, his eyes flashing. "I'd be totally remiss in my responsibilities if I'd ever let anyone believe I'd condone, let alone approve, such actions."

"Thank you, captain. No further questions."

Captain Nguyen rubbed her chin as if thinking. "Captain, do you have reason to think that Lieutenant Pullman would've had any reason to doubt your attitude on violating major regulations?"

Hayes shook his head. "No. Not a one."

"Have you ever done such a thing while in command of the *Michaelson*?"

"Taken an action in violation of regulations, do you mean? No."

"I hesitate to bring this up because of the sensitivity of the issue, but during the recent engagement in which South Asian Alliance warships fired upon a civilian settlement, you moved your ship to block the other warships' line of fire. Can you state unequivocally that such an action was permitted by your orders?"

Hayes nodded, his eyes hard. "Yes, I can."

"And in keeping with Naval regulations and instructions?"

"Yes. And in keeping as well, I hope, with the traditions of the service." Hayes paused, then added, "Captain, my actions in that incident have been reviewed by both the fleet and the area commander. Both have approved of my actions."

Nguyen nodded. "Were your officers aware that your actions were within the scope of your orders?"

"Yes, they were. I can't go into details, but my officers can all testify that I did not exceed the scope of my orders as both they and I understood them."

Lieutenant Commander de Vaca gestured for attention. "Captain Hayes, have there been any incidents on your ship of mishandling classified materials? Besides the one being tried here, I mean."

Hayes' eyes narrowed in thought. "One or two. Minor incidents involving individuals exposed to classified materials that they weren't cleared for. They were dealt with appropriately. I know we filed the necessary reports. My ship's collateral duty security manager can no doubt provide you with the details if you need them."

"Is your ship's security manager reasonably available for questioning, sir?"

Hayes pointed at Paul. "Lieutenant Sinclair. He's right there."

Paul sat straight as he became the center of attention of the courtroom. This was the last thing he'd expected to be singled out for.

Judge Campbell raised one eyebrow and eyed Paul. "Does the

member wish Lieutenant Sinclair to be sworn in as a witness to testify regarding this issue?"

De Vaca, after recovering from his surprise, shook his head. "I don't believe that will be necessary. Captain Hayes, am I correct in assuming that your ship has not been formally cited for security violations while you have been in command?"

Hayes gave a thin-lipped smile. "Yes. That is correct."

"Then I see no need for your security manager to testify to the same fact. Thank you, captain."

Lieutenant Kilgary had looked very briefly amused as Paul was singled out, but otherwise had watched Captain Hayes testify without visible emotion. Still, Paul was certain she had no doubts about his testimony. Kilgary had respected Hayes when she'd been on the *Michaelson* and could be expected to rebut any private challenges among the members over his testimony.

Captain Hayes left the court with a single nod to Paul.

Judge Campbell checked the time. "I believe this is an appropriate point at which to break for lunch. This court-martial is closed and will reconvene at thirteen hundred in this courtroom."

"All rise," the bailiff ordered as the judge and the members left the courtroom through their separate doors.

Paul stretched, realizing only now how stiff he was from sitting. He looked over toward the defense table, where both Lieutenant Owings and David Sinclair were speaking to Lieutenant Pullman. Brad Pullman appeared not in the least concerned about the morning's testimony, continuing to display a kind of cheerful confidence.

Paul shook his head and looked to where Commander Carr was just finishing stretching as well. "That seemed to go pretty well," Paul noted.

Carr glanced his way and smiled. "Well enough. The only big hitch is that issue over the list of classified materials. I'd hoped it wouldn't be a problem, but expected it would be if your brother did his job defending Lieutenant Pullman."

"You expected the defense to cause problems over that evidence?"

"Sure." Carr sighed. "It's a problem during every trial involving classified information. Somebody has to decide how many secrets we're willing to compromise in the name of protecting our secrets and punishing those who compromised secrets. It wouldn't make much sense to cause serious damage to our intelligence collection capabilities in the name of protecting them from espionage. Your brother knows that, so he's trying to hammer at that weak link and force the government to either disclose more or let that evidence drop."

"I'm guessing you're not the one deciding how much to disclose."

Carr gave a half-smile. "Right. I push for disclosing as much as possible so we can ensure a conviction, the intelligence types push for disclosing as little as possible so they can protect their secrets, and someone higher then either of us decides where to draw the line between those two positions. Fortunately, I was granted enough slack to agree to things like this special briefing for the judge."

"What'll happen there? Can you tell me?"

"I don't see why not. The briefers will give the judge as much information as they want to and see if the judge is satisfied. If the judge demands more, they'll try to provide just enough more. The problem will come if we reach a point where the judge still isn't satisfied and the briefers refuse to disclose any more. Then either someone higher up orders the briefers to give more or the judge rules the evidence inadmissible."

"How bad will that be for the government's case?"

She shrugged. "I can live with it. I'd rather not, but the coins we caught Pullman with constitute very strong evidence of espionage in and of themselves. The defense can chip away at the government's case, but they can't do much about the foundation of it except try to generate doubt at every possible point." Carr smiled again. "Not that I'm going to sit back and let them do that." She checked the time again. "I've got some things to run down. See you at thirteen hundred, Paul."

Paul didn't feel very hungry, and feared eating too much would make him sleepy for the afternoon in court. He dreaded falling asleep and being publicly upbraided by the judge while David was in the same room. So he grabbed a snack and a big coffee from the nearest take-out and sat on a convenient bench, eating slowly and watching the foot traffic go by. The outfits didn't vary that much. Almost everyone on Franklin was either in uniform or wearing an outfit associated with civilian contractors. Here and there, the clothing of ordinary civilians visiting the station made bright spots of color amid the crowds of workers, flitting in and out of sight like a few tropical birds racing through a forest of trees with bland trunks and foliage.

He'd pretty much stopped paying attention to the crowds some time ago, except as obstacles to his own movement and a possible source of superior officers he'd need to salute. Now he took a good look again, thinking that within a few more days he'd be gone from Franklin. *I wonder how Mars looks compared to this?*

Twenty minutes prior to 1300 he was back in his seat in the courtroom. "Hey, bro."

Paul glanced up at his brother. "Hey."

"Having fun?"

"It's interesting."

"Yeah." David Sinclair grinned. "Very. I saw you talking to the trial counsel. Were you guys plotting strategy against me?"

Paul just smiled back. "Maybe."

David's smile faded. "Seriously. You don't have to tell me, but I'm wondering. Are you convinced about Pullman or is the jury still out for you?"

I don't have to tell him. Maybe I shouldn't. But it's a reasonable question and I can't think of any reason not to be honest. "I'm very aware of the evidence against him, but my jury hasn't quite made up its mind, yet."

"Fair enough." David nodded greetings at Commander Carr as she walked up to the trial counsel's table, then he headed for the defense head.

Carr gave David Sinclair a look then glanced at Paul. "How's the family reunion going?"

"Not bad. But you know the big problem with family reunions."

"No."

"Lots of relatives always show up."

She laughed, drawing looks from those entering the courtroom. "That happens at my family reunions, too. Unfortunately, unlike family reunions this afternoon probably won't be too exciting, Paul. Except for the first witness."

Precisely at 1300 the bailiff once again ordered, "All rise," and everyone waited as first the judge, then the members, reentered the courtroom. "This court-martial is open," Judge Campbell declared. "Proceed with your case, trial counsel."

"Thank you, Your Honor. The United States calls as its next witness Commander Angie Moraine."

Paul tried not to flinch at the prospect of watching Commander

Moraine watching him in the courtroom. He didn't look as Commander Moraine strode rapidly down the aisle, her eyes apparently fixed on the witness stand.

Commander Moraine sat so stiffly she seemed rigid, except for her hands which seemed to be always on the verge of tapping on the keys to a nonexistent data pad. Her face was pale, her eyes darting from point to point. Commander Carr walked toward her with slow, gentle steps, as if approaching a horse liable to panic and bolt at any moment. "Are you Commander Angie Moraine, United States Navy, currently assigned as Operations Department head on the USS *Michaelson?*"

Moraine nodded rapidly. "Yes. I am."

"What was your command relationship with Lieutenant Pullman?"

"Lieutenant Pullman was, briefly, the ship's communications officer. In that capacity, he was one of my division officers."

Carr smiled encouragingly. "Then you were Lieutenant Pullman's immediate superior?"

"That's correct."

"Did you ever in any way, shape or form, order or instruct Lieutenant Pullman to carry out downloads of classified material in defiance of regulations?"

"Objection." David Sinclair gave Commander Carr a slightly sour look. "The question is phrased in a prejudicial manner."

"My apologies," Commander Carr offered. "I will rephrase the question. Commander Moraine, did you ever in any way, shape or form, order or instruct Lieutenant Pullman to carry out downloads of classified material contrary to regulations?"

Commander Moraine fixed a tight stare on Commander Carr, as if unsure whether or not she herself was being accused of wrongdoing.

"No. Certainly not. If Lieutenant Pullman said—"

Carr held up a restraining hand while still radiating reassurance. "Please, Commander Moraine. Just answer the questions put to you. If I require elaboration, I'll ask for that. Now, to the best of your knowledge, did you ever in any way, shape or form, lead Lieutenant Pullman to believe that you desired him to carry out downloads of classified material contrary to regulations?"

"No!"

"How would you describe Lieutenant Pullman's performance while he worked for you?"

Moraine hesitated again, obviously thinking this time. "There weren't any major problems. The Communications Division got its job done."

"How about his behavior?"

This time Moraine's face darkened slightly. "No *major* problems," she repeated. "A bit overconfident, but otherwise he was like my other division officers. They all needed to be whipped into shape." As if against her will, Moraine's eyes came to rest on Paul for a moment as she frowned.

"Overconfident?" Carr questioned. "So Lieutenant Pullman didn't display or express any nervousness about carrying out his job or responding to instructions?"

"No. He'd just say 'yes, ma'am' and he'd do it."

"Did he ever ask for elaboration or additional details in order to carry out his orders if he wanted to ensure he understood what was required?"

"Sometimes. Yes."

"And did he ever display any unfamiliarity with security requirements?"

"No. Not that I recall."

"Did he ever ask you to provide him with security guidance because he was unsure of proper procedure?"

Commander Moraine seemed to be relaxing slowly under Carr's gentle guidance. "No, no. Very sure of himself. Almost cocky, I'd say. That was my impression of Lieutenant Pullman."

"Then Lieutenant Pullman didn't express uncertainties about any aspect of his primary responsibility or of his other duties onboard the ship?"

"No. If anything, he acted like he was bored by instruction and training. As if he already knew everything. You know the type."

"Yes, Commander Moraine, I think I do. How did Lieutenant Pullman respond to job taskings?"

"Excuse me? I don't quite understand the question."

"If you gave Lieutenant Pullman a job to do, how did he respond?"

"He did it. Did it well enough, I suppose."

"Did he ever display or express a sense of urgency? A feeling that he had to get the job done and done quickly out of concern that you or the captain would react adversely?"

Moraine's lip curled. "No. That wouldn't be Lieutenant Pullman. He did jobs quickly because he could, I think, not because he felt any concerns."

"In your experience, did Lieutenant Pullman ever violate rules, regulations or procedures because he felt he had to in order to complete an assigned task?"

"I don't know of any such incidents. None were reported to me. I haven't been informed of anything like that. I certainly never would've approved of it!"

Commander Carr spoke soothingly to the once-again agitated

Commander Moraine. "Thank you, commander. No further questions."

David Carr also smiled as he approached the witness stand. "Commander Moraine, you just testified that in your estimation Lieutenant Pullman acted 'overconfident' and 'cocky.' Is that correct?"

"Yes. Yes, it is."

"Then would it be fair to say that Lieutenant Pullman did not act like someone with something to hide? That he didn't act like someone fearful of being caught doing something improper?"

Moraine froze again, her eyes staring at David Sinclair. Then she nodded with obvious reluctance. "Yes."

"Is it fair to say that in your opinion Lieutenant Pullman didn't act at all like someone deliberately committing acts of espionage against his country?"

"Objection." Commander Carr gestured toward the witness stand. "Defense counsel is asking the witness to speculate on matters beyond her personal experience and knowledge."

"Your Honor," David Sinclair insisted, "this is a reasonable request for the opinion of Lieutenant Pullman's immediate superior."

"Trial counsel is willing to accept such an argument if defense counsel can demonstrate expert knowledge on the part of the witness."

Judge Campbell looked at Carr with a questioning expression. "What expert knowledge would trial counsel be referring to?"

"Defense counsel asked if the witness recognized behavior similar to someone committing espionage. Trial counsel submits that Commander Moraine has not testified to ever having before encountered someone committing espionage, and therefore doesn't have any experience to use in determining how such a person acts."

"That's a good point, trial counsel. The witness is directed to inform the court of any cases in which, to her knowledge, she has worked with an individual or individuals who were later shown to be committing espionage."

Moraine stared up at the judge. "I... don't know of any, ma'am."

"Your Honor." David Sinclair held up his hands in gesture beseeching understanding. "Commander Moraine is an experienced officer. She has worked around and observed many different people for years in her career as a Navy officer. Surely she should be able to judge whether an individual is displaying signs of committing espionage."

"Trial counsel is curious as to what those signs might be," Commander Carr offered.

Paul remembered the list of items he'd been shown by NCIS before he wore the wire. Obviously, NCIS felt it had identified behavioral characteristics of spies. But then, as far as Paul could tell, Brad Pullman hadn't matched those characteristics despite being later caught with physical evidence of sabotage. Did that mean Brad was somehow probably innocent? Or did it mean the behavioral characteristics weren't actually all that definitive?

David Sinclair gave Carr a flat look in response to her statement. "Perhaps I can rephrase the question to satisfy trial counsel's objection?"

Judge Campbell nodded. "You're welcome to try."

"Thank you, Your Honor. Commander Moraine, is it fair to say that in your opinion Lieutenant Pullman didn't act at all like *you* would expect someone to act if they were deliberately committing acts of espionage against their own country?"

"Hmmm." Judge Campbell pointed to Carr. "Trial counsel?"

"Trial counsel will withdraw her objection on the stipulation that Commander Moraine's personal expectations of how someone committing espionage would act are not grounded in any practical experience or special knowledge, and are therefore purely speculative."

"Very well. The witness is directed to answer the question."

Commander Moraine glanced around in confusion. "Which question?" David Sinclair repeated it. "Oh. I don't think so. That is, Lieutenant Pullman didn't act like I would've suspected a spy to act."

"Objection." Commander Carr smiled apologetically at Commander Moraine. "Lieutenant Pullman is charged with espionage, not spying. The witness's response must deal solely with someone committing espionage."

"Sustained." Judge Campbell, her elbow on the bench and her chin on her hand, looked down at the witness stand. "Does the witness know the legal difference?" Commander Moraine shook her head. "A spy acts clandestinely or under false pretenses," Campbell explained. "That is, they're lurking, using a false identity, pretending they're someone else. Members of the armed forces in uniform aren't spies unless they put on a disguise and act under false pretenses. Lieutenant Pullman is charged with espionage, not spying, because he is not charged with acting under false pretenses. He isn't charged with pretending to be someone else in the commission of his alleged crime. He wore his proper uniform and presented himself as Lieutenant Pullman. Do you understand?"

"I think so, Your Honor."

"Therefore defense counsel's question, which is taking up a remarkable amount of time in this court and requiring no end of elaboration, pertains specifically to how you would expect someone to act if they were wearing their uniform and displaying their true identity while also working to deliver classified material to a foreign entity. Is that clear?"

Paul thought Commander Moraine was getting more confused by the moment, but Moraine nodded.

"Good," Judge Campbell stated. "Do we need to restate the question *again*?"

"No," Commander Moraine answered. "I didn't think Lieutenant Pullman acted like someone who was stealing classified material."

Judge Campbell glared at Commander Carr and David Sinclair as if daring either to pursue the question further, then pointed her gavel at David Sinclair. "*Please* continue, defense counsel."

"Thank you, Your Honor. Commander Moraine, you just recently took over command of the Operations Department on the USS *Michaelson*, isn't that correct?"

"Yes." Moraine nodded rapidly.

"When you took over command of that department, were you satisfied with the procedures in place? Were you satisfied that the department was functioning well?"

"No." Moraine glanced around half-defiantly. "No, I was not. Things had to be tightened up, expectations had to be raised, performance had to improve."

"Was it your impression that those changes had taken full effect at the time of Lieutenant Pullman's arrest?"

"No! Of course not. They'll take time. Not too much time. I won't allow that. I don't ever expect my personnel to settle for substandard performance, but getting changes across and changing attitudes can't happen overnight even with the most dedicated leadership, if I may say so." Commander Carr gestured to Paul and whispered a question to him as he leaned close, listening intently to Paul's reply, but Moraine didn't notice as she concentrated on David Sinclair.

David Sinclair nodded understandingly. "Of course, Commander Moraine. Then it's your professional opinion that the department suffered from performance problems. Security is an aspect of performance, isn't it, commander?"

"Yes," Moraine agreed warily.

"If the department was suffering from a general problem with procedures and performance, wouldn't that mean security would also be impacted? That personnel would be unsure how to handle material properly and would make mistakes in their handling of material, perhaps through no fault of their own?"

"Objection. Defense counsel is leading the witness."

"Sustained. Rephrase your question or drop it, defense counsel."

David Sinclair bowed his head briefly to acknowledge the judge's order. "Yes, Your Honor. Commander Moraine, when you spoke of a general problem with procedures and performance, did that include the handling of classified materials?"

Paul watched Commander Moraine's eyes shift. *She's thinking that if she says there weren't any problems when she took over, then she'll be blamed for anything that goes wrong and won't be able to shift the blame to her predecessor. I know she's thinking that. Which means to cover her own butt she's going to say...*

"Yes. Yes, it did include that."

David Sinclair nodded, speaking gravely. "It *did* include problems with handling of classified materials?"

"Yes. That's what I said."

"Thank you, Commander Moraine. No further questions."

"Trial counsel wishes to redirect." Commander Carr stayed at her desk and smiled again at Commander Moraine, but Paul noted that her arm muscles looked tight. "Commander, I want you to think carefully about what you just said regarding security procedures in your department. I want you to consider whether or not, on reflection, you really believe significant problems with the handling of classified material exist in your department."

Moraine looked away from Carr, her eyes shifting again. "I don't... there were problems."

"I'm not questioning your assessment that some problems may exist, but I do wish to clarify for the court whether you believe these are major problems, ones which could lead to serious violations of rules and regulations."

Her eyes refusing to settle on Carr, Moraine nodded stubbornly. "The department's performance doesn't meet my standards as of yet. Problems exist, through no fault of my own."

Commander Carr took a deep breath and Paul saw her body relax into what for some reason struck him as a fighting stance. He wondered what was about to happen to Commander Moraine.

"Commander Moraine," Carr continued in an even voice, "you've just testified that the procedures and performance of the Operations Department did not meet your standards when you assumed command of that department."

"Yes. That's the truth." Commander Moraine was wary, watching Commander Carr as if worried what her next question would be.

"Commander, is it true that you have stated that you expect the equipment in your department to always work quote perfectly unquote and the personnel in your department to always perform quote perfectly unquote?"

Moraine stared at Carr for a moment, then at Paul. Paul tried his best to look totally innocent and surprised by Carr's question.

"Commander Moraine?" Carr prompted. "Have you stated that your standards insist on perfection in all aspects of your department's operation at all times?"

Her expression still more stubborn, Moraine focused back on Carr. "Yes. I don't know if I used that exact phrasing, but I do have very high standards and I don't apologize for that. Not one bit. There's nothing wrong with expecting only the best from your personnel."

Paul tried to look at the members' table without being obvious, trying to judge their reactions. Captain Nguyen was watching Moraine with a carefully bland expression. Lieutenant Mahris was doing his best to mimic Nguyen. Commander Sriracha and Lieutenant Commander de Vaca had their eyes on the surface of the table in front of them, and Lieutenant Kilgary was covering her eyes with one hand.

Commander Carr nodded at Moraine's answer. "Do you agree that there is a very large gap between procedures and performance that fall short of 'perfect', and procedures and performance which pose the threat of significant failures, let alone major failures?"

"I don't accept that logic, commander. I don't accept any lessening of standards or expectations. I have zero tolerance for any deviance from the very highest standards."

"I see." Commander Carr canted her head as if interested in Moraine's words. "Commander Moraine, how many significant or major failures did the Operations Department suffer in the two years prior to your assuming command?"

"I... I don't..."

"Are you aware of any?"

"Not... not at this time."

"Aside from the case currently being tried here, how many significant or major failures has the Operations Department suffered since your assuming command?"

"I... There haven't been..."

"Any?" Carr prompted again. "Is it therefore reasonable to assume that the problems with procedures and performance to which you've referred were not of such severity as to pose significant risk of major failures?"

Moraine's face set into lines of granite. "I'm not prepared to say that."

"You're prepared to state under oath that serious problems existed in the Operations Department of the USS *Michaelson* prior to your assuming command and that those problems still existed as of 20 August? Even knowing that such an admission would surely trigger outside inspections of your department to ensure it can operate in a safe and effective manner?"

"Objection, Your Honor!" David Sinclair had a wondering expression. "Trial counsel is badgering her own witness."

"I noticed that," Judge Campbell remarked. "Does trial counsel intend to continue this line of questioning?"

Carr nodded. "I would like the court to instruct the witness to answer the question, since it addresses fundamental issues of the environment in which Lieutenant Pullman worked."

"I agree. Objection overruled. The witness is directed to answer the question."

Commander Moraine looked daggers at Commander Carr, who seemed totally unaffected. "I do not... believe... the problems were quite that severe."

"Please answer yes or no, Commander Moraine. Were the

preexisting problems with procedures and performance which you have testified existed in the Operations Department at least up until 20 August serious in nature?"

"This is a complex question—"

"Commander Moraine, when you relieved the prior Operations Department head and assumed command of that department, you signed a letter. The same letter every officer on a ship signs when they assume responsibilities for their division or department or ship, one which states you have assumed your duties and responsibilities. That letter is required to state significant problems, isn't it, commander?"

"Normally. Yes."

"Did you indicate the existence of any significant problems in the Operations Department in that letter, Commander Moraine?"

Moraine struggled, but finally got out one word. "No."

"With the exception of the cases alleged here, were there any cases of mishandling of classified materials within the Operations Department of the USS *Michaelson* in the two years prior to 20 August?"

"I..."

"The collateral duty security manager of the USS *Michaelson* is still present in this courtroom, Commander Moraine," Carr stated, sweeping one hand back to point at Paul, who once again wondered how it was that today he kept getting singled out in the courtroom for that reason. "Shall I call him to the stand to answer that question?"

"No! I'm not aware of any such cases."

"Then is it accurate to state that there was no evidence of a pervasive, serious problem with the handling of classified material in the Operations Department prior to and up to 20 August?"

"Yes!"

"Is it also accurate to say that you have stated no concerns regarding the safe handling of classified material within the Operations Department to your superiors on the *Michaelson*? Well, commander? Did you inform the captain or executive officer of such concerns?"

"No!"

"Thank you, commander. No further questions."

Judge Campbell had continued regarding Commander Moraine with an interested expression. "Do the members have any questions for the witness?"

Captain Nguyen looked around, her expression still carefully bland. "Anyone? No? No, Your Honor, we don't need to hear any more from this witness."

Commander Moraine marched stiffly out of the courtroom, her eyes glaring at Paul briefly before she went past. Paul let out a long breath. *If I wasn't transferring off the* Michaelson *I'd be toast. Talk about fortunate timing.*

10

After the thrill and excitement of watching Commander Moraine's exercise in trying to ensure she wasn't held to fault for anything, the rest of the afternoon turned out to be as dull as Commander Carr had predicted to Paul.

Expert witnesses were called who testified as to the exact content of security instructions and the proper procedures for handling classified material. Other experts were called, these the technicians who had swept the *Michaelson* for taps in the wake of Pullman's arrest. They'd found three, it turned out, one each in the captain's cabin, the executive officer's stateroom and Commander Moraine's stateroom. Paul found himself wondering what the odds were of a single stateroom holding two taps, one from NCIS and the other from a foreign source, at the same time. The second sweep a few days before this had turned up no new taps on the ship. Carr made sure that the fact that no new taps had been placed since Pullman's arrest was emphasized.

"Could you determine the origin of the taps?" Carr asked the chief technician.

"Not with one hundred percent certainty." The technician, whose eyes like everyone else's nowadays had perfect vision, still kept moving his hand as if fiddling with nonexistent glasses. "However, nano-scale analysis revealed a very high probability that they were manufactured at a facility in the South Asian Alliance." The technician then explained the nano-scale analysis in sufficient detail to threaten the entire courtroom with terminal sleeping sickness.

David Sinclair, for his part, kept hammering away at every possible place to try to force holes in the government's case. No, the technicians agreed, they had nothing definitively tying the taps to Lieutenant Brad Pullman. No fingerprints, not even stray DNA from flakes of skin. Apparently the taps had been periodically changed out to allow the old ones to be returned to their makers and exploited, so there was no paper trail of material from the taps to Lieutenant Pullman or anyone else.

But, Commander Carr was able to remind the courtroom again, no new ones had been placed since Pullman's arrest.

Judge Campbell, releasing the last technical witness with almost obvious relief, tapped her gavel on her bench. "This court-martial is closed. It will reconvene at ten hundred tomorrow morning in this courtroom for the continuation of the government's presentation."

After the judge and members had left the court, Paul finally let out the yawn that had been building for over an hour. Carr give him a weary grin. "I told it you wouldn't be that thrilling this afternoon."

"Not after until my boss finished testifying."

"Yes. Sorry about that. I gave her as many chances as I could to rebut her own statements about problems in her department. Did she think saying that would make her look good?"

"By the time she was done, I'm not sure she knew why she was saying what she said."

Commander Carr gave another grin. "I wasn't going to let her offer an out to Pullman. Your brother gambled that I wouldn't be hard on my own witness. He lost. It's obvious your brother is trying to build a defense that Pullman's actions were just ill-advised, not deliberately criminal."

"Will it work?"

"Not if I can help it. But given the physical evidence that exists, it's probably his best option. If he can't convince the members that somebody planted those coins on Pullman, he'll have to try to convince them that Pullman was just being stupid."

Paul looked down, frowning. "Brad Pullman's not stupid. I think David will try to say Brad got over-eager and had one of those it-seemed-like-a-good-idea-at-the-time moments."

Carr paused and gave Paul a thoughtful look. "Yes. It would match the rest of what's being said about Pullman. Thank you, Paul."

He nodded. *So here I am helping the prosecution. How do I know it wasn't a case of Pullman being too cocky, too eager to show how smart he was, being smart enough to do something he shouldn't but not smart enough to realize it'd get him in trouble? Like when he messed with those communications links? That's bad, but it's not espionage. It's not selling secrets to the enemy.*

"Have a good evening," Commander Carr added. "I expect we'll get a ruling from the judge tomorrow on whether or not we'll be allowed to enter that list of compromised classified material into evidence. If we do, we may see your captain on that witness stand again."

"Do you think the judge will admit the evidence?"

"I honestly can't make a call on that. Judge Campbell is very good at using her irascibility to mask her thoughts. We'll have to wait until tomorrow to find out what she's decided."

The courtroom emptied rapidly. Paul, knowing he had to brief the captain on the rest of the court-martial events that day, hastened back to the ship. Hayes and Captain Agee were both in the captain's cabin, doubtless discussing a few final issues on the turnover, when Paul arrived. They both listened attentively. When Paul came to Commander Moraine's testimony he had to strip his description bare of all but the most basic information. Both captains exchanged glances, leading Paul to wonder what opinions they might share on Commander Moraine, but of course neither one would ever express any negative evaluation in front of Paul.

As Paul finished, Captain Hayes stood up, too. "I guess that's all for tonight." Hayes walked briefly with Paul as they left the captain's cabin. "You'll be at the court-martial, tomorrow, again."

"That's still Captain Agee's orders, sir?"

"Yes. He'll be the only one getting briefed by you tomorrow evening." Hayes looked around. "It's very hard to believe that tomorrow I'll be relinquishing command of this ship to him. Hard to believe, but it'll be a tremendous weight off of my shoulders."

"I wish I could be at the ceremony, sir."

"You're needed in that courtroom. And you've been where I needed you when I needed you for about two years now, Paul. That's a lot more important than being at the change-of-command ceremony. You got your final evaluation from me. Any questions?"

"No, sir." The evaluation had been glowing, ranking Paul in the top one percent, and actually embarrassing him with its praise of him as an officer. "Thank you, sir."

"There's nothing to thank me for. You earned it." Hayes extended his hand. "Good luck, Paul. Look me up when you get back."

From Mars, he means. Paul shook the captain's hand, then watched him walk toward the quarterdeck. A few minutes later, Paul heard four strikes on the ship's bell in two pairs, then the announcement "*Michaelson,* departing." Very likely that was the last time Hayes would be bonged off the ship that way.

It was getting fairly late and Paul was worn out. *Worn out from today, and worn out from three years of this duty. I know exactly what Kris Denaldo meant when she talked about it.* He wandered into the wardroom and found Ensign Taylor there, kicking back with some coffee. "Hey."

Taylor raised her coffee in greeting. "Hey, yourself. Long time no see. Speaking of which, I saw our boss coming aboard after her little visit to the court-martial. She didn't seem like a very happy camper. Matter of fact, Commander Migraine looked ready to bite pieces out of the hull and spit them at people."

Paul couldn't help smiling. "I can't imagine why."

"I can. But I'd rather know the sordid truth. What happened?" Paul outlined the events in the court while Taylor smiled. "I wish I'd been there to see it. But then it was nice to have her out of my hair for a while." Taylor sighed. "You remember I finally gave her that code she's been bugging me for?"

"Yeah. You thought it'd keep her busy for a while."

"Oh, it's keeping her busy all right. The only problem is she wants me to sit down with her and go over that code line by line looking for 'errors.'"

Paul didn't know whether to laugh or punch the bulkhead. "How many millions of lines of code are there?"

"Too many. And Migraine don't know code worth a damn so she can't really identify problems with it."

"How much time have you wasted on this?"

Taylor chuckled. "Not much. See this key?" she asked, pointing to her data pad. "I push this and my chief knows to call me with word that a critical piece of equipment just broke and I've got to get there real fast and help look at it." Taylor leaned back and looked upward. "It's downright amazing how many pieces of critical equipment I've had breaking lately."

Paul sat down, shaking his head. "And I'm leaving my division under her command. Not to mention you."

"Not to worry. I can take care of myself, your relief Shwartz has her stuff together and the new guy they sent in to take Pullman's place looks like he's at least halfway intelligent. We'll keep things together."

"But you'll have to put up with Moraine for at least another year!"

"No, we won't." Taylor shook her head, then took a meditative sip of coffee. "I've seen Moraine's type before. Had a division officer a lot like her once. Commander Migraine's gonna self-destruct just like he did. People like that always do. I give her another couple of months and she'll either have a breakdown or screw up so bad she'll be relieved for cause."

"Really?" Paul stared at his coffee for a moment. "I know it's dumb, but I hate to see that happen to someone."

Taylor shrugged. "It's a waste, if that's what you mean. But Moraine got herself on this path a long time ago. You and me tried to straighten her out, remember? Didn't work, even though you were so diplomatic about it I wanted to slug you a few times. I guess they teach you that diplomatic stuff at the Academy, huh? In the same classes where you learn to drink tea with your pinky finger out?" Taylor shifted her grip on her coffee, holding it with absurd delicacy, her pinky finger extended.

Paul laughed. "I think they got rid of the pinky finger classes back in the twentieth century."

"Are you sure? I could've sworn I saw some Academy graduates drinking their caffeine-free herbal tea that way just the other day. It makes it real easy to see their rings." Taylor waved her coffee around. "Like this. 'Yoo hoo! I'm an Academy graduate! Look how well eddicated and well mannered I are!'" She pretended to pick her nose with her ring finger, then extended the digit. "'Yoo hoo! Are there any *lowly* enlisted people around to dispose of this for me?'"

"I could offer a few suggestions on what you could do with it yourself," Paul offered.

"But you won't because you're still too well mannered despite my best efforts. Well, even though I haven't been able to corrupt your young soul too much, I hope some of me rubbed off on you."

"I hope so, too." They toasted each other with their coffee.

"All rise." Paul and the others in the courtroom stood to attention. After the judge and members had entered and everyone else had been given permission to sit down again, Paul looked around, trying to gauge how things were going. Commander Carr seemed quietly confident, but then she always seemed to try to project that image in court. Paul didn't know Lieutenant Owings well enough to read his expression or body language, and David Sinclair simply displayed a sort of calm determination. Brad Pullman was the only one whose mood was easy to figure out, his confident smile and posture unaltered by events in the courtroom so far. Paul couldn't help wondering what as-yet-undisclosed defense evidence or tactic of sufficient power existed to justify Pullman's attitude.

"This court-martial is now open." Judge Campbell looked around as well. "Prior to trial counsel resuming her presentation of the government's case, the court will issue its ruling regarding the admissibility into evidence of a list of classified material identified as having been compromised to foreign entities. As a result of being provided additional information regarding the means by which the list was compiled and the criteria used to place items on that list, it is the opinion of this court that the means used are sufficiently unbiased and certain to constitute matters of fact. Therefore it is the ruling of this court that the list be entered into evidence."

David Sinclair stood. "Your Honor, defense counsel wishes to register a protest regarding this decision. While not questioning the judgment of the court or implying partiality, the fact remains that only Lieutenant Pullman's lawyers have a primary interest in obtaining the best result for their client. Yet neither defense counsel nor his assistant have been allowed to directly examine or question the means and criteria used in compiling this list. The decision to exclude Lieutenant Pullman's legal representatives from this process can only act to the prejudice of Lieutenant Pullman. Defense counsel formally requests that the court reconsider its decision and allow Lieutenant Pullman's representatives a role in evaluating the nature of the list in question."

Judge Campbell listened without displaying any reaction, then simply nodded. "Defense counsel's protest and request are noted and will be part of the record of this trial. However, the court will not reconsider its decision. In matters of national security due deference must be paid to the need to protect intelligence sources and methods. It is the judgment of this court that in the case of this list, such deference does not act to bias the case against Lieutenant Pullman. I might add that the court has a high degree of confidence that higher levels of judicial review will concur with this judgment."

David Sinclair's mouth tightened, but he nodded and sat down. Brad Pullman leaned over and whispered something to his lawyer while displaying a reassuring expression. David Sinclair nodded sharply and focused on the judge.

Paul watched the interplay, wondering if he'd really seen a flash of irritation on his brother's face when Pullman had spoken to him. *I saw it and recognized it, I think, because I grew up with David. Nobody else probably noticed. I wonder why David's annoyed with Pullman?*

Judge Campbell tipped her gavel toward Commander Carr. "Proceed, trial counsel."

"Thank you, Your Honor. The United States recalls as its next witness Captain Richard Hayes."

Paul watched in surprise as Hayes came up the aisle again. Carr must've had him standing by in case she won the ruling on introducing the list into evidence.

"Captain Hayes, I'll remind you that you remain under oath. I'm going to revisit some testimony which we couldn't complete at your last appearance. When you were informed by NCIS representatives that classified material had been compromised to a foreign entity, did NCIS identify specific items which had been compromised?"

Hayes nodded. "They did."

"For the benefit of the members, I'll explain that those items are contained on the list which the court has just entered into evidence. Captain, was one of those items your ship's operational orders for your last underway period?"

"Yes, it was."

"What was the classification of those orders?"

"Most of it was at the Secret level, but there were two Top Secret annexes."

"Top Secret being the classification used to protect information whose disclosure is defined as that which would cause exceptionally grave damage to national security?"

"That's right."

Commander Carr was standing directly in front of Captain Hayes, her arms crossed. "Can you tell the court the general nature of the information contained in those two Top Secret annexes?"

Hayes nodded again. "One was an intelligence assessment, and the other was our rules of engagement."

"What, in general, did the intelligence assessment deal with?"

"Our assessments of the capabilities and intentions of the other foreign powers who'd be operating ships at the illegally settled asteroid."

"What about the rules of engagement? What does that deal with?"

Hayes frowned in thought for a moment. "Basically, the rules of engagement tell us what we're allowed to do and how we're allowed to do it. They set the limits on our actions."

"Then by gaining access to your operational orders and those two annexes, someone would know what you expected them to do, and would know exactly what you were not allowed to do. Is that a fair summation?"

"Yes." Captain Hayes nodded heavily. "Yes, it is."

"What is your personal assessment of the actions of the warships of the South Asian Alliance during the engagement at the asteroid?"

"Objection." David Sinclair frowned at Carr. "Trial counsel is asking the witness to speculate as to the state of mind of other individuals."

"Your Honor, I am asking the captain to provide us with his professional assessment of the manner in which the South Asian Alliance warships were observed to operate. I am not asking him to speculate as to the state of minds of the officers on those ships. I am only asking his impressions of their observed actions."

Campbell frowned as well. "It seems to this court that trial counsel's question is permissible."

David Sinclair gestured toward Captain Hayes. "Your Honor, how can the witness know what other ships intended? He can only speculate."

Captain Nguyen at the witness table cleared her throat. "Your Honor, if I may."

Judge Campbell nodded. "Please do."

"Operational commanders routinely have to judge the intentions of other ships by observing their actions. It's a major part of their training and experience. It's very common not to have direct knowledge of what other ships or forces intend."

"Then you regard trial counsel's question as falling well within the professional expertise of Captain Hayes?"

"Definitely, Your Honor."

"Very well. That makes two of us. Objection overruled."

Carr nodded gravely. "Thank you, Your Honor. Captain Hayes, what was your impression of the actions of the South Asian Alliance warships during the engagement at the asteroid?"

Hayes reddened slightly, apparently still angered by the memory. "My impression, and it was a very strong impression, was that they felt they had a free hand."

"A free hand, sir?"

"Yes. They acted like they knew exactly what they could get away with, and exactly where to draw the line."

Carr began pacing back and forth in front of the witness stand. "Given what you've learned subsequently, that your orders had been compromised, do you believe that they acted the way they did because they knew what orders you were operating under?"

"Yes."

"That they felt free to act in the manner they did, bombarding the settlers on the asteroid and destroying the hijacked freighter, specifically because they knew the limits on your ability to respond?"

"Yes. I have no doubt of that at all."

"Did the NCIS representatives tell you how they believed your orders had been compromised?"

"They did." Hayes' expression had hardened as the questions dealt with events at the asteroid, and he steadfastly avoided looking toward Pullman. "They revealed that a batch of documents had been delivered to the South Asian Alliance on approximately 16 June."

"Just prior to your ship getting underway?"

"That's correct. A coded identifier on the copy of the orders in the possession of the South Asian Alliance indicated it was the same as the identifier on the orders sent to my ship."

"Meaning the copy in the possession of the South Asian Alliance had to have been copied from the orders sent to your ship?"

"Yes." Hayes took a deep breath, as if trying to calm his anger. "The NCIS representatives also informed me that another delivery of documents had been made to the South Asian Alliance on 2 August."

"Immediately following the return of your ship to Franklin Naval Station?"

"That's correct."

"Did those documents also have identifiers indicating they'd been copied from your ship's systems?"

"They did."

"What did you conclude from this?"

"That someone on my ship had been downloading classified documents and providing them to the South Asians."

"What was your reaction to this conclusion, captain?"

"I was... upset. I agreed to cooperate with NCIS in attempting to identify whoever was responsible."

Carr stopped pacing and faced Captain Hayes again. "Captain, was that your primary motivation? To identify the one responsible?"

Hayes seemed surprised by the question. "Of course."

"Not just find someone to blame. But find the one responsible."

"I see what you're driving at now. Yes. I made sure NCIS understood I wanted that investigation conducted in such a way that we caught the one responsible, not anyone else."

"Do you believe the investigation was indeed conducted to avoid catching anyone innocent and ensure the apprehension of the guilty party?"

"That's what I did my best to ensure."

"Do you believe it succeeded in that?"

"Objection. Opinion."

"I withdraw the question," Commander Carr stated before the judge could rule on the objection. "No more questions."

David Sinclair regarded Captain Hayes. "Welcome back, captain. This identifier which you say indicated the classified documents had come from your ship. Did that identifier specify where on your ship the document had come from?"

"No."

"Did it specify who had accessed the message and downloaded it?"

"No."

"Is it fair to say that nothing on those documents in any way connects them to Lieutenant Pullman?"

Hayes considered the question, frowning again. "No. It's not fair to say that. The documents came from my ship and Lieutenant Pullman was caught illegally downloading and removing similar documents from my ship. I regard that as a connection."

David Sinclair didn't let any disappointment show. "Captain, let me narrow my question. Did anything on those documents say they had been downloaded by Lieutenant Pullman?"

Hayes thought again before replying. "No."

"Did anything on those documents say they had been delivered to a foreign entity by Lieutenant Pullman?"

"No."

"When the unfortunate events took place at the asteroid, did you see any actions or reactions by Lieutenant Pullman which you would interpret as signs that he knew what the South Asians intended? Did his reactions differ in any way from those of the rest of the crew?"

"I was fairly busy with other issues than watching Lieutenant Pullman."

"But did you notice anything of that nature, captain?"

"No, not that I recall."

"Now, as to those events, you've testified that among your orders was an annex which contained an estimate of what actions would be taken by other warships belonging to foreign powers. Is that something you usually see among orders?"

Hayes nodded. "Yes. It's fairly standard, in one form or another."

"Do foreign powers also provide their warships with estimates of what our ships are expected to do?"

"As far as my knowledge goes, yes."

"Do you think it possible that the South Asian ships at the asteroid had such an *estimate*? Not actual, detailed knowledge, but an estimate?"

"Objection. Defense counsel is asking the witness to speculate on matters beyond his knowledge."

"Your Honor," David Sinclair countered, "this witness has already testified as to his *impressions* of what motivated the actions of South Asian warships. I am asking him for a similar judgment on their possible motivations."

Judge Campbell considered the question. "I tend to agree."

Commander Carr shook her head. "Your Honor, this is a different matter—"

"No, trial counsel, I believe it's substantially the same matter. I'll remind trial counsel that she introduced this line of questioning. Objection overruled. Continue, defense counsel."

David Sinclair looked back at Captain Hayes. "Captain, do you think it possible the South Asian warships were working from an intelligence estimate as opposed to detailed knowledge of your intentions?"

"It's possible," Hayes conceded.

"Is it also possible that such an estimate could've been what gave them the impression you cited, that they would be able to act without your interference?"

"Yes, that's possible. I'm not saying it's probable."

"Thank you, captain."

Carr was standing almost immediately. "Trial counsel wishes

to redirect. Captain Hayes, regarding Lieutenant Pullman's reactions while events unfolded at the asteroid, you stated you were too busy to specifically note them?"

"That's right. I don't recall Lieutenant Pullman being on the bridge."

"Do you have any memory of him at all while the South Asian warships were attacking the asteroid settlement?"

"No. I don't recall noticing Lieutenant Pullman at all during those events."

"Then to clarify, your answer isn't that Lieutenant Pullman's reactions didn't seem to differ. It's that you have no idea what Lieutenant Pullman's reactions were."

"Yes. That's exactly right."

Carr nodded slowly, drawing out the moment. "One other question, captain. Defense counsel posed to you an alternate possible cause for the confidence you say you observed in the actions of the South Asian ships on that occasion. Which do you consider more likely, that they were acting off an estimate or that they were acting from certain knowledge?"

Hayes didn't hesitate. "Certain knowledge. Estimates are all well and good, but they're only estimates. They can be wrong. They can be very wrong. You have to take that into account. The sort of confidence I believed I saw the South Asians demonstrate tells me they had certain knowledge."

"Thank you, captain. No further questions."

Captain Nguyen leaned forward, her elbows on the members' table, her hands clasped before her. "Captain, I find myself having to re-ask a question posed to you earlier. While NCIS was conducting its investigation to determine who was the source of the classified material being compromised to the South Asian Alliance, did you feel confident at every stage that the investigation was being carried out in such a manner as to minimize the possibility of an innocent person being charged or entrapped and maximize the possibility that the guilty person would be caught?"

Once again, Hayes didn't hesitate. "I would not have approved the investigation if I did not believe that to be true. I wanted the guilty person caught. More importantly, I wanted the compromising of our classified material to stop. Hauling in someone innocent of the earlier offenses wouldn't have accomplished either goal."

Nguyen nodded. "At the time the investigation began, your period of command of the USS *Michaelson* was growing short. I understand your change of command will be later today. Did you feel any pressure, internal or external, to resolve this matter quickly enough that it wouldn't be passed on to your successor in command?"

Hayes looked briefly weary, as if the burdens of his last two years had been brought to the fore by the question. "Captain Nguyen, as I'm sure you're aware, no commanding officer wants to pass on unresolved issues to his or her successor. Especially an issue of this magnitude. But at every decision point I realized that if I did not resolve it properly, then I wouldn't have resolved it at all. Telling my successor that I'd caught the right individual if in fact that person was still running free wouldn't have been doing him any favors. In fact, it'd be undermining him in a very critical way. That's a long way of saying I knew I had to resolve it right."

Captain Nguyen nodded again. "Thank you. Do any of the other members have questions?"

"I do, ma'am," Commander Sriracha stated. "Captain, you assigned Lieutenant Pullman to take over the Communications

Division. This is a job which specifically deals with much of the classified material flowing into the ship, especially the most urgent material. Did you assign Lieutenant Pullman to this position because of a particular belief in his trustworthiness?

"No, commander. I honestly can't say that. I had a division officer's job coming open, Lieutenant Pullman's record indicated he should've been competent to do it, and there was no reason to doubt his trustworthiness. No reason at that time, that is."

"Still, captain, you could have assigned Lieutenant Pullman to a less sensitive position. In engineering, perhaps."

Captain Hayes frowned and shook his head. "I could've, but even though a job in engineering might be less sensitive in the sense of less exposure to classified material, it's still a position requiring great faith in the trustworthiness of the officer. I don't have any jobs on my ship that don't require me to trust their occupants. You know that."

Commander Sriracha smiled. "Yes, sir, I do. I just wondered how you'd express it. Thank you, sir."

"Captain?" Lieutenant Kilgary asked. "I'm assuming from what's been said that there's no indication Lieutenant Pullman attempted to communicate anything to the South Asians during or immediately prior to the engagement at the asteroid? Or is there something about that which will be presented later?"

A murmur arose in the courtroom, quickly quelled when Judge Campbell gave the spectators an acidic look. Paul found himself startled as well by the question. Startled because he wondered why he hadn't thought of that himself before. Communicating with the other ships wouldn't have been easy, but it wouldn't have been impossible, either. The right software could've projected a simple code onto part of the *Michaelson*'s outer hull using the video displays which were part of the visual bypass system, or a transmitter could've been run out past the grounded outer hull, though that would've required cracking an airlock which would've set off alerts.

But Commander Carr was shaking her head and answering for Captain Hayes. "There's nothing in the government's case pertaining to that issue, lieutenant."

Lieutenant Kilgary looked surprised. "Even though as communications officer Lieutenant Pullman would've had authorized access to the visual bypass system back-up message projection capability?"

Paul felt like slapping his forehead. Well, duh.

Captain Hayes had an expression that seemed just as startled, but then his face cleared. "No, wait a moment. Pullman didn't get tapped as the new commo until after we were on our way back from the asteroid. He didn't have that access when we were out there. Lieutenant Denaldo was still commo at that time, and I know she'd have ensured there wasn't any unauthorized access of that capability."

"Yes, sir." Lieutenant Kilgary nodded in agreement. "That does resolve the question."

Lieutenant Commander de Vaca looked from Lieutenant Kilgary to Captain Hayes. "There's high confidence, then, that this Lieutenant Denaldo would've done a good job of protecting her access codes?" Both Kilgary and Hayes nodded.

Captain Nguyen checked to see if anyone else had questions. "That's it, then. Thank you, captain."

As soon as the judge dismissed him Hayes hastened down the aisle, checking his watch, and out of the courtroom. Paul checked the time as well, surprised to see how little time remained until the change-of-command ceremony was scheduled to take place. He still felt uncomfortable about not being there, knowing that Lieutenant Junior Grade Shwartz would be the one standing in front of what had been Paul's division. But it was probably just as well. Shwartz, not Paul, would be the new captain's Combat Information Center officer. He had to let go of that responsibility and start facing whatever new responsibilities he'd have in his job on Mars.

The next witness's testimony wasn't as dramatic as Captain Hayes' had been, but Paul found his information intriguing. The NCIS agent, a man Paul hadn't encountered before, testified to the results of the financial investigations conducted on Lieutenant Pullman once the proper warrants had been obtained. The last ten years of Lieutenant Pullman's financial life, both on and off the official record, had been reconstructed in exhaustive detail within a period of days. Paul wasn't sure whether he should feel reassured that the government could ferret out financial wrongdoing that well, or horrified that the government could track someone's financial life that well.

Paul stared at the displayed data. The complex diagrams, revealing a dizzying maze of interlinked financial transactions across borders and regulatory authorities, kept ending in various bank accounts whose owners had different names, but a remarkably similar set of passwords and access codes. That in and of itself meant little, until the agent revealed that a warranted search of Pullman's personal storage had unearthed a well-concealed data coin containing all those same passwords and codes under triple encryption.

Paul couldn't help staring at Brad Pullman after this information was revealed, wanting to see how Pullman would react. But except for a surprised expression and a shake of the head in denial, Pullman didn't seem especially fazed by the revelation.

There were a few purchases that hadn't apparently come from Pullman's salary, the money to pay for those things not having come out of Pullman's regular bank accounts and not being traceable to the regular government deposits of Pullman's pay. A very nice vehicle registered in Pullman's name. A state-of-the-art home theater system. A couple of gambling vacations where the house (as usual) had won a lot more than Pullman. But nothing Pullman, as a single junior officer, couldn't have afforded by using the money he earned in his own salary. Instead of using Pullman's salary, though, the luxuries had been paid for using money acquired in some other way. Paul stared again, focusing on the sums in the different bank accounts. They were nice, but even added up they didn't seem all that large.

David Sinclair tried to hammer at that in cross-examination. "Is there anything here that Lieutenant Pullman couldn't have afforded on his own?"

The NCIS agent shook his head, his expression calm. "No."

"These sums in the bank accounts. That's all you found?"

"Are you saying there's more?" the agent inquired, igniting a burst of laughter from the courtroom and a glare from the judge.

David Sinclair flushed slightly, but spoke evenly enough. "That little a sum. Those few trinkets. You're claiming that Lieutenant Pullman sold secrets to a foreign power for such modest sums? For a few items that aren't even luxuries beyond his income?"

"That's what our investigation shows."

That agent left the witness stand and another arrived to discuss the contents of other data coins found in searches of lockers reserved under various names. All of the lockers had been traced back to Lieutenant Pullman as the agents had followed threads of information from point to point. She explained and showed that these coins contained detailed plots for dead drops, locations where materials could be deposited for later retrieval by foreign agents. There were lists and photos and instructions, all of them cross-referencing each other across one or more coins so that the capture or loss of a single coin couldn't compromise any part of the scheme.

When his turn came to cross-examine, David Sinclair tried his usual question. "Did anything on these coins indicate they belonged to Lieutenant Pullman?"

"Not directly," the NCIS agent replied smoothly, "but comparative analysis of the written contents with material known to have been written by Lieutenant Pullman produced a match with a statistical certainty of ninety-eight percent."

David Sinclair gave Commander Carr a very brief but intense glower as he returned to the defense counsel's table. He knew she'd left that item undiscussed during the agent's testimony so he'd be fooled into bringing it out during the defense's cross-examination.

"This court-martial is closed," Judge Campbell announced. "It will reopen at thirteen hundred in this courtroom."

Paul stayed standing after the judge and members had left the room, once again trying to study Brad Pullman. The physical evidence presented this morning seemed both damning and conclusive, yet Pullman didn't reflect concern. *What has he got up his sleeve? What defense evidence or witness or argument is so potent that Pullman doesn't seem much worried even after being caught with all this Spying For Idiots guidebook stuff?*

"Going anywhere for lunch?"

Paul turned in surprise, seeing Jen standing beside him. "I didn't expect to see you here."

Jen shrugged. "I don't particularly enjoy visiting courtrooms anymore, but I figured you could use a break."

Commander Carr turned as well, halting when she saw Jen. "Lieutenant Shen."

"Commander."

Apparently having finished their conversation, Carr and Jen turned away from each other. Paul resisted a sudden urge to bonk their heads together, reflecting that if the two women had been a little less alike then Jen might actually have liked Commander Carr.

Jen insisted on their hiking to Fogarty's. "You haven't been eating well enough."

"How do you know that?"

"I have my own sources and methods. Order a decent meal and eat it."

"Okay, okay." Paul ate, knowing she was right, but didn't say much for a while, thoughts tumbling through his head as he tried to process everything he'd seen and heard at the court-martial.

Jen canted her head to one side and studied him. "You're awful quiet. What's bugging you?"

"I don't know." Paul frowned, then nodded. "Yeah. That's exactly it. There's all this evidence that Brad Pullman did commit espionage. Hard, physical evidence. It seems plenty convincing to me. But I keep asking myself *why* he would've done that. There's no indication at all that Pullman supports the South Asian Alliance, no indication he dislikes our government or our country or our policies on Earth or in space. No one's claiming he secretly hates the Navy. He doesn't seem to have any strong political beliefs.

All we have is money showing up in bank accounts traceable to Pullman, but we're not talking mega-bucks. Not even remotely. Nice to have money, maybe, but not even as much as he's earning as a junior officer."

"Does he look guilty? I'd expect you to know the difference between scared and guilty."

"He doesn't even look worried!" Paul clenched his fists in frustration. "No matter how much evidence I see that Pullman is guilty, some part of me keeps wondering what his motivation could've been. His real motivation. If I can't figure out *why* he'd do it, I have trouble accepting that he did it."

"Maybe he's an idiot," Jen suggested.

"That doesn't seem to be the case. He's very smart. He could handle his job on the *Michaelson* without breaking much of a sweat."

"Hmmm." Jen pondered the question as she ate. "I see your point. There's a disconnect. People don't go to all the trouble Pullman apparently did just for a little extra pocket change. Smart ones don't, anyway. Maybe he's just irrational deep down."

"Wouldn't that show up in other actions? How could he confine irrationality to just committing espionage?" Paul twisted his mouth. "Besides, if there was the remotest chance of copping an insanity plea I'm sure David would've run with it."

"Let it go, Paul."

"What? Let what go?"

"The sibling rivalry. Your brother doesn't seem nearly as hung up on it as you are."

He felt heat on his face as anger rose. "Jen, you didn't grow up with a guy who made you feel like nothing you ever did could measure up to him."

"No," she stated sarcastically, "I just grew up with a father who expected me to sprout wings and fly if the job called for it. Look, I can't claim to be an expert on you and your brother, but it's past. Let it go."

Paul picked at his food. "It's not that easy."

"Did I say it was easy? Growing up. That's the key phrase. You and I are both old enough that we ought to be able to recognize what wasn't great about our childhoods and accept it as something that was but that doesn't have to drive us for the rest of our lives. Who has a perfect childhood? David had his own pressures to deal with, believe me. Maybe he's oblivious to this day how his attitude grates on you, but so what? Why let him make you crazy?"

He found it hard to come up with an answer and didn't know if that was because it was too complex or if he genuinely didn't have an answer.

Jen touched his hand for just an instant, all the physical contact she could risk while they were in uniform and in public. "If he still wants to lord it over you, letting him get to you just means you're playing along. If he doesn't care about that anymore, then you're just shadowboxing with the past."

"I'll think about it." He saw her skeptical expression. "I said I'd think about it and I will. Because I can't think of anything wrong with what you're saying."

She grinned. "You're going to make a good husband with that attitude."

"It won't apply to every issue, I'm sure. Okay, you're so smart, tell me honestly, do you think Pullman's guilty?"

Jen looked away. "Why does my opinion of this matter?"

"Because you're smart and you know a lot about things."

"Like how it feels to be sitting at that defendant's table wondering if you're going to spend the rest of your life staring at the walls of a small cell?"

"Yeah."

She sat silent for a while and Paul let her think. Finally, she sighed. "I'm torn. I have a very strong and I know to some extent irrational bias against the government because of what happened to me. There are guilty people out there and they need to be caught. I just don't trust the government nearly as much as I used to when it comes to catching the right ones."

Paul nodded in understanding. "I feel some of the same thing. But there's a lot of evidence against Pullman. Not just the circumstantial stuff they tried to get you with, but solid caught-with-his-hands-in-the-cookie-jar stuff."

"I know." Jen played with her food for a moment. "I guess it comes down to my wondering what we don't know. What evidence might be out there that we're not seeing, that might tell another story."

"Jen, even in your case the investigators didn't try to cover up anything."

She surprised him by laughing. "Do you still believe that? All right, I'll admit they didn't actively try to cover up things. But I've been going over those reports in my free time. Don't give me that look. I've got every right to examine something that almost destroyed my life. You think the investigators dug into everything? They didn't. They asked the questions they wanted to ask. They didn't ask things they didn't want to ask. They didn't ask things whose answers they might not want to hear." Jen saw Paul's surprise. "Do you honestly think no one else wondered why that new engineering control system supposedly hadn't had any significant teething troubles? That no one else ever wondered if they ought to check to see if they could find anything contrary to the official 'everything is great' claims about that system?"

"I know your lawyer looked."

"He was a lawyer. A guy who worked hard for me and did what he could, but not someone with the specialized experience or knowledge to smell the right rats and run down the locations of their lairs. I could've done it, but I was safely locked away in pre-trial confinement and under so much stress that I couldn't think straight. Any other people who could've said 'let's question the people who actually developed this system and ask them if everything was really as great as the acquisition people in the Pentagon claim it is' didn't say anything. There were too many people who were willing to go along with what they were told when they were supposed to be investigating. Too many people who avoided looking in the 'wrong' places that might hold answers their bosses didn't want to see."

Paul clenched his fists, remembering the agony he and Jen had gone through during her court-martial. "I'm sorry."

"For what? You've nothing to apologize for. If you'd been an engineer, with the right contacts, you might've found those answers earlier, but I'd be pond scum to complain about that. You asked the questions those other people didn't. For which act of moral courage you're being sent to freeze your butt off on Mars, of course."

"That and a few other acts," Paul noted.

"Yeah. Meanwhile, whoever covered up those problems with that system remains officially unidentified and is probably still fat and happy and going to cocktail parties. All that person did was cause the deaths of lots of sailors and terrible damage to a US Navy warship, but digging that person out and making them pay would embarrass the wrong people."

"And you're afraid that might be happening to Pullman?"

"A bit. I mean, there's no way to independently challenge or verify what the spooks in the intelligence world are telling us. We have to assume they're being honest. But what if they're mistaken? What if their bosses want a conviction and contradictory information is getting swept under the rug so we never even know it exists?"

Paul sat and thought, his food now untouched. Something about Jen's argument about Pullman's court-martial and the events surrounding her court-martial wasn't quite matching up in his mind. But he couldn't figure out what was missing. "I don't know, Jen," he finally said. "I'm going to keep thinking about it."

"Good." She smiled mockingly at him. "What can they do to you? Send you to Mars?"

"There's still Ceres."

"My father's been told that if you get orders to Ceres I'll never speak to him again in this life and whatever comes after, and he knows I mean it."

"Not that he had anything to do with my orders to Mars."

"Oh, no. Of course not." Jen smiled again. "Captain Herdez is also keeping an eye out. She thinks she can block anything but what we've agreed to without tipping off anyone. The next orders you get should be the ones to her ship."

"You talked to Herdez? Willingly?"

"I've done tougher things. Paul Sinclair, if we weren't willing to go to the mat for each other we shouldn't be getting married. True?"

"True." That much, at least, he was certain of.

"When's Pullman going to present his defense?" she asked, switching topics so fast it took Paul a moment to catch up.

"This afternoon, I think. Are you going to watch?"

"No, thanks." Jen didn't quite hide a shudder. "If Pullman's defense is strong, I'm going to be thinking of how weak mine was, and if Pullman's defense is weak, I'm going to be having flashbacks to my own. I'm sure I can trust you to let me know if anything strange happens."

"Right." Paul said it even though he was feeling a bit tired of people trusting him to do things. He couldn't help wondering whether or not Brad Pullman was trusting him to do something.

11

The prosecution turned out to have only one more witness, a pert, young-looking woman named Dr. Vasquez who proved to have an almost disturbing amount of knowledge about falsifying and tampering with station access passes.

Commander Carr held up a card which Paul easily recognized as a station access pass. "Does the witness recognize this?"

The witness blinked. "It's a station access pass."

Carr stepped closer, holding the pass close to the witness. "Can you identify which particular pass this is?"

After peering at it closely, the witness nodded. "That's a pass I examined at the request of NCIS."

"What was the result of your examination?"

"The pass had been tampered with. Very nice work, using some techniques I've seen mainly in foreign intelligence services and some components of foreign origin."

Carr held the pass higher, turning to look at the members' table. "This pass was found in the possession of Lieutenant Pullman when he was arrested. Dr. Vasquez, what was the result of the tampering to which this pass was subjected?"

Vasquez smiled brightly as she recalled her examination of the pass. "It was very nice work, as I said. Didn't I? As you know, a pass reports the presence of a specific individual and in particular reports when that individual has entered certain areas of the station. Well, this pass didn't do that."

"It didn't function?"

"No, no, no! It functioned. It has to function. If station biometrics detect a human presence without a pass they'll sound an alert and locate the person. They can do that, you know. They have to for life support and station stability compensation and things of that nature. Heat emissions, carbon dioxide emissions, oxygen usage, those things and others reveal when a human is present. A person without a pass creates a sort of bubble in which no one appears to exist even though station systems can track a living presence. It instantly alerts the system that someone is wandering around without their pass. This tampered pass instead generated a series of false identities on request. The default was a sort of generic Joe Station Worker whose presence wouldn't seem unusual at any place in the station."

"The tampered pass allowed the bearer to remain undetected, then?"

"No." Dr. Vasquez seemed puzzled by having to elaborate. "Not undetected. Unremarked is a better word. A person will be detected on the station whether they have a pass or not. I just said that, didn't I? The tampered pass created identities which no one would notice. In the sense that they wouldn't care. Think of it as camouflage, allowing the bearer to blend in so that the automated systems and any human observing the read-outs would pay no attention to the person with the pass because that person would seem totally unremarkable."

"I see." Commander Carr turned the pass in her hand, looking down at it. "So the bearer of this pass could go anywhere on the station without sounding any alerts?"

"Yes. Because it also generates false security codes as needed. I don't know where they got the codes— no, wait, of course I know where they got the codes. They got them from the person they gave the pass to, didn't they?"

Carr smiled tightly and nodded. "That's correct, doctor. Station security codes are among the documents on the list of classified materials provided to the South Asian Alliance. Then you believe this pass had to have been tampered with by someone with access to the actual codes?"

"Yes, yes. No other explanation. No one could've guessed those codes. Once they had the codes they could program that pass to allow their agent to access even more areas and more secrets."

"Objection." David Sinclair pointed at the pass. "The witness is speculating."

"No, Your Honor," Carr replied. "The witness is using her expert opinion to explain the tampering done to this pass."

"She has no way of knowing—"

The rap of Judge Campbell's gavel cut off the debate. "I'd like to say something. Dr. Vasquez, do your regard your most recent statements as speculation or as technical explanations?"

Vasquez blinked again. "Technical explanations. It's the only way it could've been done."

"But, Your Honor," David Sinclair protested, "the witness is speculating as to the motivations and plan of action of foreign entities. There's no way she could know that information."

Campbell frowned at him, then at the witness. "Objection overruled. The court believes the witness's statements do not address issues outside her expertise." David Sinclair sat down, shaking his head. "Is defense counsel commenting non-verbally on the quality of the court's ruling?" Judge Campbell asked.

David Sinclair stopped moving his head. "No, Your Honor."

"Good. I'd hate to have to cite a lawyer for contempt. Continue, trial counsel."

Commander Carr held up the pass again, refocusing everyone's attention on the object. "Then, to summarize, this pass created false identities to disguise the movements around the station of whoever carried it, and contained security access codes for every area of the station?"

"Yes," Dr. Vasquez agreed. "Whoever carried that pass could go unnoticed anywhere on the station."

"And leave no record of their access to areas of the station?"

"Uh, not quite. They'd leave a record. A false one. It wouldn't be them, it'd be a record that a Joe Generic Station Worker had been there. Next time he went to the same area, the pass might indicate it was another Joe Generic Station Worker."

Carr nodded, her face grim. "And you have no doubt that these modifications must have been done by foreign intelligence sources?"

"No question. I recognized the techniques used. They're a variation of some spoofing technology our own intelligence agencies developed." Dr. Vasquez suddenly looked perturbed. "I don't think I was supposed to say that."

Judge Campbell nodded. "I feel fairly certain you weren't. The courtroom is ordered to disregard the witness's last statement. Bailiff, check with the fleet security manager on whether or not we need to provide a classified information nondisclosure statement for everyone in this room to sign. No one is to leave the courtroom until we've received an answer to that." She looked back at the witness. "Please continue and please avoid doing that again."

"Yes," Dr. Vasquez replied, nodding rapidly. "I'll try."

Commander Carr once again tried to gain attention, this time by walking right up to the edge of the witness stand. "Dr. Vasquez, who was this station security pass issued to?"

"Oh, that's easy. Lieutenant Junior Grade Bradley Pullman, United States Navy, when he arrived on station to report to his ship."

"Thank you, doctor. No more questions."

David Sinclair stayed seated, staring at the top of the defense table. Paul watched him, wondering what his brother was thinking. *He can't ask his usual questions about whether something can be tied to Pullman. That's Pullman's pass. Is there anything he can say that doesn't just emphasize the trial counsel's points?*

Finally, David Sinclair shook his head. "Defense counsel has no questions for the witness."

Commander Sriracha looked around, then spoke to Dr. Vasquez. "Doctor, don't ships' systems also read those access passes?"

Dr. Vasquez gave more vigorous nods. "Yes. Same system, smaller scale."

"Then this pass would've also let Lieut— excuse me, whoever carried it to move unobtrusively around their own ship as well?"

"In theory," Dr. Vasquez concurred.

The other members frowned at the answer, though Lieutenant Mahris' frown was slightly time-delayed by his need to ensure Captain Nguyen was frowning first. Paul knew what they were thinking as surely as if he could read their minds. *Someone sneaking around a ship. Deceiving their shipmates. Not about some minor criminal stuff but about stealing secrets. That just feels so wrong.*

Commander Sriracha blew out a heavy breath. "Thank you, doctor."

There was a brief delay then, with everyone waiting until the bailiff returned with a data pad containing a classified information nondisclosure statement that everyone had to sign. Paul signed as well, even though he was already sworn never to reveal classified information. And "never" meant exactly that. It was a source of some amusement to him that the nondisclosure agreements had been open-ended since some time in the late twentieth century. Death didn't release someone of their obligation. Neither, presumably, would the death of the universe. A billion years from now Paul would still legally be bound by the agreements he'd signed. Not that he imagined he'd be worried about that by then.

"The prosecution rests," Commander Carr announced after Dr. Vasquez had finally left the courtroom.

"Very well. Does defense counsel wish to make any motions at this time?"

David Sinclair stood. "Defense counsel wishes to move that evidence in this trial based upon classified sources inaccessible to Lieutenant Pullman's defense be ruled inadmissible and the charges based upon that evidence be dismissed."

Judge Campbell, hand in chin once again, shook her head. "Persistence is only a virtue the first few times it doesn't change outcomes, defense counsel. Motion denied. The court's ruling on the evidence will not change."

"Yes, Your Honor. The defense has no other motions."

"Is the defense prepared to begin the presentation of evidence?"

"Yes, Your Honor."

"Then begin."

David Sinclair looked toward the back of the courtroom. Paul looked as well, seeing a portable display screen being brought in by court workers. He'd never seen remote testimony before, though he'd expected to see it in this case. The cost and time commitment required to bring a defense witness up to the station made it likely Pullman's defense would make use of witnesses testifying over live communications links to Earth. "The defense calls as its first witness Dr. Steven Laskey."

There was a pause as the display was positioned at the witness stand and activated. Dr. Laskey was seated in what must be his office on Earth. Paul wondered if the view from the window in the background, blue sky and white clouds, was real or just a projection.

David Sinclair stood before the display, knowing his own image was being transmitted back to a display before the witness. "Dr. Laskey, can you state your qualifications?"

"Certainly." Laskey was a large, broad man with a bluff manner. "I'm a retired US intelligence operative. I spent thirty years working covert operations, either in the field or behind a desk."

"What do you do now?"

"I devote a lot of time to consulting on the subject of covert intelligence operations. I don't disclose secrets, but I do help those trying to portray covert ops to present a realistic picture of what it's like."

"Are you familiar with the evidence against Lieutenant Pullman?"

"Yes. What's been shown me."

"What's been shown you?" David Sinclair inquired.

"I have no way of knowing what's been kept from you, me and the court."

"Objection." Commander Carr was on her feet very quickly. "The witness is speculating without foundation."

"Objection sustained," Judge Campbell replied immediately, cutting off David Sinclair. "Defense counsel and witness are reminded to confine testimony to matters of fact."

David Sinclair looked only mildly contrite. "Yes, Your Honor. Dr. Laskey, are you familiar with the existence of software such as described in the evidence against Lieutenant Pullman?"

Laskey, apparently unabashed by the judge's rebuke, nodded. "Oh, sure."

"What can you tell us about that software?"

"Well..." Laskey shifted position, his expression thoughtful. "The description in the evidence is mostly right as to what it can do, but as to where you can get it, that stuff can be found in a lot of places."

"A lot of places? Not just in the hands of foreign intelligence agencies?"

"Hell, no. Name me a college and give me half an hour and I'll provide you with a list as long as your arm of kids with that software who're using it to steal entertainment files or to try to mess with their grades on the campus mainframe. I understand why no one wants to advertise that this software exists, but the fact is it does exist and anyone who wants it can find it without looking too awful hard."

Paul looked toward Commander Carr, but she was just listening without betraying any emotion.

David Sinclair turned slightly, so he was facing the members' table. "Anyone can get it?" he asked the witness.

"Sure. That's what I said."

"Would you regard the possession of such software as proof on involvement in espionage?"

"No."

David Sinclair let the single word answer hang for a moment before speaking again. "What about the material regarding dead-drops?"

Laskey shrugged. "It's a nice set of plans. But it's the same sort of thing you find in role-playing games these days."

"Role-playing games?"

"Yes. You know, where people pretend they're a spy or exploring some dungeon full of monsters or whatever. I've consulted on some role-playing games and there's easily a half-dozen on the market right now that contain dead-drop planning just like what's in your evidence there. Four of those games include mission planning builders that could've been used to generate exactly what was found on those coins being used as evidence."

"A game? You're saying that games are on the market which contain the same sort of dead-drop instructions as have been entered into evidence against Lieutenant Pullman?"

"Yup."

"That could've been used to create the dead-drop instructions alleged to have been in various locations which are alleged to be tied to Lieutenant Pullman?"

"Yes, sir."

"How could you, as an extremely experienced covert operative, tell the difference between real documents describing real dead-drops to be used in real spying or espionage, and something generated as part of a role-playing game?"

"I can't. I don't think anyone can."

"But," David Sinclair stated, "the plans in evidence do contain real locations on this station."

"Sure they do. That's how people build their missions in the games, by using real-world places and things. It's what the instructions recommend. It gives the players a kick to be playing spy in their own town or office complex or whatever. Go to one of the gaming conventions and you'll find people selling spy mission packages they made in their hometown."

"This physical evidence, then, these data coins with software and instructions for spying, are substantially identical to what any role-playing game devotee would have in their possession?"

Laskey nodded several times slowly. "If anything, I've seen plenty of game missions that're more complex than that stuff."

"Would you regard possession of those coins and the material on them as evidence that someone was engaged in actual espionage activities?"

"That stuff? No. If you did, the FBI would have to haul in tens of thousands of gamers."

"Do these gamers sometimes go overboard? Get so wrapped up in their game that they make use of props which are too realistic?"

"Oh, yeah. That happens. I could tell you stories."

"Are you aware of the circumstances surrounding Lieutenant Pullman's arrest, Dr. Laskey?"

"Yes. In my opinion, based on a lot experience with actually carrying out this stuff, if there was espionage involved there then someone was doing a lousy job of tradecraft."

"Tradecraft?" David Sinclair asked.

"Yes." Laskey shifted position again and grinned broadly. "That's short-hand for how to do spy-stuff right. False identities, for example. We call it tradecraft."

"But you said Lieutenant Pullman's arrest didn't indicate that he knew good tradecraft?"

"Not if he was walking off his ship with classified material on him without ensuring there wasn't anyone waiting to nab him. Careless is the best word you could use."

"Then you wouldn't interpret the circumstances of Lieutenant Pullman's arrest as indicating he was a trained espionage agent?"

"No." Laskey grinned again. "Not unless he flunked his training."

"Thank you, Dr. Laskey. No further questions at this time."

Commander Carr walked briskly toward the witness stand and faced Dr. Laskey's image. Laskey smiled confidently at her as Carr began speaking. "Dr. Laskey, let's review some of your testimony. You said software similar to that found on Lieutenant Pullman can be found from many sources?"

"That's right."

"Can that software carry out any legal functions?"

"Uh..." Laskey frowned. "No. If it carried out legal operations, people could just buy it."

"Then possession of the software constitutes evidence that someone wishes to carry out illegal operations? In other words, that the possessor has criminal intent?"

Laskey frowned again, his expression shifting as he clearly reevaluated the threat posed by Commander Carr. "I can't say that."

"But you can say the software has no legal function and anyone who wants that software could only use it for illegal activities."

"If they used it, yes," Laskey agreed reluctantly.

"And it has been previously established that the software was used during the downloading of classified material onboard USS

Michaelson, Dr. Laskey. Now, these props you spoke of gamers making. How many of them are functional?"

"I beg your pardon?"

"How many of these gaming props can actually function as sophisticated espionage tools?"

Laskey rubbed his chin, thinking. "I can't think of many, but it depends what you mean by sophisticated. You'd be amazed what kids can do."

"By sophisticated I mean a station pass modified to display all-area security clearances and false identities."

"Yeah. That's sophisticated. No. I don't know any gamer who's done that kind of thing. If they do, they keep it quiet."

"Because it's illegal?"

"That sort of thing is, yes."

"Only authorized employees of the US government are allowed to possess such devices?"

"If they're functional, yes."

"And the pass in Lieutenant Pullman's possession was fully functional, wasn't it?"

"I haven't seen it myself."

"Do you have reason to disagree with the testimony of the government's expert witness?"

"No. None that I know of."

Commander Carr nodded, her eyes still fixed on Dr. Laskey, who was watching her closely. "Now, as to your comments regarding the arrest of Lieutenant Pullman. Dr. Laskey, the basic idea behind tradecraft is to successfully accomplish missions and avoid either detection or capture, correct?"

"Yes. That's a good summation."

"Yet agents do get caught. Can you summarize the reasons for that when it happens?"

Laskey sat back, rubbing his chin again. "Ah, let's see. Bad luck. Sometimes there's no other word for it than that. Unexpected developments. Something no one foresaw that kills the mission. Sloppy execution. Somebody gets careless. Betrayal. Sometimes a combination of those things."

Carr took another step closer to the witness stand. "Then you say that sometimes covert agents are captured because they become sloppy? Careless? Over-confident?"

"Objection," David Sinclair declared. "Trial counsel is leading the witness and putting words in his mouth."

Carr held up one hand. "I will restate the question. You are saying then, Dr. Laskey, that covert agents have been known to be sloppy in their tradecraft, so sloppy it results in their capture."

"Yes. Sometimes."

"Then would it be fair to say that failure to execute tradecraft correctly is one of the causes of mission failure for covert operatives?"

"That's another way of saying it, yes."

"And you testified that Lieutenant Pullman did a sloppy job of executing tradecraft."

Laskey regarded Carr for a long moment, then nodded. "Yes, I did."

"Meaning this case would not fall outside of the situations you know of in which covert operations failed."

"Not in the broad sense, no. I won't say the exact circumstances necessarily match."

"Dr. Laskey, you testified about gamers who go to great lengths to pretend at being spies, to role-play as spies. If someone uses real espionage methods, real espionage tools, and is caught with classified material, would you describe them as pretending to be engaged in espionage, or actually engaging in espionage?"

Another pause, then Laskey shrugged. "If it quacks like a duck..."

"Please, Dr. Laskey, could you state your reply clearly for the record?"

"Yes. That is, I'd call that someone committing real espionage, or else so reality-challenged they can't tell the difference between gaming and real life any more. That happens sometimes."

"Thank you, Dr. Laskey. No more questions."

"Does defense counsel wishes to redirect?"

David Sinclair, sitting at the defense table and looking straight ahead, shook his head at the judge's question. The members exchanged looks, but none of them had questions, either. Watching them, Paul couldn't help feeling that they hadn't been impressed by the witness. It wasn't that Laskey didn't obviously know what he was talking about, but rather that his points hadn't held up under Carr's cross-examination.

David Sinclair waited as the judge thanked Dr. Laskey, and as the display was turned off and removed from the courtroom, before speaking again. "The defense calls as its next witness Lieutenant Paul Sinclair."

Paul jerked his head around and stared toward David, who gazed back impassively. Commander Carr was giving Paul a surprised look, but reading his own reaction just tilted her head toward the witness stand.

He stood up and marched to the stand, feeling a slow burn of anger building. David had ambushed him, made him a defense witness with no notice. Would it have killed David to give Paul a heads-up?

Of course, David had to have seen how Commander Carr was consulting Paul at times. Maybe the ambush wasn't all that unreasonable.

Paul sat and was sworn in by the bailiff, then tried not to stare around the courtroom. *The last time I was up on the witness stand was during Captain Wakeman's court-martial. That seems so long ago. At least then I knew it was going to happen and what I was supposed to be testifying about.* His eyes, wandering across the courtroom despite his best efforts, focused on a man and woman sitting near the back among the observers. His mother and father, who'd managed to pull enough strings using their old Navy connections to come up in time for the hastily rescheduled wedding. They must've arrived this morning and come to the court as the surest way to meet up with their sons. *Hi, Mom and Dad! You've arrived on-station in time to watch one of your sons examining your other son on a witness stand in court.*

As David approached the witness stand again, Paul made a point of catching his eye and then looking pointedly toward their parents. David followed the gesture so smoothly it probably wasn't apparent to other watchers, then locked eyes with Paul again and quirked a smile so fast it too was probably lost on anyone else watching.

"Are you Lieutenant Paul Sinclair, currently assigned to duty on the USS *Michaelson*?"

"I am."

"Do you know the defendant?"

Paul finally looked over toward Brad Pullman. "Yes."

"What has been the nature of your relationship to the defendant?"

Paul took a deep breath before answering, giving himself time to order his thoughts. "I knew Lieutenant Pullman in passing at the Academy. We were classmates and had a few classes together. The next time I saw him was when he reported onboard the *Michaelson* for duty."

"How close was your relationship on the ship?"

"We were roommates," Paul noted. "We didn't stand any watches together. We ate a number of meals together on the junior officer meal shift. We attended some training sessions together."

"Would you say you knew Brad Pullman as well as anybody else on the ship did, if not better than anyone else did?"

Paul thought about that, then nodded. "Probably. Yes."

"Did you have conversations? About work and about your personal lives?"

"Yes. Sure." Paul couldn't help remembering the conversation when he'd worn the NCIS wire and hoped that didn't show on his face.

"Did you share confidences?"

"Some, I guess. No deep, dark secrets."

"Do you regard yourself as Lieutenant Pullman's friend?"

Paul gazed at his brother's face. David was looking back with a dispassionate expression, giving no clue as to what answer he wanted. Not that it mattered, because Paul only had one answer he could honestly give. "I think we were friendly, but he wasn't onboard the ship that long and we didn't really have time to become friends as I'd define the term."

If he was disappointed by that answer, David gave no sign. "Then you wouldn't consider yourself a partisan for Lieutenant Pullman?"

It hurt to say it, in a way, because Pullman had been a shipmate. "No. I mean, I want him to get a fair shake. Just like anyone else."

David pointed at Pullman. "Prior to Lieutenant Pullman's arrest, did you ever have cause to suspect him of wrongdoing?"

That was a tough one. Paul had known of the NCIS evidence,

which had led him to suspect Pullman. Sort of. He'd really been sure it'd been Commander Moraine, though. So what was the right, true answer? "No. I personally did not suspect him of wrongdoing."

"Did you ever feel you had cause to doubt his trustworthiness?"

"No."

"Did you ever entrust Lieutenant Pullman with any special obligation, any special responsibility, freely and without worry that he'd fail to meet that responsibility?"

"Do you mean like turning over the watch to him? I did that, yes. He relieved me a few times as junior officer of the deck. I relieved him of the same watch quite a few times."

"Without any qualms?"

"Right."

David looked over at the members, then back at Paul. "During your last period of time together while the ship was out of port, a tragedy occurred. You observed South Asian Alliance ships bombarding an illegal civilian settlement of an asteroid. Did you have any opportunity to observe Lieutenant Pullman during that event?"

Paul thought hard, but nowhere in his memory of the event was any sign of Brad Pullman. "No. I don't remember seeing or hearing from him during the incident."

"Did you see him afterwards?"

"Of course."

"Did you talk about the incident with him?"

"Yes. We all talked about it. One on one and in groups. It was all we could think about."

David nodded slowly. "Did Lieutenant Pullman show any signs of unusual remorse during those conversations?"

"I'm sorry. Unusual? We were all upset."

"As if he carried some burden of guilt."

Paul paused to think again. "No. I can't say I ever noticed that." Out of the corner of his eye, he could see Brad Pullman at the defense table, a thin but firm and still-confident smile visible on his face. *I still haven't noticed that.*

"He didn't act any differently than the rest of you?"

"No. Not that I remember."

"Do you think you'd have remembered if he had?"

Paul looked over at Pullman again. "Yes. I'm sure it would've stood out in my mind."

David began walking back and forth before the witness stand. "Then the officer who knew Lieutenant Pullman best on his ship didn't notice anything amiss with Lieutenant Pullman at any time. He didn't feel any lack of trust or any concerns regarding Lieutenant Pullman. He didn't notice any reactions of Lieutenant Pullman's which differed from those of the other officers on the ship. Is that right, Lieutenant Sinclair?"

Paul nodded. "That's fair to say."

"What was your reaction when Lieutenant Pullman was arrested?"

"Shock. Disbelief."

David came closer, looking directly into Paul's eyes. "You didn't have any premonition? Any ideas based on your own knowledge and perceptions that Lieutenant Pullman might be engaged in such serious and dangerous activity?"

Another tough one. "I'd been advised of NCIS's concerns that someone on the ship might be committing espionage."

David showed a flash of surprise in his eyes, but nowhere else. "Did you believe Lieutenant Pullman was the source of NCIS's concerns?"

"No. I honestly didn't." Paul didn't look at Commander Carr.

Even if she was disappointed in his answer, he wasn't going to lie about it or try to shade the truth.

David held up his hand and began ticking off points on his fingers. "You, Lieutenant Pullman's peer, roommate and fellow worker, saw no suspicious or untoward behavior. You saw no cause to doubt his trustworthiness. You did not believe Lieutenant Pullman constituted a threat. You were, in your own words, shocked by his arrest." Then he paused and look at Paul.

Paul nodded again. "That's right."

"No more questions at this time."

Commander Carr came toward the witness stand. Watching her approach, Paul felt nervous. He'd seen Carr stroll up to a witness stand in just that fashion a score of times, then demolish the witness and shred his or her testimony. He wondered if this was what a wildebeest felt like when it saw a lioness approaching.

"Lieutenant Sinclair, do you have any reason to doubt the manner in which the NCIS investigation was conducted on your ship?"

"I don't know of any, ma'am."

"Do you know of any reason that it might have failed to identify the right source of the espionage on your ship?"

"I don't know of any specific reason."

"You testified that you knew Lieutenant Pullman as well as any officer on the ship. Just how well was that?"

"As I said, ma'am. We'd known each other in passing at the Academy. We'd just started getting to know each other on the ship."

"You weren't friends."

"No, ma'am." Paul knew Pullman was watching him, but he wasn't going to deny that truth.

"Do you believe you know him well?"

Paul inhaled deeply to calm himself, trying to think. "No."

"Not like a brother?"

Paul glanced at Carr sharply, but she betrayed no sign that the question was a dig at the fact the defense counsel was Paul's brother. "No. No, ma'am."

"Did you share personal secrets with Lieutenant Pullman?"

"No, ma'am."

"No band-of-brothers bonding?"

"No. He hadn't been on the ship long enough."

"Did you bond with other officers on the ship in that fashion?"

"Yes, ma'am."

"One? Two?"

"Uh..." Carl Meadows, Kris Denaldo, Jen before they'd become more than friends, Mike Bristol, Commander Sykes, Lieutenant Sindh. Paul's eyes strayed toward Lieutenant Kilgary at the members' table. "At least seven, ma'am."

"Do you believe you know Lieutenant Pullman well?"

"No, ma'am."

"Did you believe you knew him well prior to his arrest?"

"No." He looked over at Brad Pullman. "No, not really, ma'am."

"Thank you, Lieutenant Sinclair. No more questions."

David Sinclair stood. "Defense counsel will redirect. Lieutenant Sinclair, prior to Lieutenant Pullman's arrest would you have gone into battle with him?"

That really wasn't too hard to answer. "Yes."

"Willingly? With no qualms about having Lieutenant Pullman by your side in the face of the enemy?"

Paul stared downward, trying to remember for certain, but knowing that if he'd felt differently he'd surely remember that. "Yes."

"Then wouldn't you say you knew Lieutenant Pullman well enough to trust him by your side in the most extreme circumstances?"

"Yes, I guess you could say that."

"Were there other officers on the ship you trusted less? Officers you'd have wanted by your side in combat less than Lieutenant Pullman?"

He hated to state it publicly, but it was true. He had no idea how Lieutenant Isakov would react in combat, he thought Commander Moraine was a flake and he thought Randy Diego simply never learned nearly enough from his mistakes. Fortunately, he didn't have to name anyone to answer the question. "Yes."

"Yes, you'd rather face combat with Lieutenant Pullman by your side than with some of the other officers on your ship?"

Damn. He didn't want to malign the wardroom of his ship, most of whom were fine officers. But he was under oath. Lying wasn't an option. "Yes. Just a couple." *And please don't ask me to name them.*

"Thank you. No further questions."

Captain Nguyen regarded Paul thoughtfully. "Lieutenant Sinclair, why are you a witness for the defense?"

"I don't know, ma'am."

"You didn't volunteer this time?"

"No, ma'am." So Captain Nguyen did remember Paul from Captain Wakeman's court-martial. He'd wondered about that.

"Would you have volunteered if you'd known some information you thought could help Lieutenant Pullman's defense?"

Paul hesitated. "Yes, ma'am."

"But you know of nothing? No flaws in the NCIS investigation? No errors in the handling of evidence? Nothing?"

"No, ma'am."

He saw the look on her face and realized he'd just inadvertently confirmed Pullman's guilt in Captain Nguyen's eyes. *My damned reputation. Nguyen knows I'd speak up if I knew anything or even felt Pullman was being wronged. But I can't find any basis for saying something like that. God knows I've tried to think of anything like that.*

Commander Sriracha had something of the same look on his face that Captain Nguyen did. "Lieutenant Sinclair, correct me if I'm wrong, but do you make a presumption of competence with every new officer?"

"Excuse me, sir?"

"When a new officer comes aboard, do you give him or her the benefit of the doubt? That they're capable enough and intelligent enough and steadfast enough?"

Paul considered the question for a moment. "Yes, sir, I do. I assume that because they're officers they've proven some abilities. That's just a baseline. Once I get to know them I evaluate them on personal knowledge."

"Do you think that's what you did with Lieutenant Pullman? Give him the benefit of the doubt since you didn't know him all that well?"

Paul looked at Commander Sriracha, then nodded. "Yes, sir. I believe I did." Another nail in Pullman's coffin, perhaps.

Lieutenant Kilgary spoke next. "Lieutenant Sinclair, you testified that you'd have preferred to go into combat alongside Lieutenant Pullman over a couple of other officers in the wardroom of your ship. For the record, do you have any qualms about facing combat with your fellow officers on the USS *Michaelson*?"

"Do you mean qualms in terms of trusting them and counting on them? Not the wardroom as a whole, no. No qualms at all. Not the enlisted onboard, either. When shots were being fired by warships at that asteroid I was frankly worried about the prospect of combat, but I was glad to know who was with me on the *Michaelson* if it came to combat." *Even Garcia, who was always mad but knew his job. Even Commander Kwan, the XO, who doesn't like me but knows his job.*

"Thank you, Lieutenant Sinclair."

Paul almost thanked her back. If he knew anything, he knew Colleen Kilgary had deliberately given him a chance to publicly praise a wardroom of other officers that he might otherwise have been accused of maligning.

"No more questions for this witness, Your Honor."

Judge Campbell dismissed him, and Paul walked back to his chair and sat down, not willing to look over at Brad Pullman again.

David Sinclair stood slowly, leaning for a moment on the defense table before straightening. "The defense rests."

A murmur ran through the courtroom despite the quick rap of Judge Campbell's gavel. Paul stared at his brother. *That was it? Me and that former covert agent? Those were your only witnesses? I thought you were a really good lawyer.*

Judge Campbell glared around the courtroom until it was as quiet as a roomful of humans could manage. "Does the defendant desire to make a statement?"

Pullman started to rise but David Sinclair held out a hand to forestall him. "Your Honor, defense counsel requests a brief recess so that I can confer with my client."

"Very well. How brief?"

"Ten minutes, Your Honor."

"This court is closed. It will reopen in ten minutes' time." Judge Campbell banged her gavel, the bailiff ordered all rise, and the judge and members filed out.

The masters-at-arms came forward to escort Lieutenant Pullman from the courtroom, both David Sinclair and Lieutenant Owings following right behind. Paul watched them go, trying to read the expression on his brother's face.

The moment Lieutenant Pullman and his lawyers were outside the door the room erupted into conversation. Paul turned to Commander Carr. "Ma'am? Do you have any idea why my brother didn't do a better job?"

She gave him an arch look. "Paul, your brother's done the best anyone could do. This isn't a case built on opinions or circumstantial evidence. We've got hard evidence to back up every charge. Your brother's done his best to try to chip away at that evidence by raising doubts in the few ways he could do so. But he can't make the evidence go away. Though he did try even that where he thought there might be a chance."

"You think he's done a good job. Really."

"The best he could," Carr repeated. "Usually, espionage cases are resolved with plea agreements because they always include strong evidence. If they're good cases. Sometimes somebody gets accused of spying or espionage on the basis of flimsy evidence and those cases usually fall apart before the trial stage. But this isn't like that. I never thought we'd get to this point in this trial."

Paul shook his head. "Why doesn't Pullman look worried?"

"You tell me. You know him better than any other officer on your ship does," Carr stated dryly.

He could almost laugh at the reference to his testimony. But not quite. "Do you know why my brother sandbagged me by calling me as witness?"

"You could ask him that yourself, but my opinion is that he didn't sandbag you. Which available character reference did your brother know best? You. Who could he trust to be even-handed and not assume guilt? You. Don't look at me like that. You've got a record, Paul Sinclair. If I'd been in your brother's place I'd have called you as a witness, too."

"But I didn't help Pullman. I might've ensured his conviction."

Commander Carr sighed. "You spotted the members' reactions, eh? Putting you up there was a gamble by the defense. You might well have presented such a strong characterization of Pullman that it would've swayed some of the members. I know that's a weak reed, but I can't imagine what else the defense could do. Good for me, but I prefer a solid fight to a one-sided battle like this." Carr looked past Paul. "Friends of yours?"

He turned and saw his parents. "My mother and father."

"Ah, the Sinclair family reunion proceeds apace."

Paul pretended not to hear her. "Commander Carr, this is Commander Sinclair and... Commander Sinclair."

His mother shook her head. "Retired, both of us."

Commander Carr grinned. "You left the Navy in the hands of your son? He seems to be taking the responsibility seriously." Her smile faded. "I hope you can forgive me for trying to send your future daughter-in-law to prison."

"From what I hear you did your best to make amends when you learned of evidence of her innocence," Paul's mother replied. "I know enough about the legal system to know that's not a given with prosecutors."

"Sadly, no."

"Will you be able to attend the wedding? We're going to be a little short of guests thanks to a sudden change in schedule."

Carr gave Paul a look. "I don't think that'd be wise. There's still hard feelings toward me from the bride. I don't blame her in the least, but I don't think she needs me there to remind her of the past on her wedding day."

Paul nodded. "Commander Carr's right."

"But I hope to see your entire family outside a courtroom someday," Carr added, then she hastily checked the time. "I'd recommend returning to your seats. When Judge Campbell says ten minutes, she means ten minutes and not a second longer."

Lieutenant Pullman was already being escorted back into the courtroom by the masters-at-arms. Precisely ten minutes after the bailiff had called everyone to attention, she ordered them all to rise again. Judge Campbell settled herself, the members took their seats, then the judge eyed David Sinclair. "I'll ask again. Does the defendant desire to make a statement?"

David Sinclair stood and nodded, his face composed. "He does."

The judge gestured to Pullman. "Stand up." As soon as Pullman had come to attention, Judge Campbell began reciting the required instruction. "Lieutenant Pullman, you have the right to make a statement. Included in your right to present evidence are the rights you have to testify under oath, to make an unsworn statement, or to remain silent. If you testify, you may be cross-examined by the trial counsel or questioned by me and the members. If you decide to make an unsworn statement you may not be cross-examined by the trial counsel or questioned by me or the members. You may make an unsworn statement orally or in writing, personally, or through your counsel, or you may use a combination of these ways. If you decide to exercise your right to remain silent, that cannot be held against you in any way. Do you understand your rights?"

Lieutenant Pullman nodded gravely, though his expression remained quietly confident. "Yes, Your Honor."

"Which of these rights do you want to exercise?"

"To make an unsworn statement, in writing, Your Honor."

"Do you wish the statement to be entered into the record, or read?"

"Read, Your Honor."

"By you or your counsel?"

"My counsel, Your Honor."

"Very well. Does defense counsel have the defendant's statement?"

David Sinclair nodded. "I do, Your Honor."

"Then proceed with the reading whenever you're ready."

"Thank you, Your Honor." David Sinclair looked down at his data pad and began reading in a voice that didn't seem loud but carried clearly through the courtroom. He didn't put obvious emotion into his reading, but still managed to convey feeling. Paul couldn't help being impressed by the presentation, and realized Pullman had wisely chosen to have his statement read by a professional orator to make it sound better.

"Statement of Lieutenant Bradley Pullman, United States Navy.

"I am a military officer. I have already dedicated years of my life to the service of my country, and I hope to dedicate many more years to such service. I have agreed to place my life on the line in the service of my country. I have labored under harsh and demanding conditions in the service of my country. Now I am accused of committing crimes against that country.

"No one should believe these charges. I may have erred in various ways, through carelessness or over-eagerness or perhaps excessive dedication to getting the job done. Those are the sort of 'crimes' all junior officers commit at one time or another. They lead to mistakes, they lead to errors, but such mistakes and errors come from a desire to get the job done.

"I should have told my shipmates I enjoyed building complex role-playing scenarios. It's easy to understand how such scenarios could be confused with real mischief. But my failure to tell them that doesn't mean it isn't true.

"Many people supplement their incomes or just enjoy the thrill of wagering on professional sports. They can't openly acknowledge the source of such money, but that doesn't mean they acquire it from foreign powers.

"I ask you to accept my plea of not guilty to all charges and specifications. I do not believe the government has proven these charges. I do not believe the government has given you grounds to believe them when more plausible explanations exist. I do not believe my past service to my country will be ignored and that I will be cast aside in this fashion.

"Very Respectfully, Bradley Pullman, Lieutenant, United States Navy."

David Sinclair sat down, leaving a period of silence in his wake. Paul assumed everyone else was doing what he was, trying to work their way through Pullman's statement for what it said and didn't say. He had to admit that David's reading of the statement had given it much more power than if an untrained speaker had recited the document. But Paul was still puzzling over the statement when Judge Campbell pointed her gavel at Commander Carr. "Is trial counsel prepared for closing argument?"

Carr stood. "I am, Your Honor."

"Then let's get on with it."

Commander Carr paced slowly forward, her steps deliberate, the slow steadiness of her motions drawing attention to her. "Captain Nguyen. Members of the court. This is a simple case." She turned, raised and extended her arm, and then pointed at Lieutenant Pullman with the same slow deliberation. "Lieutenant Pullman was caught off of his ship with two data coins in his possession. The coins were carefully concealed on Lieutenant Pullman's person. One held illegal software whose sole purpose is to bypass security safeguards. The other held classified information downloaded without authorization that day from the systems on Lieutenant Pullman's ship. There's nothing inadvertent or careless about that. It can only reflect deliberate and carefully carried-out actions. Actions which violate regulations known to Lieutenant Pullman.

"Actions which may well have led to the deaths of civilians. Because other documents stolen from Lieutenant Pullman's ship are known to have been delivered to a foreign power. Documents which gave that foreign power inside knowledge. Knowledge which that foreign power may well have used to plan a massacre."

Carr's arm held steady, her forefinger still pointing at Pullman. "Lieutenant Pullman's possessions are known to have contained concealed instructions for committing espionage. The defense tried to explain such instructions in terms of games. This was not a game. There is nothing in that material which indicates it is anything other than actual instructions for successfully delivering stolen classified material to a foreign power.

"Lieutenant Pullman had in his possession a station pass which had been altered in a very sophisticated fashion. Even the defense's own witness had to concede that this was a real tool of espionage, not a prop for someone playing at espionage."

Paul was torn between staring at Pullman, whose face reflected quiet determination and who was occasionally shaking his head as Carr spoke, and staring at Carr's arm, which remained extended and leveled at Pullman like a rifle. The arm wasn't even quivering despite being held in that position for so long, making her gesture seem all the more powerful.

Commander Carr kept speaking. "Lieutenant Pullman has money whose source he can't explain. Money hidden in accounts under false names with the help of the finest money-laundering schemes known to the underground financial community. Where did Lieutenant Pullman learn such skills, and why did he go to such lengths to hide that money, and why has the defense not presented proof that it came from illegal betting on professional sports?

"Lieutenant Pullman cannot deny he was caught with the tools of espionage and the fruits of espionage. The evidence is overwhelming and undeniable. Lieutenant Pullman, for reasons still known only to himself, chose to betray his uniform, his shipmates, and his country. He sold the secrets of our country, even those protecting his own shipmates, for money. There aren't words strong enough to describe the depth of his betrayal or the damage his actions have done to his country. He should be convicted on all charges and all specifications so his cancerous presence can be eliminated from the proud ranks of the United States Navy."

Carr finally lowered her arm, still moving it slowly and steadily. Only when it had dropped all the way down did Commander Carr finally walk back to the trial counsel table and sit down.

Judge Campbell moved her gavel to point it at the defense table. "Is defense counsel prepared to present closing argument?"

"Yes, Your Honor." Paul had forgotten to look over at David to see how he'd reacted to Carr's speech, but now David Sinclair looked somber. He stood next to the defense table, not moving, but speaking in that same compelling voice he'd used to read Pullman's statement. "May it please the court, the defense holds that the government's evidence is not conclusive. There are other explanations for why Lieutenant Pullman had those materials. There are other explanations for how classified material came to be in the hands of a foreign entity. In some cases, no incontrovertible proof exists that the evidence belonged to Lieutenant Pullman. In other cases, others had access to the same material.

"It is not enough that the evidence could be read to indicate that Lieutenant Pullman *could be* guilty. No. For Lieutenant Pullman isn't just anyone accused of a crime. He is a man who has given service to his country, who has worn the same uniform as you, who has declared by his words and actions a willingness to lay down his life for his country. How can you convict such a man because he *could be* guilty? Doesn't his service require, doesn't his service *demand*, a higher level of certainty than that?

"I know the demands which military service places upon a man or woman and a family. My own parents are retired officers. The military should be demanding, for its responsibilities are great, but it must not be blind to the possibility of human error, of mistakes of judgment which do not rise to the level of criminal action.

"The defense has offered alternative explanations for the evidence against Lieutenant Pullman. Lieutenant Pullman, a man trusted by his shipmates with their lives and entrusted by the US Navy with the gravest of responsibilities on a warship, has declared himself innocent of these charges. I ask you to judge him based upon his own words and based upon your common bond. Lieutenant Pullman is one of you. His declaration of innocence is made to his fellow officers. Lieutenant Pullman should be found innocent as to all charges and specifications."

David Sinclair sat down in the silence which followed the end of his speech.

Paul, who'd watched his brother while he talked, finally looked over at the members. If he could read faces and postures at all, he saw doom for Lieutenant Pullman there. *Nice speech, David. Maybe, as Commander Carr says, the best you could do under the circumstances.* Paul studied Brad Pullman, who still seemed as calmly confident as if he were assuming the watch on the bridge of the *Michaelson*. *I've been waiting for the other shoe to drop in Brad Pullman's defense, waiting for whatever was giving Pullman that confidence, but I still haven't seen or heard it and now the case is going to the members. What's going on?*

Judge Campbell's gavel moved again, coming to rest pointed at the members' table this time. "Captain Nguyen, the members may begin their deliberations. The court-martial is closed, and will reconvene tomorrow morning at 1000 in this courtroom."

"All rise!"

Paul lost sight of Pullman as everyone stood for the judge and the members to leave, then got only a brief glimpse of Pullman's back as he was led out of the courtroom and back to the brig by the masters-at-arms. Commander Carr stayed standing, looking down at her table and idly tapping her data pad with one finger. "Ma'am?" She looked up and over at Paul in response. "How did you do that thing with your arm?"

Commander Carr looked briefly amused. "Pull-ups and push-ups and weight training."

"That was a very good speech, ma'am."

"Thank you." Something seemed to be bothering her, though Paul couldn't tell what. Then Commander Carr looked up again, toward the defense table.

Paul automatically looked that way himself. David was standing as well and looking straight at them. No. Not at them. At Commander Carr. Their eyes had met and some sort of unspoken message was being exchanged.

Carr made a warding gesture toward Paul. "I'm sorry. I need to take care of something." She hesitated. "Will I be able to contact you later if I need to?"

"Yes, ma'am. Just put a call through my data pad. That's always on. It's required."

"Good. Perhaps I'll talk to you later, then."

Recognizing the dismissal, Paul started walking out of the courtroom. At the entrance, he looked back. David Sinclair and Commander Carr had met about midway between their desks and were speaking to each other, Lieutenant Owings standing slightly to the side and listening to both. *What the hell's going on?*

12

About an hour later, after he'd already returned to his ship, Paul's data pad buzzed urgently. "Paul, this is Alex Carr. I'd like you to see Pullman in the brig. As soon as possible."

"What? The defense isn't going to want me to see Pullman."

"Actually, they do." Carr's tone gave no clue as to what was going on.

"Why?"

"I'd rather not say."

"Will Pullman's lawyers tell me if I ask them?"

"I don't know. But I assure you, they want you to talk to their client."

"This afternoon? Tonight?"

"Preferably this afternoon. As soon as it's convenient for you."

Paul waited, but Commander Carr gave no hint of other information. "Yes, ma'am. Is there anything I'm supposed to do or say?"

"Just say what you feel is right."

"I'm not sure what that is, ma'am."

"You will." Carr paused before speaking again. "Trust me."

"Aye, aye, ma'am." Paul rubbed his forehead and leaned forward a little so he could rest his elbows on his desk. His desk. For another couple of days. Most of his stuff had already been moved off of the ship and out of the stateroom which had been his cramped and crowded home for the last three years. Lieutenant Shwartz had officially relieved Paul as Combat Information Center officer and had taken over all of the ship's legal officer's duties except for the observation of Pullman's court-martial. Captain Agee, now his commanding officer, had listened carefully to Paul's report when he got back to the ship and reconfirmed Paul's orders to be there when the verdict was announced. Now, no longer responsible for his former duties and with the court-martial closed until tomorrow morning, Paul had no other tasks demanding completion.

Since I don't seem to have anything else to do, I guess I ought to follow Commander Carr's instructions. Paul stood up, grinning for a moment. *I don't have anything else to do. How long has it been since I could say that? At least since I reported to this ship!*

The brig watch recognized him again, not bothering to hide their surprise. They checked the access list twice and then phoned Pullman's lawyers for clearance before allowing Paul to sign in. Paul was escorted into the visiting room, bare but for the two chairs facing each other in the center of the room, and left there to await Pullman's arrival.

Paul sat, trying to hide his discomfort and uncertainty. What should he say to a man whom he was certain would be convicted tomorrow? Should he just flat out ask Pullman why he didn't seem more worried?

Pullman entered the room, saw Paul, grinned and started to walk toward him.

Paul stared at that confident smile. He remembered how Jen had reacted when she'd been in the brig, accused of crimes she hadn't committed. Jen, a tower of personal strength who'd nonetheless wavered under her imprisonment, showing her anguish at being charged with committing horrible crimes, her confusion at being singled out by authorities for something she hadn't done. Yet here was Brad Pullman, still radiating confidence despite the crimes he'd been charged with and in the face of all the evidence that had been marshaled against him. Without any halfway plausible alternative or any missing element that could really explain that evidence in any other way.

It flashed into Paul's mind then. That's what was different between this case and the one brought against Jen. He'd known something was missing from that evidence against Jen. Other people he'd talked to had known it, too. The engineering system in Jen's case supposedly hadn't had significant problems while being developed, where experience argued that *all* systems had such problems. Lots of people wondered about that, not just Paul. It had taken a while to find what he needed, but he and others had known what *ought* to be there and wasn't.

But he couldn't think of anything missing from Pullman's case. Anything that ought to be there and wasn't. Anything that would explain Pullman's attitude, why he'd still be confident. Except the words Ensign Taylor had spoken when Pullman was arrested. *He figured he was too smart to play by the rules... Pullman figured he was too smart to get caught.*

And too smart to be convicted.

The last shreds of doubt vanished from Paul's mind and he knew with absolute certainty. "You did it."

Pullman's smile finally wavered and he paused in mid-step. "What?"

"You son of a bitch. You bastard. You did everything they said you did."

"Paul, what the—"

"Didn't you care? You were out there with us, watching those people die on that damned asteroid, people dying because you'd sold our secrets to someone. Didn't it hurt even a little bit to watch them dying?"

Pullman had paled, his smile completely gone now. "I didn't—"

"But you still don't care. You just did it because you believed you were smarter than us. We trusted you. Out there on the ship we personally trusted you with our *lives*. And you, you lying bastard, you sold our lives. You didn't even do it because you believed you were right. You didn't even really do it for money. You sold us and your word of honor because you think it's some kind of game, don't you? A game with rules *you* don't have to play by. A game you're still not worried about losing because you think you're too smart." Paul turned away. "Guess what? Game's over, and you lost. Go to hell and stay there." He walked out, not looking back.

Everyone waited in the courtroom as 1000 came and went. Paul kept looking around, wondering where Commander Carr, David and Lieutenant Owings were. Had some last-minute evidence shown up, some proof that knocked the entire case against Pullman on its head? Paul couldn't believe such a thing could be possible. But where were the lawyers?

Pullman himself was sitting at the defense table, staring at the surface of the table without ever raising his head, finally looking like his world had caved in.

Fifteen minutes after the scheduled start of the court-martial, the door to the judge's chambers opened and the lawyers came out. Commander Carr walked briskly to the trial counsel table, apparently oblivious to the stares and murmurs of conversation her appearance had generated. David and Lieutenant Owings walked a bit more slowly to the defense table and sat down, David whispering something to Lieutenant Pullman that drew a single nod in response.

"All rise." Judge Campbell entered, looking annoyed. The members came in as well, taking their seats. "You may be seated," the judge advised everyone else. "Captain Nguyen, I regret to state that you and the other members in this court-martial may not be rendering the verdicts I know you have worked hard to reach. At the proverbial last minute the defendant has reached a plea agreement with the government." A burst of talking erupted, earning a loud rap from Judge Campbell's gavel. "Silence in the courtroom. Lieutenant Pullman, please approach the bench." Brad Pullman stood up and marched to stand in front of the judge's bench. "Bailiff, provide the defendant with a copy of the Appellate Exhibit." The bailiff walked over to Pullman and handed him a data pad.

Judge Campbell held up a data pad of her own. "Lieutenant Pullman, I have here the Appellate Exhibit which is part of a plea agreement between you and Commander, United States Space Forces, the convening authority. Is that your signature on the document and did you read this part of the agreement?"

Lieutenant Pullman looked down at his data pad for a moment. "Yes, Your Honor," Pullman replied in a flat voice.

"Did you also read and sign the second Appellate Exhibit shown there, which is also part of this agreement?"

"Yes, Your Honor."

"Do you believe that you fully understand the agreement?"

"Yes, Your Honor."

"I don't know, and I don't want to know at this time, the sentence limitation you have agreed to. However, I want you to read that part of the agreement over to yourself once again." Judge Campbell waited while Pullman read. "Without saying what it is, do you understand the maximum punishment the convening authority may approve?"

"Yes, Your Honor."

"In this plea agreement, you agree to enter a plea of guilty to the charges and specifications, and to cooperate fully and to the best of your ability with government representatives who will question you regarding the scope, nature and all other aspects of your espionage activities. In return, the convening authority agrees to approve no sentence greater than that in the second Appellate Exhibit, which you have just read. In addition, you have agreed that if you fail to abide by your promise to provide full and complete cooperation to government representatives questioning you regarding your espionage activities, it will absolve the government of any obligation to limit your sentence. Do you understand that?"

"Yes, Your Honor."

"Is this agreement contained in these two Appellate Exhibits the entire agreement between you and the convening authority? In other words, is it correct that there are no other agreements or promises in this case?"

"Yes, Your Honor."

Judge Campbell looked from Commander Carr to David Sinclair. "Do counsels agree?"

"Yes, Your Honor," they both replied.

"Lieutenant Pullman, do you understand your plea agreement?"

"Yes, Your Honor."

Campbell looked at David Sinclair. "Did the offer to make a plea agreement originate with the defense?"

"Yes, Your Honor," David replied.

The judge focused back on Pullman. "Lieutenant Pullman, are you entering this agreement freely and voluntarily?"

"Yes, Your Honor."

"Has anyone tried to force you to enter into this agreement?"

"No, Your Honor."

"Have you fully discussed this agreement with your counsel, and are you satisfied that his advice is in your best interest?"

"Yes, Your Honor."

"Do you have any questions about your plea of guilty, your plea agreement, or anything we have discussed?"

"No, Your Honor."

"Do you still want to plead guilty at this time?"

"Yes, Your Honor."

"I find that the accused has knowingly, intelligently, and consciously waived his rights against self-incrimination; that the accused is, in fact, guilty; and his plea of guilty is accepted. Lieutenant Bradley Pullman, in accordance with your pleas of guilty, this court-martial finds you of all charges and specifications: Guilty.

"This court sentences you to forfeiture of all pay and allowances, dismissal from the service, and to confinement for life.

"This court-martial is closed."

Pullman was led out of the courtroom for the last time. Paul stared at the deck, wondering why he didn't feel any sense of triumph.

Waste. That's how Taylor described what was going to happen to Commander Moraine. Maybe that's how I feel about Pullman. What a waste.

"Hey, Paul." Colleen Kilgary had left the other members, who were talking among themselves, to come over to where Paul stood. "Did you have to waste my time like that?"

"It's not my fault."

"I know. Why'd he wait so long to do the inevitable?"

"I have no idea. Did I read you guys right? Was Pullman toast?"

Kilgary nodded. "Burnt toast. We only had to talk about it for a few minutes. We would've found him guilty of everything." She reached out and slapped his shoulder. "See you at the wedding."

"Thanks." Commander Carr and David Sinclair were speaking again, Paul saw. They shook hands, then Carr came back toward Paul. "That was a surprise," he remarked to her.

"It's what we wanted." She looked around the room. "Come on. There's a few things I want to discuss with you in private."

Paul followed as Carr walked quickly to her office, then invited him in and sat down. She was hardly seated before she yawned. "Sorry. Late night."

"Working on a plea agreement, I take it?"

"Yeah." She stretched and yawned again, then noticed a message light blinking. Calling up the message, she shook her head. "My, my. Guess who's disappeared."

"I can't imagine."

"Pullman's father." She smiled wryly. "Some agents showed up to question him but he was gone. Oh, yeah, didn't I tell you? It looks like Pullman's father was the ring master for a little spy circus."

Paul couldn't think of any appropriate comments. "Nice family," he finally said.

"Yeah. The sort of family that puts the 'dys' into 'functional.'"

"I wondered where Pullman's father got the money to hire a private lawyer and send him up here."

Carr leaned back. "You weren't the only one. Counterintelligence agents have been nosing around him for a while now. Our best guess is that Pullman's daddy spent some of his ill-gotten gains in an attempt to keep anyone from learning for sure that Pullman had family ties to the espionage business. With any luck, former-Lieutenant Pullman will sing loudly and clearly enough that we'll be able to roll up any other members of the spy ring. We owe you for helping bring that about. I called you here to thank you for that."

"Huh?" Paul shifted uncomfortably. "What do you mean? I didn't have anything to do with that plea agreement."

"Oh, yes, you did." Reading Paul's reaction, Carr leaned forward again, speaking earnestly. "I knew the members of the court were ready to unanimously vote to convict. Pullman's lawyers could tell the same thing. Your brother wanted to get the best deal he could for his client. That's his job. But Pullman wouldn't consider copping a plea, even when conviction was a certainty and the possibility of him facing a death penalty was raised. He kept pretending he'd somehow get acquitted. That's why I asked you to go talk to him and that's why Pullman's lawyers agreed to let you see him."

Paul tried not to let show how horrified he felt. "You all used me? To pressure Pullman into agreeing to a guilty plea?"

"Yes! Pullman was still in deep denial, thinking he'd fooled enough people to get out of the trial without being convicted. I knew we'd convinced you of his guilt, and if you made it clear to Pullman you weren't fooled anymore it'd make Pullman crack. Because he'd realize he'd lost someone he was sure would always buy his story. That'd mean he couldn't keep on believing he could fool everyone else."

"Why didn't you tell me?"

"Because you're a lousy actor, Paul Sinclair! And very good at speaking well when it's spontaneous and sincere. I wanted you to speak your mind to Pullman, let him know he'd lost even you, and apparently you did. I'm grateful, and Pullman's lawyers are grateful. Pullman ought to be grateful. What's the matter?"

Paul made a frustrated gesture. "I didn't know. I could have at least been told I was being used against Pullman—"

"Whoa." Carr held up both hands and spoke slowly. "You do know what this plea agreement is, don't you? It's the closest thing to a win/ win this case could have. Speaking purely personally, I'd have liked to see Pullman dangling by the neck from the highest tree in North America for what he did. But we needed to know a lot of things only Pullman knows. How much information did he sell? Exactly what information? Who else was involved? What methods did he use? How many buyers were there, who were they and how did they operate? To get that, we need Pullman to talk to us.

"Now, his lawyers could tell Pullman was headed for a life without parole sentence at best. They wanted to get him something better if they could. That's why they came to me after the court-martial was closed for the members' deliberations. Pullman's lawyers got him the best deal possible. Pullman goes to jail for a long time, but if Pullman spills his guts to our debriefers then he'll be eligible for parole in thirty or forty years. That's what the convening authority agreed to, and as you know convening authorities can't make a sentence more severe but they can lessen a sentence. I still got a conviction, though, and our intelligence people get the information they need on what was compromised and how to prevent us losing more classified material. Everybody wins. Granted, Pullman's part of the win still means he'll spend a long time in prison, but he won't have to die of old age there if he cooperates as he promised."

"And all I had to do to help make this happen," Paul added, "was follow the same sort of methods that Pullman used."

Carr looked surprised. "You don't mean that, do you? Pullman chose to spy on all of his fellow officers and his country. He did it for ego and for money. You were reluctantly convinced to spy on two other officers because you'd seen convincing evidence one of them was engaged in serious wrongdoing. You did it because of your sense of duty. There's no comparison. You did good and you did right."

"Then why don't I feel like a hero?"

"Do you think anyone else does?" Carr leaned back again, sighing. "This isn't fun work and it isn't pleasant. It has to be done, so somebody has to do it. But at the end of the day it can leave you feeling like hell. You did a good thing, an important thing. Odds are, only a few people will ever know what you did to help this case along, and I'll bet that doesn't bother you."

"No, it doesn't."

"You're lucky to have someone like Ms. Shen who you can confide in and who'll stick with you. Don't lose her. I mean that. If I know anything about people I know she won't leave you unless you give her real good reason to leave."

"I'd never do anything like that!" Paul protested.

"Not premeditated, no, I'm sure you wouldn't. Paul, half the cases I deal with involve people who never intended doing anything wrong when they started out. It just sort of happened to them and before they knew it they were in deep. That applies to marriages breaking down, too. Do you think anyone plans to fall in love with another man or woman when they're already married? Some do. Most don't. They start out dipping a toe into bad acts and end up swimming in the deep end." She slapped her desk for emphasis. "I've talked to JAGs who've served on Mars. They handle a lot of long-distance divorces. A word to the wise, Paul. Don't let your marriage become one of the casualties on Mars."

"I'll remember that."

Alex Carr rose and held out her hand. "It's been good working with you and knowing you, Paul. Good luck until we meet again."

He shook her hand, feeling the strength of her grip as he realized that despite all the time they'd worked together this was one of the few times he and Commander Carr had actually had any kind of physical contact. "Do you think we'll meet again?"

"Yes. I've got a real strong feeling this isn't the last case we'll see together."

Paul stepped back and on impulse saluted. "Thanks, ma'am."

Carr returned the salute with one of her quick smiles. "Thank *you*. Take care of that woman of yours."

"Yes, ma'am."

Paul found his brother back at the hotel. David greeted him with a rueful smile. "You were right about that military lawyer, little bro. Alex Carr is a real fireball." His smile faded to a look of approval. "You won this one."

"It wasn't about me winning."

"But you don't mind me being on the losing side, do you? Hey, you beat me. It happens."

"David, it really wasn't about beating you. I wish this hadn't had to happen. I'm glad the espionage has been stopped, but I wish Pullman had never started doing it."

His brother nodded. "Yeah. Ugly stuff. Cases like this don't generate a lot of happily-ever-after endings. I wanted to tell you something, though. I've got to admit, from what I've seen up here, you've really got your stuff together. Very impressive, little bro."

Paul considered his brother, then nodded. "Thanks."

"I can't imagine driving that ship of yours around. You really do that?"

"Yeah, I really do that. Did that, rather. I detach the day after tomorrow and I won't be driving any ships again for a while."

"Oh, yeah. You'll have to tell me what Mars is like. As for Alex Carr, try to keep her up here, okay? I don't need challengers like that practicing law in my city."

"I don't think I'll have much control over that. When are you going back?"

"Two days. I couldn't book a seat on an earlier shuttle because of uncertainty about the end of the trial. Why?"

Paul hesitated. *Get over it.* "You know Jen and I had to move up the wedding on very short notice. It's tomorrow. Most of the guests and members of the wedding couldn't make it."

"Yeah. Raw deal. I'll be there, though."

"I know. The point is... I'm looking for a best man."

David frowned. "Are you asking me?"

"Yeah, I'm asking you."

"Well, damn it all." David made a fist and punched the nearest wall. "I was thinking it was past time we stopped acting like kids with grudges and was planning on making the first move. You beat me again."

"I'll try not to make a habit of it."

"What, you think you have to go easy on me?"

"No."

"Good." David smiled broadly. "To properly answer the question put to me, I'll be proud to be your best man. I understand this Jen of yours makes even an Alex Carr pale by comparison."

"Now that you mention it, she does."

Jen had, to Paul's surprise, chosen to wear a white wedding dress instead of a dress uniform. She looked like a dream come true, he thought, as she came down the short aisle of the Interdenominational Religious Worship Facility on the arm of Captain Kay Shen, and never mind that the phrase was a cliché because that was how he thought she looked. Captain Shen was staring straight ahead as he walked. Jen had discussed not inviting her father to the wedding, but Paul had talked her into it, insisting she'd regret it for the rest of her life otherwise. In the end, the argument that cinched it was that watching his daughter marry Paul would be a worse ordeal for Captain Shen than missing the wedding.

But Captain Shen managed to refrain from yelling out objections and the ceremony went off without a hitch.

There wasn't room for a sword arch outside the chapel, which was just as well considering that officers didn't carry their ceremonial swords along into space, and considering that Jen had threatened to murder anyone who carried out the traditional slap on the butt of the bride with the flat of one of the swords. Everyone held up small party favors which broadcast holographic images of butterflies flitting around the couple. Paul flinched as he discovered that the realistic images of insects had a tendency to appear to fly straight at

JACK CAMPBELL

his face, which was particularly disconcerting after spending three years in pretty much insect-free environments. Jen rolled her eyes at the butterfly display but laughed and chatted with friends who crowded around them.

"Paul! Congratulations!" Pam Connally was there, hugging him again. Paul stared at her, then at Jen.

Jen smiled back. "I just had to invite an 'old friend' of yours to the wedding, Paul."

"How did you—?"

"I knew where she worked." Jen and Pam exchanged high-fives.

Paul grinned, watching the two women talk. *How do you like that? It looks like Jen and Pam Connally are going to be friends. Maybe having a cop for a friend will help keep Jen out of trouble while I'm gone.*

Paul's mother stepped close, eyeing him suspiciously. "What's going on?"

"Excuse me?"

"Why are you and David getting along? What are you two up to?"

"Oh, that. We just wanted to see if we could freak you out."

"You're succeeding." His mother sighed. "I've hardly seen you for three years and now you'll be gone for another four."

"You've got a new daughter-in-law who'll be a bit closer."

"That's true. What a woman you chose!"

"She reminded me of you."

His mother laughed. "That's a compliment even if you didn't intend it that way! Be careful and try to stay out of trouble."

Paul smiled reassuringly. "I have no intention of getting into any kind of trouble on Mars, Mom."

"Sure you don't. Jen, did you hear that?" Jen stepped closer and nodded. "Do you believe it?"

336

"That Paul will stay out of trouble? No. Not a word."

"Good," Paul's mother replied. "I'm glad you're not entering into this marriage with any illusions. As for you, Paul, remember that Mars is full of two kinds of people: idealists who want nothing more than to conquer a new world for the rest of humanity, and malcontents who want nothing more than to get away from the rest of humanity. *Try* not to get caught in the middle."

"I promise."

The next day, Paul stood on the dock, gazing at the quarterdeck of the USS *Michaelson*. He'd stood in much the same place three years ago when he'd first laid eyes on the ship.

"What're you thinking?" Jen asked.

"That I had no idea what was waiting for me on that ship when I crossed that quarterdeck for the first time. If I'd known everything that was going to happen I would've run screaming in the other direction."

Jen gave him a sharp look. "*I* was one of the things waiting for you on that ship, Mr. Sinclair."

"I remember. You scared the hell out of me."

"I did not."

"Everything scared the hell out of me." He smiled despite the sometimes painful memories. "I guess I learned a few things."

"You done good, Paul. Now, stop thinking about the past." Jen waved Paul onward. "Go ahead."

He gazed back at her. "You don't want to come aboard? Are you sure?"

"Yeah. You don't need me tagging along while you do your final check-out, and I figure you've got the right to make any farewells alone. Besides, there's nobody left on the *Merry Mike* that I know anymore. I'll catch you back at our quarters."

Paul smiled at the thought of "our quarters." That was official now, though they'd be shoehorned together into Jen's single-person compartment. "I be back as soon as I can."

"Damn straight. We've only got forty-eight hours for a honeymoon and I intend making the most of every minute. I'm trusting you not to get involved in any trouble for the short period of time before you get back to me. Can I count on that?"

"Me? Get involved in trouble?"

"Yeah, you." She leveled an index finger at him, then smiled back. "I love you, lieutenant."

"And I love you, lieutenant."

She laughed and headed away as Paul turned to board the *Michaelson.*

He raced through the few remaining items on his check-off list. When he got to the item requiring him to see his department head, Paul used a trick Ensign Taylor had taught him to make the block turn green even though he hadn't actually seen Commander Moraine. He wasn't in the mood to deal with her this morning.

Commander Kwan, busy with something else, barely looked at Paul as he tapped Paul's data pad and sent him on his way. No love lost there.

Last but certainly not least, Captain Agee greeted Paul with a smile, then explained that since he'd only been aboard a short time, far too short a time to independently evaluate Paul, he was giving him a less than ninety days' fitness report, thereby extending the marks on the fitness report Captains Hayes had given Paul to cover the rest of his time on the ship. Barely suppressing an urge to dance with joy over avoiding a fitness report with marks set by Kwan and Moraine, Paul shook Agee's hand as he wished Paul the best.

Formally speaking, that was it. Paul looked down at his data pad. The little icon in the corner which had declared him to be a member of the crew of the USS *Michaelson*, and which had been ever-present for the last three years, was gone now. It was time to do his personal goodbyes.

Ensign Taylor high-fived Paul, offering a fond farewell and some final obscene advice for keeping Jen happy. Paul wandered through officers' country, meeting and greeting the officers he'd spent varying amounts of time knowing and working with. He could remember when each of them had come aboard, and every one of them had known him ever since they came aboard. Lieutenant Isakov was too busy to talk, naturally, and Commander Smithe was nowhere to be seen, also naturally, but the others offered sincere goodbyes. Even Commander Destin, who'd never quite gotten over Lieutenant Silver's court-martial, thanked Paul for the chance to work with him.

Having paid his respects to his shipmates in the wardroom, Paul made his final rounds of the USS *Michaelson*. Senior Chief Imari and some of Paul's sailors were in Combat and offered to-all-appearances genuine regrets at his departure. Paul didn't linger, thinking the compartment he'd once held as the center of his responsibilities on the ship already felt alien now that it no longer belonged to him but to Lieutenant Junior Grade Shwartz. He hoped the new CIC officer would do a good job of looking out for the sailors he'd once commanded.

Paul stood alone on the bridge for a few moments, thinking of the many hours he'd spent there, most of them uneventful but some full of tension and danger. He looked toward the corner where he'd been located when Captain Wakeman had mistakenly ordered the destruction of an unarmed ship. It was hard to remember the brand-new ensign he'd been then, unsure and inexperienced.

Forward Engineering felt oddly welcoming. Paul, hoping no one was watching, saluted into the emptiness. *Farewell, Chief Asher.* Then onward, through compartment after compartment, down narrow passageways grown familiar from years of travel through them, sailors wishing him cheery farewells as they passed, Paul only stopping for long again when he reached the place where Petty Officer Davidas had died. *And farewell to you, too. I hope you keep looking out for the crew. And looking out for the ship. I can't do that anymore. My time here is done.*

He walked back up to the quarterdeck. The other junior officers were waiting, lined up on either side of the brow. He faced the officer of the deck inport and saluted with extra precision. "Request permission to go ashore."

Lieutenant Junior Grade Gabriel returned the salute with a grin. "Permission granted. Fair winds and following seas, Paul." Then she gave Paul a thumbs-up and gestured to the petty officer of the watch. The petty officer activated the ship's general announcing system and bonged the ship's bell twice before declaring "Lieutenant, United States Navy, departing."

"Sideboys! Hand salute!" The two ranks of junior officers brought their hands up.

Paul raised his own arm, holding his salute as he walked between the ranks, over the brow and off of the USS *Michaelson* for the last time. Behind him, he heard the command "Ready, two!" as the others lowered their salutes.

He didn't look back at the ship, at the quarterdeck he'd first crossed three years earlier in the company of Senior Chief Kowalski, to meet for the first time Ensign Denaldo and Lieutenant Junior Grade Meadows and Lieutenant Sindh and Commander Sykes and many others. They were already gone, moved on with their careers and their lives, and now he didn't belong to the *Michaelson* anymore, either, though he knew part of him would always remain on the ship which had taken so much from him yet also seen him grow into an experienced officer.

Jen was waiting. So, unfortunately, was Mars. But he could handle that. After the *Michaelson*, he figured he could handle anything.

ACKNOWLEDGMENTS

I am indebted to my editor, Anne Sowards, for her usual valuable support and editing, and to my agent, Joshua Bilmes, for his suggestions and assistance. I'd also like to thank the special agents of the Naval Criminal Investigative Service (NCIS) with whom I worked while assigned to that command and from whom I learned much about how to catch those engaged in espionage.

ABOUT THE AUTHOR

John G. Hemry is a retired US Navy officer and the author, under the pen name Jack Campbell, of the *New York Times* national bestselling *The Lost Fleet* series (*Dauntless, Fearless, Courageous, Valiant, Relentless,* and *Victorious*). Next up are two new follow-on series. *The Lost Fleet: Beyond the Frontier* continues to follow Geary and his companions. The other series, *The Lost Stars*, is set on a former enemy world in that universe. Under his own name, John is also the author of the *JAG in Space* series and the *Stark's War* series. His short fiction has appeared in places as varied as the last Chicks in Chainmail anthology (*Turn the Other Chick*) and *Analog* magazine (which published his Nebula Award-nominated story 'Small Moments in Time' as well as most recently 'The Rift' in the October 2010 issue). His humorous short story 'As You Know, Bob' was selected for *Year's Best SF 13*. John's nonfiction has appeared in *Analog* and *Artemis* magazines as well as BenBella books on *Charmed, Star Wars,* and *Superman,* and in the *Legion of Superheroes* anthology *Teenagers from the Future*.

John had the opportunity to live on Midway Island for a while during the 1960s, graduated from high school in Lyons, Kansas, then later attended the US Naval Academy. He served in a variety of jobs including gunnery officer and navigator on a destroyer, with an amphibious squadron, and at the Navy's anti-terrorism centre. After retiring from the US Navy and settling in Maryland, John began writing. He lives with his long-suffering wife (the incomparable S) and three great kids. His daughter and two sons are diagnosed on the autistic spectrum.

A BURDEN OF PROOF
JACK CAMPBELL
(writing as John G. Hemry)

THE SECOND VOLUME IN THE ABSORBING
JAG IN SPACE SERIES

After a suspicious explosion onboard the USS *Michaelson* costs an officer his life, Paul Sinclair risks everything to expose a cover-up—and prosecute the son of a powerful vice-admiral.

"First-rate military SF. Another absorbing novel. Hemry's series continues to offer outstanding suspense, realism and characterization, and this book, no less than its predecessor, only ratchets up readers' appetites for more."
BOOKLIST

"*Burden of Proof*, like each of Hemry's books to date, is a must for any military SF fan."
SF SITE

TITANBOOKS.COM

RULE OF EVIDENCE
JACK CAMPBELL
(writing as John G. Hemry)

PAUL SINCLAIR RETURNS IN A THIRD THRILLING VOLUME

When the USS *Michaelson*'s sister ship, the USS *Maury*, is wracked by devastating explosions that destroy its engineering section, Paul Sinclair must find out what really caused the explosions. But the more he learns, the more he faces the terrible possibility that the woman he loves may be guilty of sabotage and murder.

"One hell of a series. A humdinger. The Paul Sinclair series remains at the top of my list of Great SF Books."
SF REVIEWS

TITANBOOKS.COM

THE STARK'S WAR SERIES
JACK CAMPBELL
(writing as John G. Hemry)

STARK'S WAR
STARK'S COMMAND
STARK'S CRUSADE

The USA reigns over Earth as the last surviving superpower. To build a society free of American influence, foreign countries have inhabited the moon. Now the US military have been ordered to wrest control of the moon.

Sergeant Ethan Stark must train his squadron to fight a desperate enemy in an airless atmosphere at one-sixth of normal gravity. Ensuring his team's survival means choosing which orders to obey and which to ignore…

"Gripping. Sergeant Stark is an unforgettable character. *Stark's War* reads as if Hemry has been there."
JACK MCDEVITT

"When it comes to combat, Hemry delivers."
WILLIAM C. DIETZ

THE LOST FLEET SERIES
JACK CAMPBELL

DAUNTLESS
FEARLESS
COURAGEOUS
VALIANT
RELENTLESS
VICTORIOUS

**After a hundred years of brutal war against the
Syndics, the Alliance fleet is marooned deep in enemy
territory, weakened and demoralized and desperate to
make it home.**

Their fate rests in the hands of Captain "Black Jack" Geary, a
man who had been presumed dead but then emerged from a
century of survival hibernation to find his name had become
legend. Forced by a cruel twist of fate into taking command of
the fleet, Geary must find a way to inspire the battle-hardened
and exhausted men and women of the fleet or face certain
annihilation by their enemies.

Brand-new editions of the bestselling novels containing unique
bonus material from the author.

TITANBOOKS.COM

TITANBOOKS.COM

THE LOST FLEET
BEYOND THE FRONTIER: DREADNAUGHT
JACK CAMPBELL

THE FIRST VOLUME IN THE BRAND NEW FOLLOW-ON SERIES

Captain John "Black Jack" Geary woke from a century of survival hibernation to take command of the Alliance fleet in the final throes of its long and bitter conflict against the Syndicate Worlds. Now Fleet Admiral Geary's victory has earned him the adoration of the people and enmity of politicians convinced that a living hero can be a very dangerous thing.

Geary is charged with command of the newly christened First Fleet. Its first mission: to probe deep into the territory of the mysterious alien race. Geary knows that members of the military high command and the government fear his staging a coup, so he can't help but wonder if the fleet is being deliberately sent to the far side of space on a suicide mission.

"Campbell combines the best parts of military SF and grand space opera... plenty of exciting discoveries and escapades."
PUBLISHERS WEEKLY

"Another excellent addition to one of the best military science-fiction series on the market."
MONSTERS & CRITICS

TITANBOOKS.COM